The Unwilling Bride

Candy-Ann Little

Sacred Grounds (books of a higher blend from Inknbeans Press)

© 2017

The Unwilling Bride -
Cover art by Shatzie Lee
©2011 Candy Ann Little, and Kingdom Kastle Publishing
© 2017 Candy Ann Little and Sacred Grounds (books of a higher blend from Inknbeans Press)

ISBN 13: 978-1-946841-04-9 (Inknbeans Press)
ISBN 10: 1-946841-04-8

Inknbeans Press
25060 Hancock Avenue
Bldg 103, Suite 458
Murrieta, Ca 92562

Dedication

First and foremost, I need to thank my God who has given me the ability and creativity to write this book. He has blessed my life so much and been with me throughout all my struggles. I only hope that I can bring Him honor and glory through my writing.

Secondly, I need to thank my husband and kids for supporting me, praying for me, and giving me the time I need to write.

Next, I'd like to thank family and friends who have supported and encouraged me for years. These are the people who indulge me when I'm talking about made up characters like they are real people, and haven't had me committed yet!

In addition, several special people have helped me achieve my dream. My wonderful and talented neighbor, Shatzie Lee, designed the beautiful book cover and formatted the entire novel. I also had several people who helped edit, Larry Webb, Serena Neaubacher, Vicky Schwartz, and other members of my writing group. Thank you all!

And to Jo (Boss Bean)

You have been my biggest encourager, holding my hand when I'm feeling down, and kicking my butt when I need it.

Thanks for all you do!!

The Unwilling Bride

Chapter 1
Norfolk, Virginia
September 18, 1798

The clip-clopping of horses' hooves alerted Caitlin to someone coming up the drive. She dropped the leather bag over the
balcony. It hit the ground with a dull thud. Hiking up her skirt to a
length far too improper, she held it over one arm and straddled the
railing. With both feet firmly planted on the other side of the
banister, she extended her arms trying to grasp the branch of the oak
tree that tauntingly stretched before her.

Not quite able to reach the branch, she decided to make a
jump for it. Mustering all of her determination she leapt into the air,
grabbing hold of the large bough with both arms. She dangled
precariously, trying to swing her feet up to the branch, the long skirt
wrapped around her ankles making the task difficult. The rough bark
cut through her thin overcoat, scratching the soft skin on her arms
and making the process of holding on even harder. Looking down
and realizing the height from which she dangled gave her the resolve to grip even tighter, no matter how much it hurt.

Finally swinging a leg up high enough to reach the branch,
she twisted her small torso around until she sat perched upon the
limb like a bird. Cautiously standing up, she lifted her skirt once
again. "This foolish thing is in my way." She tucked the front hem
into the sash around her waist. "There, that should hold it." She
needed both hands free to descend the tree. Tentatively placing a
foot on the limb below, she carefully progressed through the colored
leaves on her path to freedom.

She'd just passed the middle of the tree when her slipper
skidded, making her lose balance and topple. A scream pierced the
air as she fell. The branches reached out, grabbing at her clothes and

2

entangling her hair, but did nothing to stop her plunge downward. Squeezing her eyes shut, she prepared for the impact of the hard ground, but instead felt the softness of a body.

Someone grabbed her around the waist, tumbling with her and easing the collision. Caitlin lay on the ground, breathless and unable to move. Her heart raced wildly while her entire body throbbed. *I can't be dead*, she thought. *I hurt too much.* Opening her eyes, she found her older brother frowning at her. His short brown hair stood up in spikes, and grass clung to the side of his face.

"Brogan!" she squealed with relief. "I'm so glad to see you."

"What do you think you're doing?" he scolded and stood up.

"I…was umm…climbing a tree." Her legs still felt wobbly. She didn't dare try to get up.

"You could have been killed."

"I've watched you climb that tree lots of times." She didn't like him taking that parental tone.

"I do not have skirts and slippery shoes."

"I almost made it."

"Almost! You could have been seriously hurt, or even killed. Honestly, Caitlin, do you have any sense in that head of yours?"

"I have all the sense I need." She rose from the ground, pulling her skirt down. "And do not lecture me."

"Then perhaps you will listen to Father."

"Brogan, no!" She pulled at his arm. "You cannot tell him or Mama."

"Then tell me what you were doing." He crossed his arms in front of his chest, staring.

Caitlin had no choice but to throw herself on his mercy, "Running away." She plucked some leaves out of her hair.

"Trying to throw a rub in the way?"

"And what if I'm spoiling everyone's plans. No one cares about spoiling my life," she pouted. "And what are you doing over here anyway?"

"Keeping an eye on you. I knew you would try something foolish."

"'Tis no more foolish than getting married."

"Caitlin, marriage is not that unfavorable. Why must you be so dramatic?"

"I'm dramatic?" She glared at him. "It is easy for you to say. You are still unattached. How would you feel if Mama and Papa made you get married?"

"I can assure you I would not be pulling dangerous stunts."

"'It was my last resort." Her quivering lip warned Brogan of the forthcoming tears.

"Now, Caitlin, do not be upset."

"Will you help me?" she pleaded. "I can hide in the rattler and you can make an excuse to leave. Then you can drop me off outside of town." Her heart felt light once again as a new plan dawned. "If I do not get away now, I will never be free again."

"Where will you go?"

"Anywhere away from here."

"How do you plan on supporting yourself?"

"I will find a job," she said irritably. "Why does everyone insist that I cannot care for myself?"

"Because you can't," he stated matter-of-factly. "And pulling a dangerous stunt without thinking about the consequences is proof of your immaturity."

"I'm immature! Why you scatter-witted nincompoop. I knew the risks and accepted them in order to gain my freedom, just like Dwayne did."

"Our older brother willingly gave his life in the fight of Ireland. I have risked my own life several times in the pursuit of freedom, but you cannot pull dangerous stunts just to get your own way. 'Tis not the same thing." He sighed. "You are too headstrong for your own good. Take my advice, and— for once in your life— just go along with the plans."

"Would you advise Ireland to stop fighting and go along with England?"

"Nay, only you, my dear sister."

"Why do I get such counsel?"

4

"It will save all involved a lot of headaches." He plucked a twig from her tangled curls. "Now, go get your bags and I'll distract Mother and Father so you can sneak back into the house."

"And if I refuse?" she challenged, not ready to give up yet.

"Please, Caitlin, trust me on this."

"Why?" She crossed her arms. "Everyone keeps talking about trust, but no one will explain a thing."

"You will be apprised of all the factors in due time."

"You know more than you're telling me." She crossed her arms.

"I must abide by our parent's wishes, even if I don't agree with them."

"Will you promise to tell me what you can?"

"I'm sorry, Cate. It has to come from Father. Now, be quick and get in the house. Dillon is here for dinner and you need to dress."

"Oh, no!" Her last desperate effort for freedom had failed. *Why can't anything work out for me?* She stomped over to get her bags.

"Would you care for a drink?" Alin held up a crystal decanter.

"No, thank you, sir. I'm not a drinking man."

"Neither am I." He set the decanter on the table. "I'm glad to see my future son-in-law does not indulge in the spirits."

"Not drinking? Is that not a mite unusual for the Irish?"

"Aye, that it is, my lad." Alin chuckled. "We're known for our drinking, especially our preference for ale. Nonetheless, I have witnessed the destruction that liquor can do, and vowed to never allow a substance to control my life. I also believe 'tis hard to do God's work when you are drunk."

"I wholeheartedly agree, sir." Dillon fidgeted with his cravat.

"You seem a bit nervous, my boy."

"Your daughter is quite becoming and I want to make a good impression."

"Aye. Caitlin is beautiful. However, her temper surpasses her beauty. She is headstrong, independent, and at times a bit immature. I fear being the youngest and the only daughter has allowed us to spoil her."

"Children are a gift, my lord. They are put on earth to be spoiled. As for her maturity, nineteen is yet young. It will develop with age."

"Young." Alin laughed. "Most people have already dubbed her a spinster. As to her maturity, I hope you are right."

"In marriage you have to take the good with the bad, do you not?" Dillon paced a few steps with his arms locked behind his back.

"That is true. I merely want you to be informed." Alin sipped his water.

"Good evening." Kathleen seemed to materialize from no-where.

"My dear, I didn't hear you." Usually his ears were attuned to the clipping of her heels. He gave her a quick peck on the cheek.

"It is nice to see you again, Mrs. Gallagher, and may I say you look lovely this evening."

"Thank you, Mr. Cade." She curtsied as he kissed the back of her hand. A large feather from her blue hat brushed his chin.

"Since I'm soon to be your son-in-law I think it appropriate that you use my Christian name."

"Very well, Dillon. I give you leave to use mine as well." She looked at Alin. "What were you saying about Caitlin?"

"We were talking about the wedding."

"I fear this ceremony is going to be anything but a happy occasion." Kathleen's voice cracked. Her heart broke for Caitlin. "She's been through so much turmoil already. Forcing her into matrimony is something I do not want to exert."

"I know it is hard, dear. However, it's the only way to keep her safe." Alin slid his arm around her thick waist.

"I promise to take exceptional care of her," Dillon offered.

"I'm sure you will make a fine husband. That does not worry me." Her green eyes turned to Alin, taking in the handsome squared features. His short-cropped, brown hair had been replaced by gray. His face wrinkled with age. Yet, he stirred her desire every time she gazed upon him. She wanted that same love, devotion, and passion in her daughter's marriage, but feared Caitlin might never have that kind of happiness being coerced this way. "I merely wished more joy for her." She dabbed at the tears with her gloved hand.

"Being bound to anyone would never make our daughter happy," Alin stated. "She seems to have an aversion to marriage altogether. This way, at least, we know she will have a stable life with a good man."

"Caitlin does not want this marriage?" Dillon inquired as he handed her a handkerchief. "I do not want to force her hand in this matter." He knew her parents were desperate but he refused to goad any maiden into a life-long commitment.

"You are not forcing it. I am," Alin corrected. "If you do not wish to be a party to this, I'll understand. But be assured that if you do not marry Caitlin, I will find someone else."

"I do not wish to start my life with an unwilling wife."

"I understand your concern, Dillon." Kathleen softly assured him. "Caitlin may be an unwilling bride at first; however, after the vows are spoken she'll come around." She didn't want him losing interest. She liked this young man. Not only was he successful and good-looking, but he also possessed a gentle disposition— all the qualities she desired in a husband for her daughter. The one and only concern was that Caitlin would trample him. She needed a strong hand at times to keep her in line.

"I know what is best for my daughter, and she will comply with my wishes," Alin said, firmly.

"Good evening." Brogan entered the room. "Dillon, nice to see you."

"Likewise." They shook hands.

"Father, are you sure this is the best course of action?" He wanted to broach the subject on his sister's behalf.

"I see no other way." Alin threw up his hands. "We are to be deported back to Ireland. Under Dillon's name she can stay and start a new life. She will be much safer here."

"That may not be true," Dillon said. "Under the same acts that are deporting you, I'm not allowed to print anything against President Adams or the Federalist Party. To show support for any Anti-Federalist group would be breaking the law, and I could be thrown in jail. Benjamin Bache, the editor of *The Aurora*, in Philadelphia had been arrested before he died."

"Was he not the grandson of Benjamin Franklin?" Kathleen inquired.

"Aye. They arrested him and accused him of treason simply for printing an article that spoke against President Adams."

The light tapping of heels preceded Caitlin's arrival and halted any further conversation of political matters. She was a vision beyond loveliness. The turquoise crepe gown floated to the ground, extending into a small train. A yellow sash tied around the high waistline made her look even taller and more slender. The short sleeves were adorned with yellow flounce, and the same lace ran along the low curve of the neckline. Her dark red tresses were swept up in an artful chignon of ringlet curls, with a blue-green turban wrapped around her head and knotted on one side. Three yellow plumes protruded from the knot, adding a touch of elegance.

Caitlin smiled wistfully, receiving the effect she'd intended.

Dillon hesitantly stepped forward to take his bow, "Pleased to see you again, Miss Gallagher." He barely got the words out as his throat constricted.

She curtsied, bestowing upon him the best smile she could manage. Every muscle ached with the movement. "I do hope you will forgive me for being late, but I wanted to take extra care in my toilette tonight."

"You are worth the wait."

"How gallant of you, Mr. Cade." She noted his well-built stature. He wasn't exceptionally tall, but he held himself straight like a soldier. The form-fitting black overcoat emphasized broad shoulders, while black britches accentuated his lean narrow hips.

The ruffles of a white shirt ended under a brown waistcoat embroidered with black paisley stitching, and white stockings completed the ensemble. She guessed the shirt and stockings were made of silk, for this man was the portrait of high society - English society, no less.

"I am sure it would be proper for us to be on a first name basis," Dillon suggested.

"It would seem so with our wedding mere weeks away." She tried to disguise the scorn in her tone.

"We shall discuss that subject later," Alin interrupted. "Would you like something to drink, my dear?

"Water, please." A small frown furrowed in Caitlin's brow.

Alin poured the liquid into a glass. Kathleen slipped closer. "Is there some reason you cut her off?"

"I don't want her saying anything to frighten him off. Dillon seems apprehensive enough. I've hand-picked this young man, finding in him all the qualities I desire for a good marriage. I'm of the mind that an honest man would make an excellent husband. Although Caitlin seems against the idea at the moment, she will come to love Dillon as he loves her. Of that I'm confident."

"Why don't we adjourn to the dining room?" Kathleen suggested. "Dinner is waiting and surely growing cold."

"What were you talking about before I entered the room?" Caitlin asked as she laid her hand on top of the arm Dillon offered and followed her parents out of the parlor.

"Only shop talk, nothing for you to worry your pretty head over," Alin said over his shoulder.

"If I am to marry an editor of a newspaper, I should have a comprehension of his business." She smiled into Dillon's dark brown eyes.

She pressed the subject, hoping to gain an understanding of why her parents were insistent upon her marrying this man. Something was amiss and she wanted answers.

"I do not mind answering your questions." He'd answer anything when she smiled like that. "However, I do not see how the newspaper business could hold your attention for long. It is not very glamorous or exciting."

"I do not need glamour or excitement. I believe that a healthy mind leads to a happy life. And what better way to expand the mind than to learn about something new?" Caitlin sat down in the chair Dillon had pulled out for her.

"How astute of you." He took his own seat and explained the differences between the Federalists Party and the Anti-Federalist Party, as they dined on the first course.

"Tell me, Dillon, which side are you on?" Her sweet smile covered her true intentions. She planned to pry as much information from Dillon Cade as feasible under the guise of idle talk. If anyone knew her parents' plan, he did. She would use every feminine wile to extract the information.

"As a journalist, I remain neutral. The first amendment to the Bill of Rights gives me the freedom to print both sides of the story. However, the Federalists are cracking down on anyone who disagrees with their point of view, leaving editors no choice except to print one side of the story. I disagree with their strong-arm tactics."

Alin cleared his throat. "Perhaps this conversation can wait until after dinner."

"But, Papa, I find this subject truly engaging." Smiling at Dillon she said, "Please, continue."

Her green eyes aroused something inside Dillon whenever she looked his way. However, he had enough wits to realize she was trying to manipulate him. If he answered her questions carefully, he could appease her while staying under the cloak of confidentiality.

"President Adams has passed several acts that are disguised as protection acts. The sedition act silences any opposition to his party. I believe this infringes on the first amendment."

"How so?"

"Sedition generally refers to laws, acts, or words that encourage revolt against the government. I do not believe President Adams is worried about an upset of government. Mainly, he wants to silence Thomas Jefferson and the Anti-Federalist party. He has taken the Sedition Act to the extreme by requiring criminal penalties for anyone caught publishing information or opinions that disagree with him."

The conversation halted while Hilda bustled around the table. She took the tablecloth off and laid out a fresh, clean one, and then proceeded to set out the second course.

"Why is the government so worried about a revolt?" Caitlin asked. "America is not at war."

"Not officially. However, an undeclared naval war has ensued since the X Y Z affair last year. Both President Adams and foreign minister Talleyrand are trying to avoid a declaration of war, but hostilities between America and France have been growing stronger producing mistrust."

"Ireland seems to trust France. Theobald Wolfe Tone is trying to enlist their help against England," Caitlin countered.

She watched his face, searching for a hint of where he stood on that war. Surely he'd be on England's side since he had been born there. He may have lived in America for the past thirteen years, but he still had English blood running through his veins.

"True. But their help is very limited. If they had planned better, Ireland would not have lost the battle two years ago."

"The weather turned bad and prevented the fleet from arriving. France has no control over the weather." Her brother, Dwayne had been killed in that battle. She blamed England for his death, not France.

"Aye, but had they had a more experienced captain the ships would have made it."

"Perhaps, but some things are uncontrollable." She felt the hurt and anger rising to the surface. "What about these criminal penalties?" Caitlin nibbled on the venison steak cooked in a wine sauce. "If the Anti-Federalists obtain control of the government by oppressing the competition, then they are, in fact, acting as a dictatorship, and that would tread on the Constitution."

"Exactly." Dillon marveled at her discernment. She was far more than just another pretty face; she'd been schooled well. "It would undermine the entire reason we fought for independence.

Freedom and the Constitution would then be obsolete." He took a helping of potatoes and pickled green beans.

"I recognize what you're saying; however, there is one thing I do not understand." Caitlin drew her brows together and puckered her thin lips. "Mama told me we now have to reside in America for fourteen years instead of the normal five years before we can apply for citizenship. Why would the government be concerned with immigrants' status?" As interesting as she found his opinions and views, she needed to get the conversation back to her goal. "How does making an immigrant wait longer to become a citizen help with war efforts?"

"It does not." Dillon shook his head. "The Naturalization Act only makes immigrants ineligible to vote in the next election. Since Mr. Jefferson is heavily relying on European immigrant votes, it will hurt his campaign."

"It seems like all these acts have been passed to stop Mr. Jefferson's effort for the presidency." This information seemed of no use to her, although he held his end of the conversation very well. She hadn't had a discussion this gratifying since the last time she'd debated with her scholar over the Irish Revolution, two years prior.

"That is what I believe also." Dillon lathered his oyster bread with butter.

"You really should try this squash and peanut pie, Dillon," Alin interrupted. "No one cooks squash like Hilda."

"Thank you, sir." Dillon took the serving bowl. After taking his portion he handed the dish to Caitlin and smiled. He felt the temperature rise a little as Caitlin fluttered her long lashes and smiled coyly.

Hilda removed the dishes, then, once again, replaced the dirty tablecloth with a fresh white, linen cloth as she served the next course. The conversation turned to lighter matters.

After Hilda removed the dirty dishes and tablecloth, she then set out the desserts on the plain wooden table as etiquette dictated that no tablecloth be used on the dessert table. China plates were filled with an array of lemon teacakes, raspberry tarts, filbert pudding with apricot sauce and chocolate truffles.

After dessert, everyone retired to the parlor savoring cups of coffee and tea.

Caitlin smiled and played the part of a dutiful hostess. She was careful to ask only acceptable questions, biding her time patiently until the right moment presented itself. "Dillon, it is such a lovely night, I wondered if you might accompany me on walk through the garden?"

"Of course." He set his cup and saucer down and stood.

"Do not forget a wrap," Kathleen insisted. "The air is getting chilly."

"Of course, Mama." Caitlin stepped into the hall and gathered her wrap, while Dillon grabbed his topper off the hat rack.

She smiled and accepted his assistance with her shawl. "We won't be long," she said to her mother before stepping through the door that Dillon held open.

Dillon and Caitlin walked along the moonlit path until they came upon a bench nestled beneath the Spanish trees. "Can we rest here?" Her entire body felt like it was on fire. She didn't know if her muscles would make it any further.

"Of course, my lady." He helped her sit. "Are you feeling all right?"

"Aye." She looked up at the sky. "The moon certainly is luminous."

"Indeed, very brilliant, but it pales in comparison to your beauty."

"Why, sir, if I did not know better I'd say you are flirting with me."

"You do not find it fitting for a man to pay attention to his bride-to-be?"

"If his attentions are genuine."

"I assure you, my attentions are nothing but honest." Taking a seat beside her on the tiny bench, he inhaled the sweet scent of rose water wafting from her delicate skin. "You truly shine brighter than the stars."

Caitlin's laughter mingled with the sounds of the night. "I perceive, sir, that you overindulged in the spirits before supper."

"Your beauty intoxicates me."

Caitlin cocked her head and admired the man sitting beside her. His curly brown hair had been pulled into a ponytail, allowing full view of his face. The soft, silvery light cascading from the moon highlighted his high cheekbones and angled features. Fine lines etched his eyes and mouth, giving him a distinctively hand-some quality. "Am I to assume that a man as handsome as yourself has failed to find other beautiful women?"

"I have met a few."

"And have you told these others the same lines you're repeating now?"

His dark eyes danced with mischief. "Do you not think me sincere?"

"Nay."

"Why, your beauty reminds me of a poem.
'If a star were confined into a tomb,
Her captive flames must needs burn there,
But when the hand that lock'd her up gives room,
She'll shine through all the sphere.'"

"Henry Vaughn. I'm impressed with your selection." She could identify with being confined to a tomb. *That is what marriage would be like.*

"Do you like Vaughn?" Dillon asked.

"Aye. But I'm more partial to Shakespeare."

"I find him a bit too tragic for my taste."

"To each his own." She found the conversation about poetry intriguing. His easygoing disposition and quick wit were refreshing compared to the childish boys who'd previously courted her. "I have one for you.

"'Tyger! Tyger! Burning bright

in the forests of the night,
what immortal hand or eye,
dare frame thy fearful symmetry?'"

"A more modern poet. William Blake is a favorite of mine."

"I also like the writings of Robert Burns."

"Ah! The famous Scottish poet." He smiled showing his perfect teeth.

Caitlin felt a flutter in her stomach – an experience only felt once before. The first time she'd accompanied her father to Dillon's printing shop. At fifteen, she'd felt a flutter every time he smiled, but quickly dismissed the tingling sensations as a child's infatuation. Now, looking at him as a prospective husband somehow changed his appearance. Even though he had an incredibly handsome face, he was still the person trying to take her freedom away.

"May I be permitted to ask a question?" She calmly met his gaze.

"Of course."

"Why have you asked for my hand in marriage?"

"Ah, Caitlin. I should have known you'd get straight to the point." The quiet sounds of the night disappeared as he contemplated his answer. He couldn't tell her that he'd agreed to the marriage for her protection. Not only would that give her parent's plan away, it might be a lie. Marrying him could well endanger her life. He had no idea how far the Federalists would go in trying to seize power. They could decide that simply imprisoning editors would not be harsh enough, and execute them for treason.

He took in her gentle features and brilliant green eyes, sparkling brighter than the stars filling the autumn sky. "You are very beautiful. Any man would count himself fortunate to gain a jewel as rare as you."

"So I'm to be another possession to you?"

"Not at all," he said. "I will cherish you."

"You do not even know me."

"I'd like to rectify that."

"I still do not understand why the haste? Why not court me in the normal manner?" She had to hold her temper and be patient. Loosening her tongue now would only produce disaster. Feeling confident about gaining the information she desired from him, she smiled, playing her part perfectly.

"I know everything is happening quickly. However, I do intend to win your favor." Reaching inside his overcoat he produced a neatly wrapped package. "If you will accept a gift from me."

Caitlin's stunned silence amused him. "I really should not," she protested. "But I do love presents." Her eyes gleamed as her fingers hastily unwrapped the package. "Oh, Dillon. It's exquisite."

"It meets with your approval?"

"How could it not?" She'd never seen a piece of jewelry like it. A large square diamond was set in the center of a silver brooch with small, round ones encircling it.

"May I pin it on you?"

"Of course." She handed him the brooch.

"Are you sure you like it? You seem a bit uncertain." He fastened it to her shawl.

"It's lovely— only so expensive. I'm not sure I should accept it."

"It is not improper for a gentleman to buy his bride a gift."

"But I haven't accepted your proposal yet."

"Oh." His dark brows shot up. "Your father informed me that we are to wed in two weeks."

"He informed me of the same thing. However, I'm of legal age to do as I like." She stood and a jolt of pain shot up her back. She clenched her teeth, thoughtlessly smoothing the front of her dress as she walked a few steps away. The intimacy forced by the little bench played havoc on her nerves.

"Are you in pain?"

She turned to face him. "My slipper is a bit tight and pinches my toes."

"I see." He stood, not moving from his spot, yet his wide shoulders seemed to loom over her. "Are you sure you are not bruised from the fall?"

She smiled sweetly, keeping her gaze level with his. "Whatever are you talking about?"

"Brogan told me about your botched escape."

"That rat!" She crossed her arms and winced.

"Is marriage that unfavorable?" He stepped closer. "Or is it I that you loathe?"

"I do not wish to be united with anyone at this time."

"I see." Dillon spread his legs and folded his arms behind his back. "Have you told your parents?"

"I require your assistance in that matter." She smiled. "You can tell Papa that you have changed your mind and you do not wish to marry me." She fluttered her lashes. "He'll listen to you. I just know it."

"Am I to assume that they did not hearken to your protests?"

"They are both being so stubborn." She stalked over the rose bushes, ignoring the pain and delicately picked a bloom. "You, Mr. Cade, are my last chance." She played with the soft petals.

Hearing the desperation in her voice made him regret the situation altogether. He'd been fearful about taking a bride against her will, no matter what the circumstances were. Nonetheless, after carefully examining the facts, he had decided it would be the best course of action. The major problem would be convincing Caitlin of that.

"I understand your reservations…"

"You understand?" She whirled around pricking her finger with a thorn. "How can you understand anything when you are a party to this madness?" Tears gathered in her eyes.

"I can imagine how you feel," he said, softly. "If the boot was quite on the other leg, I'd feel the same way."

"But you would never be in this position because you're a man."

"And you suppose that men never have feelings of hopelessness? That we do not feel forced into situations? My dear Caitlin, why do you think men go to war?"

17

"Perhaps they feel compelled to defend themselves, but when the battle has ended they have freedom to show for their efforts. Certainly more than I will ever have."

"Caitlin." His gentle tone eased her anger. "I do not want to force you into anything."

Her eyes brightened. "You'll talk to Papa?"

He closed the distance between them. "There are circumstances that compel me to do this."

"You won't help me then?" Her green eyes bore into his. She saw tenderness and even pity residing in his brown orbs, but something kept him from yielding to her wishes.

"I wish I could." He watched a tear drip onto the rose, mingling with the drops of blood that marred the white petals. "You've hurt your finger."

She looked down, unaware that she'd even been pricked. The thorn in her heart hurt more than her finger. "'Tis nothing."

He lifted her slender hand to inspect the wound. "I don't have my handkerchief," he said as a few more drops fell. Instinctively putting her finger to his mouth, he sucked the wound, totally unprepared for the jolt that surged through him.

Feeling the electricity also, Caitlin jerked her hand away. "You, sir, are a rake," she said breathlessly. "You try and bamboozle me into marriage just so you can have your way with me."

"I have no such intentions."

"Then why the haste? Something is amiss and you are cognizant of it."

"You are correct, Caitlin. There is more to this matter. However, I am not at liberty to say anything."

"You can compel me into wedlock but cannot tell me why? How noble of you, sir!" Anger mounted until her smooth, pale face became inflamed.

"I can assure you if there were any other way of protecting you, I would take it. But particulars have tied both your parents' hands, and mine. We are only doing what we feel is best."

"Best for whom?" she sneered. "My parents seem content having me hang on your sleeve. Have I become such a burden to them that they no longer wish me around?"

Dillon grabbed her shoulders, spinning her around until he peered into her eyes. "Your parents love you. It is why they are doing this."

"And what about you, Mr. Cade?" Her eyes pierced his soul. "Why are you willing to oblige yourself in the confines of marriage to someone you barely know?"

He pondered his answer for a long moment before softly saying, "'Tis my duty."

"What do you know of duty? You, sir, have no honor." She shrugged free of his clasp, crying out in pain. "If you had any sense of honor or duty, you'd explain the situation to me. Do I not have the right to make my own decisions?"

"Perhaps in a perfect world, but not in a country fearing war with France." He felt an overwhelming urge to pull her close. Instead, he clasped his hands behind his back.

"You are nothing but a nincompoop if you think I'm going to marry you!" His silence aggravated her even more. "You see yourself gallantly coming to my rescue, whereas I see you as nothing more than a prig, stealing my freedom. I doubt you plan on stopping at my freedom, either. Do you intend to steal my virtue as well?" She paced back and forth as her wrath elevated. *Couldn't he do more than demurely stand there?* "Do you intend to violate me?" she yelled.

"I would implore you to lower your voice, Caitlin. Someone may overhear."

"Are you afraid someone will think you a cad for taking advantage of an innocent? Or do you presume that once we marry I am your property to do with as you see fit?"

"I merely…"

"Oh, save your useless breath." She threw her hands up in the air. "Your eloquent words will not work on me. I tell you truly, Mr. Cade, I will not bed you of my own accord. I'll not even wed you of my own consent."

"I understand your apprehension, Caitlin." He sighed. "I can assure you I will not take advantage of you."

"Right!" She crossed her arms. "You will not see it as such because a husband is to own his wife. Some men count their wives as nothing more than slaves."

"Perhaps some men, but not I." He wanted to assuage her fears. "I will treat you with the utmost respect."

"Do you think reciting poetry, using flattery, and giving expensive gifts will impel me to your side? I can truly say that it will not. You, Mr. Cade, are my enemy and all the money in the world will not convince me otherwise."

She ripped the brooch off her shawl, tearing a hole in the delicate fabric. "Take your bribe back." She threw it at him.

He ducked out of the way just in time. Dillon watched the dejected look cross her rounded features. Understanding that she'd behaved out of anger and fear, he felt compelled to dismiss the act of temper. "I am truly sorry, Caitlin."

"Sorry for whom?" she sniffed. "Certainly not for yourself. In two weeks you will have a virgin bride to ravish as you please, and I will have no say." The horrid image propelled forward with so much vigor that she could no longer stand the sight of this wretched man. "I hate you, Dillon Cade!" Picking up her skirt she dashed for the comfort of her room.

Chapter 2

Dillon mounted the stairs, following the melancholy sounds of the pianoforte. When the song ended he lightly tapped on the door.

"Come in."

Dillon stepped through the door and met Caitlin's startled gaze. "I thought you were Mama," she said.

"Your father gave me permission to speak with you." He stepped forward, leaving the door open. "You play very beautifully, my lady."

"I have not been able to play my best lately." The bruises from her failed escape attempt made moving difficult. Sharp pains emerged every time she hit the keys too hard. Standing, she asked, "How may I be of assistance to you, Mr. Cade?"

"I thought we discussed that the other night." Dillon stepped closer. "You may call me Dillon. The formal address will not do for a husband."

"As you wish, *Dillon.*" She stressed his name with more sourness than a hundred lemons could provide. Although there were several more names she'd like to attach, she held her tongue. "I am sure you did not come all this way to discuss address."

"Nay. I wanted to clarify something from our conversation a few nights past."

"There is nothing left to say."

"If I may make one thing understood?"

"If you must." She sighed. The sooner he finished his prattling, the sooner she could go back to sulking.

"It is obvious that you do not wish to speak to me, so I will make my comment brief." His medium-sized frame stood straight and his arms were in their usual position behind his back. "I only wish to alleviate your fears of being ravished. If it would suit you to have separate bedrooms then I will not object."

"Truly?" Caitlin couldn't hide her shock or relief.

"It will accommodate me just fine." He bowed his head. "Good day, my lady."

"One moment."

He turned to face her with his hand on the doorknob.

"What made you change your mind?"

"I have done no such thing. You presumed something that simply is not true. No matter what you may believe of me, I am not a rake or a cad. I will never force myself upon a young maiden, my wife or not." With a curt nod he left.

Caitlin paced the room letting his comments sink in. *So he will not force me into the marriage bed.* That piece of knowledge should have settled her mind, and yet, now she felt spurned. He seemed overly zealous in obliging this element of their marriage. Perhaps he didn't wish her in his bed. Stopping in front of the whatnot shelf she picked up a small figurine. *So what?* she mused. *As long as I do not have to appease the enemy.*

"I have a present for you." Kathleen set a large box on the bed.

Caitlin wanted to stew more, however curiosity got the best of her. She closed the book that she'd been pretending to read and walked over to the bed.

"Open it," Kathleen instructed.

"Oh, Mama, it's lovely." Caitlin pulled out a beautifully decorated ivory satin gown.

"Try it on and see how it fits." Kathleen clapped. "I cannot wait to see you in it."

Caitlin knew this to be her wedding gown, and although the craftsmanship looked unmatched to any dress she'd ever laid eyes on, it also reminded her of the impending doom. "I do not feel like changing right now."

"But we have to leave time for alterations, if any are needed." Kathleen wouldn't take no for an answer. "Turn around I'll unbutton your gown."

"I suppose I have no choice in this, either."

"Nay, my daughter."

Caitlin subjected herself to her mother's care and soon was garbed in the formal dress. The high waist of the chemise allowed the satin to hang freely as it flowed down, forming a long train in the back. A cream crepe overdress printed with tiny flowers of pink, lavender, yellow, and silver delicately drifted over the satin. A silver silk shawl crossed at her bust, then wrapped under each arm forming a bow in the back. Flowers stitched in silver thread adorned the hem of the gown.

"It fits perfectly," Caitlin noted, fanning her hands over the cool, creamy material. "I cannot believe I fit into your wedding dress."

"Oh, 'tis not my wedding dress."

"It's not?" She had wondered why it didn't smell musty.

"I could never have afforded a dress this magnificent when I married your father."

"Then where did it come from?"

"The seamstress made it."

"How did she sew it so fast? I've only been engaged for twelve days. This had to have taken longer than that."

"She started it a few months ago."

"A few months ago!" Caitlin whirled around, nearly knocking over her mother, who'd been arranging her train. "You've been planning this for months and yet I was not informed until a few weeks ago."

"We didn't want to drag the situation out. Your father and I thought it best to notify you closer to the nuptials so you would not be unduly perturbed."

"My, isn't that considerate?" She arched a red brow. "Don't allow me to worry over the nuptials, just coerce me into them."

"Caitlin, we have already been over this and I do not wish to discuss it anymore." Kathleen turned her attention back to the garment. "Do you think you will be warm enough in the short sleeves?" She played with the silver flounce. "I thought about long ones, but I loved the lace on these cap sleeves."

"It will be fine." She didn't want to drop the subject, yet no one listened anyway.

"Now all that is left is the headdress," Kathleen stated.

"I do not have to put the whole outfit on right now."

"But I want to see you in it."

"You will see me in two days."

"Indulge me."

Kathleen set a chiffonet headpiece on top of her auburn curls. The silver gauze ruffled down the sides and back, held in place with a bandeau of colored flowers. "'Tis perfect."

As much as Caitlin hated the idea of the wedding, she did feel like a princess in the gown. Her wardrobe mostly consisted of the middle class materials: linen, crepe and cotton. The luxurious feel of the satin lifted her spirits, a little. "I should have known it was not your dress. I never imagined you this slim." She got one last barb in.

"That is a rude remark," Kathleen scolded. "For your information, I was very slender when I married. Age and having three children have added to my frame."

"I do not intend to ever be plump," Caitlin needled.

"Perhaps you will not, however you cannot stop time."

"No, but I won't have any children."

"Oh, Caitlin, I wish you would think about this issue. But, once you are married it will be your life to live."

"I am glad to hear I have a say about something in my life." She took her headpiece off.

"You are making this decision out of anger. I ask you to reconsider once you have calmed down."

"Why? Just so you can have grandchildren?"

"Life can be very lonely, Caitlin. Children can fill that void. Where are you going to be in your old age without children?"

"Right where you and Papa put me." Her eyes narrowed.

Kathleen fought back the doubts forging forward, causing mass confusion as to what was right. On one hand, they had to physically protect Caitlin. On the other, her daughter would be condemned to a loveless marriage without any children. *Which way of life would be best?*

The sun slowly slipped over the horizon, causing the sleepy town of Norfolk to awaken to a bright pink sky scattered with perfect cotton-like clouds. The warm rays touched the ground, drying up the last drops of dew clinging to the grassy fields, tobacco crops, colored trees, and delicate flowers.

The air, feeling a bit chilly now, promised to warm up as the day wore on, leaving in its wake the most ideal weather for saying one's vows. That is, of course, if one wanted to recite the words that fettered one for life. Caitlin's apprehension mounted with the rising of the sun; it brought life to the day she'd been dreading.

Rolling over, she forcibly punched the feather pillow, taking out her frustrations while trying to flatten the lumps. "Why even bother?" she sighed. "I have not slept all night, it is useless now." Throwing back the quilt, she slipped out of bed and walked to the window, recalling the dream that had recurred all night long. "Oh, Dwayne," she softly muttered. "What are you trying to tell me?"

His voice had appeared in her sleep, as if he had been reaching out from beyond the grave, trying to console her tormented heart. "Keep the faith, *Catie pie*. Keep the faith." Catie Pie. No one had called her that since his death.

Her eyes wandered over the lush green lawn that extended to the edge of the forest. The golden sun appeared over the tops of the trees, casting a majestic mood over all of Virginia. This type of day typically would have stimulated her. However, Caitlin's gloomy mood wouldn't be lifted even by a spectacular sunrise.

A light rapping brought her out of her musings. "Come in."

Kathleen entered. "I thought you would still be sleeping." She crossed the room to stand next to her daughter. "Such a beautiful day."

"I suppose."

"It's going to be a perfect day for the wedding."

Caitlin made no response. She'd begged, pleaded, and cried for two weeks to no avail. Sometimes crying so hard that now the well spring of tears seemed to be dried up. There were no tears left only a quiet resolve to forge ahead.

"Darling, I wish you could enjoy the day just a little."

"That will never happen." Caitlin smoothed out some wrinkles from her nightdress. "I will go through with the nuptials, but do not mistake my compliance for acceptance. This day is nothing more than bondage to me. I will go to the altar with my head held high, but a heavy heart."

"Is there nothing I can say to convince you otherwise?"

"Aye." She leveled her gaze to meet her mother's. "You can explain the situation. Everyone informs me that this is for my own good, yet they refuse to inform me why."

"You deserve some answers, but I won't go against your Father's wishes. We will explain everything in due time."

"In due time!" Caitlin threw her hands up. "This is the morning of my wedding. How much longer must I wait?"

"Until after the ceremony."

"Why?"

"We do not want to cause undue stress."

"Oh, come, Mother! You cannot hide behind that cloak forever. If you truly did not want to cause me distress then you would not be forcing my hand into marriage. And most certainly not to the enemy."

"Why not think of Dillon simply as a man instead of someone who is English?"

"I will think of him simply as my enemy." Caitlin smoothed out some wrinkles in her nightgown.

"Is that not harsh for someone you hardly know?"

"Is it not harsh forcing me to be leg-shackled?" Caitlin paced a few steps. "You and Papa did not inform me of the wedding until a few weeks ago because you were afraid I would talk you out of this ridiculous idea."

"Or, try to run away." Kathleen smiled at the shocked look on Caitlin's face. "We knew you wouldn't take this quietly."

"How did you know?" Caitlin crossed her arms. "Brogan! That rascal told you."

"Brogan said nothing. You are my flesh and blood. Do you not think I know how your mind operates?" Kathleen pulled up the sleeve on Caitlin's night dress to reveal a faded bruise. "Besides, I noticed the bruises and scratches."

"It was the only way to keep my freedom." She pulled her arm away and stalked back to the window. "Even that attempt failed. It seems I am destined to become Mrs. Caitlin Cade."

"I like the sound of that, don't you?"

"Humph!" Caitlin elevated her perky nose. "I like Caitlin Gallagher just fine."

"Therein lies the problem. The Gallagher name has become too dangerous. It is associated with treason in Ireland."

"What has that to do with America?"

"America may view us as a threat. Under the name Cade you will be protected."

"Nonsense!" Caitlin defiantly folded her arms.

Kathleen lifted her chin. "'Tis our job to keep you safe."

"Do I not have a say in the matter? After all, it is my life."

"If circumstances were different," Kathleen stated. "However, we must play the hand that has been dealt us."

"I do not like this hand."

"Neither do I. Nonetheless, it is what God has given us. Besides, you could have been dealt a worse hand."

"How? I am being forced into a marriage with an Englishman to protect me from a government I'm starting to despise as much as England. You think there is a bright side to all this?"

"Dillon is a fine looking gentleman. If you must be tied down, at least you have someone worth looking at."

"Mother!" She covered her ears. "I do not wish to hear such talk."

"Come now, Caitlin. You are about to be married, and we have never had our talk."

"You need not waste your breath. Our marriage will be one in name only."

"Time has a way of changing hearts. Perhaps, someday things will be different."

"Never!" Caitlin whirled around. "I will never sleep with the enemy."

Kathleen knew better that to try and reason with her. When Caitlin got in moods like this you couldn't rationalize with her. At least she would go through with the ceremony. That seemed about as much as she could expect. "Why don't you get ready? The enemy is here."

"Why is he here so early?"

"He has come to take the morning meal with us."

"Great." She arched her brows. "What a way to start the worst day of my life."

The courtyard buzzed with activity as everyone prepared for the upcoming ritual. Chairs and tables were set in place, bouquets and centerpieces artfully arranged, the garden cleaned and weeded, all while the smells of the wedding dinner wafted through the air.

Caitlin couldn't believe the number of people working, and the transformation that occurred in their garden. "Who are all these people?" she asked her mother, stepping onto the terrace.

"Dillon brought some helpers along with the dishes from his house. The neighbors have also loaned us their place settings and linens," Kathleen informed her.

Alin kissed her cheek. "Good morning, my pet."

"What is so good about it?" Caitlin asked. "I had no idea so many people were coming. I thought it would be a private affair."

"Nay, my lady." Dillon's soft rich voice floated behind her. "I hope you do not mind that I have taken the liberty to invite some associates and friends."

Spinning around, Caitlin found herself facing a most dashing image. Although he was simply dressed in a white cotton shirt and brown knee length pants with white stockings, he presented a most admirable sight to behold. "Of course, I don't mind, Mr. Cade. After all, it is your wedding also. I wonder why we are not having the ceremony in the church if everyone is coming."

"Not everyone is coming," Kathleen explained. "Having the ceremony in town would cause quite a stir if the town folk were not invited. Having it here is more private."

"It is really just a few associates from work and the nearby neighbors. I hope that meets with your approval," Dillon said.

"It is not my affair to care about." Caitlin shrugged. "Whatever, you want, Mr. Cade."

"We are about to wed in a few hours, perhaps you can start calling me Dillon."

"I do not know you well enough to use your Christian name."

"Whatever makes you feel most comfortable, Miss Gallagher."

"Come now, Dillon, you are being far too generous." Brogan slapped him on the back. "Cate is only being difficult. You need to have a firm hand with her."

"It is my wedding day, and I will behave however I wish." She crossed her arms, petulantly. Apparently everyone in her family had fallen under some kind of spell, for no one, except her, seemed to care that he was English. *Have they all forgotten Dwayne so readily? Forgotten the fighting, and the lives that were lost in the battle for freedom? And what about fleeing for our lives?*

They'd uprooted everything and moved to America because England considered them traitors after finding evidence that her brothers were in the United Irishman Organization. The whole family might have been killed as traitors if her father hadn't been a lawyer with high contacts. Instead, they'd been exiled from their home. And now, her family willingly accepted this man with open arms.

"Are you taking a seat, Cate?" Brogan's voice interrupted her thoughts.

"I am not very hungry."

"It is just nerves," Kathleen insisted. "But, you do need some nourishment, and Hilda cooked your favorite."

"Cracklin' oat cakes." Caitlin brightened.

"Aye. With maple syrup."

"Well, I am a little hungry." She took a seat. "How did Hilda manage all this cooking by herself?"

"My cook is assisting her. Other members of my staff are helping to prepare, also." Dillon sat across the table.

"We are having all your favorite dishes, and Dillon's, too." Kathleen smiled. "'Tis going to be a grand marriage feast."

"Just grand," Caitlin huffed.

"What a lovely day for a wedding," remarked a tall slender girl with dark ringlets cascading down her back. She joined the family.

"Sarah." Brogan stood, mesmerized by her beauty. Even in a simple blue walking dress, she looked ravishing. "I did not know you were joining us."

"I am the maid of honor, you goose." She flounced over to the table, the blue ribbons on her straw hat bouncing with each step.

"I am so glad you're here." Caitlin jumped up and hugged her best friend fiercely.

"Of course I'm here. Who else would stand up for you on your wedding day?"

"But I did not ask you," Caitlin stated, confused.

"I took the liberty of asking Sarah, figuring she would be the most logical choice. You were so busy with all the other details that a maid of honor slipped your mind," Kathleen elegantly lied. Caitlin hadn't prepared one thing for the wedding. Instead, she had chosen to sulk for the entire two weeks.

"Of course I would have asked her, had I thought about it." Caitlin felt a little foolish. She now wished she'd invested a little more time into the planning. "Sit next to me, Sarah." She indicated the empty chair.

Dillon and Alin stood, waiting for the women to be seated. Both girls sat down, followed by the men.

"So tell me, Mr. Cade, how did you manage to snag our dear Caitlin so quickly?" Sarah asked boldly.

"I...umm..." Dillon cleared his throat. "The hand of fate."

"A very forcible hand I might add," Caitlin sighed.

Sarah frowned at Caitlin, "I guess I just never pictured Mr. Cade as your husband." Then, smiling at Dillon, she said, "No disrespect intended, Mr. Cade."

"None taken, and please call me Dillon. I consider any friend of Caitlin's a friend of mine."

"Thank you, Mr. Cade. I mean, Dillon." She blushed slightly. "I have known you as Mr. Cade for so long that I may have trouble remembering your Christian name."

"Do not fret about it. Call me whatever you like."

"That, sir, could be a dangerous proposition," Caitlin smirked.

"Depends upon who is calling the name." His dark eyes held her gaze, his heart skipping a beat.

Sarah's arrival elevated Caitlin's mood. They chatted and giggled while eating the morning meal. Caitlin asked to be excused when she finished, wanting to prepare for the ceremony.

"Might I have a private word with you?" Dillon wiped his mouth and stood.

"Of course." Caitlin smiled, tautly.

They found a secluded spot in the garden. "I fear there is a matter we must address."

"What?"

"During the nuptials there is a part where we must kiss."

"I am aware of that. I have been to a few weddings in my lifetime."

"How do you want to proceed?"

"I do not comprehend what you're asking."

"Should we kiss or not?"

"Oh. I see." She looked thoughtful for a minute. "I must say that I do feel uncomfortable with all these guests. I had been under the assumption that only immediate family would be at the ceremony. However, since all the guests have no idea that we are marrying in name only, I see no reason why we must tell them. We will proceed with the nuptials as typically planned."

"Are you saying that kissing me would not be unfavorable?"

"I shall struggle through it."

"If it would ease your fears, we could practice before the ceremony." His dark brows rose with challenge.

"I cannot believe you would suggest such a thing." Caitlin feigned shock. "You, sir, truly are a cad."

His deep chuckle glided around the garden like a gentle breeze, settling in her heart. "Merely a suggestion."

"What did he want?" Sarah asked once they were ensconced in Caitlin's bedroom.

"Can you believe he had the audacity to ask me if I wanted to practice our kiss?"

"You're telling me you have not kissed?"

"You can close your mouth, Sarah. It is not a big deal."

"But you are going to be wed in a few hours."

"And we shall kiss during the ceremony."

"How romantic," Sarah gushed. "You're going to have your first kiss on your wedding day."

"Only you could find romance where there is none."

"But Dillon is so handsome. I cannot believe you haven't kissed him yet. And I most certainly cannot believe you are marrying him."

"It is nothing." Caitlin brushed it off.

"Nothing!" Sarah's blue eyes widened. "Every girl in town has had a crush on Dillon Cade, including me. You have captured the most eligible bachelor this town has ever had."

"And I thought you were pining after my brother."

"You know that my intentions toward Brogan are true. However, as a young girl, Dillon Cade was the object of my fantasies."

"You can marry him, if you like."

"'Tis too late. One, my heart now belongs to Brogan, even if he does not want to marry me. And two, you have stolen Dillon's heart."

"I would not say that." A knock on the door interrupted their conversation.

Kathleen swung the door open. "I have come to help you dress." She brought in two bouquets of red and white roses.

"Mrs. Gallagher, the bouquets are lovely." Sarah took them and set them on the dresser.

"Thank you. Now you'd better hurry and get ready. The ceremony will be starting soon."

Caitlin stood in front of the mahogany cheval mirror admiring the handiwork on her gown, while her mother fussed with the silver shawl. "There. Perfect."

"You look so beautiful," Sarah gushed. "This is the most gorgeous gown I have ever seen."

"I feel like a princess," Caitlin admitted, pinning up a few more curls.

"You look like one, too." Kathleen stepped back, admiring her daughter.

"Your dress is something new," Sarah observed. "Now we need something old, something borrowed and something blue."

"Do not forget the six pence in your shoe." Kathleen held up the round coin.

"Oh, Mama. I do not believe in those silly superstitions."

"Nonetheless, it doesn't hurt. Now slip this in your shoe." Caitlin rolled her eyes as she put the coin into her silver slipper. "I also have this." Kathleen pulled a blue handkerchief from her reticule. "My mother gave it to me the day I married your father. She carried it the day she married your grandfather."

Caitlin took the piece of faded blue lace, running her hand over the embroidered flowers adorning the edge. "Beautiful."

"I stitched your initials and the date in this corner." She pointed to the letters and numbers. "Here are mine and your father's. And that is your grandparents."

"That leaves the fourth corner for when your daughter gets married. What a great family tradition," Sarah exclaimed.

"That leaves something borrowed." Caitlin quickly changed the subject.

"Here." Sarah took her earrings out and handed them to Caitlin.

"But these are the pearls your parents gave you when you turned sixteen."

"I know. But you are only borrowing them. I expect them back."

"Thank you." Caitlin hugged her best friend. "And thank you, too, Mama."

"But what about something old?" Sarah asked.

"I believe the handkerchief covers both," Caitlin said.

"I have one more thing to give you. I believe it covers old." Kathleen handed her a small box. "It will match perfectly with your dress."

"Where did you get this?" Caitlin gasped as she opened the package.

"It is a present from Dillon."

"But I threw it at him in the garden."

"You threw an expensive piece of jewelry like this?" Sarah asked.

"He made me angry."

"Caitlin Gallagher, that temper of yours is going to get you into trouble someday," Sarah scolded.

"'True." Kathleen agreed as she pinned the diamond and silver brooch on the middle of the shawl. "I fixed the clasp and sewed the rip in your shawl."

"This is old?" Caitlin asked.

"'It is a family heirloom. It belonged to his mother," Kathleen explained.

"He didn't tell me that."

"Did you give him a chance?"

Caitlin responded with silence.

A loud knock preceded Alin's gruff tone. "Ladies, we must hurry. Our guests are waiting."

Sarah opened the door, and Alin stepped inside. He stopped short when he spotted Caitlin. "You look beautiful." He fought back the tears. "My little girl is all grown up."

"There is still time for you to change your mind." Caitlin made one last attempt.

"This is best for everyone." Alin held out his arm. "Come, I have a daughter to show off."

Caitlin nervously walked down the path formed by the chairs, grateful for her father's sturdy presence by her side. Sarah and Brogan were already at the altar offering more support. Mustering enough courage, she glanced at Dillon and felt her breath stall. He looked like a typical dandy, clad in an ivory satin frock with black beads embroidered in a swirl design along the edge of the jacket and cuffs. A matching waistcoat was closed with block buttons, and he'd tied a black cravat around the collar of his white silk shirt. His ivory satin breeches ended with white stockings and black, square-toed shoes. The magnificent craftsmanship of the suit paled in comparison to the stature of the man wearing it. The tailored jacket spanning the width of his shoulders narrowed, revealing his thin waist and hips. She wondered if he wore a corset, as some men did, to achieve that perfect waistline.

Dillon breathed a sigh of relief when Caitlin came into view. Although she'd been pleasant during the morning meal, he wondered if she might back out at the last minute. *So far so good.*

His heart swelled with pride as Caitlin walked toward him. She seemed to outshine the sun, which danced and played with the fiery curls dangling beneath the silver headdress. Although she appeared to be a most willing bride on the outside, he saw the hesitancy and anger residing in her eyes. He only prayed that God would alleviate her apprehension someday.

Alin pecked her on the cheek and whispered, "This *is* for the best. I love you."

"I love you too, Papa." A tear teetered on her long lashes. The unspoken plea, *don't make me do this*, was squelched when Alin passed her gloved hand to Dillon and took his seat next to Kathleen. Handing her bouquet to Sarah, she placed both hands into Dillon's grasp.

He gave her hands a gentle squeeze for reassurance, which ignited a tingle that spread through her body, turning her pale cheeks pink. Her first instinct was to pull away; however, she'd have to wait until the end of the ceremony.

The sun stood high in the sky, warming the fragrant air that swirled around the occupants in the garden. The tinkling of water from a large fountain spouting crystal liquid into a small pool served as the backdrop for the couple. The red, gold, and yellow color scheme of autumn further complimented the choice of cream satin for the bride.

She smiled stiffly as they went through the ritual, reciting the sacred words and praying. When it came time for the ring, she slipped her glove off and gasped when Dillon slid the huge diamond on her third finger. After a few words of instruction, the preacher pronounced them man and wife and told Dillon to kiss his bride.

Caitlin felt the heat from his body as he stepped closer, placing an arm around her waist. A smile played upon his lips, "Are you ready, my sweet?"

"Make haste and get it over with," she groaned. The corners of her mouth turned down, but her head obediently tilted up. She closed her eyes, bracing for the kiss. Both were unprepared for the spark that charged between them when their lips met. Caitlin's eyes flew open, and she would have backed away if the steel arms around her waist hadn't tightened, keeping her anchored to that spot. He kissed her tenderly at first, gently moving his mouth above her own, producing sensations that were overwhelming and exciting. A soft moan escaped as her mouth responded to his lips.

The gnawing in the pit of Dillon's stomach grew like wildfire causing his desire to quickly burn out of control. He deepened the kiss forcing Caitlin's mouth open and greedily tasted the treasures inside. His kind, gentle lips turned fierce with longing and passion. Pulling her soft body even closer against his hard muscled chest produced emotions that rampaged through his soul, tormenting his body.

Caitlin hesitantly complied at first, but soon found her own hunger rapidly intensifying behind the reluctant facade. She wound her arms around his neck inching as close as possible. All other feelings fled, leaving behind a craving that only his touch would quench. Eventually, confusion emerged from somewhere deep in a crevice of her heart, reminding her that Dillon was her enemy.

Managing to find some strength in her feeble limbs she pushed at his rock hard chest, breaking the mysterious spell they'd fallen under. A shaky hand flew to her mouth, touching the warm wetness left behind. She was thankful he didn't immediately withdraw his hands from her waist or she'd have toppled over. His kiss seemed to suck the strength from her body and mind. She felt a little embarrassed. Having never been kissed like that before, she didn't know if her reaction had been appropriate.

Dillon vaguely heard the crowd cheering as his senses slowly returned. Remembering they were still in front of their wedding guests, he wondered what they thought of such a passionate display. He'd only meant to give her a little kiss to seal the vows. How had it turned into an ardent demonstration of emotion?

Chapter 3

"That was one passionate kiss." Brogan slapped his brother-in-law on the back.

"It was only for pretense," Caitlin declared.

"It looked real to me," Sarah stated, handing Caitlin her bouquet.

"Looks can be deceiving," Caitlin insisted, although her legs still felt unsteady.

"I am practically out of breath from watching you." Sarah blushed.

"Why, Sarah, I do believe your cheeks are as red as your dress," Caitlin teased.

"Your cheeks have a glow as well," Sarah pointed out, "and it makes you even more beautiful."

"She's right, Cate." Brogan kissed her on the cheek. "You look beautiful."

"I would say breathtaking." Dillon offered his arm. "Shall we go greet our guests, Mrs. Cade?"

Her back stiffened at the use of her married name, but now wasn't the time to discuss it. "Of course, Mr. Cade." Her cold eyes met his. Slipping her arm through his, they walked up the aisle, ducking the handfuls of grain tossed at them.

Caitlin smiled compliantly as she met the guests, accepting their compliments and the wellspring of good wishes. She seemed the picture-perfect bride, hugging and kissing friends and family, showing off the large diamond in her ring, and dutifully standing close to Dillon as he slipped his arm around her slim waist.

"Oh, darling, that was beautiful." Kathleen hugged Caitlin so tightly she couldn't breathe. "I cannot believe my baby is married."

"I am not a baby anymore," Caitlin quipped. "And I would not be married if you and Papa hadn't forced me into it."

"Nonetheless, it was a lovely ceremony." Kathleen dabbed at the tears in her eyes.

"I have to concur," Alin interjected. "My little girl has grown into a beautiful young lady."

"Oh, Papa." Caitlin hugged the man that had always been her pillar of strength. Inhaling the smell of musk and cigar smoke that was uniquely her father's scent helped to bolster some courage to face the rest of the day. "I do not understand any of this," she cried into the crook of his neck.

"I know, sweetheart. We will explain everything when the time is right."

"I've already taken the vows, can you not tell me now?" Salty drops fell from her confused green eyes. She'd submitted to the hasty wedding without any knowledge of the circumstances, trusting only in her parents' protection. For some odd reason, they were transferring that guardianship to Dillon, and she wanted to know why.

Alin wiped the tears from her cheeks. "Later. Right now I want you to enjoy your wedding day."

"I don't believe that will happen." Triumph filled her heart as Dillon stiffened at the remark.

"It could if you weren't so stubborn," Alin scoffed.

"'Tis your Irish temper I possess."

"Aye. I wish you'd gotten more of your mother's sweet nature."

"It will have to be enough that I possess her looks."

"It is enough." He kissed her cheek and proceeded to shake Dillon's hand. "Take good care of her."

"I will, sir."

The guests took their seats at the tables, while Hilda and Martha directed the servants with the food preparations. After Dillon and Caitlin took their place at the head table, everyone enjoyed the feast. Caitlin drained her glass of wine during dinner and asked for a refill.

"I did not realize you had a preference for alcohol," Dillon commented.

"You barely know me, sir. There is a lot you do not realize."

"True. However, I'm anxious to find out." The wrinkles deepened around his eyes as he smiled.

"Do not be too anxious, *my dear*." Her voice dripped with sarcasm. "There are certain things you will never discover."

"Perhaps. Perhaps not."

"What do you mean?" Her eyes widened with astonishment. "You agreed that our marriage would be in name only."

"Aye, madam. However, I have heard that liquor reduces inhibitions."

Her red brows arched elegantly. "Do you presume that a few glasses of wine will make me more inclined to accept the invitation to your bed?"

"Perhaps."

"I can tell you truly, sir, the only way you'll ever have me is by force. No amount of liquor will change that."

"Shall we see?" He picked up the bottle to refill her glass.

Caitlin had never been a drinker and could not argue about the effect it would have on her. Covering the top of her glass she said, "I believe I'll have to keep my wits if I do not want to be violated by you."

His soft laughter mingled with the murmuring of the crowd. "I like a woman who knows her limitations." He set the bottle down.

"It is not my limitations that I'm worried about," she scoffed.

"I can assure you, madam, that I am aware of my limitations, as well."

"Is that why you are not drinking?"

"A man cannot think clearly when his head is muddled with spirits."

"That is true, however, I believe there are times in life when an unclear head can serve you far better than a clear one."

"Such as?"

"A prisoner being forced into confinement."

His thick brows formed a frown.

"It would serve me better not remembering anything from this day," she continued.

"Might serve me better, too." He smiled wickedly. "You would not recall anything from the nighttime."

"Humph!" Caitlin angled her pointed chin out. "You, sir, are worse than a cad. You're the devil himself."

His lighthearted laughter sparked contempt in Caitlin. She was not amused by this situation and most definitely wouldn't let him goad her into fulfilling his wishes.

"I have decided to have that drink after all." She obstinately filled her glass and then tipped it in a silent salute.

When dinner ended, they cut the bride's cake and passed it out for everyone to enjoy. The leftover cake was packed up, ready to be sent home with the bridal party. This tradition usually represented good luck to the newlyweds. However, Caitlin did not think that Brogan, Sarah and her parents could pray hard enough to bring good wishes to this union.

Next, Dillon threaded a piece of cake through a large ring. The entire group counted out loud as he made it to seven before the cake broke. Applause erupted, but Dillon felt disappointed that he hadn't made it to nine – the magical number for this tradition. Of course, what did it really matter, since it would take more than cake, wishes, and superstitions to help this marriage? It would take the hand of God Almighty, himself.

"Oh, Caitlin, this fruitcake is the best. And the marzipan is the sweetest I've ever tasted," Sarah stated as she dug through the piece of cake on her plate.

"It seems Hilda has outdone herself," Caitlin responded. "Why are you smashing the cake?"

"I'm looking for the ring or the horseshoe." Sarah turned questioning eyes to her. "Hilda did put the charms in the cake, did she not?"

"I'm not sure."

"I do not see anything in this piece. I need another slice."

"Sarah, you do not need charms."

"But the ring will bring me love, and the horseshoe brings good luck. I must find one of them."

"Why?"

"For good luck. I am also going to sleep with a piece of the cake under my pillow tonight," she added. "If I dream about Brogan then maybe we will wed next."

"Sarah, those superstitions do not work. I am sure my brother will marry you, but it will not have anything to do with cake or lucky charms."

"It won't hurt, either."

"I know Brogan loves you. It will only be a matter of time before he asks for your hand."

"I hope he does it before I'm an old maid."

"You put too much stock in the formalities of society. You are far from an old maid." Caitlin had never understood the romantic, wishy-washy side of her best friend. Sarah never had a thought of her own. She always followed the rules and superstitions set by others.

"Well, I just want to make sure." Sarah went to get another piece of cake.

The orchestra swung into a festive tune and some of the guests headed to the designated spot for dancing.

Dillon wanted a dance with his beautiful bride, even if coerced. "May I have this dance, Mrs. Cade?" He extended his hand.

"Of course." She swallowed the last drops of wine, feeling a tingling spread throughout her body, which helped bolster the fraudulent, joyful mood. Dancing was the last thing she wanted to do, but the charade had to be kept up until the end. *I hope it's over soon*, she sighed.

As they went through the steps of the dance, Dillon asked, "How do you feel?"

"Words cannot express my feelings." Actually, she had the words; it just wasn't ladylike to use them in mixed company.

"You have had several glasses of wine. I do not want you getting sick in front of the guests."

"Are you worried about your reputation?"

"Nay, Mrs. Cade, it is the reputations of you and your parents that worry me."

"I can assure you that my reputation will be just fine." She smiled, knowing that he didn't approve of her drinking. "There is one more thing I wish to discuss."

"Anything, my lady."

"I do not like your constant use of "Mrs. Cade." Just because you are partial to the name does not mean the whole world is. Caitlin will suffice."

"You do not fancy taking the name Cade?" Dillon challenged.

"I do not fancy taking any man's last name. However, I loathe your English name most of all."

"I'll be obliged to call you by your Christian name, if you do the same with me."

"Sir, you drive a hard bargain." Being on a first name basis with this tyrant was the last thing she wanted. However, being reminded constantly that her last name was now English seemed far worse. "It is as you wish, Dillon," she reluctantly agreed.

The dance ended and Caitlin used the excuse that she was out of breath and needed a rest to leave the dance floor. She went back to the table and poured another glass of wine.

Allen approached Dillon as he stood off to the side of the dance floor watching the other couples happily maneuver through the steps.

"Do you think it's a good idea for your wife to be imbibing so much?"

"Nay, sir. I tried to caution her, but that made her fix upon it even more."

"I'll have a talk with her."

"If you don't mind my saying, sir, I think it would be best to let her alone. Caitlin is stubborn and must learn the consequences of drinking on her own. Besides, I feel we have all made more than enough decisions on her behalf."

"I suspect you're right, lad."

The music swelled into an Irish jig and Caitlin's feet tapped along with the beat. Her feet weren't the only things that felt light. Her head seemed to float along like a cloud beside her body, and her spirit soared higher than the tops of the tall pine trees. She slipped through the crowd to stand by her father and Dillon.

"Papa, come dance with me." She tugged at his arm.

"You know I'm not much of a dancer," he moaned. "You and Dillon looked good out there."

"It is my wedding, and I want to dance with you."

"All right." Alin followed Caitlin onto the dance floor and fervently tried to keep up with her.

When the song ended, Alin tried to leave but Caitlin wouldn't let him. The next song started and he found himself surrounded by couples and had no choice but to join in the wheel.

Kathleen decided to get a dance with her new son-in-law. They joined everyone on the floor and soon switched partners with Caitlin and Alin.

Alin gladly went into the arms of his wife, however Caitlin was more reluctant. The overwhelming proximity of her spouse left a feeling of weakness that caused her knees to wobble, and set her head spinning. Their kiss at the altar had left her feeling the same way. She tried forcing the memories away, but the haze under which her brain operated made this task difficult.

Caitlin looked around the crowd, watching the couples gladly glide to the music. She spotted Brogan and Sarah, their hands touching as often as they dared without risking Sarah's reputation. The attraction between them could be felt. *They make such a handsome couple*, she thought. The black frock coat and breeches of the same color emphasized Brogan's tall, bulky physique. His light brown hair was a contrast to Sarah's dark tresses, which had been piled high in ringlet curls and held in place by a bandeau of red and white flowers. The Greek-style dress flattered her tall, slender frame while the red complemented her dark complexion.

She felt a little envious of the pair. *It must be delightful dancing with the person you love instead of this ton from England.* She had always wanted to experience that kind of attraction, and now would never have the chance. The kiss sealing her vows would be as close as she'd ever get.

Starting to feel the tears swell behind her eyes, she excused herself and went in search of another drink. *I don't know what all the fuss is over this stuff,* she contemplated before draining another glass. The former tingling in her limbs gave way to numbness and made her feel better. She could almost forget that she'd married her greatest foe.

Her pink lips curved contentedly when she noticed the puckered frown on Dillon's oval face. "A few more drinks and I'll show him," she stated to herself. What right did he have telling her not to drink? What right did he have marrying her? She'd show him. She'd show them all!

The afternoon sun lowered in the sky causing the huge maple tree to cast its shadow over the guests as they danced and had fun. Even Caitlin seemed to be enjoying herself. Dillon assumed the relaxed attitude was due to the wine coursing through her veins, and the fact that he'd kept his distance, but the time had come for them to leave. He worried that Caitlin would make a spectacle of herself. Dillon proceeded to the dance floor to fetch his drunken wife.

"There you are." Caitlin announced loudly as she fell into his arms. "I was beginning to think you'd abandoned me."

"I would never do that."

"That's my husband," she muttered, "gallant to the end."

"I try, madam." He gestured for Sarah.

"So tell me, Mr. Gallant," she slurred, "what are you getting out of this marriage? I mean, why would you tie yourself down with a wife, especially when we will never even be intimate?"

"I see the wine has loosened your tongue." He held on to her as she swayed. "This subject is best left to be discussed privately."

"Oh, I see. You do not want me embarrassing you. Well, you should have thought about that before you went through with this charade."

Sarah hesitantly approached, not wanting to eavesdrop, but Dillon motioned for her again. "Can you help Caitlin up the stairs? It's time to toss the bouquet."

"I can manage the stairs on my own." Caitlin squared her shoulders and proceeded unsteadily to the house, feeling woozier than she wanted to admit.

Dillon gently laid his hand on Sarah's forearm. "Whatever it takes, do not allow her to ascend the stairs alone. I fear she may fall and get hurt."

"Aye, sir." She noted the concern in his eyes. "I am under the impression that something is going on here. This is not a love match, is it?"

"Nay. However, I'm not at liberty to give details."

"I understand, and I'm not asking for any. I only wanted to let you know that Caitlin couldn't ask for a better husband. Your concern is evident and I appreciate the way you have handled her behavior tonight. Most husbands would not have been so lenient."

"Caitlin is having a hard time right now. I'm sure she will come around in time."

"Aye," she skeptically replied, then hurried off to catch up with Caitlin.

This staircase never seemed so long before; Caitlin mused as she struggled to climb it on unsteady limbs. Gripping the wood railing with one hand and her bouquet in the other left her no way to lift the train of her dress. She tried holding up the hem of her gown with one hand, but her equilibrium was off and she swayed, teetering on the edge of the step. Thankfully, Sarah steadied her and now held the dress up out of the way. They reached the landing while the group of unwed maidens gathered below, eagerly waiting to catch the bouquet.

"This is a stupid tradition," Caitlin muttered. "I didn't catch the bouquet at Caroline's wedding. Bonnie was supposed to be the next one to get hitched."

"Her turn will come," Sarah reassured her. "You were just luckier than she."

"Luck!" Caitlin harshly laughed. "I feel about as lucky as a rabbit's foot."

"A rabbit's foot is very lucky."

"Not for the poor rabbit."

"Hush now and throw the bouquet," Sarah urged.

Caitlin tossed the flowers over her shoulder. She heard the scrambling below then applause erupted from the crowd. Not being able to look at the fool who'd caught the bouquet, she closed her eyes, which also served to fend off a wave of nausea.

The grandfather clock chimed four times, bringing an onslaught of tears to Caitlin's eyes. Each chime thudded through her head and caused her stomach to revolt. "I feel sick."

"I'm not surprised, from all the spirits you have consumed," Sarah scolded.

"Now you sound like Dillon."

"Well, someone should have talked some sense into you before now. It is not ladylike to drink."

"Save the scolding for later. Right now I need fresh air."

Sarah helped her maneuver down the steps where Dillon waited to assist her outside. He helped Caitlin into the back of the carriage, instructing the driver to hurry home. The motion from the horses lurching forward, however, proved too much for her weak stomach. Covering her mouth she tried to hold back the nausea.

"Feeling ill, my pet?" Dillon chuckled at the vicious glare she tossed him.

The sun filtering through the gray clad sky dimly made its way into the equally gray bedroom that hosted its new mistress. With a groan, Caitlin rolled over and vomited into the bucket placed next to her bed.

A light rapping on the door intensified the shooting pain behind her eyes. "Who is it?" she barked.

"Your husband." Dillon's voice drifted through the door.

"What do you want?"

She heard the door squeak open. Dillon warily crossed the room and stood at the foot of the bed. "How are you feeling, my sweet?"

She tried to glare but the response produced tears in her blood shot eyes. "I think I'm going to die," she moaned.

"You will not die; however, you will be sick for a while." He dipped a washcloth in the porcelain washbasin, wrung it out and placed it on her forehead.

Caitlin reveled in the coolness for a few seconds before her pride reared up. Ripping the cloth off, she threw it back at him. "I do not need your help." Embarrassment combined with discomfort caused her tone to sharpen. "You probably think I'm a lushy, and now God is punishing me."

Not wanting to add to the turmoil, he replied, "I think you are a woman who celebrated her wedding day. You just over-indulged in the spirits a bit."

Caitlin's eyes flashed. "I wanted to forget that I was married."

"Did it work?"

"For a while. I do not recall much from the end of the wedding feast." As the thought slowly dawned on her, she sat up straight in bed. "How did I get here? And who undressed me?" *Has he broken his word and taken advantage of me?* The sudden movement caused her squeamish stomach to revolt once again. She almost felt too sick to care if he had ravished her.

As the remnants of dinner heaved into the bucket, Dillon filled a glass with water and handed it to her.

She shook her head. The thought of anything in her stomach, even water, intensified the queasiness.

"Drink it." He pressed the glass into her hand. "It will help you feel better."

She gingerly took a few sips, which washed the disgusting taste out of her mouth but did little to ease her headache or upset stomach.

"And to ease your mind," Dillon reassured her, "Lucy put you to bed last night."

"Who is Lucy?" The thought of a stranger undressing her wasn't any more pleasant than the thought of Dillon doing it himself.

"Your personal maid."

"My what?"

"Lucy assures me that she's skillful in arranging hair and is up to date on all the latest styles."

"I have a personal maid?" *Just how deep did his pockets go?*

"Aye, my pet. She will be back in a little while. I let her have a break since she has been tending to you all morning."

"What time is it?" The questions forged through her hazy mind.

"Almost half past ten."

Caitlin rolled her head back onto the pillows and closed her eyes. "I have never slept this late."

"I believe you will be spending the better part of the day in bed."

"I take it you've been through this before?"

"Only once, but it was enough to deter me from partaking in spirits again."

"Once shall be enough for me also. That is, of course, if I survive."

50

"You will survive. Trust me." He handed her the wet cloth again. "Put this over your eyes. It will ease the ache in your head."

Normally Caitlin would have put up a fight, but she didn't have the strength today. Besides, the cool cloth did feel good. "Are you going to say it?"

"Say what, my lady?"

"You told me so."

"Nay. I tried to warn you of the effects only to protect you from this misery you're facing now."

"I should have listened." Removing the cloth, she looked into his brown eyes. "Why did you not try harder to stop me?"

"It is not my desire to impose my will or beliefs upon you. You are obviously a very spirited and well-educated young lady, quite capable of making decisions on your own, when you are not being so stubborn."

She wanted to argue the matter, but somehow he had disguised the insult with a compliment. "You must be a poor debater if that is the best insult you can produce."

"No insult intended."

"I would normally quibble with you, however, my head is pounding and a ringing forms in my ears with every word. I fear I must wait until my health returns before I can dispute with you."

"I await the day with anticipation." He ceremoniously bowed. "Good day, madam."

"Good?" She'd have laughed outright if the throbbing in her head would quit.

Chapter 4

Caitlin wrapped the robe around her slender body, securing it with a belt. The blue cloth did little to fight off the chill, but it offered more modesty than the white cotton nightgown. She cautiously walked down the dimly lit hall. Peering into the rooms whose doors stood ajar made her feel a bit guilty, as if she were snooping around a stranger's house, yet this was now her home.

The rooms were practically empty, furnished with the barest of necessities. No pictures hung on the walls. There were no fancy curtains adorning the windows and no fashionable rugs on the floors. A gray, drab feeling hung around the entire house. It didn't look or feel like the households she'd grown up in. Her mother had always managed to transform the meekest house into a warm, loving, carefree, and hospitable home. The fireplaces were lit in every room, warding off the chill, and making unexpected guests feel welcome. This place felt more like a dungeon.

Crossing to the other side of the hall, she peeked into a bedroom. Unable to see clearly, she pushed the door open wider. This room had personal touches, making it feel more comfortable than the others. The crackling fire engulfed the room in a warm, cozy glow.

"How are you feeling this morning?"

She jumped as Dillon's voice startled her. "Better. I merely feel like a team of horses ran over me, but I no longer think I'll die."

"That is good to hear," he laughed softly. "So how do you like Regal Hall?"

"It is a bit chilly." Caitlin crossed her arms, feeling self-conscious about her state of dress.

"Are you cold?"

"A little." She rubbed her palms up and down the length of her arms.

"Where are your slippers?" He questioned, noticing her bare feet.

"I have not found them."

"Are your trunks not in your room?" His tone was sharp.

"Aye." She didn't want to admit that bending over the chests made her feel sick. She still felt too weak to do much of anything.

"You cannot walk around Regal Hall without something on your feet. You will catch your death."

"I wouldn't if there were some heat in this place."

"It will be warmer downstairs, but you must find something for your feet. I do not have many carpets in the house."

"You don't have many furnishings at all."

"I have what I need."

"Why is this room nicer?"

"'It is Lucy's room. I believe women are better suited for decorating and such."

"Why not hire someone to fix it up?"

"I am pleased with it the way it is. Does it not meet your approval?"

"There's nothing regal about it unless you like dingy and gray. This house could use a sprucing up. Some paint and new curtains would go a long way. Not to mention a few carpets."

"I believe decorating is best left for the woman of the household. The house looked like this when I bought it, and I have not bothered to change anything. I shall leave that task up to you, my dear."

"What?" Her green eyes filled with excitement. "You want me to decorate your house?"

"It is your home now also," he reminded her. "I want you to do whatever you wish. You can renovate the whole interior if you like."

"That could be very expensive."

"Money is no object," he assured her. "This house is in your hands. Now, shall we have breakfast?" He offered his arm.

"Perhaps I should dress first." She pulled the sides of her robe up higher around her neck.

"Nonsense. This is your home, and I will have you take the morning meal in whatever you please."

"I would feel more comfortable in a morning dress."

"You look beautiful just as you are. Besides, Martha will be angry if we are late."

Hastily running a hand through her long tresses, she felt the tangles and snarls. She looked a fright. Nonetheless, it was nice to hear a compliment. "I am pretty hungry."

"'Because you did not have any solid food yesterday."

"You assured me that chicken broth wouldn't upset my stomach like solid food." She slid her arm through his.

"Did I lie?" he asked as he led the way downstairs.

"No. However I am famished today."

"That is the price to pay for indulging in too much wine."

"If you do not mind, sir, I'd like to never bring up the subject of my foolish behavior again."

"As you wish, madam."

They entered the dining room where smells of sausage, bacon, eggs, hoe cakes, oatmeal, and biscuits greeted them. The overpowering aroma made her feel faint. Dillon put a steady arm around her waist, guiding her soft form into a chair. He liked the feel of her womanly body pressed against his.

"Perhaps you should start with something light," he commented. "How about a cup of tea?"

"That would be nice."

The tea not only settled her stomach but also stimulated some warmth in her cold body. She shivered slightly from the sensation of its heat.

When the bulky maid came back into the room, Dillon directed her to find Lucy and have her go through Caitlin's things until she found the slippers. "Bring another wrap for the mistress also," he ordered.

"Yes, my lord." She curtsied and then went off to do his bidding.

"Do you want some butter or honey for your hoe cakes?" Dillon held up the china boat.

"No, thank you. It will be better to eat light this morning."

"I suspect you are right." He looked at her plate. "You have managed to eat quite a bit. It will help you feel better." He held up a biscuit. "Want to try one? Martha is well known for her flaky pie crusts and rich breads and biscuits."

"How can I not try one with such a glowing report?" She took one, declining the butter he offered.

"I must get to the shop," Dillon announced. "Feel free to look around, but do not overdo it. You have a house full of servants at your disposal, so take it easy."

"I believe I will take a nap. I still have a slight headache."

"Excellent. I will be home at noon for supper. Good day, my lady."

After a nap and a long bath, Lucy brushed through her hair, pinning it up and placing a white cottage cap over the auburn pile. Adorning herself in a blue muslin morning dress, Caitlin toured the house, making mental notes and forming her plans to transform the house into a regal palace. Deciding that the parlor and dining room, being the entertaining rooms, should be the first rooms converted, she then took a look around the kitchen.

Martha, however, disliked the intrusion and stated so. She'd run the kitchen for twelve years and wasn't about to hand the authority over to some stranger, even if she happened to be the master's wife.

Caitlin, knowing her way around a kitchen, had spotted several things that did not meet her approval. She ruffled Martha's feathers by insisting the leftover flour on the kneading board should be scraped back into the "emptyings" jar.

"There's bits of dough mixed with that flour."

"The crumbs will not hurt anything and that's a lot of flour being wasted."

"It isn't that much flour," Martha insisted. "I have never put scraps in my starter. The bits of dough will make my pancakes and biscuits lumpy."

"My mother and Hilda managed our kitchen that way, and you'd be hard pressed to find better bakers in all of Ireland."

"Perhaps that's how things were done in your homeland, but you're in America now. I'd remind you to remember that." Martha crossed her thick arms in front of her large chest, bringing the discussion to an end.

"We'll see what Dillon has to say on the subject." Caitlin never let anyone else have the last word in an argument. However, she heard Martha mumbling under her breath as she left.

Caitlin found the rest of the staff reserved but more open to her presence. Their curiosity overrode any resentment they may have felt. The astonishment at their master's hasty marriage to a woman he barely knew melted the moment he'd carried his bride over the threshold. Even though the poor thing had been sicker than a dog, you couldn't hide her undeniable beauty.

"How was your morning?" Dillon unbuttoned his benjamin and hung it on the coat rack, placing his hat on a peg next to it.

"Quite productive," Caitlin beamed. "I have decided which rooms I want to redecorate first."

"That was fast." Dillon assumed she would take a while to become comfortable with the house before jumping into the task of redesigning the rooms.

"I am not one to waste to time," she stated. "I have several ideas of what I want to do. However, since I've never done this before, I may have to hire someone to assist me."

"Whatever you need." He felt his heart skip a beat as a smile brightened her face. He'd give up all his money to keep her happy.

"I need to go into town first thing tomorrow. Perhaps Mrs. Johnson can recommend someone."

"I would prefer you not to go into town just yet."

"Why?" Her smile faded.

"You do not have a chaperon."

"If you recall, I'm now married and do not need one. I'm perfectly safe going into town alone. Besides, Lucy will be more than happy to accompany me."

"It is not a question of your safety."

"Then what is it?" Hostility engraved her tone.

"I would like to be present and decide on the person we hire."

"Oh." That wasn't an unreasonable request. After all, he was paying for the remodeling; he should have a say in the decisions. "Would you like me to go over my ideas with you?" Her tone softened.

"Nay, madam. As I said earlier, decorating is best left in the hands of a woman. I merely want to oversee the hired help."

"That sounds reasonable."

"I am not an unreasonable man."

"That remains to be seen." A reasonable fellow wouldn't have forced her into marriage. A reasonable man would have helped her out of the predicament when asked. He would have seen her need for independence and left her alone. "However, you're right on this subject. I would not have the first clue how to hire a worker."

"My schedule will be busy at the shop tomorrow, but maybe the day after I can drive you."

"That will have to do." She pretended to pout. "But, I can do nothing else until then."

"I promise to take you to town as soon as possible. Until then, maybe a tour of the outside grounds will occupy your time."

"Oh, yes." She smiled eagerly. "Can we go after supper?"

"If it will please you, my dear." Her enthusiasm surprised him, and delighted him.

"There is one other thing I wish to discuss with you." Inhaling deeply and smoothing out a few wrinkles in her morning dress, she continued, "It's about Martha.

His laughter made her look up. "I shall speak with her, although I'll be wasting my breath. Martha's used to running the household."

"Am I not the mistress of the house now?"

"Aye. But you have to make some allowances. It will take time for the two of you to learn to work together."

"No wonder she runs the house with an attitude like that!" Caitlin quipped. "She's a servant. You must have a firm hand in dealing with her."

"I have not needed a firm hand with her before." Though he didn't like the remark about Martha only being a servant, he didn't say anything. She was fifteen years his senior and had been like a mother to him.

"Have you been married before?"

"You know I have not."

"Then this problem never arose before?"

"As I said, I will have a talk with her." His crisp tone told Caitlin not to pursue it any further.

"As you wish, sir." Her mockery intensified with a small curtsy. Dillon taking a servant's side over hers only made the resentment grow stronger. She was his wife, even if in name only. That should have borne more status than the hired help.

Caitlin tied the yellow ribbons of her straw bonnet then checked her appearance in the gold-framed convex mirror. The yellow and blue flowers adorning the hat matched perfectly with the blue and yellow checkered pattern of her Roman style dress. Pinching her cheeks to give them a rosy glow, she smiled slightly.

What's taking him so long? She tapped her small pointed slipper impatiently. It had been three days since he promised to take her into town. Not only was she eager to get started on the house, but he had also agreed to buy her some new dresses and bonnets.

Shopping always put her in a good mood. However, qualms tugged at the back of her mind. This was her first trip out as a married woman. The hasty nuptials no doubt left people with lots of questions, and she wondered how best to answer them. Although she and Dillon had made a pretense at the wedding to appear as a happy, devoted couple, she couldn't keep that charade up forever. At the same time, she wasn't sure people could tolerate the truth. Although arranged marriages were common among the upper class, the middle and lower classes married more for love. After all, they didn't have large fortunes, old names, and empires to merge together.

How could she tell her friends and acquaintances that her parents had arranged the marriage? That she'd been goaded into this situation for reasons unbeknownst to her? Even though her father said it was for her own protection, as of yet, he had not elaborated as to what she was being protected from.

"Mr. Cade is bringing the carriage around," Lucy stated, as she hurried into the hall. "I found your blue pelisse. Will that do?"

"Fine." She slipped her arms into the coat.

"This matches perfectly with your dress," Lucy assured her as she hooked the silver latches. Making a trip around Caitlin, she brushed away some wrinkles on her back and shoulders, wanting her mistress to look perfect. She wanted everyone to see what a good job she was doing. "You are the portrait of beauty." Anxiously reaching up, she fiddled with a stray curl.

"Will you stop fussing?" Caitlin smacked her hand away.

"I'm sorry, Mrs. Cade."

"And stop calling me Mrs. Cade."

"Yes, ma'am."

The dejected look crossing the young girl's face instantly made Caitlin regret being so snippy. "I did not mean to yell at you. You are only a few years younger than I am. It seems ridiculous for you to keep referring to me as Mrs. Cade. My name is Caitlin."

"Yes, Mrs....I mean Caitlin." Her blue eyes brightened but still seemed clouded with dissatisfaction. "You don't feel it improper for me to use your Christian name?"

"You will soon learn that I do not like following the rules. I like doing things my own way. If I felt it improper, I would not have suggested it in the first place."

A smile brightened the girl's face. She not only had the prettiest mistress in town, she also had the nicest. "Yes, ma'am."

"What?"

"I mean, Caitlin."

"That's better."

The door opened and a gust of wind whipped around the hem of her skirt. "Are you ready?" Dillon asked.

"We are waiting on you." Caitlin straightened her back and headed to the door.

"Sorry I took so long. A problem arose in the stable."

"Nothing serious, I hope."

"Not at all. Everything is fine." He helped Caitlin and Lucy into the carriage. When both women were settled, he climbed up and sat across from Caitlin.

"You have been very mysterious about the stables," Caitlin noted.

"How so, madam?" He cocked his head.

"You did not show me the stables when we toured the grounds the other day."

"I assumed that ladies detest the smell of stables."

"You assumed wrong about this lady," she quipped. "I enjoy being around horses. As a matter of fact, I had a horse in Ireland. I even groomed him myself."

Dillon's lighthearted chuckle filled the small space. "I should have realized you would be different." His deep-set brown eyes regarded her closely. "So, the smell does not offend you?"

"Nay." She sat erect, trying to look sophisticated and keep her body from swaying as the horses pulled the heavy load over the bumps in the dirt road.

He shifted in his seat, stretched his legs out, crossing them at the ankles. The brush of his legs instantly made her mind go back to their wedding day and the kiss. A chill swept through her as she remembered how close their bodies had been, and what he tasted like. *Oh, foolish girl!* she reprimanded herself. How could a mere look or simple brush of his body send her mind back to that kiss?

"Are you cold?" Dillon asked bringing her back to the present.

"Just a little." She felt her body shaking.

"Here." He tossed her a blanket.

"Thanks." She wrapped it around her legs, but knew it would do little to ease the chills. They weren't caused from the cold wind. "When are you going to show me the stables?" she asked, averting her attention.

"As soon as I have a day off."

"Who knows when that will be?"

"We have been married less than a week and you're already complaining that we do not spend enough time together." A small smile played on his lips. "I would have thought that would be more to your liking."

"It is," she stated. Casting a glance toward Lucy, she cautiously continued. "I merely meant that I am anxious to see the stables. Perhaps I can tour them by myself?"

"Afraid not, my dear. It would be too dangerous."

"I know my way around stables," she insisted.

"I'd prefer you to wait for me. I will take you as soon as I can."

"Whatever you say, *my lord*."

"Now that we have that out of the way," he winked at Lucy, "is there anything else on your mind?"

"As a matter of fact, there is." She fixed him with a stare. "What are we going tell people about our marriage?"

His thick brows drew together making his face even more handsome. "Whatever you want, my dear."

"It's your marriage, too," she reminded him. "Just once I'd like you to have an opinion on something."

"I told you my point of view on the stables and now you're miffed."

"I'm not miffed," she stated indignantly, "I am merely curious."

"I'd rather have you angry."

"Why?"

"Then we could kiss to make up." Her horror-stricken gasp made him laugh.

"Truly, sir, you are a philanderer."

"How can I be a womanizer? You are my wife!"

In name only, she wanted to remind him, but due to the fact that Lucy was riding with them she simply said, "I am sure I'm not the only woman you have said that to."

"Perhaps not. However, you are the last."

Now it was her turn to laugh.

The smell of wood and spices greeted Caitlin as she entered the general store. A tall, thin lady with gray hair looked up from her writing when she heard the door and shuffling feet.

"Caitlin!" Her wrinkled face crinkled even more with her smile.

"Good day, Mrs. Johnson."

"I didn't expect to see you so soon after your wedding."

"We are doing some remodeling and wondered if you know anyone who could assist."

"Oh. Yes. Just wait right here and I'll get Mr. Johnson. He handles things like that, you know." She bustled off into the back room.

It annoyed Caitlin that women never discussed things like business. Everyone knew it was Mrs. Johnson, not her husband, who kept the store going. Yet she hurried off to get him as if he were the one in charge.

As she stood there stewing, Dillon and Lucy joined her. His tanned cheeks were reddened and his hair tousled from the wind. A few long strands escaped from his ponytail, curling as they dangled down, brushing his shoulder.

"Did you talk with Mrs. Johnson?"

"She's getting Mr. Johnson as we speak."

Mr. Johnson came out of the back room, tucking the tails of his shirt into his trousers. His short-cropped hair stuck up in all directions. "Good day, Mr. and Mrs. Cade."

"Good day to you, sir." Dillon shook his hand. The two went off to talk business while Mrs. Johnson showed Caitlin and Lucy the new fabrics that had arrived.

"Isn't this one just lovely?" Mrs. Johnson held up the roll of green velvet.

"Oh. It is." Lucy ran her hand over the soft fabric.

"It is beautiful," Caitlin agreed, "but I fear it's too expensive."

"Too expensive," Mrs. Johnson chuckled. "That coming from someone wearing a diamond the size of a small mountain."

Caitlin glanced down at her hand, still not accustomed to wearing the ring. It was a constant reminder that she no longer controlled her own life. She now belonged to Dillon. The metal felt cold and hard. "It is only a piece of jewelry."

"Only a piece of jewelry." Mrs. Johnson elbowed Lucy and roared with laughter. "Wish I could afford so fine a diamond."

"Diamonds cannot make up for happiness," Caitlin stated. "In the end, love is the only thing that matters."

"How very poetic of you," Mrs. Johnson observed. "But you fared better than most. You got Prince Charming and money to boot."

"That remains to be seen."

"True. You're just getting to know each other. It takes time to build a good marriage. However, you snagged the most eligible bachelor in town. Not only is he rich, but he's the most dashing male within twenty miles."

"Mrs. Johnson!" Caitlin gasped. "You mustn't say such things."

"You're married now. You know what goes on between a husband and wife."

"That is beside the point." She fidgeted with her gown, running her hands over the cool, cotton fabric, smoothing it out. "Lucy should not be hearing talk like that."

"Fiddlesticks." Mrs. Johnson waved her hand. "She is approaching the age to marry. Then she'll find out firsthand what all this talk is about."

"Hush now," Caitlin insisted.

"I'm only saying that you should be grateful to finally get hitched. The whole town is abuzz about you getting married so quickly. And poor Henrietta is just beside herself. She..."

"Did you find anything you like?" Dillon cut in.

"There are so many wonderful patterns here, I have not made up my mind as of yet." Actually, they'd been talking and she hadn't even seen all the bolts of fabric.

"Why don't we go to the tailor's shop and look at some styles of dresses. Perhaps then you will have a better idea of which fabrics you would like."

"That is a good idea." Caitlin was grateful for an excuse to leave.

Lucy helped Caitlin into her pelisse. They bid the Johnsons good day and stepped outside. The wind played with her hat, trying to lift it into the air. She held onto it as they made their way across the street and down the boardwalk.

"Did you get any names?" Caitlin asked.

"Not really. Mr. Johnson was not very clear."

"Mr. Johnson never has a clear head when it comes to business. But he seems to give his card games a lot of attention."

"Caitlin! How do you know that?"

"Everyone in town knows he gambles. He's too lazy to work and that's his only means of support."

Dillon abruptly stopped walking. "Even if it is true, you mustn't say such things out loud."

"Why not? Mrs. Johnson speaks her mind."

"Mrs. Johnson has many years on you, and earned the right to say as she pleases."

"She has never spoken to me so boldly before."

"You were the daughter of Alin Gallagher before. Now you are my wife. People are going to treat you differently."

"Why must women always be associated with men? The daughter of ... the wife of ... the sister of. Why can't we simply be who we are?"

"What did Mrs. Johnson say to rile you up so?" Dillon asked, knowing it didn't take much.

"She went on and on about how I should be grateful that you married me. Suggesting that I snagged you. Like you are some prize and I am nothing but a heap of dung."

"I'm sure that's not what she meant." He wanted to ease her hurt feelings. "Mrs. Johnson adores you."

"Then why must she be so unkind? She seemed to care more about Henrietta than about me."

Dillon tensed, "What did she say about Henrietta?"

"Not much." Caitlin turned to Lucy. "Do you know anything about her?"

"I know Henrietta was cross when she heard you were getting married. I think she fears becoming an old maid."

"Serves her right." Caitlin smiled smugly. "She's never been nothing but mean to me since I moved here." For the first time she, felt glad about being married, even if it was just animosity toward Henrietta.

They went into the shop and Caitlin looked over sketches of dresses. As the women talked about which fabrics best suited the styles, Dillon had a surprise visitor.

"Master Cade," A young boy of about sixteen entered the shop. "I've been looking all over town for you." He took his hat off.

"Well, Johnny, you found me. What is the matter?"

"The printer isn't working again."

"You boys can't fix the problem?" Dillon asked, irritated.

"We tried, sir." He played with his hat sheepishly.

"All right. I'll be there in few minutes."

Dillon turned to Caitlin. "I fear I must go. I will be back to pick you up as soon as I can." He quickly brushed a kiss across her lips, taking her by surprise.

After picking out three dresses and discussing fabrics and patterns, Lucy and Caitlin hung around the shop for a while waiting for Dillon. After getting restless, they decided to go for a walk and ended up back at the general store.

"Caitlin, this hat would be perfect with the purple dress." Lucy held up the white top hat with purple plumes.

"The colors do match closely." Caitlin untied her bonnet and fitted the top hat over her array of curls. "I do like it, but it's a little high. I'm use to smaller hats."

"But it looks so stylish," Lucy insisted.

"You're right. Perhaps I'll splurge."

"Oh, Caitlin. I can't wait to see you in the entire outfit. You will look so stunning." Lucy trotted off to find some other trinket that would please her mistress.

"You shouldn't allow her to use your Christian name like that," Mrs. Johnson commented. "It's not proper."

"She is my charge and I will decide what is proper." Caitlin took the hat off. "I want to purchase this."

"You never do anything properly." Mrs. Johnson took the hat and headed to the front of the store.

"What is that supposed to mean?" Caitlin followed, tying her bonnet.

"Just like your wedding. You didn't court the proper length of time. You barely had an engagement and then you were married."

"You can take my courtship up with my parents. They are the ones who planned the whole thing." Caitlin felt the temperature of the room rising as her anger level elevated. Not only had she been coerced into wedlock, now she was being blamed for the hasty ceremony.

"Of course, they had to rush everything." Mrs. Johnson insisted. "They wanted the nuptials to take place before you started showing."

"You think I'm in the family way?"

"Everyone knows what a rushed wedding means."

"Then you may inform everyone they are wrong. I am not now, nor will I ever be with child."

"You're not having a baby?"

"No, you goose."

"'For the best, I suppose. It would break your poor mama's heart to know a grandchild was on the way and not be around to see it."

"What foolishness are you talking about now?"

"They will be long gone to Ireland," Mrs. Johnson informed her.

"They cannot go back to Ireland."

"Don't you know?" Confusion registered on the wrinkled, old face. "They have no choice. The government is forcing them back."

"Why?"

"It has something to do with the some kind of law the President passed."

Caitlin felt the room spinning as the pieces of the puzzle started fitting into place. "That's why they forced me into this marriage?" She was too preoccupied to respond to the shocked gasps that erupted from the few people in the store. Her mind was centered on Dillon, her parents, the government, and the Sedition Acts. All these things had conspired, impelling her into a marriage with the enemy.

Chapter 5

Anger and resentment shook her to the core. She ran out of the store, leaving behind her coat and Lucy. She never even felt the blustery bite of the wind as it gripped and tugged the hem of her dress. The windy conditions made the progress slow, but fury spurred her on. The breeze pulled and loosened the ribbons of her bonnet, pushing the hat back so that it flopped and dangled behind.

She burst through the door of the printing shop looking like a wild cat. The three men jumped and spun around, astonished at the sight. Caitlin stood in the doorway, the wind still clawing at her dress, her untamed, red hair flying in every direction, her pale face reddened to the color of rubies, and her eyes blazing like emeralds set on fire.

"You!" She pointed to Dillon. "You have been in on this from the beginning." Taking a few steps inside, she let the wind slam the door shut.

"Caitlin, calm down," Dillon urged.

Untying the ribbons, she threw the hat aside, and continued her aggressive pace forward. "You knew my parents were being deported back to Ireland, and yet, you said nothing." Her eyes narrowed with rage. "Is that why you agreed to marry me? You think you're saving me? Did you think I'd fall into your arms and claim you as my knight in shining armor?"

"I... I... only..."

"Shut up! I don't want to hear any more of your lies."

"I never lied to you." His tone remained calm.

"You never told me the truth either."

She stood close, her face only inches from his. Anger and violence swirled, mingling with hurt and confusion. "When were you planning on informing me?"

"That was up to your parents."

"I see. Blame everything on them."

"It was their decision, Caitlin."

"You!" She pointed in his face. "You are the problem. If it weren't for you and your country, we'd have never been in this mess in the first place."

"I'm an American now. I no longer consider myself from England."

"An American!" She tried to regain some control of her emotions, but they were too far gone. "America is sending them back. This country is no better than England. You are my enemy twice, Dillon Cade. I hate you!" The thunderous sound of her palm meeting Dillon's face resounded in the room. No one dared even breathe until the shuffling of feet ended with the slamming of the door.

"Caitlin, wait!"

"Ma! Pa!" Caitlin's frantic voice rose above the pounding of horse hoofs as she headed toward the house at breakneck speed. Pulling back on the reins, she recklessly brought the steed to a halt. Her careless dismount was slowed when the hem of her skirt caught on the pommel. She tugged on the material until it ripped, freeing her from the saddle. When her feet hit the hard earth, she fled into house yelling, "Where are you?"

Kathleen was the first to meet her in the foyer. "Caitlin! What is the matter?"

"How could you?" She asked the question tearfully. All the angry words and accusations fled from her mind.

"How could we what?" Alin's deep voice surrounded her.

She looked toward the doorway to see her father dressed in brown breeches with a matching leather vest. His gray eyes were silently penetrating, while his face was set in a firm look, ready to defend his actions. The same look he wore when defending a client in court.

"How could you not tell me about Ireland?" she exploded.

"We were planning to." Kathleen advanced with outstretched arms.

"When?" Caitlin avoided the embrace.

"How did you find out?" Alin asked.

"It does not matter. The only thing that matters is you pushing me into marriage without telling me the truth."

"We wanted to protect you." Kathleen wrung her hands.

"Protect me!" Caitlin threw up her hands. "Making me marry my enemy is not protecting me."

"Dillon is not your enemy," Alin reminded her, "and his name will keep you safe in America."

"Do you believe I'd want to stay here without you?" Her heart ached. The pressure increased, forcing the tears to slip out the corners of her eyes. "Why didn't you tell me?"

"I did not want to spoil your wedding day. We planned on talking to you the next time we saw you." Alin handed her a handkerchief.

"You didn't want to spoil the worst day of my life? You should have informed me before the wedding." She blew her nose. "Everyone knew. Brogan, Dillon, even Mrs. Johnson. I was the only one without a clue, yet my life is affected the most."

"I knew I shouldn't have left you alone." Dillon's voice startled her.

Whirling around, she stared in amazement at his disheveled appearance. Although his tight-fitting pants and matching black jacket were tailored to fit his manly form like a glove, they were covered in dust. His cravat was crooked, and his curly brown hair had loosened from the string and hung in disarray. His split lip had swollen and dried blood still clung to the corner of his mouth. She would have laughed out loud at his untidy appearance if she hadn't been so upset.

"If it were not for that stupid printing press breaking…"

"If it hadn't broken, I'd still be in the dark," Caitlin yelled. "I'd still not know why I had been forced into marrying you. And, I wouldn't know that my parents were going back to Ireland. And,

I most certainly wouldn't have found out what a lying scoundrel you are."

"Caitlin!" Her mother gasped. "You will not speak to your husband that way. I brought you up with better manners."

"Manners! What good will they do me?" She laughed scornfully. "You don't need manners living with the English or the Americans. They're both nothing but a lot of pigs."

"'Tis enough," Alin yelled. "I realize you are upset, but that does not give you leave to be rude."

"Then what does?" She glared at her father. "You did not think it rude to make plans about my life without informing me."

"What we did, we did to protect you," he insisted.

"I am old enough to make my own decisions." She pointed to herself. "I should have been given a choice. You should have trusted me enough to tell me the truth." Hurt flashed in her eyes.

"I'm sorry I did not discuss the matter with you, but I feared you'd be rebellious and not understand." Alin put a hand on each shoulder. "You are not my little girl any more. I failed to see that, but I must bear this burden alone. Both Dillon and your mother wanted to tell you. Even Brogan informed me I was handling the situation wrong. Now I see they were right. I only pray that you will forgive me someday and know that I love you and want the best for you."

"And Dillon Cade is the best you could find?"

"He is a fine man and will give you a good life." Alin's eyes shifted to Dillon. "Not many men would suffer the abuse you've inflicted."

"Only because he's a spineless nincompoop."

"Caitlin!" Kathleen's cheeks reddened with embarrassment, matching her red gown. "I have had quite enough out of you." Looking at Dillon she continued, "I'm truly sorry for our daughter's behavior."

"No need to apologize. She's very upset," Dillon noted.

"'Tis no reason to be mean." Kathleen looked ready to swoon.

Caitlin's irritation reached the breaking point. Why didn't her parents realize her hurt and anger? Why was Dillon the one defending her? "I do not need you to defend me." Her eyes shifted from Dillon to her father. "And I do not need you to protect me."

"It was our job." Alin studied her a moment before asking, "If I had told you everything, would you have agreed to the wedding?"

Her silence was the answer.

"That is just what I thought," he sighed.

"I hope you do not think I'm staying here when you go back to Ireland. I'm going home with you."

"No. You will stay here with your husband," Alin commanded.

"But I want to go with you," Caitlin pleaded.

"Ireland is far too dangerous. You will be safer here."

"I don't want to be safe," she cried. "I want to be with you."

"I have already lost one child. I will not risk the life of another." Alin's gray eyes filled with compassion as they fell on his weeping daughter. "It will be hard for your mother and I, as well."

"What about Brogan?"

"He's going back."

"You're willing to risk his life?"

"I have no control over Brogan. Sons are different than daughters."

Aye, men get to do whatever they please while women are told what to do, she thought contemptuously. "Is there nothing I can say to change your mind?"

"Nothing." Alin fought the tears threatening to fall.

Caitlin wanted to fight harder. To plead more earnestly. However, she recognized the determined look on her father's face, and knew the effort would be fruitless. There was nothing left to do but quietly accept her fate.

"Caitlin, we must get the horses back to town," Dillon urged.

Wearily looking at him, her heart filled with disdain. *How could he be so insensitive? My life is unraveling and he's worried about the horses.* Of course, the thought never occurred to her that she had taken the mare without permission.

Dillon held the reins as Caitlin mounted. Trying to sit sidesaddle without the proper saddle was almost impossible. Slipping and sliding on the leather as she adjusted her skirt almost made her fall off.

"How did you ride all the way out here so fast without falling off and breaking your neck?" Dillon asked.

"I didn't ride sideways."

"I fear we'll never make it back to town with you sitting like that. You'll have to ride astride."

Caitlin altered her posture until she straddled the horse in a most unfitting manner for a woman. "Must you watch me?"

"I do not want you to fall." He hadn't realized that he'd been staring. Although she sat in the most unusual position for a woman, he found the unconventional position quite alluring.

"I told you, I do not need your protection." She kicked the horse and left Dillon standing there staring after her.

"I'm not trying to be your protector," he said, riding up alongside her.

"Then what are you doing?"

"Trying to be your friend."

"I do not need your friendship either. Your friendship is with my father, not with me."

Not wanting to push the subject further, Dillon rode beside her in silence.

The ride was slow and quiet, leaving Caitlin time to ponder the situation. It also left her feeling the bitterness of the autumn air. Hostility and hurt kept the cold away before, but now the frosty conditions bit through the thin fabric making it hard to ignore.

"Are you cold?" Dillon asked.

"I le… left the s… s… store in such a fit th… that I for… forgot my p… pelisse."

"Here, use my frock." He reined the horse to a stop and slipped off his jacket.

Her first instinct was to refuse the gesture. However, the bitter cold left her no other alternative. She snuggled into the jacket, grateful for the warmth. The faint scent of Dillon drifted up and for an instant she forgot her anger.

It was late by the time they returned the horses to their proper owners. After retrieving their carriage and Lucy, they headed home. The last pink rays of the sun marred the horizon, its dim light producing an eerie backdrop for the oak, maple, and pine trees, as they cast their shadowy branches across the face of the square house like a puppet show. Evening shadows played around the corners of the large, stately dwelling, turning the tan bricks into a lonesome shade of gray. The light fog rising from the ground encompassed the property like a cloak. Not even the candles lighting the two straight rows of windows could dispel the gloom. Or, perhaps, it was merely Caitlin's misery that made the entire picture look so dismal. Either way, this Georgian style house was the last place she wanted to be.

Upon entering the house, they were met by Martha, who stood with her large arms crossed in front of an even larger chest, ready to scold them for being late. However, her attitude softened when she noticed the frightened, desolate look Caitlin wore. The disheveled appearance of both Caitlin and her master piqued her curiosity, but a warning glance from Dillon cautioned her not to seek answers.

"I've kept dinner warm for you." Her tone sounded more motherly than outraged, which is what she'd felt a few minutes before.

"Thank you, Martha. But I fear I'm not feeling well. I think I will go to my room." Caitlin started toward the stairs.

"Would you like me to bring up a tray?" Martha offered.

Caitlin turned around. Dread and sorrow displayed in every line of her face. "That is very kind of you. However, I have no appetite."

The house seemed to groan under the weight of its new mistress's broken heart. The feeling reached out from every nook and cranny, pressing down upon Caitlin like a millstone.

"I can bring you up some soup and tea." Martha couldn't let her go to bed without something to eat. It must have been the destitute look on Caitlin's face that caused her motherly instinct to kick in. She should have been miffed that she'd prepared supper and they hadn't made it home in time to eat.

"No, thank you. I just want to be alone."

"Do you need help getting ready?" Lucy asked.

"It's been a long day and you are probably hungry. Have your supper. I can manage by myself."

Finally ensconcing herself in the bedroom, she leaned against the door. "Alone at last." The small fire in the hearth dimly lit the room, producing little warmth. It would need to be stoked soon or it would burn out, but she didn't have the strength to do it. She didn't even have the energy to get out of her gown.

Feeling weary, she fell across the bed and wept. Bitter tears of remorse, agony, and betrayal streamed down her cheeks. She'd lost everything that ever mattered in her life. Her home and friends in Ireland. Her brother, Dwayne. And now her parents and Brogan. "I have nothing left," she sobbed. Nothing but Dillon.

Caitlin awoke, shifting on the bed to allow her numb arm to bend. She lay on her back while her eyes adjusted to the dark. The fire had died, and only a few embers still smoldered in the pile of ashes. Stumbling to the mantle, she searched for the tinderbox and lit the lantern by the bed. The lone flame cast ominous shadows around the large room.

The damp night air hung heavy in the room and dug through the thin layers of fabric, causing Caitlin to shiver. She bent and twisted, trying to undo the row of buttons that ran down the back of her dress. Unable to reach all of them, she silently chided, *why didn't I have Lucy come help?* Her agitation only mounted when she realized that it was late and Lucy would no doubt be asleep. "How am I going to get out of this thing?"

She quit fiddling with the buttons and went to restart the fire. Perhaps some warmth would ease the dampness.

"Caitlin." Dillon called through the door. "May I enter?"

"Go away."

Ignoring her command, he opened the door. "I see the fire has gone out." He took the piece of wood that she held. "I'll stoke it for you."

"I know how to do it." Anger and resentment still resided in her tone.

"I'm sure you do." He gently met her gaze. "However, you have had a rough day and this is a duty I can perform."

"Then do it." She crossed her arms. "It is your house anyway."

"'Tis your home now also."

"It is my prison and naught else."

"Is there nothing I can do to alleviate your apprehension?"

"Nothing," she said pointedly. "Unless..." a thought struck her, sparking a flame of hope. "Unless you allow me to leave with my family." The flame grew into a full-fledged fire, if only she could convince him to help her. "Oh, Dillon! You could tell my father that you do not want to be in this arrangement any longer. Since we have not consummated the marriage it will not be a problem legally."

Dillon poked the fire a few more times and replaced the poker in the stand. Slowly turning, he met her excitement with a somber tone. "I cannot do that, Caitlin."

"Cannot or will not?"

He watched the spark of hope die from her eyes, and hated being the one to bring her disappointment. "Your father and I have already discussed this."

"And what I feel or think does not matter?" Contempt crept back into her tone.

Dillon much preferred the way she said his name when trying to persuade him of something. "I can tell you truly that if there were another way to keep you safe, I would let you go."

"What concern is it of yours if I'm safe or not?"

"As I told you earlier, I consider you a friend."

"You barely know me."

"That is true, but we will have a lifetime to get to know each other."

"Not in my lifetime." She crossed her arms.

"I only hope that someday you will change your opinion." He held up a hand to stop her protest. "You have already stated your position. I do not need to hear it again."

Miffed, she twirled away from him trying to hide the angry tears welling up. She would not let him see her cry.

Dillon watched her fiery hair dance through the air and noted several undone buttons on her dress. "Shall I get those buttons for you?"

"What?" She faced him again, surprised.

"Since Lucy is asleep, and I am here, I can undo them."

"You will do no such thing."

"It is a husband's duty."

"I can manage by myself."

"I see you are struggling."

"Then I will sleep in my dress."

"Nonsense. It's damp and dirty. You will catch a chill."

"What do you care?"

"I do not wish to come home to a sick wife. Now turn around," he demanded.

Caitlin was taken aback by his commanding tone. It was the first time he'd used it with her. "You will not touch me. Next thing you'll be taking liberties."

"I assure you, madam, I will not take any unwanted liberties. I only wish to undo the buttons, then leave."

Although she did not want any help from him, the prospect of him leaving sounded inviting. She presented her back to him. "Make haste."

Dillon moved the soft tresses to the side, and deftly undid the buttons. The pressure of his hands sent tingling sensations down her back. His fingers felt hotter than the fire blazing bright in the hearth. She shivered from the contact. What was it about the proximity of this man that always set her on edge? A simple touch ignited feelings she'd never had before.

"And you wanted to stay in this dress all night. You're already shivering." Dillon's hand steadily went down her back, slowly undoing each button. He noticed her pink skin under the thin cotton shift and ached to undo more than just the buttons.

"Well, thanks to you I will be out of it soon." She tried to control the tremor in her voice.

An image of her standing in front of the fire without a stitch of clothing crept through his mind, intensifying the pressure in his gut. If he didn't leave right this minute, he'd never be able to keep his promise. He hastily bid her goodnight and left.

Caitlin sat at the table having the morning meal when a loud knock sounded through the house. A few minutes later Sarah bustled into the room.

"Oh, Caitlin, have you heard?" She rushed into Caitlin's arms. "Brogan is leaving."

"Aye. I found out a few days ago."

"How can he go? How can he just leave and not care what happens to me? Did I ever mean anything to him?" Tears spilled out of her blue eyes. "Will I ever see him again?"

"Of course, you will." Caitlin tried to answer the barrage of questions. "Brogan cares for you very deeply. He would not be going if he did not have to."

"Yes, he would." Sarah shook her head. "He cares more about that organization than me. He said that was the reason we could not marry. His business is not finished in Ireland."

"The United Irishmen will defeat England soon, and then Brogan will come back. You will get married and have lots of children. Everything will work out because the two of you are meant to be together." Caitlin tried to soothe her best friend, but knew the possibility of death surrounded all her family members.

"Oh, Caitlin!" Sarah sat down. "I'm so afraid. I do not want him to go."

"I don't, either," Caitlin said forlornly. She'd already lost one brother, and now the threat loomed over her loved ones once again. *Why can't England just leave us alone?*

"Caitlin, I'm so sorry. Here I am going on about myself and never once considered your feelings. Why, I am the worst friend in the world." She stood up, fiercely hugging Caitlin. "What must you be going through? You are losing your entire family."

"I will be fine. I'm optimistic that I'll see them again." She may have said the words, but didn't feel them in her heart. She only wanted to make Sarah feel better.

"You are the strongest person I know," Sarah smiled faintly. "I only wish I had half your strength."

"It is not strength, it's determination that keeps me going."

"You have the most determination of anyone I know." The masculine voice startled both women.

"Mr. Cade." Sarah spun around.

"I am sorry I startled you."

"It's quite all right, sir. I just didn't hear you."

"He seems to materialize from nowhere," Caitlin quipped. "Almost like a ghost."

"I assure you, my dear, I am no ghost." He brushed her cheek with a dutiful kiss.

"Of that I'm sure." No ghost could produce the sensations she felt from his touch. Even though his lips barely touched her skin, the jolt felt like lightning. Shock mixed with joy at the sensation. How could she feel happiness at his mere presence? She had not seen him in days, being mostly confined to her room. Although boredom and loneliness had brought her down to breakfast, she had to admit that seeing Dillon's face and hearing his gentle tone soothed her soul beyond words.

"Sarah, would you care for a bite to eat?" Dillon noticed Caitlin's nearly untouched plate and wanted her to finish. She'd barely eaten anything since the news of her family's departure. In fact, he'd been surprised to see her downstairs at all, even though it was a very pleasant surprise.

"No, thank you, sir." Sarah sat back down in the chair, her legs too weak to hold her up. "I am too distraught to eat anything."

Although unaccustomed to dealing with women's emotions, Dillon felt he had to do something. Witnessing the devastating emotional effect this situation had on his wife made his gut twist. "You must keep your strength up."

"Why?" Sarah wailed. "The man I love is leaving and I'll never see him again."

"It is true he's leaving, but you will see him again," Dillon reassured her.

"Not if he gets killed."

"Brogan will do everything in his power to stay alive. Just as I will do everything I can to bring him back home."

"What can you do?" Caitlin questioned.

"Your family has to leave under the Alien Enemies Acts that President Adams passed. I am working with the Anti-Federalists to elect Thomas Jefferson as next president. Under his leadership, he can overturn these acts."

"Then my family could come back to this country?" Hope glimmered in Caitlin's green eyes.

"That is what I am working on."

"I do not understand this political stuff," Sarah confessed. "All I want is for Brogan to be safe and stay here."

"His safety is in the Lord's hands. But as citizens we can all do our part to bring him back home." Dillon patted her hand. "I believe everything will work out just fine. You must keep your faith."

"I hope you are right," Sarah sighed.

Chapter 6

The sun peeked out from behind the gray clouds, trying its best to brighten the late October sky. The earlier rainstorm had not only dampened the ground, but drenched Caitlin's resolve as well. She stood looking out the window, watching as the last few leaves desperately clung to the oak and maple trees. The nearly bare branches reached up toward the sun, while the thick trunks were anchored to the ground by the roots that had embedded themselves in the soil for many centuries. Although most of the leaves had fallen, forming a blanket over the ground, the boughs magnificently stretched their twisted arms out as if they were still elegantly clothed. They were neither ashamed nor embarrassed, for this was their home and they were comfortable. Caitlin envied those trees. They knew where they belonged. Their roots spread along the ground and went as deep as time itself. They would die if they were ever uprooted.

A light knock interrupted her thoughts. She turned from her contemplation and faced the door. Dillon stood there looking quite dapper dressed in brown the same shade as his hair, which was tied in the usual ponytail.

"May I come in?"

She nodded and watched as he closed the distance between them.

"What are you looking at?"

"Nothing much." She turned back to the window. "Just noticing the trees and how dead they look right now."

"Aye, but they are not. They will bloom again in the spring."

"I know. It is amazing to think something that looks so dead can still be living."

"Life courses through the trees where we cannot see it. The roots are buried under the ground and nourish it from the inside."

Placing his hands behind his back, he continued as if instructing a classroom full of children. "Just like us. We have to take food into our bodies to produce our outer strength."

"I am well aware of how trees and people receive their nourishment." She rolled her eyes. "I just do not understand why the trees have to lose their leaves and look so lifeless through the winter."

"Only God can answer why He created the trees the way He did. We must trust that He had a reason for it."

Her red brows gracefully arched over her green eyes. "Was there a reason you came to see me?"

"I merely wanted to see how you are doing."

"As well as can be expected under the circumstances."

"Are you seeing your family off?"

"I am not." She unconsciously smoothed the wrinkles from her morning dress.

"'They are your family and you should do as seems right. However, I'd encourage you not to let your anger rule your heart."

"And what do you know about matters of the heart?" Her chin protruded arrogantly.

"I know that the heart can be easily broken. And that the pain and despair can last a lifetime if we allow it." A strange look flashed in his warm, brown eyes.

"You make it sound as if we have a choice." She turned to stare out the window once again. "I did not have a choice in anything that has happened in my life. I was uprooted from my home and moved here because of my brothers' association with the United Irishmen Organization. Then I was forced into wedlock. Now because of that commitment to you I am not free to go with the rest of my family." Anger spiked her tone. "So you see, Mr. Cade, I have no choice."

"You do have a choice." His voice was soft. "You can choose to allow bitterness and hate to fester in your heart and destroy your soul. Or, trust that God has a plan."

"I am starting to wonder if God even exists," she scoffed.

"Do not let stubbornness cause disbelief. It will only lead to destruction."

She said nothing.

"My dear, you have two choices. You can sit around brooding, or do something about it."

"And what can I do about my circumstances?"

"That is an answer you must seek for yourself. But I can tell you that when life dealt me a hard blow, I chose to do something about it."

"Exactly what did you do, Mr. Cade?" Her sarcasm did not go undetected.

"I opened the printing shop."

Her brows furrowed in confusion. "How did printing a paper help you?"

"I use my paper to promote justice and inform people of dangers in our society."

"Like President Adams' Sedition Acts?"

"Exactly."

"How does printing your view of politics help anyone?"

"It's not just my view. I print everyone's side. It is not about who is wrong or right. Most citizens do not know what is going on in politics or criminal activities unless they read about it." He took his stance with his feet apart and locked his hands behind his back. "That is what I do with Norfolk News. I print the stories that keep people informed."

Caitlin pondered this statement before asking, "If starting the printing shop was your way of dealing with injustice, am I to assume that your trouble had something to do with a newspaper?"

Dillon paused a long moment before answering, as if debating whether or not to reveal the information. After all, he'd never enlightened anyone about his past. And Caitlin certainly did not make trusting an easy thing. She resented him and all of England. However, they were husband and wife, and building a life together must start with trust. Perhaps if he took the first step, she'd warm up to him.

"My mother was killed years ago. The only thing harder than her dying was all the gossip that surrounded her death."

Caitlin's mouth dropped in dismay. "Your mother is dead?" The cold, insensitive words escaped before she could stop them. The pained look they produced on Dillon's face made her regret them immediately. No matter how much she disliked him, she never wanted to inflict pain on him. "Oh, Dillon, I'm so sorry. I… just…I thought your parents lived in England."

"My father and stepmother live there." He said the words with disdain.

Caitlin was hesitant to ask any more questions, but curiosity got the best of her. "What happened?"

Dillon wanted to share his heart with her but the words lodged in his throat. He had not talked about the situation in over eighteen years. "She was murdered."

"Murdered!" Caitlin gasped.

Dillon flinched at the horror visible on her face. It was his job to protect her, not produce terror. "I should not have blurted that out. This subject is far too harsh for a woman."

"Don't be a goose." She recovered from the initial shock. "You of all people should know by now that I am much stronger than the average woman." She brushed her auburn hair back and fidgeted with the front of her yellow dress. "I will admit shock at the thought, but I do want to know what happened. And how did that lead you open a printing shop?"

Dillon hesitated only a moment. He found that talking to Caitlin and opening his heart eased the pain he'd hidden for so many years. "My father is a very influential man, and he'd made a few enemies. No one knows for sure what happened. My mother was found stabbed to death in the back street of an alley. All kinds of rumors started that she was having an affair and her lover killed her. Some even said that my father killed her in a jealous rage."

"Was she having an affair?"

"I do not know for sure, but I never believed it. She was the most honest, loyal and trustworthy person I had ever known." His liquid voice got softer as he remembered his childhood.

"What about your father? Do you believe he had something to do with her death?"

"That was the most scatterbrained theory of all," he sneered. "Anyone who knew my father knew that he was the provider of the family, not the nurturer. He spent so much time at the office and on business trips that he did not even realize he had a family. I doubt he would have cared if she did have an affair."

"Sounds like your parents did not have a very good marriage." She felt a twinge of guilt for growing up in such a loving home.

"My mother was always faithful and loving towards him, even when he would forget plans they had made. She would go to parties by herself. Or, more times than not, just stay home. She always justified his behavior because he had to work so hard to give us the things we wanted."

"They never found the killer?"

"Nay, but the gossip got around. We never got our side of the story out. The town busybodies painted my mother as a two-timing, adulterous whore, and my father said nothing to dissuade otherwise. The police never found any evidence of an affair. If they could have gotten the facts out to the public, maybe the rumors would have stopped."

"Perhaps, but sometimes not even the truth will stop rumors."

"True." Dillon paced a few steps, placing his arms behind his back. "I vowed never to let injustice win again. I moved here and became an apprentice. When I opened my shop, I promised myself that I would fight to be fair, and print only the truth. I give people information so they can make informed decisions." He stopped pacing and turned to face Caitlin. "I will continue to do so no matter what the law says."

"I believe you have accomplished your goal." She smiled slightly. "I just do not know what I can do."

"Something will come to you." He smiled, then gently added, "The biggest regret I have is not saying good-bye to my mother." He got a faraway look in his eyes. "She tried giving me a kiss before she left, and I brushed it aside. I was too old to be treated like a child. At fourteen I was tired of her treating me like a baby. She left that day without so much as an 'I love you', or 'good-bye' from me. 'Tis an unsettled feeling I have carried for all these years. It is unfinished business." He looked directly into Caitlin's eyes. "Do not make the same mistake." He walked to the door. "I will have the carriage ready in case you change your mind."

Dillon and Caitlin scanned the crowd searching through the sea of colored clothing, horses, carriages, and cargo. Norfolk port was a beehive of activity as people bustled around the dock, loading and unloading large freight containers.

Groups of people gathered around the massive, stately ships, waiting for the passengers to disembark. The mixture of wealth and poverty were never more evident than at the docks. Elegant men and fashionable ladies dressed to the nines were among the dirty, tattered, and altogether-unkempt breed of the underprivileged.

The stench of dirt, horse manure, and sweat mixed with the salt from the ocean to produce an unbearable odor.

"Do you see them?" Caitlin asked through her lace handkerchief.

"Not yet." Dillon jumped to the ground. "Perhaps we will see them at the dock. There are too many people standing around to find anyone." He held up his hand to offer assistance. "Be careful, 'tis muddy."

Caitlin held up the hem of her walking dress, trying not to step in any puddles as they weaved their way through the throng of people. However, the yellow muslin gown was spotted with mud by the time they reached the plank.

"I see them over there." Dillon pointed.

Following his finger, her gaze fell on Sarah and Brogan embracing. Sarah's dark, curly tresses were pinned up under a gray felt hat with three black plumes. Her black palisse opened over a gray dress. As they approached, Sarah noticed them and ran to give Caitlin a hug.

"I did not think you were coming." It was evident that Sarah had been crying all night. The dark circles under her eyes were swollen, making her sockets look sunken into her head. A red nose matched her bloodshot eyes.

"I had not planned to, but Dillon talked me into it."

"I did no such thing. The decision was all yours."

Caitlin shot him a look as if to say *like I had a choice after that story you told.*

"I'm glad you came. No matter whose idea it was."

"I'm glad, too." Brogan hugged Caitlin tightly. "I would be mad at you forever if you did not say good-bye."

"I guess some things will never change." She forced a little smile. "You are always mad at me for something."

"I will miss you, Catie pie."

"Caitlin!" Kathleen called, "Oh, my beautiful little girl. You did come to see us off after all." She hugged Caitlin enthusiastically, almost knocking off her white and yellow hat.

"Aye, Mama. I could not let you leave without saying good-bye."

Kathleen cupped her hands around Caitlin's face, looking directly into her eyes. "You are a grown woman now, and no longer need us to care for you. I wish you all the happiness that life can hold. Promise me you will take care of yourself and your husband. And promise me you will continue going to church every Sunday."

"I promise, Mama." Although she silently cringed at the husband part, she knew it was her duty.

"Cate." Her father stepped up, unsure of what to do or say.

A long moment stretched between them.

"Oh, Papa!" Caitlin threw herself into his arms. "I forgive you." Deep down she was not ready to forgive him yet, but she had no more time to ponder it. They were leaving and she wanted a clear conscience.

"I am truly sorry for everything." Alin fought back the tears. "You have been through so much turmoil for someone so young." He stepped back to get a better view of her face. "God always has a reason, Caitlin. Do not ever forget that."

"I won't." Tears fell from her green eyes. "I am going to miss you."

"As I will you, my child." He kissed the top of her head and turned to Dillon. "Take good care of her."

"I will, sir." Dillon shook his hand. "As if my life depended on it."

"Your life does depend on it." Brogan slapped Dillon on the back. "When we come back, my little sister had better be the happiest gal in town or I will come after you myself." He winked at Dillon.

"With a threat like that hanging over my head, I shall double my efforts."

"I would like to ask another favor of you." Brogan's eyes drifted over to where Sarah stood with her parents. "Will you watch out for Sarah as well?"

"Consider the task done." Dillon shook Brogan's hand.

"Thank you. I would not trust her welfare to just anyone."

"I count it a great honor that you trust me with not only your sister's care but Sarah's also."

Kathleen and Alin were saying their round of good-byes to their friends. Brogan was back by Sarah's side, speaking with her parents. The brief moment alone gave Caitlin the opportunity to speak with Dillon.

"You seem to be shouldering an oversized load today." She watched him from the corner of her eye.

"How so?"

"First, I am handed over into your care. Now, Brogan wants you to look after Sarah."

"Sarah has her parents to care for her. I neglected to point that out to Brogan because he wants to physically do something. It's his way of dealing with the pain. I also figured that since she is your best friend, I would be helping you out as well."

"Why should you care what happens to my family?"

"It is my family now, too."

After another round of hugs and more tears, Brogan gave Sarah a kiss, not the sort a beau would give, but the deep, long kind of a husband. Shocked onlookers gasped at the passionate display, including Sarah's parents. Brogan figured if he died, he would do so with the taste of the woman he loved on his lips.

The kiss ended and Brogan huskily whispered, "That should hold you until I return."

"If you return." She turned red rimmed eyes on him. "I love you."

"I love you, too." His voice quivered slightly. "That love will bring me back to you. Count on it." He sounded determined. "Good-bye, Sarah." He forced his muscles to move away.

"No. Don't go!" Sarah screamed after him and dissolved into a fit of tears. Her legs weakened, unable to support her and the massive weight of her heartache.

Brogan quickened his pace. If he didn't hurry and get on the boat, he would never have the strength to leave. He only wished his chest didn't feel as if it were in a vice grip.

Caitlin watched as her family walked over the old, wooden plank that led to the ship. Tears sprang to her eyes, and her heart thudded against her chest with the intensity of a hammer. *How am I going to survive without them?*

She stood on the dock, watching *The America* maneuver in the murky water. The large, red paddle wheel easily slicing the water like a knife in butter, moving the magnificent white ship trimmed in blue toward the Atlantic Ocean, carrying her family away from her.

The cranking of the paddle wheel faded being replaced by the chatter of people, wagon wheels churning and horse hooves crunching over the road. A low rumble of thunder echoed in the distance. Dillon slid his arm around her waist but said nothing. They watched in silence as the ship diminished in size. Caitlin still hoped it was all a bad joke. The boat would turn around and bring her family back. It had to be a practical joke. It hurt too much to be real. She'd thought the same thing about Dwayne's death, but that had been real also. The final shred of reality dawned on her. "Will I ever see them again?"

"I believe you will."

"You sound so certain." She finally took her eyes off the ship and looked at Dillon. "I am not certain of anything anymore."

"I understand how you feel."

"I suppose, in a way, you might. But you left England because of your mother's death and of your own free will. I was forced to flee Ireland by the government of England."

"I did not leave because of my mother," he corrected.

"Then why did you leave?"

"I believe I have divulged enough information about myself today." He heard another patch of thunder and noticed dark clouds rolling in. "Are you ready to go?"

She shook her head and turned back to view the boat. The massive *America* was nothing but a spot on the horizon.

"You are going to cause me to break my promise."

"How so?" Her eyes never wavered from the ship.

"I promised your father I would take care of you. If you get sick, you will prove me incapable of the job."

"I cannot bear to leave yet." She strained her eyes. Searching for the ship but it blended into the water and gray clouds."

"The boat is gone, Caitlin." He tugged at her elbow. "Let's go home."

"My home is in Ireland."

He tried to understand her mood. He remembered feeling out of place when he first arrived. He also knew the helplessness of having to leave the land you grew up in. Although he'd made the choice to come to America, his decision was based on other people's actions.

"Shall we go before it starts raining?" he urged one more time. "Besides I have a gift for you that might perk you up."

She scowled at him. "What is it?"

"You have to come with me if you want to see it."

"I am not in much of a festive mood, and I don't want to play games."

"It isn't game. I assure you that you are going to love it." His brown eyes twinkled.

"All right." She finally gave in. "But if I do not like the surprise, I am going to knock you in the noodle."

What are we doing out here? Caitlin wondered as she followed Dillon to the barn. The last thing she wanted was another tour. Although she had wanted to see the stables, they held little interest to her at the present moment.

"My dress is getting ruined," she complained.

"I will buy you a new one."

"Why are we out here?"

"To get your present."

"In the barn?" She tried thinking of something she'd want from a stable but nothing came to mind.

"Aye." They reached the barn. "Wait here a minute while I go and see if everything is prepared." He disappeared through the large red door.

"He certainly knows how to capture my interest," she mumbled and snuggled down into the warmth of her pelisse.

She heard the neighing of a horse, then a loud bang followed by shouts and shuffling feet. Upon entering the barn, she had to stop and let her eyes adjust to the dim light. Caitlin followed the sounds down the rows of stalls, stopping at the sight of a wild horse pinning a man to the wall. Her heart beat even faster after realizing that Dillon was the one in danger.

One of the barn hands tried to calm the horse. "Easy there. No one is going to hurt you." The horse snorted and stomped its hoofs in response.

Caitlin turned to the nearest barn hand and questioned, "What happened?"

"Mr. Cade tried to lead this mare out of her stall. She got spooked and started bucking. Now he's trapped in there until we can find a way to calm her down."

"What spooked her?"

"Who knows. It doesn't take much with this one. She's the most temperamental animal I've ever seen."

"Caitlin?" Dillon called. "Go back to the house. It is too dangerous for you out here."

"Looks to me like you're the one in danger," she said, smugly. "Besides, you dragged me out here, and I am not leaving until I get my present."

"As you can see, I am a little busy right now. You will have to wait for your gift." The horse whinnied again, stomping her feet. Dillon pressed back against the wall.

"I shall wait right here." She wasn't about to leave him when he could get hurt or even killed.

"Stubborn females," Dillon muttered.

The horse becoming more agitated started prancing in the small square. Dillon was crammed into the corner of the stall as far as he could go. If the horse kicked up her heels, she'd get him right in the head.

"Please, Caitlin, go in the house," he pleaded. If something happened to him, he didn't want her to witness it. *Oh, Lord, a little help from you would be appreciated*, he prayed. *Calm this horse down. She is your creation after all.*

"I am not leaving," Caitlin announced determined. "I might be able to help."

That statement drew snickers from the men.

"I can do more than just stand around," she said indignantly. The rustling of her skirts stopped their laughter.

"Do not go any closer, Mrs. Cade."

"My husband needs help and you are doing nothing about it."

"We are waiting until the mare calms down. Then we can coax her out."

"In the meantime, Dillon could get kicked." She started toward the stall.

"Caitlin! No!" Dillon yelled.

"I refuse to stand around and watch you get killed." Turning her attention to the horse for the first time, she saw a small, gray mare. Her memories floated back to Ireland. She'd owned a gray pony once. "Besides, I'm very good with animals."

"'Tis your people skills that need some work." Dillon commented off-handedly.

"Humph!" Ignoring his remark, she stepped closer to the animal. "Easy girl."

At first, the horse made more commotion, but then she stopped. Picking up her ears she softly whinnied.

Caitlin stepped closer, "It's all right. I will not hurt you." The horse stopped prancing, straining her ears as if she heard a faint sound in the distance. "It's a good girl." Caitlin continued forward. "Would you like some oats?" She looked back at the helper. "Get me some oats."

The horse backed up a little, but still didn't give Dillon enough room to move. Caitlin had to get the horse turned around before he could make an escape. She took a handful of oats from the pail the worker offered.

"Here are the oats." She dared to take another step. "My horse back home used to love oats." She seemed to be reliving good memories as much as talking to the horse.

Dillon wanted to tell her to stop, but he didn't dare say a word and upset the horse anymore. His pulse raced wildly, and beads of perspiration trickled down his back and neck. He felt more fear for Caitlin than for himself. One wrong move and she'd get herself killed.

The horse sniffing the oats started to turn. Dillon shifted to the other corner as the horse moved.

"That's a girl. You want these oats, do you not?" As Caitlin cautiously approached, the horse sniffed a few times, smelling something other than the oats. As if Caitlin's presence alone calmed her.

"Caitlin, be careful," Dillon warned.

"You be careful," she countered. "Start easing out of there. After she turns completely around, you will be able to make your move."

Dillon slid along the wall a few feet. Waiting. Praying.

"You are beautiful," Caitlin cooed. "You remind me of my horse."

The horse turned and faced Caitlin, sniffing her out-stretched hand that held the oats. Dillon quickly, but quietly, exited the stall.

Caitlin stared as the horse sniffed and sniffed but never ate any of the oats. There was no mistaking those large, dark eyes, and well-defined cheekbones. This was her horse. "Spirit?" she whispered.

"Aye," Dillon said, "your present."

The horse whinnied, throwing her head back, recognition glowing in her eyes.

"Oh, Spirit!" Caitlin threw her arms around the neck and cried into the gray hair. "I have missed you so much."

The horse nuzzled up against her head as if to say the same thing. However, the blue plumes in her hat proved to be too much temptation for the mare. She started to nibble on one.

"You bad girl," Caitlin teased. "I see you have not changed one bit."

"She's the most ill-tempered beast I've ever seen," the young worker complained.

"And Connemara ponies are known for their good temper-ament," Dillon jested.

"She has always been feisty. That is why I named her Spirit." Caitlin rubbed her neck. "However, I have never known her to be so unmanageable."

"She has had a long trip. I am sure she will calm down once she gets used to the place." Dillon dared to pat her neck. "She is a magnificent creature."

"Aye." Caitlin laid her cheek against Spirit's neck and combed her fingers through the long mane. "How did you find her?"

"Your father helped me. He knew the family who bought her when you left Ireland."

"They wanted a horse for their son. She was the perfect size for him."

"I guess Spirit was too spunky for him. The boy was too scared to ride her. They were more than happy to sell her when I made an offer."

"But why did you purchase her?"

"She was to be a wedding present for you. However, she was late arriving."

Caitlin bestowed a genuine smile on him. "'Tis like having a piece of home right here with me." The dim light made her tears shimmer like diamonds. "Thank you, Dillon." How did this man always seem to know what she needed?

Chapter 7

Caitlin rode atop the gray pony as gracefully and elegantly as a queen. The horse was compact and well balanced with a free, easy movement that made it look like it floated over the ground. The sure-footedness and natural athletic build of the animal aided in the ability of jumping.

Caitlin set up temporary jumping grounds, much to Dillon's dissatisfaction. His heart leapt in his throat every time she jumped a fence, but he said nothing. She seemed to get a thrill from jumping, and he'd seen a different side of her since the horse arrived. She was carefree, civil, and actually smiled, something he hadn't expected to see in the two weeks since her parents left.

He wasn't sure if her personality change was because of Spirit, or that she might be taking a liking to him. She had seemed genuinely concerned about his welfare when he'd been trapped in the stall. Whatever made the difference, life was starting to calm down. Dillon felt comfortable and happily settled into his new routine.

Since Caitlin started joining him more at mealtimes, he found himself coming home for supper, and not going to the eatery, or skipping the meal altogether. He didn't stay as late at the shop. He enjoyed coming home to a cooked dinner and some companionship.

Of course, that did lead to one problem. His feelings for her were growing stronger. But he had no idea how she felt. The desire that shot through his body every time he looked at her felt harder to control. He wondered if he would be able to keep his end of the deal much longer.

Caitlin sat by the hearth, the warm glow of the fire illuminating her auburn hair. She carefully pulled a needle and thread through the fabric, knotting it and pushing it up again. Dillon watched her rhythmically repeat the process a few more times. Then her brows wrinkled.

"What is the matter?"

"I cannot get this section right," she sighed.

"May I take a look?"

She looked up, surprised. "It's only embroidery."

"I am aware of that."

"What do you know about stitching?" Even her father had never taken a vested interest in the art of sewing.

"I know a little." He smiled. "My mother used to let me help when I was young."

"You are welcome to take a look." She held out the hoop.

He studied it for a few minutes before saying, "Ahhh. Here is your mistake." He pointed to a row of stitching. "You miscounted the spaces in this row."

"Where?" She grabbed the hoop out of his hands. Studying the area, she saw the mistake. "Bother! Now I have to redo all of it." She started ripping the stitches out.

"Do not fret. Everyone makes mistakes."

"I shall never get it done at this rate!"

"What is it anyway?"

"It's a picture for the wall by the door."

"Oh." He was surprised.

"Is that all right?"

"Of course, my dear. I had not realized you were working on something for the house."

"Aye. The walls are so bare. I thought a few things to decorate would help it look more lived in." She hesitated a moment before broaching the subject. "Dillon, I do have a matter I wish to speak with you about."

He set his book on the table and gave her his full attention. "This sounds serious." She'd never initiated a conversation before.

"It is about the matter of redecorating the house."

His thick, brown eyebrows shot up. "What about it?" She'd been so angry after finding out about her family leaving that the subject had been dropped.

"Do you mind if I still do it? I know we talked about it once, but nothing got started."

"Why would I mind? I told you the house is in your hands."

"That was before my family left." Before she'd slapped him, insulted him, and just plain ignored him. "Perhaps you have changed your mind."

"Nay." He earnestly studied her. She truly did seem more relaxed now. Perhaps someday she would consider this her home too. "I will place an ad in the paper for a contractor."

Her face brightened. "Thank you."

The door squeaked open and Dillon looked up from the press. His agitated expression softened when he saw Caitlin. His breath caught in his throat. The purple fabric floated down to the floor like liquid silk. A high white hat with three matching purple plumes completed the look. Her white wrap was held in place by a brooch.

"Am I disturbing you?"

"Nay, I am only fixing the press again." He wiped his hands on a rag. "I did not know you would be in town today."

"I wanted to surprise you," she strode forward, "and show off my new dress." She twirled around so he could get the full effect. "What do you think?"

Beautiful, he thought. "Worth every cent."

She smiled, her cheeks a rosy glow from the cold. "The other dresses will be ready in a week or so."

"I am sure they will be of the same fine craftsmanship."

Caitlin moved closer to get a better look at the press. A young boy standing nearby hurried to the other side of the room.

"You'd think I have the smallpox's the way he ran away," Caitlin commented.

"Well, my pet, you did leave quite an impression on him the last time you came in."

"I was angry and upset." Hurt and loneliness still burned in her eyes.

"I know. However, Johnny is young and very timid. It may take a while for him to warm up to you."

"Are you printing the paper?" She noticed his large, brown leather apron covered in black ink. There was a spot on his cheek also. She wasn't accustomed to this casual appearance. He wore long brown pants and a plain white shirt, cuffed to his elbows.

"Nay. The paper does not come out until Thursday so we print it on Wednesday."

"When is the deadline for submissions?"

"Tuesday. Why do you ask?"

She smiled, fluttering her long, thick lashes. "I have given some thought to your suggestion. And have come up with an idea to help my present predicament." Her gloved hand went to the brooch she wore.

Dillon followed the movement and recognized the piece of jewelry. "You are wearing my mother's brooch."

"Aye, it is a lovely piece. I am sorry I threw it away so carelessly the night you gave it me. I had no idea it meant so much to you." She looked up with sincerity in her eyes. "The story you told was truly enlightening and inspiring. So much so that I have written a piece I wish you to publish." She took out a piece of paper from her reticule.

Dillon unfolded the paper and read the writing. An expression crossing his face that Caitlin couldn't recognize; when he finished reading, he looked up and said, "It's very good."

"Truly?"

"Aye, well written and very concise, straight to the point."

"Then you will print it?" Her face brightened with eagerness.

"I would suggest a few changes first."

"What?" Her tone took on an edge, ready to defend whatever he found wrong.

"I am assuming that you want me to print this anonymously?"

"Yes."

"Then you need to make a few minor changes. If I print this as it is, everyone will know you wrote it. By saying 'the Sedition Act forced my parents back to a hostile country,' people will automatically know it is you. To my knowledge no other families have been sent back. And here," he stepped closer and pointed, "instead of writing 'I,' start out by saying 'a family I know'. "It will not be lying because you do know them, but it won't give away your identity either."

"I see what you mean." Caitlin studied the paper. "I shall work on it some more." Looking at Dillon she asked, "Will you print it then?"

"Absolutely." He cocked his head. "It is surprising you are taking my suggestions without a fight."

"I may be stubborn, but I am not stupid." She smiled. "Besides they are very good suggestions."

"If you want, I will look over the revised edition tonight."

"That would be nice."

The clanging of the door drew their attention away from each other. "Sorry it took me so long," Lucy bustled in, "but Henrietta started talking with me. It's the oddest thing, she never talks to me."

"Knowing Henrietta, she wants something. It's the only time she's ever nice to anyone," Caitlin commented.

"I do not understand what she could want from me."

Dillon stiffened when her name came up. Before Caitlin could ask about it, a commotion in the back of the room caught everyone's attention. Johnny lay sprawled on the floor with boxes and papers scattered around.

"Are you all right?" Dillon asked.

"Aye, sir." He stood up, straightening his clothes. His eyes met Lucy's but then quickly looked away. His cheeks turned a bright red. "'Twas only carrying some boxes of paper back to the storage room. I didn't see the table."

"Next time do not carry so many boxes at once. You are going to hurt yourself one of these days."

"Aye, sir." Johnny started gathering up the papers, too embarrassed to look at Lucy.

"I better help him clean up the mess." He nodded toward Lucy. "I will see you both later."

However, Lucy was busy watching the young man pick up the papers.

Dillon gave the handle one more crank and watched as the pieces of wood flattened the paper against the coffins.

Caitlin eagerly waited.

"Be careful. The ink is still wet," he cautioned as he held up the paper for both of them to look at.

"You are only printing one?"

"This is the proof sheet. I have to check it for mistakes. After we make the corrections on the machine, then we will print more copies."

"How many copies do you have to print?"

"Our subscriptions are up to one hundred."

"It is an amazing feeling— seeing something you have written in print," Caitlin said with pride. "I bet it would be even more satisfying seeing your name printed after the article."

"That is too risky, my pet. Perhaps the next article will bear your name."

"Next? I have no more ideas."

"I am sure you will think of something." He winked. "If you keep it up, you could become a regular black letter gentry."

Caitlin laughed. "I doubt that. I am not a writer."

"You wrote this, did you not?"

"It is just a short opinion."

"It may be short but will have people talking." He fidgeted with some small square objects.

"What are you doing?" The press fascinated Caitlin. She'd been in the shop many times with her father, but never had the audacity to ask questions about how it worked.

"Setting the type." He looked up and explained. "That is putting the letters in proper order. I saw a few mistakes and I'm correcting them."

"Mistakes like, this word is spelled wrong?"

"Exactly."

"Did you notice that the letter A is upside down in this word?" She pointed.

"I have not gotten that far."

She flipped through the pages. "The E is missing altogether in Ireland."

"What line is that?" Dillon diligently worked over the press.

"I do not know," she said puzzled.

"Sorry. I forgot I was not working with Johnny." He showed her how to count the lines. "This is the first line, second, third and so on." He moved his finger down the page. "The lines are set in columns. This is column one, two and three." Her nearness momentarily distracted him. She stood so close that her chest almost brushed his arm when she inhaled. The fragrance of flowers mingling with soap drifted up creating an intoxicating scent. He liked the smell of cleanliness. He liked the smell of her.

"So, this letter is on line twelve, column two." She looked up excitedly. "This is just like a puzzle." Dillon's intense stare made her feel a little unsettled. She quickly lowered her gaze back to the paper, her long-lashed lids covering her green eyes.

Dillon mentally shook himself. "Only you could find a game in work." Her sense of playfulness was one more thing he liked about her.

"Life is work," she commented. "If you do not look for fun, it will become boring."

"Truer words have never been spoken." Dillon laughed, enjoying her company. He felt a strange sensation whenever she took interest in his life.

He bent over the printer, moving and replacing letters as Caitlin read the lines and columns with errors. "There, the text should be correct." He grabbed two large, round pads, soaking them with ink. Caitlin earnestly watched, like a child viewing someone making candy. "This is called inking." He stamped the two pads over all the letters several times to insure he didn't miss any spots. "The more ink you use the darker the print."

When he finished inking, he laid a piece of paper over the letters. A hard, flat board covered the paper. Then he clamped the board down to secure it so the paper wouldn't move. When this was all done, he moved to the side of the machine and started cranking the handle, covering the 15 by 20 inch paper with words. Next, Dillon carefully clipped the paper on a line. "We shall let it dry for a while. Then we can read and see if there are any more mistakes."

"That is a lot of work for one copy. You have to do this ninety-nine more times?" Caitlin seemed astonished.

"Setting the type is the most time consuming part." He informed her. "After the paper is error-free the process goes much quicker."

"I never realized so much work went into the newspaper."

"It is a lot of work, but when you can make a difference the effort is worth it."

"What if you do not make a difference?"

"The day I cease to make a difference is the day I close my shop."

In spite of his weak-minded ways, he had a determination that she liked. *Perhaps he isn't such a dim-witted goose after all.* She smiled to herself.

A young girl entered the shop, her pink dress brightening the drab, dull shadows that lingered after dusk. She removed her bonnet, patting her blonde hair back in place, and hung the hat on the rack next to the door.

"Henrietta, to what do I owe this visit?" Dillon managed to hide his surprise.

"I just came to compliment you on another wonderful edition." She stepped forward, hoping Dillon would notice the low-cut neckline. A smile curved her red painted lips when his gaze drifted down. "I especially liked the opinion piece."

"There were several. Which one drew your attention?"

"Come now, Dillon, don't play coy with me." She smiled seductively. "You know which one I'm talking about."

"I am sure I do not."

"The anonymous one that everyone is talking about." She stepped near the press, running her long, thin hand across the frame. "We all know your little wife wrote it." She spit out the word wife as if it were something distasteful.

"You know I am not at liberty to say who wrote the letter." He clasped his hands behind his back, fighting to control his emotions.

"It's only me and you here. I shall not tell a soul." She puckered her lips, pressing the index finger against them.

"An editor never reveals his sources."

"Do you not trust me?"

"Why are you so intent on finding out the identity of the writer?" He had to be leery. His business and maybe even his life depended on it.

"Merely curiosity." Recognizing that determined stance she switched gears, trying a different approach. "The only reason I ask is that, well, if you are accepting women writers, I would like to submit something."

Dillon silently groaned. She'd come to him before with articles to print but none of them were good. "I have never turned down a good piece of writing, no matter the gender."

"You certainly never printed any of my pieces." She pouted, obviously missing the point.

"Your submissions were not opinions; they were intended as a column. For which, I cannot afford to pay."

"Dillon Cade, you should be ashamed of yourself," she stated, outraged. "I never asked you for coin. I wrote those papers from the depths of my heart only wishing to see them printed." Actually, she'd only used them as an excuse to see Dillon. "You wounded me deeply when you rejected them. And, now you tell me the real reason was because of money."

"I am sorry if I hurt your feelings." His tone softened. "I understand how personal writing can be. I did not mean to imply that the only reason I rejected your submissions was for money." He paused, forming his words carefully. "Your writings did not fit the format of this paper."

"I don't understand."

"This is a newspaper. We report information that is pertinent to the reader concerning government, and local activities. Your submissions were more of a personal basis."

"And what is wrong with that?"

"It does not fit under the context of news."

"If I wrote about something else, would you publish it?"

"I would carefully consider it."

A smile brightened her face. "Oh, Dillon, I knew I could count on you." She pulled some papers from the jeweled reticule hanging around her wrist. "Will you take a look at this?"

Dillon took the papers noting that she stood much closer than need be. As he glanced over the first paragraph, she leaned in, rubbing a breast against his arm. "Henrietta, what are you doing?" He jumped back a step.

"Watching you read." Her blonde brows knit together, giving her an innocent look.

"I do not like people reading over my shoulder."

"What else don't you like, Dillon?" She closed the space between them, brazenly brushing against him one more time.

"Teach me what you like. I'll do anything." Her husky voice surrounded him. Tempting and inviting him to take her.

"Henrietta, what has gotten into you?" Confusion darkened his face. She had certainly flirted before but had never been this brash.

"What's wrong, Dillon? Do you not like what you see?" Her pink skirt swayed around his legs as she stepped even closer. "Or do you not understand my proposition?" She looked him square in the eyes. "I am offering myself to you."

"I understand the proposition. I just do not understand why you are making it."

"Because you've gone and married that little twit! I can no longer afford to be subtle." Hurt mixed with the anger.

"Do not speak so unkindly about my wife," he mildly warned.

"Why are you so concerned for her? She does not care about you."

"You should not speak about subjects of which you have no knowledge." His tone was gentle but still reprimanding.

"Ha." Her pointed chin jutted out. "I know that your marriage was arranged by her parents. If you hadn't been goaded by her father, you would have married me."

"I have never mentioned marriage with you." He did not want to hurt her feelings, but she'd built up some fantasy about the two of them. Although she was fair to look upon, he hadn't been able to get past her immaturity.

"You did not have to use words. Your actions were enough."

"What actions are you talking about?" He'd been very careful to avoid any pretense of flirting when she was around.

"We had dinner together. We talked all the time. I could feel the attraction." Her hazel eyes blazed in the dim light. "You would have gotten around to proposing sooner or later."

"I am sorry if my actions have caused you distress." Although they had dined together a few times as friends, he'd purposely avoided intimate situations like socials and parties. Their conversations centered around chance meetings at the

General Store, or when she'd stop by the shop with something to publish. He really could not see where she'd gotten the idea that he planned to propose.

"'Twas not your actions then that caused my distress. It is your rejection now that wounds me." She turned away, wiping at the tears. She'd almost gotten him to kiss her by pretending to cry once. "Here I am throwing myself at you, making a complete fool of myself. And you just let me go on when you have no intention of accepting me." Her words came out between sobs.

Pulling a handkerchief from his pocket, he stepped closer and held it out to her. "I am truly sorry."

She took the accepted handkerchief and dabbed at the corner of her eyes. Looking up into his eyes, she made one last attempt. "I can offer you what Caitlin can't or won't. Keep that in mind when you're lonely." With head held high, she walked away leaving Dillon to his chaotic thoughts.

"What are you reading?" Dillon entered the parlor.

"*A Sicilian Romance*." Caitlin sat on the sofa with her feet curled beneath the white fabric of her dress. A matching cottage cap covered her red curls.

"I like Ann Radcliffe." He also liked the domestic picture she presented curled up by the fire, reading.

"Have you read it?" Caitlin asked, shocked.

"Several times, but I liked *The Italian* better."

"I have not read that book. It was only published last year. Although Papa did allow me to splurge on books sometimes, we never got new ones."

"It's in my study if you would like to read it."

"Are you serious?" Excitement flashed in her smile. "I cannot wait to read it."

Dillon took a seat, sighing out loud. He'd been on his feet all day and sitting down was a welcomed relief.

Caitlin noticed his tired eyes. "I believe Martha kept your dinner warm. Would you like me to get it?"

"Food sounds good, but I am too tired to walk into the dining room.

"I could bring it in here."

"That would be nice."

Caitlin crept down the long hall, shielding the candle with her hand. She was so intent on being quiet, and keeping the flame lit that she never noticed the shadow approaching.

"Caitlin, what are you doing?"

Her startled eyes flickered in the candlelight. As if running into Dillon wasn't unnerving enough, it was now compounded by the fact that he stood nearly naked, droplets of water gleaming on his skin. His darkened hair hung in wet ringlets, brushing the tops of his bare shoulders.

Caitlin's eyes roamed over the wide shoulders and bare chest, following a path down to his narrow hips, where the line from his form-fitting breeches started. She blushed a deep red, and dared not look any farther. She had never seen so much of the male body. It was more intriguing than she imagined.

The idea of reaching out and touching his chest burned its way through her body making her fingers itch. However, she quickly smashed that stray notion. If merely looking did strange things to her body, she didn't knew what would happen if she actually touched him.

"I... I could not sleep so I thought I would get a book."

"Why are you sneaking around?" Dillon dried the back of his head with a linen towel then hung it around his neck. The white ends hiding most of his chest from view.

"I was not sneaking," Caitlin said aghast. "I did not want to wake anyone. I had no idea anyone would be up this late."

"Why are you carrying a single candle instead of a lantern?"

"Why are you lurking around the place with no light at all?" she countered.

"I know this place well enough to get around with no light." He gave her a lopsided grin. "Can I be of assistance in searching for a book?"

"I can manage, thank you." She wanted to get away from him. The scent of soap and man surrounded her like a thick mantle, strangling intellect and reason.

"I insist. I do not want you fumbling around the house in the dark. You could get hurt. Besides, I know where the library is."

"If you must assist me then lead the way."

Her only thought as she followed him through the house was that she now knew he did not wear a corset, that fabulous body was all his own. The Bible said that man was made in the image of God. Caitlin wistfully wondered what God must look like if Dillon were a mere image.

Chapter 8

Caitlin felt irritated over the next few days, though she couldn't discern a particular reason. She'd woken up gloomy and could not shake the feeling. Not even her morning ride on Spirit lessened her animosity. Of course, the person she directed her anger at was Dillon.

He sat in the dining room having the morning meal when Caitlin strolled in. The cool, November air had darkened her cheeks to a ruddy red. They almost matched her hair, which was hanging down to her tailbone in a ponytail, swaying with the movement of her hips.

Dillon seemed absorbed in watching the tresses easily swing across her back. He'd only seen her hair down a few times. She normally kept it pinned up under a cap or headdress. He liked how the fiery color contrasted with her light skin. It was thick and full, reminding him of evergreen bush set ablaze. A picture of Moses and the burning bush filtered through his mind. He wished he could run his fingers through it.

Caitlin moved across the floor, her gray riding habit rustling with each restless step. Plopping down in the chair, she busied herself with filling a plate. She buttered a biscuit then opted for honey instead of the usual preserves. Although Martha's biscuits melted in her mouth, and needed no extra sweetening, Caitlin still liked to indulge.

"'Tis a bit nippy to be riding today," Dillon commented.

"'Tis never too cold to ride."

He could smell the autumn wind in her hair and feel it emanating from the gray cloth of her dress and matching spencer; at least she had the sense to wear a jacket. "You are going to catch a cold if you keep riding in this weather."

"Aye, my lord," she taunted. "Am I to seek your permission for everything I do?" She hated being controlled.

Dillon's forehead wrinkled as he contemplated what he'd said to put her on edge. "I merely wish to watch out for your health." He may be a man but he was familiar with the recent trends in women's fashion. They'd gone from wearing heavy, warm fabrics like velvets, brocades and wools, which kept the winter chill away, to wearing light, thin fabrics like cottons, crepes and muslins. Although he liked the all-natural look, lighter materials combined with the absence of hoops and petticoats made women more susceptible to colds and influenza. In fact, so many women had died that the malady had been dubbed 'the muslin disease.'

"I do not need you worrying about me. I can handle myself."

"I am your husband and I do worry."

"You are my warden and naught else." Her eyes narrowed, crinkling around the corners.

"I don't know what has set your bristles up," Dillon calmly countered. "But I would appreciate you talking the matter over with me instead of calling names."

"Aye, my lord. Whatever you say, master." She fluttered her lashes in mock compliance. "While I'm at it, may I use the privy when I am finished?"

Dillon decided it was best to remain silent. If he said anything, it would only be fuel for sparring.

Caitlin, however, refused to be ignored. "I see the cat has gotten your tongue again."

"I merely wish to avoid a fight." His dark gaze held hers. "And for some reason you seem intent on battling this morning."

Of course it would be just like him to back down, she thought angrily. "And for some reason you seem to take pleasure in telling me what I must and must not do."

"I am doing no such thing. I merely want you to be careful so you won't catch your death."

"What do you care if I die?"

"Caitlin, what is the matter?" Dillon gently probed.

His tender tone eased her jangled nerves. She wanted to talk to him, confide her heartache, but she regarded him as part of the problem. If it weren't for him, she would be with her family right now. Anger rose, overshadowing any feelings of sensitivity. "My problem is you. I am trapped here with nothing and must abide by your wishes."

"You are not trapped, and you have plenty. If you wish for more, I will buy it."

"Therein lies the problem. You have everything. I have not a sixpence to scratch with." She crossed her arms. "I gave up my freedom the day we exchanged vows."

"I must get to the shop. I do not have the time to debate this matter with you." He stood, wiped his mouth and placed the linen napkin next to his unfinished plate. "We can discuss this at length later this evening if your mood has improved."

Dillon smacked the press with a hammer harder than needed, and sent the tray rolling, taking his frustration out on the broken machine instead of Caitlin. "Fiend seize it!"

"Twill not help fix the press if you keep hitting it so hard," Johnny stated hesitantly. He'd never seen his boss so agitated before.

His apprentice looked ready to scurry for cover. "I am sorry, Johnny. 'Tis' a foul mood I'm in today."

"Aye."

"I am tired of fixing this press."

"The wood is old, sir."

"'Tis not only the tray that is old. Something seems to break every time we go to press."

Johnny may not have been the smartest kid in town but he realized that Dillon's sour mood was more than just the press. He figured it had something to do with his new wife. However, he wasn't about to ask. "Why don't you buy a new one?"

"'Tis a thought. But something that expensive must be accompanied over on the ship. I do not feel like taking a trip to England."

"Why not?"

He'd never stepped foot back in his homeland after crossing the sea to America. His reasons for leaving were still there. "I am too busy." With that statement he ended the subject. "Let's run a draft and see if this thing is working yet."

Caitlin and Martha were battling again. The rest of the staff scurried out of sight after witnessing her indignation. Martha would not be bossed around by a rude, spoiled child. She didn't care if it was her master's wife.

"I will not take orders from you." Her large arms were in their usual position— crossed under her chest.

"I am the mistress of this house, and I will see you fired for your insubordination," Caitlin stated.

"Humph." Martha tossed her head back, giving her large frame a lofty air. "I have been tending this here house for years. You weren't nothing but a child when I started looking after Master Cade. If anyone is gonna do any firing around here, 'twill be him."

"We shall see about that," Caitlin countered. "Perhaps Mr. Cade is used to living in filth but I refuse to. There is no reason these dishes shouldn't be done and the food put away. The milk will sour if not put back on ice."

"And I told you that I'll get to it when I have time. The weather is cooling off and milk won't spoil like it does in the summer." The standoff had begun.

"If you have too many duties, then I will hire more help."

"No!" Her thick hands went to hips. "I ain't having any strangers in my kitchen."

"'It is not your kitchen," Caitlin reminded her. "And if you don't want hired help, then I can lend a hand."

"Are you hard of hearing?" Martha stepped forward, towering over Caitlin. "No strangers in my kitchen."

Although Martha was twice her size, Caitlin never backed down. "I am hardly a stranger. I am the mistress of this house."

"In name only."

Caitlin's mouth dropped open in shock. "How dare you!"

"'Tis the truth." Martha's eyes narrowed, pinning Caitlin with a sharp stare. "I may not be the most educated person around, but anyone with a set of eyes can see that the two of you don't share a bedroom."

"Whether true or not, 'tis not the servant's place to say anything." Furiously gathering her skirts Caitlin stormed out.

Dillon rubbed his brow where a dull ache formed. The ache wasn't half as dull as the day had been. Caitlin was still stewing in her room. She had not bothered to come down for dinner. And Martha's sunny disposition told him that the two had had another disagreement. The rest of the household went about their duties quietly. It seemed the whole house had been affected by his bride's somber tone.

He wanted to talk to her but wasn't sure that would help. She didn't seem ready to open up. Perhaps it would be best to let the mood pass. However, life felt pretty lonely without her around. Their marriage may be in name only, but the companionship appealed to him. He enjoyed their conversations. She seemed truly interested in his work, asking questions and intently listening to the trials of his day.

He glanced at the empty chair in the parlor, the one Caitlin should have occupied, and felt a tugging in his heart. A feeling he didn't comprehend. He missed watching the glow of the fire dance through her auburn waves. He also missed the way her white brow wrinkled when she was in thought or perplexed. The slant of her green eyes watching as he told a story, and her light laugh drifting through the air whenever she let her guard down. He had not realized that he'd become so attached to these little things. Only now, when they were absent from his life, did he recognize the emptiness. *Does Caitlin feel this emptiness too?* He wondered. *Does she still regard me as her enemy?*

Caitlin tarried extra-long in her toilette, making sure that Dillon had left for work before descending the stairs and going into the dining room. Upon seeing the clean table, she ventured into the kitchen and found Martha finishing up the dishes.

"Where is the morning meal?"

"I just finished putting it away."

"But I have not had any yet."

Martha shrugged her wide shoulders. "You took so long that I assumed you wouldn't be eating. And we can't have the food spoiling, now can we?"

Caitlin rolled her eyes, frustration welling. "I would appreciate something to eat." She tried keeping her tone level.

"Then fix something. I ain't stopping you."

"'Tis your job."

"I'm the cook. I ain't your personal maid."

"You purposely put the food away before I could eat."

"I'm only following your orders." Martha set the last dish in the sink. "If you don't like the looks of my kitchen, then stay out of it."

"'Tis my house and I will go where I please. You have no right telling me where I can and cannot go in my own home."

"'Twould not be a Christian thing for me to tell you where to go."

"Ohhh!" Caitlin's fists tightened into balls at her side. "Get me something to eat right this minute!"

"I'm busy, as you can see. I don't have time to dish out food for lazy, selfish, children."

"Lazy!"

"If you'd been up earlier and down here on time you could have had your morning meal while it was hot. As it is, you will have to settle for leftovers and get them yourself."

"Why…you!" Caitlin felt angry enough to attack her. Thankfully, Lucy's entrance distracted her.

"What is going on in here?" She placed herself between the feuding women. "I can hear you yelling all the way upstairs."

"Your mistress here wants something to eat and I'm too busy to fix her a plate," Martha sneered.

"Well, now, I can remedy that," Lucy stated. "You go have a seat in the dining room and I'll bring you a plate."

When Caitlin only stood there, glaring at Martha, Lucy gent-ly put an arm around her shoulders and guided her to the dining room. Coming back a few minutes later, she chided Martha. "Why don't you ease up on her?"

"Why?"

"You haven't liked her since the first day."

"'Tis nothing to like," Martha scoffed.

"You could find something if you gave her half a chance." Lucy unwrapped the biscuits and placed a couple alongside the sausages and cold grits. "Poor thing has been through a lot."

"So has Master Cade, but you don't see him being rude to people."

"Mr. Cade has had more time to deal with his problems. Caitlin is still trying to put the pieces back together." Lucy picked up the plate, heading to the door. "Her whole family is gone," she said and disappeared.

"I still think she's a spoiled brat," Martha fumed to herself. Although she'd felt compassion a few weeks ago, when she first heard about Caitlin's family being forced back to Ireland, she found it hard to be sympathetic right now. They were in a battle of wills, and only one of them could win.

"Lord, what am I to do?" Lucy had informed him of the animosity growing between his wife and cook, though, as of yet, neither one of them had said anything. Should he step in and try to solve the problem? Or let the two of them work it out? When it came to female troubles, he was at a loss. On the other hand, he doubted that two independent and headstrong women could work out the problem without interference.

Dillon knocked on Caitlin's bedroom door. When she didn't respond, he said, "I know you're in there."

"I do not wish to speak with you."

"Quit being so stubborn. There is a matter we need to discuss."

"What is it?" She jerked the door open, realizing she'd never have any peace until he had his say.

"'Tis about the house." He waited, hoping she'd invite him in. However, she stood in the doorway with her arms crossed. "A fellow is coming by on the morrow to look around and give a quote on the renovations."

"Fine. Is there anything else?"

He fidgeted with his collar. "I wish to speak about the contentions between you and Martha."

"I knew she'd run and tell you." Caitlin furiously rubbed the front of her gown. "No doubt you are on her side."

"Martha has not said a word to me. And I am not on anyone's side."

Caitlin stopped her fussing and looked up to meet his penetrating gaze. "How did you hear about our fight?"

"'Tis not important. But I would like to hear what happened."

"Why?"

"I cannot have a peaceful house if my wife and cook are always at odds. We must find a way to deal with this matter."

"Then fire her."

A dark cloud crossed his squared features. "That is not an option."

"See? You are taking her side."

"Martha has taken care of me since I arrived here." His voice turned soft. "She filled the void that my mother's death left."

Caitlin had no argument for that, but she was not about to be taken in by sympathy for his dead mother. She had her own grieving to do. "Then there is nothing left to say." She turned and started to shut the door.

"Caitlin, do not shut me out."

His soft plea tugged at the corner of her heart. She stopped, silently debating with herself. She just didn't trust him enough to allow him access to her heart. She'd never had a broken heart and intended to keep it that way. Yet, a small part of her wanted to confide all of her woes. Wanted to feel his arms wrapped around her, wanted to hear the comfort of his voice as he uttered soothing words. The need for survival reared up, diminishing any tenderness. "Goodnight, Dillon."

He felt the jab of disappointment as he heard the click of the closing door. At least she hadn't slammed it in his face. He'd notice a slight droop in her shoulders before she said good night. *Maybe I'm making some progress after all.* He hoped.

Caitlin hurried into the parlor, stopping the flow of conversation.

"Ah, here's my wife now." Dillon extended his hand. "Caitlin, I'd like you to meet Mr. Barclay."

"Nice to make your acquaintance." She curtsied.

"The pleasure is all mine." He smiled stiffly, which looked out of place on his round face. Mirthless, dark eyes examined her through thick, round spectacles. "I was unaware that you'd be joining us."

"I am sorry to be late, but my errands kept me longer than expected." Shoving a red tendril under the blue capote, she settled down on the settee, smoothing out the wrinkles in her blue gown and rearranging her skirts.

"You will mostly be dealing with my wife. I have put the renovation in her hands." Dillon breathed a sigh of relief at her entrance, fearing she had changed her mind and didn't want to take on the task. But, she'd arrived willing as ever to tackle the job. She was so unpredictable. That was one of the intriguing points about her personality. She made life more animated and lively.

"That is highly unusual," Mr. Barclay objected. His chest puffed out like a rooster. Caitlin thought the buttons on his waistcoat would spring off. "I assumed I would be working with the head of the house."

"I fear I have no talent in this matter." Not feeling proficient in the matter is why he'd never done the work in the first place.

"'Tis highly improper for me to be alone with a lady." His old-fashioned ideals wouldn't permit the idea of a lady doing a gentleman's job, especially one of this nature. It was a big job requiring a skilled, keen, and competent thinker, not the wishy-washy, fanciful, and dense disposition of a woman.

"Caitlin is far more suitable for the job than I." Dillon's tone was mild but the note of command couldn't be missed.

"As you wish, sir." Although he sounded none too happy about working with a woman, he wasn't about to lose an account of this size.

"As to impropriety," Dillon continued, "I will be present as much as possible, not to mention the house full of staff members. Caitlin will have her personal maid with her at all times." Pausing, he looked to her for acceptance. She nodded her approval.

"I understand." Barclay's cold, hard, eyes drifted in her direction. *At least she's pleasing to the eyes*, he mused. If he must work with a half-wit, it was better to have a pretty one.

With that settled, the three toured the house as Caitlin filled him in on the details she wanted attended to right away, starting with the dining room and downstairs parlor.

"'Tis customary to start with the upper floors and work down."

"I'm sure that is true, Mr. Barclay, but we do not entertain on the upper level. I want the downstairs rooms finished before Christmas."

"'Tis not possible," he said astonished. "Christmas is only seven weeks away."

"I believe it is your job to make it possible," Caitlin countered. "If you start down here these rooms will be done long before then.

"Surely you jest." His mouth dropped open.

"Not at all." Moving past him, she entered the living room. "This room will not need much work. New curtains, an area rug, a coat of paint, or perhaps wallpaper, I have not made up my mind yet." She paused, looking up to the ceiling. "The molding is in good condition, and the floor is sound. The only thing I desire to be replaced is the mantle over the hearth." Turning a bright smile on him she added, "Do you not agree?"

"The floor is sound and the molding is in good condition," he agreed, surprised at her knowledge of construction. She wasn't as dimwitted as he previously thought. "But it will still be time consuming."

"I assume you will be working with a crew." Caitlin tilted her head slightly, observing him from slanted green eyes.

"I have men to help."

"Excellent. You'll get this room done in no time." Walking past the men she added, "Now for the parlors, both the upstairs and downstairs will require more work. There are floor boards loose and rotten molding around the windows." She went into the hall and started up the stairs, leaving the men no choice but to follow.

"Mr. Cade, I urge you to reconsider. I simply cannot work with your wife." He whispered in a gruff voice. His reluctance mounted, realizing he'd never be able to squeeze more time and money out of the project. Caitlin knew exactly what she wanted and how long it would take to get it done. He'd never encountered a man with such precise calculations.

"Why not?" Dillon questioned.

"She expects too much in such a short period of time. Not to mention, her manners need some work. She doesn't behave at all like a proper lady."

"I'd thank you to keep your opinions about my wife to yourself." Dillon's brown eyes blazed. "As to her capabilities, she has more than proven herself adequate for this task. I trust you will learn how to work with her or not take the job."

"As you wish, Mr. Cade." His receding hairline enlarged his round face, giving more space to turn red at the indignant response.

"If you need to hire additional help to accomplish the task, then do so at my expense. Or, if need be, I will hire more workers on my own."

"No, sir." He met the challenge. "If I need more help, I prefer to do the hiring. Too much chaos is created when you have two crews trying to complete the same assignment."

"Just make sure the project is done on time."

"Yes, sir."

"He does not seem happy about working with me," Caitlin commented after escorting Mr. Barclay to the door.

"I am sure he will come around in time." Dillon smiled. "He's just not accustomed to working with women."

"I believe he is accustomed to swindling people."

"Come, now. Let's not be rude."

"Why not?" she asked. "'Tis only my bad manners and unladylike behavior."

"So you overheard that comment." His chortle rubbed the already raw wound.

"I do not wish an incompetent nincompoop like him to do any work on this house."

"He is not incompetent, my dear. He comes highly recommended."

"Nevertheless, I do not want him stepping foot in here again."

"You are upset. You will see reason once you calm down."

"I, sir, do not intend to calm down. Nor do I want to work with the likes of someone so mean and nasty."

"Caitlin, you cannot go through life firing everyone you do not get along with."

"You could if you had any backbone."

"I do not agree with every article I publish in the paper, but I must be fair and impartial. You have to learn to get along with people even if you don't like them."

"If you want to justify being spineless by calling it fair and impartial, you can. I, however, am not a journalist. I see things in black and white and call them as I see them. A spade is a spade, and a coward is a coward."

"And you think Mr. Barclay is mean and nasty?"

Caitlin put her foot on the first step, but quickly turned around at that comment. "Exactly what are you implying?"

"I am not implying anything. I am saying that your tongue is sharper than a two-edged sword. You can shred a man to pieces with it." Hurt flickered in his eyes. "You, Caitlin Cade, are the meanest, nastiest person I have ever met."

"How dare you!" she screeched. "I am your wife."

"Then start acting like one!"

"I do not have to stand here and listen to this." She lowered her voice, hoping the servants weren't listening. "You knew full well that I wanted no part of this charade." Her green eyes misted. "But you insisted on pursuing this marriage and agreed that it would be in name only. Now you stand here, insulting me because I am not behaving as your wife. Perhaps I would be apt to be kinder if you ever took my side."

"I am on your side, Caitlin. I stood up for you with Mr. Barclay, did I not?"

"Of course you do with a stranger but you won't take a stand against a simple cook."

His silence only fueled her anger. "See what I mean? The hired help are more important to you." She turned to go up the stairs but he grabbed her arm, twirling her around.

"You and Martha are going to have to work this out on your own. I will not be in the middle."

"Of course not, you take the cowardly way out. Do not get involved then you don't have to make a decision. You can continue being fair and impartial."

"You need to grow up, Caitlin. Only children run and sulk in their bedrooms, expecting someone else to defend their bad behavior." He leaned closer tightening his grip when she tried to pull away. "Adults must learn how to work problems out on their own."

His breath rushed past her cheek, nipping the tip of her ear causing tingling sensations. She felt the same sensations travel up her arm, where his hand still held her in place. She could feel the heat of his skin through the cotton sleeve. How could her body react so intimately when his touch was anything but gentle?

Angry at her body's response and the harsh words he spoke, she lashed out. "You, Mr. Cade, can go straight to the devil." Struggling to free her arm and not able to, she raised her other hand to slap his face.

He clutched her wrist in his hand. "Oh, no you don't," he seethed. "I have put up with your rude behavior long enough. I have given you the benefit of the doubt because I have felt sorry for you. I have made all kinds of excuses and pardoned your contemptuous acts all in the hopes that you'd come around someday." Bending her arm behind her back, he leaned so close that his chest brushed against hers. "But no more, Caitlin. I will not put up with your behavior anymore." His tolerant temperament had been stretched to the limit.

His body felt like a torch as he pressed closer. Even in anger he still felt desire for her. What was it about this woman that set his pulse racing and every nerve on edge? Unable to control his own body, he claimed her lips.

She struggled against him, but that proved futile and only ignited the flames already devouring her body. Anger and desire merged into one emotion. Everything else faded away leaving only this moment impressed in their minds.

Caitlin knew she should push away, step back, or do something to end this madness, yet her body didn't budge. His kiss left her immobile and thirsty for more like the scorched fields drinking in the rain after a summer drought. She felt a chilling sensation when his hands released her arms. A moment later they were gliding up her back, creating a whirlwind of emotions. She wound her arms around his neck, clinging to him helplessly, her fingers played with his curly mass of hair. She felt faint from lack of oxygen but didn't move or take any steps to stop him.

Dillon finally broke the kiss, silently chiding himself for taking such liberties. Looking into her startled green eyes he saw something else, although he was not sure what. Love. Hate. Desire. Anger. These emotions so closely mirrored each other that it was hard to tell which one she felt. He certainly felt confused about his own feelings. "I am sorry, Caitlin." He turned on his heel and left.

Chapter 9

A clap of thunder startled Caitlin awake. She groaned and rolled over feeling annoyed at being awakened so abruptly. Her annoyance wasn't just with Mother Nature; it was also directed at Dillon. Since the ill-fated kiss four days past, he hadn't been around. He stayed away all day, not coming home until well after she'd retired for the night. Not that she missed him, but he could at least have the courtesy to help with the decorating. After all, it was his house. He'd left her alone to deal with Mr. Barclay, and things weren't going smoothly.

Sliding into her slippers and donning her robe to fight off the chill, she went to the hearth and threw a log onto the nearly depleted fire. After stirring the ashes with the iron poker, she felt the warmth radiate through her body as the fire flourished to life. The glowing embers brought to mind the kiss.

Oh, that kiss, she fumed, angrily jabbing at the fire once more. Why couldn't she get it out of her mind? *Am I going mad? Am I losing my senses?* She could find no other explanation. One minute she was angry with him, the next she was kissing him. A dull ache formed between her breasts, and her cheeks flushed at the sensations his lips had produced. Both times he'd kissed her, she'd done nothing. Humiliation flared like a wildfire when she thought about how her body responded. What was it about him that turned her into a weak-minded nitwit?

"Mr. Barclay, would you care for some coffee or tea?" Caitlin smiled prettily.

"Tea would be nice." Lines creased his round forehead as he studied her. She certainly looked like the same person he'd worked with over the past week, but she didn't act the same. The sourly, contemptuous, vixen had been replaced by a smiling, gracious, lady.

"Would you like sugar?"

"No, thank you."

"Here you are." Caitlin handed him a china cup and matching saucer. "Please have a seat." Her small hand indicated the chair next to her.

He nervously glanced about, his small dark eyes searching for a chaperon.

"Lucy will be here soon. There was a matter that needed her attention."

"Perhaps we should wait until she arrives."

"Nonsense. Do I need to have fear of you, Mr. Barclay?"

"I'd never harm you," he staunchly defended.

"Are you perhaps fearful that I may harm your person in some way?" Her green eyes glowed bright with the challenge.

"That's preposterous." He drew his shoulders up to his full height of five feet eight inches, sucking in his round stomach slightly with offense.

"Then, please, have a seat. I have a matter I wish to discuss with you."

"Is everything to your liking?" He sat down, awkwardly balancing the cup and saucer. She had done nothing but complain since the project started. Bluntly barking orders at his men, and arguing with him as if she were in charge. And, since the master of the house hadn't been around, he could do not but hold his seething temper in check. However, this morning she had descended the stairs with a smile upon her lips. Her mood was light and gay as she complimented him on the work, letting him take control, even asking him for advice. Did she now have another complaint?

"Everything is coming along splendidly." She smiled, hoping to stroke his ego. "But I wish to seek your opinion on a matter."

"How may I be of service?" He set his tea on the table and gave her his undivided attention.

"'Tis about this mantle. I have a large project in mind and hope you can help." She crossed the room, running her hand along the rough, wooden top.

"'Tis why I'm here, madam."

"Now, I have not talked with my husband yet. He has been so busy at the shop." She paused. After receiving his nod of understanding, she continued. "So the plans are not definite, but since time is of the essence, I thought you could start the process and have a few quotes ready. If my husband does not agree, then we will drop the whole idea." Although she chafed at the idea of running to her husband, she knew the statement pleased Mr. Barclay, who strongly disapproved of women taking the lead. Not to mention, the project was quite expensive.

"Tell me what is on your mind and I'll see what I can do."

Caitlin smiled, satisfied that she had finally accomplished the task of wrapping him around her finger.

Caitlin paced in front of the hearth in the downstairs parlor. She'd endured another meal alone and feared the evening would be spent in solitude as well. She would have gone completely out of her mind if it hadn't been for the work on the house keeping her busy during the day.

The household remained fiercely loyal to Dillon and therefore wary of her intrusion into their lives. The battles with Martha didn't bolster the servants' confidence in their new mistress. Lucy, being a new hireling, was loyal to Caitlin, but she'd been slipping out in the evenings to visit with her family, which left Caitlin completely alone. With Sarah being heartbroken over Brogan's departure, she didn't venture out much, and Caitlin felt like she'd not only lost her family but her best friend too.

Her heart ached with loneliness. She felt the bitter strains of longing and oppression crushing down upon her, reaching their snarled claws around her heart and squeezing until she thought she'd crumble under the weight of depression. Oh! What was a girl to do? Heaving a sigh, she shook her head as if to clear away the muddle. By dint of will she forced the feelings to flee, squaring her shoulders in firm resolve, not allowing another dark mood to overcome her. It was easy to succumb to grief and depression when you were all alone.

"Good evening, my lady."

"Dillon." The name slid past her lips with an excited gasp. She'd never been so glad to see him.

"Am I disturbing you?" He'd watched her pace across the floor with a frown creasing her brow.

"Nay. You merely took me by surprise. You have not been around lately."

"I have had a lot to do at the shop." Even as he casually offered the excuse, he knew it was not true. He'd needed time to collect himself. To find a way to control the burning desires that surged through him. If he failed to find a suitable way to contain this hunger, he'd never be able to keep his promise of a name only marriage. His only other option was to change Caitlin's mind.

"'Tis what I thought." She sighed, running a hand down her green dress, focusing on the wrinkles and biting back a sharp comment, not wanting to offend the one person she could have a conversation with. "I am sorry about my attire. I figured I would be alone again tonight so I dressed more comfortably."

"You look beautiful." He noticed the black lace edging the sleeves and neckline was fraying, and the elbows showed signs of frequent use. But the dark green complimented her red hair, making her eyes even more vivid. "Besides, I too am dressed casually."

Even when dressed simply in brown pants and a white shirt, he still made an imposing figure. The width of his shoulders filled the small space of the doorway. He stood in his usual position with both hands behind his back, feet spread apart. Caitlin's eyes eagerly took in his appearance but she said nothing, fearing words wouldn't get by her constricted throat.

Dillon could have sworn he saw something pass in her eyes. But what? Tenderness. Serenity. Perhaps loneliness. That would likely better describe her state of mind. Whatever it was, it caused him to falter a moment. Hope welled up. Could he perchance win her affections? Stepping forward he held out a package that was behind his back. "'Tis for you, my lady." He definitely could read the surprise in her green orbs.

"What is this for?" She took the box.

"A peace offering." He watched as she deftly unwrapped the present.

"Oh, Dillon." She held the leather bound book in one hand while running the other over the engraved letters of the title, *Lyrical Ballads*. "'Tis beautiful."

"'Tis the newest book of poetry by Samuel Taylor Coleridge and William Woodsworth."

"I love poetry," she stated.

"'Tis my way of apologizing. I hope you can forgive me for the fight we had."

"The fight was not the problem." She met his eyes. "All married couples fight." The memory of that kiss hung heavy between them.

"Married couples also kiss." He met the challenge head on.

"Not ones in name only." Her chin jutted out.

The barb hit its mark. "I do not know what came over me. I am truly sorry."

Her eyes lowered back to the book. She knew the gift was expensive, and he did seem sincere. She also realized her fault in the fight. He'd told her she needed to grow up and handle her problems like an adult. He was right. Her mother had always gotten more work out of the servants using a gentle hand and kind words. 'Twas just her foul mood that made her act unreasonably. As for the kiss, she still had no idea what had happened there. However, she would extract a little revenge before accepting his apology.

"I could not possibly accept this. 'Twould be the same as accepting a bribe."

His dark eyes clouded with confusion. "'Tis nothing like a bribe," he softly expressed. "I merely wanted to buy my wife a gift."

"Really? Seems that you have already taken liberties and may expect more should I accept this." She held up the book.

"I have already stated that I regret my mistake. The book is a small token of my apology and nothing more." With hands clasped behind his back, he paced a few steps away. "I require nothing in return."

"You require nothing more because you have already taken what you wanted." With a swift motion, she tossed the book onto the coffee table with a loud thud. *Oh, it felt so good to spar with someone.*

What was it about this woman that could completely obliterate his calm disposition? His jaw tensed slightly before he spoke. "Pray tell, what exactly have I taken? 'Twas a simple kiss and nothing more."

Caitlin felt a sharp jab at the statement. There'd been nothing simple about that kiss, at least not on her part. She'd had simple kisses by a few of the boys who'd courted her. But she'd never been kissed by a man before. The awkward, clumsy attempts of boys could never compare with Dillon. Anger pricked her heart. He'd kissed her senseless, leaving her feeling confused and humiliated. Now he stood there claiming it was simple, as if it hadn't meant anything to him.

"You have taken my freedom and gained yourself a wife. One who must obey your every command and bend to your will. A wife who has been confined with taking care of the duties of the household while you gallivant around town."

His heartfelt laughter took her by surprise. "You, my dear, will never conform to anyone's will, least of all my mine. And I seriously doubt that you have ever obeyed any command." Crossing his arms in front of his chest, he stared at her.

"Humph!" That stubborn chin came out once again.

"Dare I say that if the decorating is too heavy a burden to bear, I am sure Mr. Barclay will be more than happy to assume the responsibilities by himself." Dillon shrugged his shoulders. "He disapproves of your involvement anyhow."

"No doubt he will take forever and rob you blind by the time he's done." Caitlin turned toward the fire, stretching her hands out to the warmth. "I did not say it was a burden I couldn't handle. 'Tis just a burden, that's all."

"The same kind of burden that marriage is?"

"The household duties are not half as burdensome as marriage." She heard the shuffling of his feet and then felt the warmth of his body as he stood close behind her.

"What is so oppressive about marriage, Caitlin?" His whisper brushed her cheek. "Do you not live in a nice house with a free hand to do as you please? Is your wardrobe so drab? Your belly empty? Do you want for anything?"

She closed her eyes, forcing her heartbeat to calm before answering, "'Tis more to life than possessions. There are things like love, loyalty, trust."

"I am capable of giving you all those as well." It took every ounce of his will power not to reach out and touch her. His breathing became irregular and his heart picked up speed. "If you would only accept them."

Caitlin spun around in astonishment, her gown swishing out like a cloud before settling back down against her long legs. "I could never love someone I did not trust."

"Have I given you any reason not to trust me?" His hoarse whisper raced along her nerves, setting her on edge.

"You, Dillon Cade, are my enemy." Although she said the words, the conviction behind them was lacking.

"I would like to be your friend."

Her eyes bore into his. "We cannot be friends. We are already husband and wife."

"That does not mean we cannot have friendship," he challenged. "Good marriages start with friendship and companionship."

"Ours did not start that way," she reminded him. "I was forced into wedlock, and I have no idea why you willingly went along with the plan."

"To save you." His mild voice pleaded for understanding. "'Twas the only way, Caitlin."

His gentleness roused compassion in her. "You did not tell me the truth before the wedding."

"As I have stated before, that decision was up to your parents. I had no control over it."

She couldn't hold that argument against him forever. Her own father had admitted that it was fully his idea to keep her in the dark about their departure back to Ireland. "Perhaps you had no control, but the fact remains that you forced me into this position. The only thing I have to offer is respect."

It was now Dillon's turn to be taken by surprise. That was more than he'd anticipated. "Many solid marriages have been based on less than that."

"Was your parents' marriage built on respect, or did they love each other?"

"I am not sure about my father, but my mother was in love." His mother had foolishly loved his father to the extent of heart-breaking ignorance.

"My parents, too, married for love." She cocked her head in thought. "Where does that leave us?" She posed the question. "We both grew up in families built on love. Now we are thrown together by the hand of political parties."

"I've come to learn, Caitlin, that circumstances happen for a reason. 'Tis best to make the most of it." He stepped closer. "I accept the fact that you respect me and I intend to build upon that."

Her auburn brows arched upward. "What exactly do you intend to build?"

"A solid, loving marriage."

Her mouth gaped open.

"The problem is we never had a courtship," he stated. "I intend to woo you until you fall hopelessly in love with me."

"Surely you jest."

"Nay, madam. I intend to make you my wife in all possible ways, including winning your heart."

"You will never win my heart," she stated with assurance. "'Tis safe to guess that the only thing you really want is a partner to warm your bed." She crossed her arms defiantly. "And that I will never willingly give you."

"We shall see." His brown eyes sparkled with mischief.

"Truly you are a cad!"

His laughter filled the room. "Nay, madam. I am merely a man besotted by your beauty."

She found it hard staying angry with him when he laughed, for his laughter seemed to pick up her spirits. Even so, she put on her best front. "'Tis plain to see where you have spent the last four days," she chided. "The local tavern is the only thing that has besotted you."

"Nay, my lady. I have not stepped foot in there." His laughter sobered. "I do, however, have to admit that my reasons for staying away did not pertain only to work." He looked her in the eyes. "I did not know what to say to you. I feared you'd never forgive me for my indiscretion."

"Your presumption was correct." She lifted her nose haughtily in the air. "I have no intention of forgiving you." She crossed the room, picking up the book from the table. "What was your real purpose for this gift?" she questioned. "To ask forgiveness, or win my affections?"

"I must confess, a little of both."

Caitlin paused a moment, processing his words. Why did the prospect of him seriously courting her cause a fluttering in her stomach? Surely she didn't want the attentions of this traitor. She couldn't let her guard down. However, life had been pretty lonely the past few days. With her family gone, she had no one to turn to.

No one except Dillon. Without him she felt totally and utterly alone. Could she open her heart just a crack? Could she forgive him? Forget he was born in England? Could she put her convictions aside?

"I thank you for the book of poetry." She finally managed to speak. "I accept it and your apology. However, I cannot encourage you to continue your pursuit. 'Twould be a waste of your time. I will never change my mind." Hesitantly looking at him, she continued. "I appreciate your honesty so I feel it only appropriate to return it."

"Thank you for accepting my apology, and my gift. It brings me great pleasure to please you, madam." He gallantly bowed. "As for the other matter, I will not give up so easily."

"Suit yourself," she quipped. "'Tis your time that you'll be wasting."

"'Tis never a waste of time when it comes to matters of the heart." His lips twisted into a grin. "Is there anything else I can do for you?"

"Actually 'tis another matter I wish to discuss." She'd almost forgotten the reason she'd waited up for him. "I have an idea for the fireplace." She sat down in a chair placed in front of the crackling fire.

"I have already told you to do as you please."

"But 'tis expensive and not really necessary."

He crossed the room taking a seat beside her. "Can Mr. Barclay accomplish the task?" He gently took her hand.

"Aye. I have already spoken with him." She felt a warmth spreading from her hand, moving slowly up her arm, causing her heart to palpitate faster, "but I told him to hold off until I talked with you." She needed to think and the tingling sensations were now spreading to her brain. Withdrawing her hand, she stood and paced to the fireplace.

"I have already stated that I do not care about the cost. Do as you please. I will talk with Mr. Barclay tomorrow."

Her green eyes brightened. "Oh, Dillon, thank you." She turned to face him. "'Twill be beautiful." Her excitement shined brighter than the fire burning in the hearth.

"You're welcome, my dear." His smile physically seemed to touch her. "I do have one other item of business."

"What is that, my lord?"

He lost his train of thought at those words and felt his heart lurch to a screeching halt. She'd never uttered *my lord* except sarcastically. He wasn't sure she even realized what she'd said. "Umm…" He shook his head trying to concentrate. "The only room I ask you to not touch is my study."

"I think we can manage that." His generosity astounded her. This was his house, but he'd given her freedom to do as she wanted.

"I hope you understand how much it means having you work on the house. If the burden is too great, I will hire someone else. I have left Regal Hall in your hands because I have complete faith in you. I only hope to one day win the same kind of trust from you."

"We shall see, my lord."

"With that thought to warm my heart, I will bid you goodnight."

She smiled coyly. "The useless utterances of your tongue never cease, do they?"

"Not when I'm after a prize so great."

"You're a scoundrel," she teasingly scolded.

"And I shall always be so." His departing laughter drifted through the air.

"Good morning, my dear." Dillon held up the ceramic pot. "Would you care for a cup of tea?"

"Aye." She took the cup and saucer. "Thank you."

"What are your plans for the day?"

"Same as every day for the past week, working on the house."

"I thought perhaps we could go for a ride."

"I truly have too much work."

"Mr. Barclay is more than capable of handling things by himself for a few hours." She found an excuse every time he wanted to do something. He'd never win her heart if he couldn't get her alone. "Besides, I thought we could do some shopping in town." He'd sweeten the pot a little.

"I cannot think of anything I need." Once she set her mind on a task that's all she thought about until it was finished.

Dillon held up a piece of paper. "We have been invited to a dinner party at Thomas Jefferson's."

Her fork clanged against the plate. "Thomas Jefferson? The Vice President?"

"The one and only." Dillon smiled. "I have met him a few times. I'm helping with his campaign. This is really more of a political function, but wives are welcome. I think you would have fun."

Caitlin couldn't have been more astonished if the President himself had invited her to dinner. Her husband had more connections than she realized. A man as timid and mild as he didn't seem the type to have such powerful contacts. Of course, she was finding out that beneath the placid façade was a powerful force that no one should underestimate. "I guess if I am going to meet Mr. Jefferson, then I could use a shopping trip."

A few hours later Caitlin and Lucy were admiring the new selection of hats while Dillon priced some supplies for the shop. After a long discussion with Mr. Johnson, Dillon joined the women. "I like that one."

Caitlin tied the red ribbon and cocked her head in the mirror. "'Tis a bit too bright, don't you think?"

"Perhaps it is a little overpowering, but red is my favorite color."

Untying the bow she set the hat back on the rack. "Did you order the supplies you needed?"

"Most of them, but I have to run over to the shop and get some measurements. Will you two be all right for a few minutes?"

"We will be fine." Caitlin waved him away. "Hurry back. I am hungry."

"All right." Dillon started for the front door when a group of women bustled into the store. Henrietta's hazel eyes lit up when she noticed him. "Why Dillon Cade, fancy running into you."

"Henrietta."

His reply was short and she didn't like that at all. Casting a glance around the store she noticed Caitlin. He was more inclined to flirt when his wife wasn't around. As it stood she'd have to be bolder to capture his attention. She smiled, glad she'd taken extra time in preparing herself, having wetted her slip so that it clung snugly to her legs. Although the cold weather made wet petticoats miserable to wear, she liked how the look revealed not only her long legs but her womanly curves as well. "I was just talking about how I never saw my article in your paper." Talking about the shop was the only way she could ever engage him into conversation.

"As I told you earlier, your work just doesn't fit with this type of news," he sighed. When would she realize that she wasn't cut out to be a writer?

"Oh, I thought perhaps you could take a risk and publish it anyway. Maybe just to see how people react to it." Batting her lashes she laid a hand on his arm. "Couldn't you do it as a personal favor to me?"

"The newspaper business does not work that way." He folded his arms behind his back, causing her hand to slip away.

Although miffed at his reaction to her touch, she wasn't about to give up. "Well, then, maybe I'll stop by the shop later and drop off another article I've been working on. I believe this one is more in line with what you want."

Silently groaning to himself he politely answered, "I will be happy to take a look. I will not be in the shop today, so just leave it with Johnny."

"Is something wrong at home?" This man practically lived at the newspaper shop. She'd often wondered how much work it took to put out a weekly paper. Certainly it didn't require someone to put in the hours he did, but she could always count on finding him whenever she wanted. The idea of him not being as accessible made her heart twist a little.

"Everything is fine. We are remodeling and I'm needed at home."

"I see." The twist turned into a full-fledged flop. She hated the idea of Caitlin living in that huge house with the man she loved, even if it was an arranged marriage. She should be living there not that Irish trash! "I'm glad to hear nothing is wrong." Her tone was tight. Pasting a smile on her face she leaned in and whispered, "Let me know if I can ever be of any assistance to you."

"Caitlin is handling the project just fine, but thanks for the offer."

Henrietta smiled seductively and brushed her chest against him. "I think you'll find that I'm better at a lot of things."

"Darling, there you are." Caitlin smiled sweetly, slipping in between the two. "I thought you were going to hurry back so we could get something to eat. You know how all this shopping just plumb tuckers me out. But what am I to do? I have to find a new hat for Mr. Jefferson's dinner party."

"Sorry, I got held up."

Turning fiery eyes to Henrietta, she smiled tautly, "How nice to see you, Henrietta. I hope you won't think me rude, but my husband and I are in a bit of a rush."

"Not at all," she lied. "Dillon and I were just going over some business matters. I'm sorry to detain him."

"No harm done, but you better hurry, dear." Caitlin slowly, purposefully laid her hand on Dillon's chest.

Henrietta's hazel eyes darkened when she saw the flash from Caitlin's large diamond. The bitterness only grew after noticing how possessively Dillon slipped his arm around Caitlin's waist. The little twit wasn't stopping with getting Dillon to wed her. She'd have him bedded soon also. *I'll have to put my plan in motion before that happens.*

Chapter 10

"Where is Lucy?" Dillon asked after they'd been seated in the tavern.

"She met some friends. I told her she could spend a few hours with them."

"This is more of what I had in mind. I wanted some time alone with you."

"Really? I expect Henrietta to join us any minute." Although she'd played the part of a loving wife for her rival's sake, she wasn't putting on any airs now.

"Jealousy does not become you." Dillon took a drink of cider from his wooden mug.

"I am not jealous." Her small nose elevated a few degrees. "I would have to have feelings for you in the first place in order to be jealous."

Her defensiveness told him he was right, but pride wouldn't allow her to admit it. "I see. Perhaps you are merely shallow and superficial."

"How dare you."

"Why are you getting upset?" Leaning back in his chair, he casually stretched out his legs, crossing his ankles. "I am only trying to find excuses for your rude behavior."

"'Tis nothing wrong with my behavior. Yours, on the other hand, could use some lessons."

"I do not recall being rude."

"Insensitive is more like it." Crossing her arms defiantly she hardened her heart against the sharp pains stabbing it. Why did the thought of him being in someone else's arms bother her so?

"I do not know what you're talking about."

"Don't play dumb with me, Dillon." Caitlin kept her tone level, but hurt flashed in her eyes. "If you want to keep a light skirt like that, you're welcome to her. However, you could have the decency to control yourself in public."

"There is nothing between me and Henrietta."

"'Tis not what it looked like in the store." She sat back, crossing her arms. "Do you allow every trollop to rub against you in such a way?"

"I do not allow anyone rub against me." Cocking one dark brow he added, "Of course, I'd make an exception for you."

"'Twould be a cold day in Hades before I'd ever rub against you, especially after someone like her has touched you." Bitterness laced her husky voice.

"I have no interest in Henrietta. We were just talking, that's all."

"Oh, that's right. You two were discussing business, was it not?" Her cynical smile said volumes. "Exactly what type of business are you two involved in?"

"We are not in business." Dillon leaned forward, placing his elbows on the table. "She was trying to convince me to publish an article she wrote."

"She seemed to be doing a lot of convincing," Caitlin quipped. "No wonder you spend so much time at the shop." She'd never said anything but his staying away for an entire week still played upon her mind. Had he been with Henrietta the whole time?

"I work late because it takes a lot of time putting out a weekly paper. Do you know it takes twenty-five hours just to set the type? Since Adam moved, I have only Johnny to help and he's an apprentice."

"I suppose your little mistress is not much help around the shop?"

"Henrietta cannot even write, let alone run a press."

"She has never struck me as the scholarly type."

"Trust me she's not. I wish she would give up the notion of being a writer."

If Henrietta were his mistress, he should have some kind of feelings for her. At the very least be supportive. Although the thought of being a better writer caused a small thrill to run through her, at the same time she felt distressed. "So, you think I'm a good writer, just a bad wife."

"Caitlin, you are a terrific wife."

"You do not have to lie, Dillon." She'd been unfairly pressured into this marriage, and had been anything but kind. She couldn't even blame him for turning to someone else. "We may have a name-only commitment, but I would like to have honesty between us." Anger had died leaving behind truth. "I realize that men have well certain needs. Since I'm unable to fulfill that part of our marriage, I can see why you would turn elsewhere."

Dillon's heart tugged forcibly at the disappointment he saw on her face. "You have not failed in any part of this marriage." Reaching across the table, he took her slender hand. "I know how hard this situation is for you. I am not some brute that cannot live without a woman's companionship. I am willing to wait until you are ready."

She wasn't sure if it was his touch or his words, but something melted her heart. She wanted to believe him. "What if I am never ready?"

"There is more to marriage than physical contact. I have enjoyed our time together just as it is." A quirky smile touched his lips. "Well, maybe I could do without so much fighting." Placing a kiss on the back of her hand he added, "Milling with you is not very romantic."

Caitlin surveyed her surroundings. Although daylight streamed into the large room through the windows, it didn't brighten the drab, dingy feeling. Servants bustled around, placing dishes of food and tankards of ale on the wooden tables that were crammed with the lunch crowd. Smells of roasted pork, lamb, and beef floated in from the kitchen, while the active buzz of conversation sounded like a nest full of bees. "'Tis a little crowded to be romantic."

"I know. It's not the gentry tavern but the food is good." Though he came from wealth, Dillon seemed more comfortable with common folk then the upper class. "Besides, I get more business in here."

A small smile lifted the corners of her mouth. "You really love your work, don't you?"

He paused a moment before answering. "I do love printing the news, but I do not wish to make it the only thing in my life. I want to have time with you. And, perhaps, someday even have children. I will never put my job above my family the way my father did."

"What happened to having a celibate life?"

"I said perhaps, someday," he clarified. "Having a family has never been high on my list, or I'd have married years ago. But, now 'tis something I have been considering. 'Would be nice to have someone to pass the business onto."

"I must make it clear that I do not ever intend to have a family. I fear our goals for this marriage are traveling down two different paths."

"I am not going to pressure you into anything. I am just saying that things change with time. God can change hearts. His plan for marriage is that two hearts become one. Perhaps our thoughts and ideas will merge onto one path sometime in the future." Looking deep into her eyes he asked, "Promise me you will not reject the idea out of spite."

"Contrary to what you have witnessed, I am not a spiteful person."

"Then you will seriously consider my proposal?"

"I will, but do not put too much hope into the idea." She looked down at her folded hands. "I do not think I will ever trust anyone enough to open myself up completely and have a physical relationship."

He digested that a moment before answering. "Caitlin, as I have stated previously, I will not force you into anything. You are young, and it is only natural to have insecurities about intimate situations. I believe as you mature, your outlook will be different. I shall be waiting when that day arrives."

"You sound positive about that."

"I am. You wouldn't have been so jealous if you did not care, even just a little." He winked.

"You, Mr. Cade are full of yourself."

His deep chuckle lit up his brown eyes. "I like the shape of your mouth when you pout."

Her astonished gasp made him laugh even harder.

Caitlin watched the bare trees stretch their empty arms toward the gray, cloudy sky. The vibrant colors of autumn now lay on the ground in shades of brown, disintegrating, rotting, and being trampled by horse hooves and carriage wheels.

The lap robes and warming pan didn't seem to fight off the chill with much success, although she surmised it would be even colder without them. Perhaps her discomfort was because she wasn't used to traveling such long distances. They were now on day two of their journey.

"Are we almost there?" Lucy didn't want to complain, but she was cold, tired, and stiff. She knew her mistress felt the same way, yet, somehow Caitlin managed to handle the trip with dignity and grace.

"We'll reach the inn in a few more hours. It will be one more day before we reach Mr. Jefferson's." Dillon smiled at the boisterous sigh. "Would you like to stop for a while?" The question was directed at Lucy however his attention was on Caitlin.

"Yes," Lucy quickly answered.

"I would not mind stretching my legs also." Caitlin demurely smiled under Dillon's intense stare.

Lucy watched the exchange of tenderness pass between them; she didn't care what the town, or staff said about them. She felt certain their marriage was more than platonic. Quiet, affectionate moments like this one spoke louder than all the gossip.

Dillon pounded the carriage wall three times, and the wooden wheels began to squeak as they ground to a halt. A cold breeze whirled in when the door opened. The occupants wondered if stretching their stiff muscles was worth venturing out.

Dillon got out first and offered assistance to Lucy. Caitlin wrapped the fur robe tighter around her shoulders and accepted Dillon's hand. As she started to descend, the horses impatiently pranced, causing the carriage to sway. Caitlin stumbled on the step. Grabbing the hem of her gown to keep it from tearing left her no hands to steady herself. A rush of cold air stung the delicate skin of her face as she propelled forward.

Dillon grabbed her around the waist, pulling her close and blocking the fall. She slid down the length of his body until her feet touched the ground.

"Are you all right?" Worry lines creased his eyes.

Shaken from the fall, and the sensual movement, Caitlin didn't answer, but nodded her head slightly. Leaning against Dillon not only for support, but for warmth, she reveled in the security of his arms. Their bodies merged into one. They forgot everyone and everything, including Lucy, who had started to rush to her mistress' aid, but stopped short, feeling like an intruder on an intimate moment.

Lucy decided to head over to the second carriage to talk with Johnny. Spending time alone with the handsome apprentice was the only bright spot in this whole trip.

Dillon and Caitlin stood there for several moments. The sound of horses whining, over the howling of the wind brought Caitlin back to her senses. Mustering enough courage, she pulled away from the embrace, shivering as the cold air replaced the warmth of Dillon's body. "Thank you for your assistance."

"'Tis why I'm here, madam." He bowed low. "We should be moving on. I will go find Lucy and the rest of the crew." Dillon left Caitlin to attend to her needs while he searched the woods.

After everyone was assembled and the carriages were on their way again, Dillon entertained the women with stories about his childhood. It seemed in no time at all they arrived at the inn.

They had lodged in a large town the night before. The big, roomy inn had been stately and pristine. This little, ragged place wasn't any bigger than a medium size house, and it was set in the middle of no-man's-land. Chickens, pigs, and goats ran loose around the yard.

"I know 'tis not much," Dillon whispered, "but it is the only place for another five miles."

"'Tis fine." Caitlin smiled, and mounted the wooden steps, stepping over a sleeping dog on the porch.

"Velcome. Velcome." The short, slender hostess opened the door, and shook both Dillon and Caitlin's hand enthusiastically. "It's goot to have company." Her Dutch accent and deep tone seemed out of place for someone so small.

She ushered the group into a small, dingy room with a large wooden table. The fire in the hearth roared as the smells of dinner filled the house. "Vould you like to settle in the rooms bevore supper?"

"No, thank you. I'll give you a hand," Caitlin offered.

"No. No. You are guests." The small woman waved her comment away.

"I'll help the boys put the horses away." Dillon left.

Despite the protests, Caitlin helped set the table. When the men came back in, the meal was ready. Everyone sat down and Dillon asked the blessing. "Our Father who art in Heaven. Hallowed be thy name. We thank you for the safety so far on this trip and pray for continued well-being. We also thank you for the provisions of lodging and food. Amen."

Everyone's spirits seem to lighten as dishes of roasted chicken, mashed potatoes, green beans, biscuits, nuts, and dried fruit were passed around. The conversation and storytelling continued long after dinner ended. Everyone enjoyed the fun filled atmosphere as they sat around the hearth.

Finally calling it a day, Dillon led Caitlin up the rickety stairs. "I am sorry I could not acquire separate rooms— space is limited. They only have two bedrooms." Dillon opened the door and Caitlin stepped into the small, simple room. "However, I did manage separate beds."

Except for the two beds on opposite walls, one dresser, a beaten up washstand, and a thin, torn rug on the floor, the room was bare. "And I thought your place was stark." Caitlin smiled wistfully.

"I know it's not much. 'Tis only one night we must stay here."

"Is Mrs. White bunking with Lucy?"

"Aye. They're in the other bedroom. The men are on the floor in the living room."

"I still do not understand why you brought Mrs. White along. I do not need two personal maids."

"Mrs. White is here for Lucy. I fear she is too young to be unattended."

"Am I not capable of being her chaperon?" The defensive tone warned of a storm brewing.

"My dear, you are more than capable. But I did not want you to be saddled with all the responsibilities. Besides, Mrs. White begged me to come."

"Are you not in control of your servants? They run over you like a pack of wild horses."

Dillon smiled at the playful pitch of her words. "If she is looking after Lucy, we shall have more time alone."

"You have managed that quite magnificently. I am now cornered in this room all alone with you."

"You are not cornered, my pet." Dillon hung his overcoat on a peg in the wall. "You are sleeping across the room."

"Is a mouse safe from a snake when it's across the room?"

His effortless laughter echoed off the bare walls. "You needn't worry about me, my dear. This snake is full."

"Been feasting on some other helpless victim, have you?"

"I would hardly call you helpless," Dillon quipped. "You could slay a man with that sharp wit of yours, not to mention your tongue."

"You like my wit?" Caitlin was so taken aback that she ignored the tongue remark.

"Your brilliant mind is one of the things I love most about you."

Caitlin definitely liked the path of the conversation and wanted to pursue it further, but a knock on the door interrupted.

"I just vanted to check and make sure everything vas okay." Their hostess stood with hands clasped in front of her dirty and blood stained apron.

"Everything is fine." Caitlin's gracious smile lit up the room.

"Goot. Goot. I also vanted to say that I prepared hot vater for a bath, if you'd like one."

A quick surveillance of the tiny woman told Caitlin that she wasn't fond of bathing. And, the condition of the house didn't leave much hope for a clean washroom, or tub. However, she didn't want to hurt the woman's feelings when she'd obviously gone through so much trouble. "A bath would be wonderful."

"My husband is getting the vater now. You may come down as soon as you'd like."

"Thank you. I'll just gather my things and be right there."

With a quick curtsey she was gone.

The room was pretty much what Caitlin expected - small, dingy, and a little drafty. Although the brass tub was old and worn, it was clean.

Caitlin soaked in the water luxuriating in the warmth, as it soothed her aching muscles. It might not have been the prettiest bathroom she'd been in, and she didn't have any of the scented soaps and oils like at home, but this bath was the best she'd ever taken. She had never needed one as badly as today, not only to wash away the dust and grime from the trip, but she was grateful for the time alone.

Not having a minute to herself on the trip left no time for thinking. She wondered how Mr. Barclay was coming along with the house. The work had been progressing nicely over the last few weeks. Mr. Barclay had lost his contempt and listened to her suggestions and ideas— as long as she consulted with Dillon first.

That irked her for a while, but soon she found it wasn't so difficult to ask his permission, especially when he granted her every desire. Dillon's enthusiasm made it easy to try and please him. Every now and then she would catch him watching. His eyes held so much admiration; it sometimes caused her to blush, something she'd never been prone to do.

Truth be told, she'd kept herself so busy that thinking was next to impossible. She didn't want to think. Not about her marriage. Not about Dillon. And most certainly not about the feelings he induced whenever he was near. It seemed hard to believe that in the last week, since Dillon acknowledged that he wanted to woo her, they had only had one fight. Of course, Henrietta was the center of that argument.

Dillon swore that nothing was going on with her. She wanted to believe him, and he'd never given her cause to distrust him. However, she'd heard bits and pieces of gossip around town. For some reason everyone thought Dillon had planned to marry Henrietta. And, that Caitlin had swooped in, scooping him up and carrying him away like a hawk stealing a chicken. What she didn't understand is why the town folk would be saying that if it weren't true.

She wasn't dense enough to think that Dillon hadn't had relationships before her. After all, he was a very handsome man. That, coupled with his easy-going personality and generous spirit was enough to draw any woman to his side. She'd often wondered why he wasn't already married. His admission that he hadn't wanted to be tied down did not mean he hadn't had companionship. If he had been interested in Henrietta, why hadn't he married her?

Even though he'd married Caitlin, he could still continue a relationship with Henrietta. After all, they had both agreed to a name-only marriage. Dillon had been more than eager to suggest it. Caitlin had assumed he'd had another woman all along. So, why did he come to her now wanting a courtship? And, worst of all, make her love him?

No, she couldn't be that careless and give her heart to a man who would only toss it away when the next little trollop passed by. Although Dillon seemed to be a true gentleman and wouldn't do that sort of thing, she just didn't know him well enough yet. She had to keep the wall up. Not wanting to lose her identity was taking second place to not wanting a broken heart.

The water grew cold and Caitlin slipped out of the tub. She wrapped a linen towel around her head, then patted the drops of water from her body as quick as she could. Donning her nightgown and robe, she hurried up the stairs, wincing as each step creaked.

Lucy met her in the hall. "I heard you coming."

"I believe the whole house heard me. I tried walking softly, but the steps are so old."

"Do you want me to assist with your nightly toiletry?"

"No, you go back to bed. I can handle it."

"As you wish, Mrs Cade." Lucy dipped into a quick curtsey and hurried into her room.

"Mrs. Cade," Caitlin muttered as she continued down the hall. "I see Mrs. White has been talking to her."

Entering her room, she found Dillon putting more logs on the fire. The heat from the hearth sent a shiver through her cold body, making her teeth chatter.

"There you are. I was just about to send Lucy to fetch you. I feared you hit your head and drowned in the tub." Dillon took her hand. "You are freezing. Come sit by the fire."

"S.. Sor.. ry, it.. took so long." She sat in the chair offered.

"Did you enjoy your bath?"

"Y... yes."

"Good. Now sit here and warm up. This place is old and drafty."

As she sat there warming up, Dillon took the towel from her head. "What are you doing?"

"Your hair will dry faster if it's down." Walking over to the chest he started digging through it. "Where is your hair brush?"

"'Tis in there somewhere."

After finding it, he came back and started brushing through the tangled mess. Gently he applied stroke after stroke until the knots came undone.

"You have a gentle touch," Caitlin whispered. "Lucy isn't even that good."

"I aim to serve." He winked. "Now lean forward and bend your head down."

Caitlin did as commanded, and he continued to brush the long tresses, getting the tangles out from underneath the thick mass of hair.

"That feels so good," she murmured.

"Then sit back and I shall show you something else."

Tossing her head up sent her hair flying through the air like flames. Skeptical green eyes watched him, while questioning red brows arched.

"'Tis not what you're thinking." Dillon laughed. "Just sit back and relax." Coaxing her back, he gently slipped his fingers into her hair, messaging her head.

Caitlin tried to keep silent, but the "ohh's and mmm's" keep slipping out. "That feels wonderful."

"Do you want me to do your shoulders also? It will loosen the muscles."

"Sure. Why not?" She'd never felt so pampered. Closing her eyes, she leaned back against the high-back chair and let Dillon work his magic.

"Do you have a gown on under this robe?"

"Of course." Sitting up she pinned him with a stare. "Why do you ask?"

"I could do a better job on your shoulders without the bulky robe."

"Ohh." She felt a little awkward.

"'Tis up to you." He went back to rubbing her shoulders.

Caitlin had to trust him at some point. He was only trying to make her comfortable. Besides, she had her thickest gown on, so he wouldn't be able to see anything. "I guess it wouldn't hurt to take the robe off. I cannot sleep in the thing." Standing up she slipped the robe off and tossed in across the room. It sailed through the air and landed on her bed.

"Nice throw," Dillon commented.

"I used to play rounders with my brothers." She sat back down. "I was pretty good at marbles also."

"I bet." The image of her running around bases and throwing balls at boys didn't surprise him. Dillon continued his massage.

"You are great with your hands," she moaned.

"It must come from working with the press all day."

"You are not this gentle with the press. If you were, maybe it would not break so often."

"Perhaps I'd be gentler if it were as beautiful and warm as you."

"Too bad your sweet talking could not fix the thing," Caitlin teased. "I am surprised you have not talked the press into printing out the paper all by itself."

"Too bad that was not possible. Then I could spend more time at home with you."

"As if you would be happy sitting around with nothing to do."

"If you were there, I'd have something to do," he whispered in her ear.

The light wisp of his breath shivered down her neck, while his hands continued kneading her shoulders. Fighting hard to control her mind, she responded in barely a whisper of her own. "What would we do all day besides fight?"

"Oh, I could think of a few things." Sliding his hands over the rounded part of her shoulders, he then moved them down her arms.

Caitlin felt the warmth of his hands through the cotton fabric of her gown. The sensations surging through her body reminded her of the few times they'd kissed. For some reason the urge to feel his lips on hers intensified. When his mouth pressed against the delicate skin on her neck, she physically choked back a moan. Closing her eyes she leaned back, enjoying the feelings his hands and lips produced. She felt her body melting like wax on a hot summer's day.

When his hands grew bolder and his tongue slid across her skin, she suddenly jumped from the bolt of shock. She was out of the chair in seconds, shaking her head as if to clear away the muddle that engulfed her brain.

Looking at Dillon she saw the conflicting emotions cross his face. He too, seemed unable to speak, as if he were trying to gather his scattered wits. She watched the desire slowly being replaced with guilt, and knew that an apology was coming.

She held up a hand to stop it before he even uttered a word. "Do not apologize, Dillon." Her voice was soft and shaky. "'Twas just as much my fault."

Dillon's dark brows rose in surprise. "'Twas not your fault, Caitlin. You must believe that I never intended this."

"I do believe you."

"Really?"

She watched the firelight dance across his furrowed brow, and almost laughed as the innocent, panicked look, changed to amazement. "Really. You have been nothing but a gentleman on this entire trip. I think we both got caught up in our emotions, that's all." Before he could explain or apologize any further, she went to her bed and threw back the threadbare covers. "I suggest we get some sleep. We still have a long trip ahead of us."

"Aye, that we do." Dillon stoked the fire for the night without a word. She'd brought the conversation to an end more efficiently than Martha ran the kitchen. *Thomas Jefferson should think about hiring her for his campaign manager*, Dillon mused.

Excitement pulsated through Caitlin as she craned her neck out the carriage window, watching the house looming larger and larger in the distance. The long dirt lane led them up the rolling slope of Virginia's picturesque mountain, where Monticello sat.

"It is absolutely breathtaking," Caitlin breathed in awe.

Dillon only smiled as he watched the afternoon sun illuminate the childlike wonder in her green eyes.

There was nothing to say for the stately, Roman neoclassic house spoke eloquently enough for itself. The red brick of the building sharply contrasted the white columns holding up the large gabled roof of the portico. The white railing running along the second and third stories of the house looked as if it were caging in the four chimneys protruding from the roof.

As if the house wasn't beautiful enough, the scenic views surrounding the structure seemed to scream tranquility. The lush greens of the lawn and numerous trees looked unusually out of place for this late in November.

As the caravan neared the house, Caitlin's excitement suddenly switched to fear. Turning worried eyes upon her husband she nervously bit her bottom lip.

"What is the matter?"

"I just realized that I do not know what to say or how to act."

His soft laughter seemed to ease her soul more than the gentle words he spoke. "Do not be so anxious, dear. Mr. Jefferson is only a person. Besides, you have been raised in the customs and manners, have you not?"

"I have. But I've never had the chance to use them around such influential people. The man is Vice President, for goodness sake. He wrote the Declaration of Independence, and is the future candidate for President. There you sit acting like he is any normal man."

The carriage stopped and panic spread to every fiber of her being. In just a few moments she'd be inside the famous Monticello. She'd have to speak to Mr. Jefferson. Or, was it forbidden for women to talk without the permission? *Do I curtsey first, or thank him for inviting us? Oh! I wished I'd paid more attention to my studies.* She'd been more interested in arguing over why women had to behave like obedient dogs, than actually learning how to act. Now, she feared looking like a fool. Would Dillon be angry if she embarrassed him?

"Oh God, please help me," she whispered.

Chapter 11

Caitlin's trepidation increased as she stepped through the east front door into the entrance hall. Tall windows that were more reminiscent of doors allowed a copious amount of sunshine in to brighten the room. The rays bounced off the wooden floor and darted around the two toned room, making the whitewashed upper half look as pure as new fallen snow, while bringing out the vivid yellow-orange of the bottom portion. A large white balcony not only connected the two mezzanine wings, but also served as a display area for a Mandan buffalo robe and other animal skins.

The entrance hall was not only a waiting area it was also a museum of interesting facts related to American history, western civilization, and Native American cultures. Amongst the art displays and busts of prominent people were Indian artifacts including pipes, jewelry, and clothing.

"Mr. Jefferson certainly has a fondness for dead things," Caitlin commented, as she looked at a display of bones.

"Mr. Jefferson has a fondness for history," Dillon replied. "See this map?" He pointed to a yellowing piece of paper. "This map was made by his father, Peter Jefferson, and Joshua Fry." Looking up to the balcony he pointed to the buffalo skin. "If you look closely there is a battle scene painted on that robe."

A sound of commotion drew Dillon's and Caitlin's attention to the front door. The rest of their party bustled into the entrance hall.

"Oh, Caitlin have you ever seen anything so grand?" Lucy twirled around, excitement flashing in her blue eyes. "Even the ceiling is decorated," she observed.

Caitlin tipped her head back and focused on the eagle and star pattern. "I had not even noticed that."

"Oh, Caitlin, I can't believe I am really standing in Mr. Jefferson's entrance hall."

"Ahem." Mrs. White loudly cleared her throat.

"I mean... Mrs. Cade." Lucy hesitantly looked at Caitlin then back to Mrs. White, who smiled in appreciation at the formal use of the surname.

Caitlin could see the dilemma that Lucy faced. Obviously, Mrs. White had instructed her to use the proper address. Although Caitlin could understand the logic behind the command, she still didn't like someone trying to take over her authority.

"Mrs. White, I have given Lucy permission to use my Christian name. I also give you leave to do the same."

"No. Ma'am, 'tis not proper." Her stocky build seemed to widen as her broad shoulders went back in a huff. "I will address you as Mrs. Cade or Mistress." The wrinkles around her gray eyes deepened as the challenge was made.

Caitlin mentally counted to ten then calmly answered, "Do as you please." She smiled sweetly. "I realize that you have a certain way of doing things."

Mrs. White nodded her head and hid a smile of triumph. She was bound and determined to teach this young'n some proper manners.

"As mistress of the household, I expect my orders to be followed. If you do not wish to address me as Caitlin, then do not. But, you cannot impose your will onto other people. If Lucy has no problem addressing me by my given name as I have asked, then you should not contradict me. It is confusing for Lucy and for the other staff." Caitlin folded her arms across her blue, velvet spencer and stared at Mrs. White. "Do I make myself clear?"

"Aye, ma'am."

"Very good. Now, why don't you two go see how the men are coming along with our trunks?"

With a small curtsey, Mrs. White left, followed by Lucy, who now wore the triumphant smile.

Suddenly feeling Dillon's eyes on her, she turned, meeting his gentle gaze. She couldn't decipher his emotion. He didn't look angry. Neither did he look happy.

"I'm sorry if I was out of line."

A small smile warmed his face. "You were not. A servant should never usurp your authority."

"You are not upset with me?"

"You handled the situation perfectly. You let her know that you were in control without being harsh."

"If you approve of my dealing with Mrs. White, why do you look so disturbed?"

"I am perplexed." His brown eyes grew intense as he asked, "Why are you so intent on not using my last name?" He'd felt like they were growing closer, especially since he'd come forward and told her that he wanted a real marriage. Although she needed more time, he'd noticed a softening in her attitude. However, the adamant refusal of his name made him wonder if he had not imagined the difference in her. Did she still view him as the enemy?

"I do not like being called Mrs. Cade." She walked over the case holding the maps and pretended to study them. "'Tis no reason, I just prefer Caitlin." She turned to face him. "'Tis nothing against you. I never liked being called Miss Gallager either. It's so formal, and I am not a formal person."

A heavy weight lifted. "I see." He smiled. "As long as it is not a personal thing against me."

"I assure you, 'tis not."

The entrance of a tall, thin, black man interrupted the conversation. "Sir, ma'am." He bowed his graying head to each. "Mast'ah Jefferson will be detained long'ah than he thought. He said to show you to your rooms, and he'll be with you presently."

They followed the servant through the massive rooms, admiring the enchanting décor, and the exquisite architecture.

"This, here, will be your room." The servant showed them into an elaborately embellished, octagon shaped room.

Caitlin surveyed the trellis wallpaper, white fireplace, and gold framed portraits. The whole room had a French feel. "'Tis beautiful."

"Mister James and Mistress Dolly often stay here when they visit."

"The Madisons' have slept in this very bed?" Caitlin pointed to the alcove bed.

"Yes, ma'am."

She found it hard to contain her excitement as she pondered who else might have used this room. After the servant left, Caitlin hoisted up her dress and ran across the room, leaping onto the bed with a giggle.

So enthralling was her laughter that Dillon didn't bother to reprimand her for unladylike behavior. Besides, her carefree spirit was her most enduring quality. He'd never be the one to crush it.

"I'm sure it will not be long before Thomas calls for us. Do you want to freshen up?"

Caitlin rolled over, fluffing the pillow under her head. "I'd prefer to take a nap." She stretched, and yawned. "This bed is so soft. You should try it."

"I have already tried it, my dear."

She propped herself up on her elbow. "Is this the room you stayed in?"

"Once. I have had a different room on each visit."

"How many times have you been here?"

"Three." Dillon noticed a little pucker creasing her brow. "Is something bothering you?"

"I just realized that there is only one bed. Do you plan on sleeping in here?"

"Most married couples do sleep in the same bed."

"You have not made other plans?" She jumped off the bed in a snit. "If I must remind you, *husband*, our marriage differs greatly from other marriages."

His soft laughter only spurred her anger more. "I will not be laughed at!"

He stifled his mocking tone. "I am only teasing. Something you seem to partake in quite often."

"Then you do have other plans."

"Not as of yet. However, the problem can be easily remedied, all the while making our marriage look legitimate."

"How?"

"I will simply tell Thomas that my snoring is bothering you. He will then ensconce me in another room."

"That sounds reasonable enough." She admired his logic. He had a way of handling every situation in the most respectable and dignified manner. Of course, it made him seem stuffy at times. However, the more she grew to know him, the less stuffy he seemed. He had an uncanny way of undoing every preconceived notion she held of him.

Without warning, Dillon charged across the room, grabbed her around the waist, and catapulted them through the air. Her scream died as the impact on the bed forced the air out of her lungs. Opening her eyes, she found Dillon smiling.

"Just what do you think you're doing?"

"I wanted to try out the bed."

"You could have done so without scaring the wits out of me?"

"That was the fun part." Dillon laughed.

"You, sir, are a cad." She pushed him away. "A rake. A no good, pompous dandy."

His laughter made even her pretense at anger disappear. She started laughing with him. "'Tis not something I expected from you."

"You bring out the unexpected in me." He tenderly smoothed back a curling tendril of her hair.

His rough hand gently scraped the soft skin of her cheek, producing a shudder that slowly seeped into her spine. She tried to force the feeling away. *I won't feel anything but hatred*, she silently reminded herself. The venom of hatred was fading, being replaced with something stronger. Something compelling. Something so different and foreign that it scared her to death.

Caitlin stepped through the double doors of the Tea Room. The evening rays of the sun spilled into the room through the large windows, bathing the unpainted plaster walls in shades of pale pink and orange. The soft, muted colors subdued the apprehension seeping through her body. She placed a hand over her stomach and took a few deep breaths, trying to curb the anxious excitement that churned inside. She started smoothing out imaginary wrinkles from her red silk dinner dress, while rehearsing her greeting for the hundredth time.

The sound of feet and male voices brought her head up with a snap. The gold fringe on the red Turk, perched atop her curls, swayed slightly. She'd have to remember to not move her head so much since the crescent shaped hat didn't have a ribbon and was only held in place by long pins.

The details of her well-prepared greeting fled completely with the entrance of the two men. She stared in utter wonderment at the tall, slender stranger next to her own husband. His fading, red hair was pulled back into a neat ponytail just like Dillon's, and although the cut of his suit expressed a wealth of power, it didn't give his physique the domineering, sexy quality that exuded from Dillon. Although Thomas Jefferson was much taller, he didn't have the width of chest and shoulders that Dillon possessed. This effect made him look gangly. However, his serious, watchful eyes said he was a force to be reckoned with.

"Mr. Vice President, may I present my wife, Caitlin."

"I'm pleased to meet you, Mrs. Cade." Jefferson extended his hand.

"You too… I mean… I'm pleased also." Somehow her hand ended up in Jefferson's hand.

"You do me a great honor, madam." Jefferson pressed a light kiss on the back of her gloved hand. "I cannot remember the last time my presence has made such a beautiful, young lady as yourself stammer." His smile was sincere, but without the warmth and light-hearted manner that Dillon had.

"I am sorry, sir if I seem addle-minded." Caitlin blushed. "I have never been in the company of someone so powerful. The honor is truly mine, Mr. Jefferson." She curtsied.

"Why, Mrs. Cade, you have the honor of being married to one of the most influential men in all of Virginia," Thomas Jefferson stated. "Surely you are used to it by now."

Caitlin wanted to argue that Dillon merely owned a newspaper shop. Thankfully she realized the folly of the statement before it left her mouth. She was well aware of the regulations of society. She must adhere to them, even if she didn't agree with them, especially in the presence of the potential future president.

Biting down hard on her tongue, she managed a smile and said, "Aye, my lord 'tis true. However, being married to Dillon gives me a different perspective. He is just an ordinary man at home."

Thomas gave that statement some consideration before smiling. "You will come to find that underneath all the flair and pompous airs, we are all ordinary men."

Caitlin arched a red brow and smiled coyly. "Then we had better get this visiting done quickly. I want to become acquainted before the illusion of honor and prestige wears off."

The sudden burst of laughter set her heart at ease. "Well, then, my dear Mrs. Cade, tea will be served promptly." He clapped his hands and the servants started bustling around. "I thought we could take a tour of the house after we eat if you are up to it."

"Oh, that would be lovely. 'Tis such a beautiful house. I cannot wait to see more of it." Caitlin's excitement was contagious.

"This is my 'most honorable suite'." He extended his hand in a sweeping motion to reveal the important busts of his friends and heroes. "Besides dining, it's my favorite place to read and write."

"I can understand why. The view from here is inspiring." Caitlin sat in the chair he offered her.

The slaves wheeled two carts to the table and everyone filled their plates with finger sandwiches, dainty desserts, nuts, and dried fruit. Tea and coffee were served. The decanters were then left on the table for refills.

"That is the most unique coffee urn I have ever seen," Caitlin commented.

"I designed it myself," Jefferson informed her. "I have also had special goblets made."

"Is there no end to your talent?"

"I truly hope not, Mrs. Cade."

Dillon and Jefferson talked mostly about work through the course of the meal. Jefferson explained about the Kentucky Resolutions he'd written, which presented a severe attack against the Federalists and opposed the Alien and Sedition Acts. Furthermore, James Madison was working on a similar Resolution for Virginia. Caitlin listened to them talk about politics and campaign strategies before the conversation turned to the famous Theobald Wolfe Tone.

She knew that Mr. Tone had been captured the month before. Although he'd managed to get support and supplies from the French army, the uprising ended as a military catastrophe. The Irish and French armies combined had still been severely outnumbered by the British.

However, Caitlin held out hope that Mr. Tone would escape. Surely, God wouldn't allow a man as dedicated as Tone die, not when there was so much work still to do. Didn't the Bible say that God is our strength, and he will deliver us?

Caitlin kept silent throughout most of the conversation, nodding and smiling, only voicing an opinion or asking a question once in a while. As tea time wound down, the conversation turned back to topics more suitable for women - such as the meal, the dinner party the next evening, and the remodeling of the house.

After the dishes were efficiently cleared away, a frozen dessert was brought out. Caitlin had never seen anything like it. She wasn't even sure which piece of silverware to use. Anxiously watching, she waited until Thomas picked up his spoon, then she did the same.

"Wait until you taste this, Mrs. Cade." Jefferson took a spoonful. "Mmm. Perfect."

Caitlin's eyes darted to Dillon. He smiled reassuringly and took a bite as well.

She took a small spoonful. An unknown flavor burst on her tongue. The sweet, creamy confection slid down her throat, chilling a path to her stomach. "This is the most delicious thing I've ever tasted," she crooned.

"It's ice cream," Thomas informed her. "I developed a taste for it when I was in France and couldn't live without it. I bought some vanilla beans and started growing them right here at Monticello."

The slight scent, that she assumed must be the vanilla, tantalized her taste buds. She dug into the dessert, almost shoveling it into her mouth.

"I would recommend slowing down. You can receive a terrible headache if you consume it too quickly," Jefferson warned.

"I am sorry. I did not mean to be such a glutton." Her pale cheeks flushed with humiliation

"No need to feel embarrassed, Mrs. Cade. 'Twas my first reaction the first time I ate the frozen concoction. I merely wanted to prevent the same outcome I suffered."

"Thank you for your concern, Mr. Jefferson." Caitlin smiled then finished the rest of the dessert more slowly.

"I do hope you will forgive the mess. I am extensively remodeling the entire third floor," Jefferson said as they toured the house. "I redesigned the upstairs about two years ago, and it's still under construction."

"Oh! We are redecorating Regal Hall. Perhaps I can gather some ideas. Your taste is extraordinary."

"Thank you for the compliment."

Caitlin's admiration increased as they walked through the house. Not only was Jefferson the most influential man she ever met, but his talents in architecture and style superseded anything she'd ever seen. He'd not only designed the house, but invented a lot of the devices in it. His talent for inventions seemed to be only surpassed by his love of books.

Caitlin found the library to be the biggest she'd ever seen. "How can one man read so many books?" She questioned as she perused the shelves filled with leather bound volumes. "Where does he find time?"

"Perhaps he has not read them all," Dillon offered. Although he had quite an extensive library at home, he felt inadequate when compared to Thomas Jefferson.

"Dillon, do you want to see the plans for the dome that will be built?" Jefferson never even looked at Caitlin.

Caitlin didn't even have time to be miffed at the sudden shift in the conversation, before Dillon defended her. "I am sure Caitlin would be delighted to see the plans. She is the one in charge of Regal Hall. I have had neither the time nor inclination to oversee the task. She's proven herself far more capable than I."

"Your wife has a good head on her shoulders." Jefferson winked at Dillon. "I like that quality in women."

"I also have good ears and happen to be standing right here."

"Please, forgive me for being so rude. 'Tis been a long time since I've enjoyed the company of a young lady. I fear my manners are a bit rusty." Jefferson smiled and bowed slightly.

"Apology accepted, if I can see the plans."

"Follow me and I shall show you the diagrams."

If Caitlin had been amazed by the architecture of the house so far, this dome far exceeded her expectations. "What a wonderful concept. But, what will you do with a room surrounded by glass?"

"Perhaps it will be an extra bedroom, maybe an office. I have not decided what to do with it yet. I fell in love with the concept and decided to build it."

"I noticed that several rooms are this octagon shape," Caitlin commented.

"Yes. There's something about the shape that appeals to me."

"It is so unique." Caitlin went off to the corner talking with Jefferson, leaving Dillon by himself.

He'd started to wonder about the wisdom of defending Caitlin. Her sharp mind seemed to attract Jefferson's attention. *Perhaps I should have let him keep treating her as an inferior*, he sighed. *Then Caitlin would be by my side, not another man's.* Dillon tried to control the unruly feelings recoiling through him, but they only increased as the tour continued.

Upon entering the parlor, Caitlin noticed several game tables positioned around the room along with sofas and chairs. The unpainted, plaster walls were covered with gilded framed paintings. But the truly, eye-catching focal point of the room was the parquet floor, which Jefferson had designed himself.

A pianoforte and a harpsichord were situated in the corner with several music stands. Caitlin walked over, running her hand along the smooth, cool wood of the musical instrument.

"My wife loved to play the pianoforte," Jefferson informed them.

"Caitlin plays very well," Dillon boasted.

"I like to play the violin," Jefferson informed them. "When I was courting Martha, I came to call one day and two other suitors were waiting in the hall. When we started to play together, they became angry and left. Apparently we played together so well that even they knew we were a perfect match." Jefferson's tone softened as he remembered his late wife.

"You never found another woman that played music as beautifully?" Caitlin noted his loneliness.

"I do not have the time for courting. Perhaps you could do me the honor of accompanying me tomorrow night. We can play a duet at the dinner."

"Me?" Caitlin spun around in surprise. "Mr. Jefferson, 'twould be an honor." Excitement pulsated through Caitlin's body, beaming out of every pore. Her eyes were bright. Her cheeks flushed. Even her smile was wider. Dillon could have sworn that beams radiated from her ear openings. Of course, this only served to make her more beautiful, therefore adding to his agitation.

He had married the most beautiful woman, yet, she didn't — nor would she ever — love him. No matter how hard he tried. Nothing would wash away the stigma of English blood.

Caitlin's idle chatter echoed down the long hall as they made their way to the bedroom. "Can you believe that he wants to play a duet with me?" She pointed to her chest. "Me, Dillon." She twirled around, her red skirts billowing out. "I must start practicing at once."

"You play beautifully, my dear. Do not be so anxious."

"But this is Thomas Jefferson. I shall never play as well as him."

"You have never heard him play. Perhaps he's only mediocre."

"Are you jesting?" Her awe of the man continued. "The man has a brilliant mind. Did you see all things he has invented? Do you wonder what it must feel like to imagine pictures in your mind and shape them into existence? Oh, and his love of music and books! He is the smartest man I have ever met."

Dillon had never experienced resentfulness before. But as the iron claw of jealousy tightened around his gut, that was all he felt. He resented the fact that Thomas was born in the United States while he'd been born in England — the sworn enemy of his wife. He also resented his brilliant mind and resolute attitude. Although these qualities were good for a future president, they may well intrude into his relationship with Caitlin. The need to defend his position as husband intensified, along with the yearning of wanting his wife to come to love him.

"I find it hard to believe that you have been so inspired by a man who defends slavery." He held open the door to their bedroom.

Caitlin swept past him, the scent of rosewater wafting around her like a thick cloud. Once in the room she spun around to meet Dillon's eyes. "I do not understand the problem. You are working with the man, helping him to get elected at the next election."

"I strongly disagree with his position on slavery. For the man who wrote 'all men are created equal' to keep slaves proves hypocritical, do you not think?"

"If slavery is so unsavory to you, why are you helping his campaign?"

"Because it's the only way to bring back your family."

Caitlin merely stared, unable to say anything. She hated when he said things that she couldn't argue with. The man constantly amazed her. Finally finding her voice, she asked, "So you are helping elect the next president even though you do not agree with his policies?"

"I must confess that I have always been more conservative. Except for these acts, I have always been behind President Adams. He has instituted these acts only to silence Jefferson and other opponents, but in doing so he has overstepped the boundaries of the Constitution. Most Americans are turning against him because of this one fault." Staring deeply into her green eyes he continued. "I can assure you that if there were any other way to bring your parents back, I'd do it, but supporting Jefferson is the only way. Once he is elected, he will have the power to overturn the Sedition Acts. Then your parents can come home."

Caitlin's heart raced. Her breathing became uneasy. Why must these symptoms occur whenever he looked at her like that? Taking a deep breath, she tried to clear her mind. "So you are going against your personal principles to help my family?"

"'Tis the only way." Dillon spread his feet, locking his hands behind his back. Although this was his normal stance, tonight it served to keep his hands under control. The only thought running through his mind was the feel of her soft, smooth skin.

Breathing deeply wasn't working, so she turned away, walking over to the washbasin. Pouring water from the porcelain pitcher into the large bowl gave her time to collect her thoughts. Not knowing how to handle the unknown feelings recoiling through her body, she resorted to a familiar tactic. "I find it hard to believe that you could criticize a brilliant man like Mr. Jefferson and then stand there thinking you are some hero, admitting that you are giving up the very principles you believe in just for my family. Am I to swoon over your generosity?" She spun around, anger sparkling in her eyes. "Do you think I will fall into the marriage bed with you just because you have done this great and noble deed? 'Tis only so in your sight, sir. I find it outrageous that you'd abandon morality and principles for any reason."

Dillon felt as though she'd slapped him in the face. He didn't know which stung more, her defense of Jefferson, or the belittling of his moral standards. "'Tis the thanks I get for helping you?"

"I never asked for your help. When I did ask for assistance, you refused. If you'd gone to my father, you could have stopped the nuptials."

"Even now that you know everything that transpired, you still do not see why your parents and I took this course of action. What will it take to get through that thick, stubborn head of yours?" Anger and exasperation seeped into his tone.

"I do not now, nor will I ever, see why I had to marry you. I would have been just fine in Ireland with my family. Instead I'm stuck in a foreign land married to a blockhead."

Dillon's brown eyes turned hard. The muscle ticking in his jaw accelerated, looking ready to explode. He stepped closer. "Woman, you could weary the self-control of a monk."

Caitlin took a step back in fear. She'd never seen him so angry.

"You may not like the idea of being married, but whether you approve or not the vows have been spoken. I expect you to behave as a proper wife." Unclenching his jaw slightly he asked, "Have I not been a good husband? Have you not an unlimited expense account? Are you not arrayed in the finest fashions? Have you a clue how much your clothing costs? Why, that hat alone cost as much as the entire dress."

Caitlin bristled. "I have been a proper wife. If you are talking about the marriage bed, may I remind you, Mr. Cade that you agreed to the circumstance before the wedding. I would be nothing more than a strumpet if I bedded you for expenses and clothing."

"I am not referring to our little arrangement. I am talking about acting respectably in public, especially around other men."

"How dare you!" Her fists tightened into two balls. "You parade your mistress in front of the whole town then accuse me of improper actions."

"Oh, for the love of...!" Dillon physically felt his stomach knot. "We are back to Henrietta again. You will do and say anything to make me angry. You constantly twist facts to make you look like a victim and me the villian. Well, I have had enough! You have pushed me too far." Grabbing his dinner jacket, he stalked to the door. "You want to be on your own? Fine. I am not giving you any more money. From now on you will have to work and pay your own expenses."

Caitlin jumped at the slam of the door. Usually fighting left her feeling invigorated. Tonight she only felt scared and a little lonely. She'd never seen him so angry. However, she had the impression there was something else going on.

The empty room surrounded her, anger still residing in the corners. She shivered at the thought of sleeping alone in this strange house. She wanted Dillon back. He always made her feel safe even though that was one of the reasons she disliked him so.

Caitlin surveyed herself in the long, gilded mirror that hung on the parlor wall. It was one of a matching set. Mr. Jefferson explained that the two mirrors helped enhance the light in the large room.

Although right now lighting was the farthest thing from her mind. She was determined to have a grand time, no matter what Dillon said or did. Running a nervous hand over the creamy satin of her wedding dress was useless since there were no wrinkles.

Lucy kept the clothing in immaculate shape. She sighed, replaying the fight from the night before. She had been spending frivolously.

"You look beautiful."

Caitlin saw Dillon reflected in the mirror. His brown curls pulled back in the usual ponytail. "You wore the suit from our wedding?" Her throat seemed tight.

"It's the finest suit I own. I like your hair without any headpiece. Your vibrant curls are all you need to adorn your head."

"You should watch such talk, sir. A lady could misconstrue that as a compliment."

Dillon's thick, brown brows arched in silent amusement.

Caitlin merely spun around and stepped past him. Dillon followed her to the dessert table. Looking at the array of pies, cakes, and other sweets only made her feel fuller. She didn't have room for one bite, however she wanted to divert her attention away from Dillon. Choosing a sweet meat pie, she nibbled at the corner. "Delicious," she moaned. "Only the best will do for Mr. Jefferson."

Dillon stiffened at that remark. He didn't know why he felt so angry towards their host, certainly not because of the difference in political views. He'd been here several times and accepted the slaves as part of Jefferson's household. Why did watching the slaves who'd prepared the feast and now served it, bother him so much? Why did his wife even speaking Jefferson's name twist his gut?

"Mrs. Cade, there you are." Thomas Jefferson approached with his tall, lanky frame clothed in black, his red hair hidden under a white wig with two large curls on each side. A black, leather tie held the fake ponytail in place. "I'd like to introduce you to my youngest daughter, Mary."

"Pleased to meet you," Caitlin curtsied.

"Please do not be so formal," Mary laughed. The blue, empire dress brought out the blue in her eyes, making them sparkle with warmth, which immediately set Caitlin's fears to rest. "Mr. Cade, do you mind if I steal your wife for a while? It is so nice to finally have someone my own age to talk with."

"Of course not." Dillon smiled.

"Do not be off too long. Mrs. Cade has promised to play a duet with me," Thomas reminded her.

Mary linked her arm through Caitlin's, and they wove their way through the crowd. Mary started introducing Caitlin around. Eventually Caitlin's anxiety decreased, and she started enjoying herself.

"Your wife seems to be the center of attention," Jefferson noted.

"She's always been corky," Dillon agreed. He watched as she laughed and talked with everyone. Her brilliance filled the room. How could men not take notice of her? She wasn't really doing anything to attract attention. So why did he not like the way men looked at her as she walked by?

Trying to combat these unexplained feelings felt useless. He felt himself becoming more agitated by the minute. When a slave, dressed in formal attire, offered him a glass of wine, he accepted. Taking the goblet from the silver tray, he tentatively sipped the dark, tart, drink. The strong alcohol taste overpowered his senses, reminding him why he didn't drink.

However, when he noticed Caitlin gliding across the dark and light checkered floor on the arm of Thomas Jefferson, he drank the mixture down in one gulp, grabbing another glass.

As the evening continued, Caitlin laughed and talked with everyone in the room. As she became the belle of the ball, his demeanor became even more sour. And, when she played the pianoforte while Jefferson accompanied with the violin, he stalked out of the parlor, went into the study and poured a glass of brandy. The only thing stronger than the whisky coursing through his veins was his anger.

Chapter 12

Caitlin happily hummed as she took off the silver ear bobs and put them in a box. Lucy bustled around the room picking up discarded garments, folding and putting them away.

"Wasn't tonight the most romantic night ever," Lucy sighed.

"It was a very grand party," Caitlin agreed.

"You were the prettiest lady there."

"'Tis an exaggeration. There were many beautiful ladies."

"For sure, it's the truth. Even Johnny agreed." Lucy set about unpinning Caitlin's hair.

Caitlin noticed Lucy's eyes brighten in the reflection of the mirror. "Did you and Johnny have a nice time?"

"Oh, yes." Lucy nodded vigorously. "We watched everyone dancing for a while, then we went into the garden and danced. There was something magical about dancing underneath the moon and stars."

"I take it you were properly chaperoned?" Caitlin may be unconventional, but she wasn't a fool. Some rules were set in place to protect you and must be followed.

"Oh, yes. There were slaves all over the place. We were never truly alone. It just felt that way."

"Very well, then. I'm glad you had a nice time."

Lucy finished with the pins then picked up the large, silver brush. "Caitlin, what do you think of slavery?"

Caitlin's green eyes started in the mirror. "Why do you ask?"

"It just seems so sad to me." She ran the brush through Caitlin's red locks. "I mean, not only do the slaves not get paid for all their work, but they don't have any say over their own lives."

Caitlin could certainly identify with that. She'd had no control over recent events in her own life. The scariest feeling in the world is the loss of control. She couldn't imagine being born into a world where you never had any say over anything that happened to you.

"I think it is sad too," Caitlin conceded. "But there are people who think it's an acceptable lifestyle. There is nothing we can do about it."

"But is that not why we vote people into office? So they can change things?" Lucy finished braiding Caitlin's hair.

"I suppose you're right. Voting people into office with the same ideals as you could change things, but some things are left up to God." Caitlin stood and Lucy helped her into the cotton robe, and then went to her own room.

Caitlin paced the room, waiting for Dillon to return. Of course, the possibility of him going directly to his room was great, but she thought he'd at least make an appearance and say good night.

Dillon stumbled down the hall, running into a table and knocking over a vase. It crashed to the floor with a shattering force that rumbled through his eardrums. The crystal crunched under his feet as he continued to swagger down the hall towards the bedroom. Knocking hard on the door, he didn't wait for a reply before barging in, stumbling over his own feet.

Caitlin spun around, surprised. "Dillon what are you doing?"

"I have come to bid thee goodnight." The stench of alcohol saturated the air. His words blurred together so badly she found it hard to understand him.

"I see you have been dipping rather deep tonight." Caitlin held her breath.

"Only a few drinks." Dillon swayed slightly. The room spun out of control. An ache formed between his eyebrows. He knew it would only get worse by morning.

"Look at you!" Caitlin said appalled. "You cannot even stand up."

"I'm standing up. 'Tis you that are swaying." He stifled a laugh. "As a matter of fact, I see that I now have two beautiful wives."

"Will you get serious?" Caitlin crossed her arms.

"Serious, you say." His words were drawn out. He tried standing straight, but nearly toppled over. "Perhaps, my second wife will be serious enough to be faithful."

"You are talking nonsense." Caitlin rubbed her temples, trying to ease the stress. "Go back to your room and sleep off the alcohol."

Stumbling towards her, he grabbed her upper arms, as much to keep from falling as in anger. "You do not tell me what to do." Rage glared in his eyes turning them hard as stones.

"Dillon, you're hurting me." She tried withdrawing from his grasp.

"So what? You do not seem to care when you hurt me." His hands tightened. "You do not care about anybody, except yourself." The struggle knocked him off balance.

Caitlin escaped his grip and stepped back. Fear welled inside. She didn't know if she should make a run for the door, or calm him down. Not wanting to cause a scene, she chose the latter.

"Dillon, you are not yourself tonight. Why not discuss this in the morning when things are clearer?" Her tone was gentle.

"Things are crystal clear," he said. Looking at her through blurry eyes, he realized what a fool he'd been. She'd never come to love him. "When we get home, I shall start divorce proceedings."

"What!" Shock tightened around her chest. "I don't understand, why?"

"I cannot fight you anymore, Caitlin." His tone softened, a tinge of regret adjoining each word. "You have made it perfectly clear that your affection will never be towards me."

"You accepted that when we married."

"Do you have any idea how hard it was watching you tonight? You can spread your charm over an entire roomful of men, but cannot spare a shred of tenderness for me." He shook his head. "I cannot live with your animosity anymore." Stumbling to the door, he left.

Caitlin stood in stunned silence for a long time. Emotions rolling around like a thunderstorm. She should be glad. This is what she'd wanted for the last seven weeks. So, why was fear the dominating emotion?

Had she pushed too far? She had recognized the jealous streak, and purposely flirted and teased tonight just to irritate him. In hindsight that may not have been the wisest move. But he'd certainly made her angry enough with Henrietta.

As the anger subsided, loneliness and despair hit with a one-two punch. *How can he just throw me out with nowhere to go?* He knew her family was gone. Could he be that heartless?

He wasn't in his normal state of mind, Caitlin thought, trying to comfort herself. *It was the alcohol talking.* She felt confident that once he sobered, he would change his mind. He probably wouldn't even remember the conversation by morning.

Thomas Jefferson sat reading while Caitlin finished her morning meal. Dillon entered, quietly taking a seat.

"Good morning." Jefferson looked up from his book. "How did you sleep last night?"

"Fine, thank you." He poured some coffee.

Caitlin noticed he took very little food. Remembering how queasy her stomach had been after drinking, she empathized with him. He looked remarkably well considering how awful he must feel. She hadn't even gotten out of bed the day after their wedding. The only distress he showed was to wince when a slave dropped a handful of silverware and they scattered across the floor, clanging like a bell.

Caitlin finished her meal, while partaking of small talk with Mr. Jefferson. Dillon didn't have much to say. The cloud of tension surrounding him seemed to smother the entire room.

"Mrs. Cade, perhaps you'd like to see the gardens today?" Thomas asked. "It is not as beautiful as in Spring and Summer but it's passable."

"I would like that very much."

"I fear we must leave today," Dillon informed them.

"I thought you were staying for a few more days." Thomas inquired. "Are you sure you are up to the long trip home?"

"I shall be fine. Some urgent business has come up that requires my immediate attention."

"I hope nothing too serious," Thomas said.

"We shall see." Dillon looked at Caitlin. "We will leave as soon as you're packed."

Caitlin wondered if the urgent business was her? His attitude wasn't any better this morning. Was he hurrying back to divorce her? Could she change his mind? *Oh, Lord, what am I going to do?* Overwhelming panic brought tears to her eyes. *Please change his heart, she prayed.*

The Bible taught that God was in control. She'd been so angry over the recent events that she'd stubbornly ignored God. Now, He was the only one who could help her. She would never understand why God had allowed the war and her brother's death. Being forced from Ireland, and then separated from her family, had only added to the animosity. The final straw had been being pushed into a marriage she didn't want.

Now, all she wanted was to stay secure in the marriage. Would God help her after all the anger she'd built up towards him? Would Dillon forgive her as well?

Mr. Barclay and his men were finishing up for the day when Dillon and Caitlin arrived home. The last thing Caitlin wanted to do was tour the house and check on the progress. She felt exhausted, sore, and had too much on her mind to worry about the redecorating. However, Mr. Barclay beamed from ear to ear, and she didn't want to disappoint him.

Pushing her irritation away, she focused on the task at hand, knowing a sour temper wouldn't get her anywhere, except kicked out the door. Dillon had been right. Becoming an adult meant learning how to control situations calmly, rationally, and respectably. With that in mind, she gave her brightest smile and graciously accepted the invitation to inspect the rooms.

Dillon tagged along watching with admiration as Caitlin efficiently put the household in order. She juggled directing the servants, and complimenting Mr. Barclay on a wonderful job so effortlessly that she seemed to belong in Regal Hall as much as he. A gleam brightened her eyes as she praised the men on having completed the parlor and dining room so quickly.

It was a pity that things hadn't worked out. The staff had come to like, or more appropriate, respect Caitlin. Even Mr. Barclay had fallen under her charm now. If he didn't know better, he'd have sworn she looked pleased to be home. Of course, that was merely a dream. A delusion. One he'd have to let go of. As much as it hurt losing her, he knew she'd never be happy here. He just didn't have the heart to keep her against her will any longer, even if it was for her own good.

The transformation of the parlor still took Dillon by surprise. The firelight danced upon the wooden floor, making the coat of polish gleam like new. The turquoise paint seemed to change moods just like Caitlin. Changing to a subdued blue, whereas, the sunlight bouncing off the bright walls made it look more green.

Caitlin had been quieter, almost downhearted since the return home. He would have figured she'd be walking on the clouds. After all, he'd promised to give her the freedom she so desperately wanted. Who could know what thoughts rolled around inside her head? The complexity of that woman gave him a headache.

Dillon took a seat on the new gold and turquoise sofa. Gold velvet curtains hung on the windows. And thick throw rugs carpeted the floor. A crystal dish had been placed on the table with dried flowers in it. Pinching some of the stuff between his fingers, he sniffed surprised that he liked the smell.

"'Tis potpourri," Caitlin informed him as she entered carrying a vase of flowers. She placed the crystal vase on a table across the room, the yellow roses adding the right touch of color. "Made with a mixture of dried flowers, herbs and spices." She took a seat opposite him. "When the real flowers start to die, I dry them. I can reuse them and they aren't wasted."

"'Tis a practical matter?" Dillon liked that side of her. It was the one area they had in common. There was nothing showy or overdone in the decorating. The rooms had a lively, high-spirited feel with warmth and elegance. It certainly reflected Caitlin.

"Aye. Plus it makes the room smell good." She pulled out the cross-stitching and went to work.

"It does smell nice," he agreed. The little touches made a difference.

Uneasy silence stretched between them. Although they'd been home for several days, they'd managed to avoid each other. This was the first encounter and neither knew what to say. Someone had to make the first move.

Caitlin looked up from her stitching to find Dillon watching her. "What?" She arched a red brow.

"We need to talk."

The serious tone dashed her hopes of pretending nothing was wrong. "I knew I should not have come in here," she mumbled.

"We cannot avoid the issue forever."

"I do not understand why this is coming up at all?" She set the hoop aside. "Are you upset that I was flirting? Then let me start by apologizing."

She paused only briefly at the stunned look on his face. "I am sorry I made you so upset. I did not realize that some innocent flirting would affect you so much. Please, Dillon, please forgive me."

Dillon sat immobile for a few seconds before clearing his throat. "I did not think I would ever see the day when you would admit to being wrong, let alone apologize."

"I am sorry." The clenching of her jaw warned that she wanted to say more, but held her tongue.

"'Tis all you have to say?" Dillon quirked his brow.

She hesitated. "I do not wish to upset you further."

"This certainly is not the girl I married," he teased. "The Caitlin I know would let me have it with both fists."

"Is that what you want?" she asked. "To upset you so you have an excuse to kick me out? Then you can run to your little Henrietta and pretend I don't exist. Is she putting you up to this? Does she want you to marry her? 'Tis what this is all about, is it not?" Tears welled, turning her eyes into shimmering gems. "You do not want to be strapped with the responsibility of a wife anymore. Does it ease your conscience to make it my fault?"

"I am not making anything your fault," Dillon defended. "Why are you bringing up Henrietta? She has nothing to do with this. I am giving you your freedom. Is that not what you want?"

"My freedom?" Caitlin stood. "And where shall I go? I have no family, and you know it. What shall I do? I have no skills."

"I beg to differ. You have great skill in writing."

"I have written one piece."

"An article that had the whole town, and probably all of Norfolk, talking."

"I would not go that far." Caitlin tried not to smile at the compliment, but a strange sensation rushed through her. "People have forgotten about it by now."

"That does not mean you cannot write something else."

"So after you divorce me, are you going to help establish me as a writer?" She tried to keep the hurt out of her tone but wasn't successful.

"Caitlin, I am confused. I thought this is what you wanted, the chance to be free and make your own money. You will not be trapped in a marriage with your enemy any longer."

"And I thought this marriage is what you wanted."

"It was. It is." He threw his hands up, frustrated. "I do not know what I want any more. I just know that I cannot continue like this." He stood, pacing over to the fireplace.

Caitlin walked up behind him, putting her hand on his shoulder. "You accepted this marriage in the beginning, what changed?"

He paused before answering, his eyes clouded with torn emotions. "I fell in love with you." Turning around, he took her hand in his. "I cannot live with you hating me any longer. Not when I want you so much. Not when my heart beats for you." He placed her hand over his heart. "Do you feel that? My heart races at the very touch of your hand. Every poem I read reminds me of you. Every song is about you. I cannot keep the distance between us anymore."

Caitlin felt the warmth of his body. The irregular beating of his heart. Even the uneasy laboring of his breath seemed to grab her. She felt as if the fire had jumped out of the hearth and landed on her. The warm, fuzzy sensation almost smothered her until she couldn't breathe. Withdrawing her hand she stepped away, trying to regain some composure. "If this were to become a real marriage, would you stay in it?"

"It has gone beyond that. I told you, I would never force you into my bed. Not by any means."

"What if I were willing?"

"You are not." Dillon locked his hands behind his back. "You do not even like me touching you."

How could she explain what his touch did to her body, when she didn't understand it herself? "Do you think you are the only one confused?" She tried reading his expression. However, he managed to mask his emotions well.

"I am sure you are just as confused as I."

"Then I beg you not to kick me out, at least not yet. Just give me a little more time."

"My dear, Caitlin, I am not kicking you out. I am only giving you the freedom you so desired." Staring into her eyes, he said softly, "I cannot bear being the one to bring you unhappiness."

"What if I do not want my freedom?"

"Are you saying you want to stay in the marriage?" Shock registered in his eyes.

"'Tis exactly what I'm saying." Walking over to him she placed the palm of her hand on his cheek. "You are the kindest, gentlest man I have ever met. Any woman would count herself lucky to be your wife."

Dillon was so taken aback by the affectionate words and gentle expression in her eyes he couldn't speak. He took her hand from his face and kissed it. "If you only knew how much those words mean to me." Dropping her hand, he stepped back and turned toward the fire. His hands locked behind him. "But I am not sure why you are changing your mind? I am offering you everything you ever wanted. Perhaps, 'tis only fear that is keeping you here."

"I cannot give a truthful answer," she admitted. "I am not sure what is going on."

Turning to face her, he smiled slightly. "Thank you for that honest answer. Perhaps we had better not make any hasty decisions."

"I agree."

"Well, that must be a first." Dillon laughed. "We finally agree on something."

"It cannot be that uncommon." Caitlin shrugged. "Married couples have to agree sometimes."

"I suppose." Dillon turned serious. "'Tis one other matter we must clear up." He looked directly into her eyes, almost reaching her soul. "I need no other woman. Put the thought of Henrietta out of your mind."

"I shall try." Why did she feel a tug at her heart every time she pictured him with someone else?

"I suggest we get some sleep and continue this conversation when we are both rested."

"Again, I agree."

"Then I bid thee good night."

She watched him leave. Feeling too restless to sleep she stayed in the parlor a while longer. She picked up the Bible off the table and sat down by the fire. *Thank you, Lord, for changing Dillon's heart, and mine. If it's not too much to ask, help me find a way to show Dillon how I really feel.*

Caitlin waited patiently for Dillon to leave for work. He seemed to be in no hurry this morning. Although the tension had eased somewhat, it was still awkward between them, but she had a plan to remedy that.

God had certainly answered her prayer. She'd been awake most of the night forming her plan. Although she felt scared, she had peace that God would provide the courage she needed, and help her complete the task. After tonight, Dillon would know her heart like no other man had ever known.

Dillon finally finished his morning meal and left. Caitlin went in search of Martha, finding her in the kitchen, kneading dough.

"Martha, may I speak with you for a moment?"

"Depends on what you want. If it's about reusing the flour scraps, then, no, I ain't got any time."

"'Tis nothing to do with flour, however some counsel on Dillon's favorite meals would be useful."

Martha stopped kneading the dough, giving Caitlin her full attention. "Just what do ya have cooking in that brainless head of yours?"

Caitlin stiffened at the insult but held her temper in check. She knew Martha was baiting her. She couldn't give in to anger at the moment. "I have no idea why you are so against me, but I do not have time for petty arguments. I need your help." Looking Martha in the eyes she asked, "Can we set aside our differences for Dillon's benefit?"

Martha shrugged her wide shoulders. "Depends on what it will benefit him."

"I need you to help me plan a special dinner for him. If you leave his favorite recipes, I'll do all the cooking."

Martha's loud cackle rolled through the house like thunder. "You think I'd be fool enough to leave you alone to prepare the food for my master?"

"I'm quite capable of cooking," Caitlin defended.

"That ain't the problem. It's what else ya might add to the meal that worries me."

"How dare you!" The sting of the accusation hit her hard. "I'd never do anything to hurt Dillon."

"Seems to me you have it pretty good. You've been out spending his money like crazy, buying fancy dresses, and hats. You've certainly spared no expense in redecorating this place, meanwhile complaining about my not using flour scraps in the baking." She crossed her large arms.

Caitlin felt the tension between her eyebrows. *Why did this woman have to be so difficult?* "I am sorry I said anything about the flour, but I do not understand how those simple comments turn me into a murderer. As you have pointed out, Dillon has given me everything I want. So, why would I want to kill him?"

"Maybe cause offing him would leave you a very wealthy widow. You wouldn't have to answer to a husband anymore." Uncrossing her arms, she placed both hands on the sides of her ample hips. "I ain't leaving you alone with my master. No way! No how!"

Caitlin rubbed at the pressure in her forehead, mentally counting to ten, trying to rein in her anger. A sharp tongue wouldn't get her anywhere. *Lord, please help me with this situation.*

Feeling a calm settle over her, she replied, "Martha, I realize we got off on the wrong foot. I would like us to start over again. That is why I am coming to you for advice. You know Dillon better than anyone. I want tonight to be extra special for him. I also want it to be a surprise. Will you help me pay him back for all the kindness he has shown to me?"

Martha mulled the thought over for a few seconds. "All right. I will help you, but Lord God almighty help you if'n anything happens to Dillon." Looming over Caitlin, she said with a sneer, "I'll come after you."

"Understood. Now we must hurry to accomplish everything before Dillon returns tonight."

Caitlin convinced Mr. Barclay that since his men had worked so hard and were way ahead of schedule, they deserved some time off. After working a half day, they wrapped up and left at two o'clock.

Caitlin had been busy in the kitchen all day. Although she assured Martha she could handle the cooking, Martha insisted on helping. At first, she'd been upset at the persistence of the cook, but after a while she was glad for the help.

Martha managed to keep herself busy with canning and preserving of vegetables and fruits, but she was close by to keep an eye on Caitlin. However, she soon realized that Caitlin was no stranger to the kitchen.

The two women spent most of the afternoon in the kitchen, stopping briefly to have their own supper at noon. By the end of the day, they seemed to have a bond, or at least, an understanding of each other. Caitlin missed her mother, and memories of their shared times together in the kitchen spilled out during the course of the day. That was the one soft spot that Martha held for Caitlin.

As the women worked side by side, even Martha loosened up telling stories about Dillon, now and then, slipping some personal stories in about her own life.

With Martha's help dinner was done sooner than planned. That left her more time to get ready. She took a long, hot bath and washed her hair, knowing it would take several hours before it dried completely.

Lucy helped her dress in the purple and white gown. That seemed to be Dillon's favorite. She left her hair down and Lucy artfully arranged the tresses into a cascade of auburn curls.

"Thank you, Lucy. That looks beautiful." Caitlin hugged her.

"More than your hair is beautiful. You look more radiant than the sun."

"Oh, stop that flattery and get going. Your parents must be excited to have you home tonight."

"Aye, it just feels kind of strange. I know I've only been here for two months, but it feels like a lifetime ago since I lived with my folks."

"I know the feeling. So much has happened over such a short period time. I guess that is what is referred to as growing up."

The two descended the stairs as Martha came out from the kitchen. "Well, now everything is done except the spoon bread. Don't put that in the bee oven until Dillon gets home. 'Tis best served warm and there's no telling what time he might'n be home. The pumpkin soup is by the hearth keeping warm. Just stir it now and then. And, the raspberry tart and lemon tea cakes are cooling."

"I'll manage." Caitlin stifled a laugh.

"It won't matter anyhow. Master Dillon isn't a picky eater. I've done burnt things that he went on and ate without a word." Martha laughed. "I don't expect he's gonna worry about eating anyhow. Not with you all dolled up like that."

"I just want everything to be perfect." Caitlin nervously brushed her palms down the front of her dress.

"Stop that fretting," Martha admonished. "You look fine and dinner will be perfect."

"I hope so." She had a lot riding on tonight. Her whole future was at stake. Would she be able to pull off a romantic tryst? She wasn't sure Dillon even wanted this. Was she being too brazen? Silently praying for courage and strength she again felt peace about this course of action. This is what God told her to do. But, what if she'd misread the signs?

"Oh, stop this." She chided herself. "I have the plan in motion. Nothing left to do but go forward." Take the leap of faith.

All the fires had been stoked and she was lighting the last of the candles and lanterns when Dillon came home. Nervous butterflies took flight in her stomach. However, their flight was short lived. For the look on Dillon's face told her this was the right thing to do. The warmth and tenderness in his eyes gave her the courage she needed.

"Where is everyone?" He took off his overcoat. "Except for the lad who took my horse to the stables, I did not see anyone."

"I had everyone go home early. As a matter of fact, the boy will leave as soon as he has finished with your horse."

"What is all this?"

"I wanted to surprise you. I made your favorite supper, and I did not want any interruptions."

"No interruptions, huh." He stepped closer, wanting to hold her. To kiss her. Then stopped short. "You look so beautiful and I'm a mess." His pants and shirt were smudged with ink.

"I have a bath waiting for you upstairs."

"Really?"

"I still have some things to prepare. The food should be done by the time you finish bathing."

Dillon took the stairs two at a time. After dumping the hot water into the brass tub he relaxed for a few minutes, trying to figure out what was going on. He certainly liked coming home to this after a hard day of work.

After drying off, he noted that she'd even set out his favorite pants and shirts. How in the world did she know that? He dressed then went back downstairs.

Caitlin was in the dining room, spreading rose petals on the table.

"It smells wonderful," he commented.

"I hope it isn't dried out. It has been kept warm for a while."

"I'm sorry I was late. I did not know you were going through so much trouble for dinner."

"'Twasn't much trouble, especially with Martha's help. I wanted to prepare it by myself but she would not let me."

"I am surprised she let you in the kitchen at all." He laughed.

"Believe me, it was not easy. But, I think things will be better now."

"Is there anything I can do?"

"You can light the candles on the table while I get the first course."

As she ladled the soup into the bowls, she wished she'd taken Martha's suggestion on having someone here to serve. Now, she would be stuck running back and forth between the kitchen and dining room. How could they have a serious conversation if she was always getting up? But, she didn't want anyone around. No prying ears or peeping eyes.

"Candles are lit. Anything else I can do?" Dillon entered with a smile.

"Perfect timing. You can carry this tray out to the table."

"We could take all the courses out now, so you will not have to make so many trips."

"Great idea."

They loaded up the meal onto the large, silver trays, and carried it out to the table.

"Oyster loaves, roasted pork stuffed with apples, fried cucumbers. How did you know all of my favorite dishes?"

"Martha." She smiled. "She even helped me pick out your outfit."

"I should have known."

The meal progressed and they laughed and talked. Dillon was so caught up in the atmosphere that he forgot all about the bad news he received earlier. He only wanted to enjoy every minute of this night.

After dinner, they went into the parlor where Caitlin served dessert.

"I do not think I can eat another bite," he protested.

"We can save it for later. How about some tea or coffee?"

"Coffee would be great."

She poured a cup and handed it to him. "Do you want to read some poetry?"

"Sure." He picked up the volume he'd given her as a gift.

"I marked my favorite poems."

He flipped it open to the dog-eared page. Clearing his throat he began. "'Love' by Samuel Taylor Coleridge.

'All thoughts, all passions, all delights, whatever stirs this mortal frame, are all but ministers of Love, and feed his sacred frame.'" He cleared his throat again. "Caitlin, why did you pick this poem?"

"Because it says what I feel."

"You have no right to torture me this way." Bitterness edged his voice.

Had she miscalculated his feelings for her? "I thought this is what you wanted." She fought the panic welling inside her. Standing up she walked over to the hearth, trying not to cry.

"Caitlin, I'm sorry. I did not mean to be so gruff." He came up behind her. "But you cannot lead me on like this. 'Tis not fair. Not after I told you how I feel about you."

She spun around, looking him in the eyes. "But, I am trying to tell you how I feel, and you are not listening." She stepped closer. Taking his hand she placed it over her heart. "You accused me of not wanting your touch. That is not true. Do you feel my heart beating, Dillon? When you are this close, I cannot breathe. I feel so overwhelmed that I am scared to death. Can you feel that?" His hand scorched her skin.

Dillon's pulse raced so fast he couldn't breathe either. He couldn't even think, but, somehow he managed a response. "Caitlin, 'tis not safe. You must let my hand go now. Touching you makes me go crazy." He tried to pull his hand away but she clung on tight.

"I want you crazy," she whispered.

He heard the heavy sigh in her tone. He felt the beating of her heart pick up pace, matching his own rhythm. "Caitlin, I cannot allow you do something you will regret."

"Losing you is the only thing I will regret."

That was the last shred of self-control he possessed. Embracing her waist he pulled her close, fiercely kissing her sweet lips. She matched his kiss with a fierceness of her own. He buried his hands in her hair, inhaling the fragrance as he kissed a trail down her neck.

The sensations produced by Dillon's touch muddled her mind more than hard cider. She didn't think about what was happening. She only rode the tide of emotion that swept her into another world. Kiss for kiss, touch for touch, they explored each other's bodies finding only perfection and delight. Just the way God intended between a husband and wife.

Chapter 13

Dillon watched the flames hungrily licking the logs, devouring the wood in a consumption of heat. The warmth blanketed his already sweltering body. He felt a kinship with the logs. Caitlin's passion produced such fierce desires that his body felt on fire at a mere touch. He lay next to her, his emotions smoldering like a heap of ashes.

Averting his gaze from the hearth to Caitlin, he saw her lying on her back, eyes closed, but not sleeping. He watched the rhythmic heaving of her chest, not knowing what to say. Although she'd maneuvered this encounter, he had no idea what she felt. Doubts and misgivings raged like waves in a hurricane.

Rolling onto his side, he propped his head up with his elbow on the floor, for the first time studying Caitlin's face. He noticed a tear trickle a path down to her earlobe. A quick glance of the room revealed the discarded clothes strewn about, taken off in the heat of passion. When he noticed the blood staining the rug he panicked.

"Caitlin, did I hurt you?" He sat up with a start. "I'm so sorry. I should have been gentler."

Caitlin opened her eyes, his horrified expression making her laugh. Reaching up she touched his cheek. "I am fine, Dillon."

"But the blood?"

"'It is normal for the first time."

Logic settled in. "Why are you crying?" He held his breath not positive he wanted the answer.

Caitlin sat up. "'Twas different than what I'd expected." She maneuvered her body slightly, trying to cover her nakedness. "I guess I was not prepared for the intensity."

"Nor was I," Dillon admitted. "But it does not have to be like that every time." He didn't want to scare her off.

"I was not afraid, and it didn't hurt much." She blushed, slightly.

"No second thoughts or regrets?"

She shook her head, never looking him in the eye. This shy, unnerved Caitlin was a completely different woman from the headstrong, outgoing girl he knew.

"My bath is still upstairs. I shall warm more water so you can bathe." He grabbed his pants and stood up.

Caitlin grabbed her gown, relieved to be dressed. "This was not quite what I had in mind when I planned this evening. I am truly grateful I had the foresight to ensure privacy."

His light laugh eased the tension. "So am I."

She smiled, looking him in the eyes, now that they were armed with clothing. "We were supposed to go to the bedroom."

"It does not matter." He tucked a stray curl behind her ear.

Circling his waist with her arms, she hugged him tight, liking the feel of his hard, flat chest pressed against her. He was so strong and safe. Feeling protected by him was another emotion that confused her.

By the time she pinned her hair up and gathered the fragrant soaps, Dillon had the bath warmed. Caitlin soaked in the tub, enjoying the warm sensations of the water. Remembering the way her body felt when Dillon touched it.

A knock on the door startled her out of the musings. "Come in."

Dillon hesitantly stepped over the threshold. "I wanted to make sure you were all right."

"I'm fine." She cocked head, smiling. "You may come all the way in."

He walked over to the tub. "Do you want me to wash your back?"

Her back wasn't in need of washing. However, she wanted to have Dillon touch her again. "'Twould be nice." She leaned forward, handing him the rag.

He lathered it with the flower scented soap and applied it to her back. "Are you sure I did not hurt you?" His gentle voice sounded scared.

"Positive," she sighed. "Just a little sore— that is to be expected the first time."

"I should have been more tender." He soaked the rag, squeezing it at the nape of her neck. His eyes followed the rivulets of water sliding down her smooth, creamy skin. Reaching out, he ran the tip of his finger down the same path. "I promise to control myself next time."

Caitlin shivered from his touch. "I do not want you to ever hold back," she whispered. "The passion works both ways. I feel it just as deeply as you."

The smooth, husky tones of her voice slid over him like butter melting on biscuits. The catch in her breathing made his pulse quicken. His mouth suddenly went dry. He watched the drops of water glide down her body, gently splashing into the tub as she stood up.

"Oh, Caitlin." All self-control fled. Wrapping his arms around her wet body, he drew her into a deep kiss, lifting her out of the tub.

Caitlin awoke and reached for Dillon but found she was alone. Squinting at the window, she tried to judge the time of day, but the shutters had been closed tight against the late November wind. The small amount of light slipping through the wooden slates wasn't enough to tell the time.

"Sleeping beauty awakes." Dillon entered the room carrying a tray, "Just in time."

"What is all this?"

"I figured since you went through so much trouble to make dinner last night that I would make the morning meal." He sat the tray down on the table by the bed. "How do you feel?"

"I'm famished, but other than that, I could not be better."

"It isn't much." Dillon lifted the linen towel. Aromas of scrambled eggs, bacon, toast, coffee and tea wafted through the air. "I fear I burnt the toast a little."

"Everything looks wonderful. Besides, who can complain when getting served in bed?" She took the cup of tea he offered. After taking several sips she looked up and smiled. "You know a girl could get use to this."

"'Tis my plan." He sat on the bed, next to her. "To spoil you, so you'll never want to leave." He took her cup, setting it on the tray.

"'Twould be best to be careful what one wishes for," she leaned forward, giving him a kiss, "It may come true."

"I believe life will never be dull again."

"I certainly hope not." Lounging back against the pillows, she smiled, "I shall do my best to keep dullness away."

"You shall not have to work all that hard." He watched her green eyes brighten with amusement. Her fiery hair tumbling around her shoulders in a tangled mass of curls. Her mere presence dispelled the glum, dreary, drudgery of life. "You have a light that seems to follow wherever you go."

"And you, my lord, have a silver tongue. Which you wield very skillfully."

"As long as it keeps you by my side." He kissed her again.

"And what shall I use to keep you by my side?" Caitlin seductively allowed the sheet to slip down.

"Woman, you are a temptress." Dillon raised one dark brow. "However, I must get to work. We are behind schedule as it is. I shall try my hardest to be home early tonight."

"I suppose duty must come first." Her long, exaggerated sigh hinted at boredom.

"I fear that is true. Besides you have work to do as well."
He gave her a lopsided grin. "Mr. Barclay will not be put off
again."

"I cannot wait until the house is finished so we can be
alone."

"We will have all night to be together." Leaning over, he
kissed her one more time. "Good-bye, love." Grabbing some burnt
toast from the tray, he headed out the door.

"You sure are in a good mood today, boss." Johnny hadn't
seen Dillon this happy in months. "Seems odd, especially after the
tragic news about Mr. Tone's death."

"Aye, my boy. My mood has nothing to do with Mr. Tone.
It is a sad day indeed. He was a great man. I'm honored to have
known him."

"Are we printing his speech in the paper?"

"Aye. I believe his speech will inspire everyone."

"How did your wife take the news?"

"I never got the chance to tell her." Dillon smiled. "We had
other distractions last night."

"What could be more important?" Johnny asked.

"When it comes to adults, it is best not to ask too many
questions," Dillon laughed.

"What is this speech about?" The female voice startled both
men.

"Blast it, Henrietta. Will you stop sneaking up on me?"
Dillon demanded. Johnny slipped, unnoticed in the back of the
shop.

"I didn't sneak," she defended with a pout. "Why are you
so sour anyway?"

Dillon took a deep breath, trying to calm down. "I am busy
right now." He didn't have time for her whining. And, he most
certainly didn't want Caitlin to know she was there. They were just

becoming close.He wouldn't risk the blissfulness they'd shared last night on petty jealousies.

"I won't take much of your time." She pasted on a smile with her bright pink lips, but was not pleased with his distant tone and attitude. "I only wanted you to take a look at this." She handed him the folded linen paper.

"What is it?" He held up his ink stained hands. "I will never be able to read it if I touch it now."

"An article about the social."

"How can you write about it when it hasn't happened yet?" Dillon was more than perplexed. His tone was edged with frustration.

"Exactly my point. It's announcing the event."

"Everyone in town already knows about it."

"You could still take a look at it." Her pout developed into full-blown dejection.

"All right. Set it on my desk and I'll get to it when I have time." Without another word, he turned back to the press.

Clearly miffed, she stomped across the room, tossing the paper onto the cluttered desk. She wanted to spend more time talking. He seemed to be giving her less and less attention since he'd married that Irish chit. Suddenly she brightened with enthusiasm as she formed a plan.

"Dillon Cade, you should be ashamed of yourself," she scolded. "Why look at this desk. I do declare it's the messiest thing I have ever seen."

"I do not have time to worry about the appearance of my desk. I have a newspaper to get out."

"You know what you need?" She didn't wait for him to answer. "A secretary to help you with organizing things." She started rearranging papers. "See, I can help you do lots of things around here."

"I do not need a secretary, or anything else."

"I would not charge much. Why, I'd even be willing to work for free." The seductive tone matched her swaying hips, as she sauntered across the room, positioning herself next to Dillon.

"I believe what little payment I'd expect would be most enjoyable for you." She pressed the soft curves of her body against his.

Lord; give me patience, please! Dillon silently prayed, hoping to alleviate the anger boiling inside of him. He was pinned between the press and a daft woman, void of understanding.

"Henrietta, back up and give me some room. 'Tis not proper to be so close."

She took two small steps back. "I was only showing you what I have to offer."

"I have already said that I'm not looking for any help. If you need money, I suggest you find a husband."

"Being married isn't the only way a girl can be compensated."

Clearly angling to be his mistress, she had certainly dressed for the part. With her low cut, tight forming dress, and painted face, she'd fit right in on the streets. Dillon surmised that is where she might end up if she didn't get her act together.

"'Tis the only way for a proper young lady," he warned.

She could tell by the hard look in his eyes that her persuasion wasn't working. "I fear you aren't ready for my talents yet. However, I am a patient woman. You'll tire of your little *arrangement* soon enough. I'll be waiting for you when you do."

Before Dillon could say anything, Johnny came in from the back room.

"Johnny, how nice to see you again." She smiled brightly, turning around to face the intrusion.

"It… it is?" he stammered.

"Of course it is. Why, I was just telling your boss that what you need is someone to help keep things clean and organized. What do you think?"

"I… I don't know, ma'am." Johnny looked down at the floor. He couldn't figure out why she was being so nice. Whenever he ran into Henrietta in town, she would make fun of him and call him names.

"Why don't you talk your boss into it." Turning to Dillon she ran her tongue across her upper lip. "We could have so much fun together." With her black skirt sashaying, she made her way to the door.

"Think about my offer, Dillon."

The whole house had been in a buzz of activity all day. Mr. Barclay and his men worked on the remodeling while Caitlin oversaw the combining of the two bedrooms. All her things were taken into Dillon's room. She didn't think the chore would have taken so long, but combining all their things in one room proved to be a giant feat. Things had to be sorted, separated, and rearranged. Caitlin had been busy all day, only stopping to eat supper at Martha's insistence.

"Thank you, Martha. I must confess that I feel much better after eating."

"Can't have you going around starving yourself. You're already a mite too thin now." Martha removed the dishes from the table.

"I just want to have the room completed before Dillon comes home. The task is taking longer than I'd expected."

"You have plenty of time." Martha waved her chubby hand. "Master Dillon won't be home for a long time."

"He said he'd try to be home early."

"Don't get your hopes up. The paper comes out in two days." She finished loading the cart with dirty dishes. "Ye may be having dinner by yourself. But I'll make sure it's hearty. You need to keep your strength up for when the master does get home."

"Martha!" Caitlin set the linen napkin down. "You shouldn't say such things."

"Humph. Why not, 'tis true."

"Certain things are not proper to discuss."

"Since when do you care about proper?"

"Some things are private."

"Then, I guess it wouldn't be proper to say it's about time the two of you stop playing cat and mouse, and get down to the business of making a marriage."

"You're incorrigible."

Martha's loud cackle echoed through the house. Caitlin couldn't help smiling as she retreated.

After answering Mr. Barclay's questions, she went back upstairs to the bedroom. Needing to find more room for her clothes, she started searching through the dresser drawers. She found two stacks of letters. One set was tied with a blue ribbon, the smaller set with red. She also found some paper, a few quill pens, an inkwell and a blotter.

Knowing she shouldn't read the letters didn't stop her curiosity. Besides they were married. *Is it still considered an invasion of privacy if you're married?* Deciding that it wasn't, she untied the blue ribbon. The folded pieces of paper had poems scratched onto them. She only read a few. Then retied the ribbon and went to the stack tied with red ribbon. These letters appeared to be from England, probably from his father.

A little bit of envy ran through her. She hadn't received any letters from her family since their departure made her anxiety heighten. She didn't know if they were alive or dead, maybe even thrown in prison somewhere.

She brushed the tears away, and tried to focus on the positive. She'd said prayers for them every night. Surely God was protecting them. Her faith felt stronger as it grew. She felt her childhood faith blossoming into something real. No longer did she view God through her parents, or the preacher's eyes. She now had her own understanding, her own views. God felt real in her heart his love alive in her life.

Slowly opening the letter, she read the brief letter from his father. Not much had been said in it. Then again, Dillon had said they weren't close. The next letter was written in a different handwriting. The large, loops and swirls suggested a woman's writing. Caitlin thought twice about reading this one. Was it from an old girlfriend? Maybe someone who still hoped to one day marry Dillon.

That thought made her angry. Opening the letter she read the lengthy contents. Relief filled her when she realized it was from his stepmother. However, anger, disappointment and hurt merged as she continued reading. Stuffing the letter back in the pile, she retied the ribbon then threw the pile on the floor.

Deciding to forget that she'd even seen the letter, she went back to cleaning out the drawer. However, the anger and humiliation wouldn't be appeased. She'd have to talk with Dillon tonight.

Finding a loose piece of paper, she picked it up, carefully weighting the idea of intruding again. She hadn't liked the last letter. However her stubborn curiosity reared to life again.

The contents of this letter were more devastating than the last one. Caitlin felt the room spin. She gasped for air, as if the breath had been knocked from her chest. "This can't be true," she murmured. "This can't be happening."

Dillon found Caitlin in the downstairs parlor, pacing back and forth like a caged animal. Her determined gait and rigid face foretold a storm brewing.

"Caitlin?"

She stopped pacing, clearly taken aback by his presence. "I did not hear you enter."

"I'm not surprised. You seemed deep in thought. Whatever is the matter?"

She held up the folded letter. "When were you going to tell me about this?"

"Last night."

"I do not recall you mentioning the fact that Theodore Wolf Tone killed himself after being found guilty of treason." Caitlin crossed the room, waving the envelope. "Did you not think I have the right to know? This affects my entire family. How could you keep something like this from me?"

"If you remember, we were busy with other things. I did not want to spoil the evening." Dillon took his stance with his hands locked behind his back, looking like a soldier preparing for battle.

"'Twas purely selfish motives that drove you to secrecy?" Caitlin's animosity rose. "'Tis my life we're talking about, my future. Is that not more important than a night of passion?" She spun around in a whirl of anger.

"That is not fair," Dillon stated, calmly. "You planned the evening. I merely wanted to wait until the right moment to bring up the subject." Unlocking his hands he walked up behind her, setting his hands, gently on her shoulders. "I thought I was your future."

The hurt in his tone softened her heart. "You are, Dillon." She turned around, allowing herself to find comfort in his embrace. "I'm only worried about my family. I was also hurt that you would keep something so important from me."

"I'd never do anything to intentionally hurt you." He ran his hand through her hair. "I planned on telling you tonight. Besides, his last words to the court will appear in the paper. The whole town will know about it then."

He hugged her tight, feeling her animosity melt away. "I, too, am worried about your family."

"You are?" Her voice muffled against his chest.

"Aye. We are married. So your family becomes my family."

"Then must I also adopt your family?" She looked up into his eyes, noting the hardness that replaced his usual mirth.

"Some families are not worth the effort, my dear. I would never punish you by forcing my family on you."

"You hate your family that much?"

"I would not go that far." Dillon pushed away, pacing over to the hearth. "We are just not close."

"You never talk about them. Except for the one time when you told me about your mother, you have never said anything else."

"There is nothing to tell. Besides, you have not opened up about your family either."

"True. But I have spent most of our marriage hating you for forcing me into wedlock." Caitlin walked up behind Dillon, slipping her arms around his waist and resting her cheek against his back. "You can hardly expect a girl to open up to her enemy."

"Am I still your enemy?"

"Do you have to ask? Was not last night enough proof for you?"

Dillon turned, staring into her eyes. "Some people can have intimacy without any feelings."

"I believe you are speaking of the male population, sir. Women do not treat such matters lightly."

"I could argue the point, but will not waste the time. Especially if that means you have feelings for me."

"If I admit to having feelings, will you open up about your family?"

"I have already said there is nothing to tell." His tone chilled the room.

"Have you not kept in contact at all? Not even with letters?" She persisted.

"Why are you pushing this subject?" He turned around, looking into the fire, lost in thought.

"I am sorry. I did not mean to pry into matters that are none of my business."

"I did not mean that." Dillon sighed. "My family is your business. I just do not like talking about them, especially my stepmother."

"Is she the truly wicked stepmother, like in Cinderella?"

"She made that character look like a kitten."

"Do they know that we are married?"

"Why are you feeling so insecure? Do you think I'm trying to hide you?" He chuckled. "Will it make you feel better to know I sent a letter to them?"

"'Tis not insecurity, but curiosity. What do they think of our hasty marriage?"

"Why so many questions?" Suddenly a light dawned. "You read the letters, didn't you?" Clasping his hands behind his back, he muttered to himself. "Yes, of course. It all makes sense now. The letter about Tone's death was in my drawer with the letters from my father. You were snooping and found them."

"I was not snooping," Caitlin denied. "I happened upon them by accident."

"Did you manage to unfold and read them all by accident as well?"

"I only read a couple. Please do not be angry with me. I did not mean to pry. I was just curious."

"I am not angry. I merely wished to protect you from the unpleasantness."

"Then you do not agree with your stepmother. She said some awful things about me."

"I care little for her opinion and sent a letter back telling her so."

"As long as you do not heed to her advice."

"Never." Dillon gathered her in his arms. "You should not have read those vicious, cruel rantings." Dillon gave her a long, slow kiss. "Does that put an end to the distress, and uncertainty?"

"Somewhat. Although I may need just a little more convincing."

They kissed again.

"How's that?"

"I'm swooning," Caitlin moaned.

"I doubt that could ever happen."

Without warning, she claimed his lips in a heated kiss that touched both of them more deeply than words could explain. "How is that?" she asked, breathlessly.

"I believe that now I'm swooning." Her passion sparked feelings he didn't even know he possessed. "However, I have one question." He kissed a trail down her neck. "Why were you searching my drawers in the first place?"

She heard the question, but her mind couldn't keep up with the sensations his hands and lips produced. "Ummm, I needed more room for my clothes." She had almost forgotten the purpose of cleaning out that drawer.

Dillon suddenly stopped kissing her throat. The absent of his mouth left her feeling cold. "Is something wrong?"

"You moved your clothes into my bedroom?"

"Is that all right?"

"You move quickly once you make up your mind."

"I wanted to surprise you. I can move back to the other room if you prefer."

"Not on your life." Dillon swooped her up. "Let's go look at our room."

Dillon turned the handle of the press, causing the paper to move forward. The tinkle of the bell above the door alerted him of a visitor.

"Caitlin, what a nice surprise." He walked over but stopped short of kissing her. "I have ink all over me. I do not want to ruin your dress."

"Pish-posh." Caitlin waved her gloved hand. "I care not about this old thing. Besides, it will give me an excuse to go shopping for a new one." Leaning forward their lips touched briefly. "Why do you have the bell?"

"It is only a precaution. I have had some visitors sneak in lately. I thought it would be best to not be surprised by anyone. You never know who may come through that door."

"I hope you do not mind us dropping by. We were in town and I thought I would surprise you." She cocked her head toward

Lucy, who was chatting away with Johnny. "Besides, Lucy was looking for an excuse to see your apprentice."

"You need no excuse to come by. 'Tis always a pleasure to see you." Dillon wiped his hands on an old rag, saturated with gasoline. Watching the two youngsters, he decided it was time for a break.

"Hey, Johnny, why don't we break for supper a little early?"

Caitlin saw Lucy's eyes brighten with enthusiasm. The unspoken question made her blue eyes even brighter than normal. "Go ahead and take your break also."

"Thank you, Caitlin." The two rushed out the door, the bell echoing after their footsteps.

Caitlin surveyed the shop. "I see 'tis been a while since you have cleaned."

"What is it with women and cleaning?" Dillon sighed. "I have to get the paper out. I do not have time to clean."

Walking over to his desk, she leafed through the clutter of papers. "What's this?" She held a piece of paper. "It looks like an ad for something."

Dillon read the scribbled handwriting. "I've been looking for that. It was supposed to go in tomorrow's paper. It will have to wait until next week, now."

"I cannot figure out how you find anything. Not only is the desk a mess, but there is no organization. All ads should go in one spot. It would save you a lot of headaches if you knew where things were."

"That is true. But, I have not the time." Dillon pecked her cheek. "Perhaps you would like to clean my desk."

"It will take a while."

"I'm sure you are up for the task."

"'Tis my wifely duty." She laughed.

A short time later Caitlin had the desk cleared and stacks of papers organized. Her brow furrowed as she read a letter. "This is an odd ad about the social next week."

"Blast it!" Dillon cursed under his breath. "That is not an ad. Henrietta stopped by and wanted me to print that."

Caitlin stiffened. "Why did you not print it?"

"I did not even bother to read it."

"Is that supposed to make me feel better?" Fighting back tears, she turned away from him.

"Caitlin, do not be upset." Dillon wanted to console her, but his hands were stained. "I swear nothing is going on. She keeps bothering me about printing her articles, but I will not do it."

Caitlin wanted to trust him. She had no reason not to. These insecurities kept creeping up. Needing time to think, she looked for an excuse to escape. "I need some boxes." She went into the back room.

Henrietta was about to enter the shop when she noticed Caitlin cleaning off the desk. The little twit! She fumed. Every time she turned around, there was Caitlin. Henrietta wanted to enter the shop, but since Dillon had hung that bell, she couldn't come and go unnoticed. However, the two appeared to be fighting. When Caitlin went into the back room, she crept around the back into the alley. Finding the window to the back room, she pushed up on the pane. Luckily, it wasn't locked. She opened it only a few inches, but it was enough to hear the conversation. Pressing her ear against the wooden frame, she listened for voices.

She put a gloved hand over her mouth to stifle a giggle when she realized they were fighting about her. However, her mirth turned to anger as Dillon entered the room and the conversation continued.

"I did not print the article because it is not a good idea," Dillon said.

"The idea is not all that bad. The social is a big event," Caitlin countered.

"I run a newspaper, not a gossip column," Dillon explained. "I do not see the point in announcing something that everyone already knows about it."

"What about the people from out of town? An announcement could draw newcomers. Not to mention, it is still news. Anything that happens in town is considered news. Why do you insist on only printing politics? You could increase the number of subscriptions if you included things women wanted to read as well."

"But the men already purchase the paper. Women can read it when they are done."

"What about the women who are not married?"

Dillon thought for a moment. "You have a point there."

Henrietta couldn't believe that Caitlin and she agreed on something. If Caitlin won the argument, then Dillon would print her piece. After he realized what a wonderful writer she was, he'd come crawling— no, begging— her to love him. She felt her plan was falling into place.

"The problem is, I do not have time to go all over town looking for subjects that women would be interested in. Besides, I don't even know what interests them."

"So, you hire a woman on the staff." Caitlin smiled. "Someone who could keep the place clean, and look for tidbits of information."

Henrietta's heart beat quickened. Surely Dillon would hire her for the position.

"Are you up for the job?"

"Me?" Caitlin arched a red brow.

"You are the perfect person. After all 'tis your idea."

"But I am your wife."

"Does that mean we cannot work together? I will even pay you. That way you will not feel trapped in the marriage." A sarcastic smile touched the corner of his mouth.

"I figured you would want Henrietta to be your assistant." She was not about to let him win the verbal war.

"Caitlin." He sighed. "I want nothing to do with her. Not personally, or in business. Besides, I need someone who can actually write. Not the incoherent ramblings she produces."

"Are you sure you want to be stuck with me all day long?"

"I want you by my side all day and all night." Dillon's suggestive tone turned serious. "I love you, Caitlin. I want no other woman in business or pleasure. I will heed your suggestion, but only if you agree to be my partner."

"We are already partners at home." She crossed the room, succumbing to his embrace. "I'm just not sure about mixing business. We may tire of seeing each other so much."

"I shall never tire of seeing your beautiful face." To prove his point, he kissed her.

A loud crash, followed by a clang, startled them apart. Dillon went to the window but saw nothing. "Must have been a stray cat."

Chapter 14

"Can you believe that tramp!" Henrietta stormed down the street. "She's destroyed everything I've worked for." Completely oblivious to the eyes staring at her, she continued her tirade. "She has not only coaxed Dillon into her bed, but now is taking my place at his shop. That should be my article he's publishing. Incoherent ramblings!"

Hurt and anger cut like a sharp knife shredding her pride into tiny pieces. She'd never win Dillon now that Caitlin was giving him what he needed. All attempts of throwing herself at him were for naught. Humiliation overwhelmed her.

How could Dillon find her beautiful? What man could find that Irish trash attractive? "She's nothing but a puny stick with pasty, white skin. And, that hair! They'll pay," she vowed. "They'll both pay!"

"From my earliest youth, I have regarded the connection between Ireland and Great Britain as the curse of the Irish nation, and felt convinced, that while it lasted, this country would never be free or happy. In consequence, I have determined to apply all the powers which my individual efforts could move, in order to separate the two countries...I have sacrificed all my views in life; I have courted poverty; I have left a beloved wife unprotected, and children which I adore, fatherless. After such sacrifices, in a cause which I have always considered as the cause of justice and freedom – it is no great effort at this day to add my life."

Caitlin set the paper on the table, wiping the tears away. "It is hard to imagine after a great speech like that, Mr. Tone killed himself with a penknife."

"I suppose he felt more honor in taking his own life than allowing England to take it from him." Dillon settled his hand on top of hers.

"Do you think he's in Heaven?" Caitlin inquired.

"I suppose so. Why do you ask?"

"Because he killed himself. Doesn't the Bible teach that killing is a sin?"

"True, but it also teaches that Jesus died for our sins. Therefore, all sin is forgiven, if you have trusted Jesus as your Savior."

"So, you think God forgave Mr. Tone for taking his own life."

"I believe God forgives all the sins of war."

"I don't understand why God is allowing all of this tragedy." Caitlin was still struggling with her faith. She'd started to see God's hand leading when she prayed for help with Dillon. God granted that prayer. Yet, in something as important as this war, He didn't seem to hear anyone's prayers. The war was still going and Ireland wasn't free.

"We cannot always understand God, Caitlin. His ways are higher than our ways. But, we must have faith that He is in control. Everything will work out according to his plan. God directs our lives. We must learn to follow his path, no matter where it leads."

"Even if it leads to death?"

"Aye. Even unto death. Or, into a marriage with your enemy." Dillon's brown eyes sparkled, mischievously.

"You, sir, are still a cad."

"Aye, but I'm your cad."

"'Tis true. I suppose I'd better get used to it."

"Aye, my love." Dillon leaned across the table, giving her a tender kiss. "You are stuck with me for the rest of your life."

"Until death do us part?"

"Death is the only thing that could take me away from you."

"Oh! Excuse me." A surprised voice exclaimed. Dillon and Caitlin drew apart, startled by the interruption.

"Sarah!" Caitlin exclaimed. Crossing the floor in a swift motion, she had her best friend in a hug before another word could be spoken.

"I am sorry to intrude. Mrs. White told me to come in."

"No intrusion at all." Dillon stood. "Come join us."

"No, thank you. I have already had my morning meal."

"Sit down. We have so much to talk about." Caitlin led Sarah to the table. "How about a cup of tea?"

"'Twould be lovely." Sarah sat down, noting the glow around Caitlin. A glow that hadn't been there the last time she'd visited. "Thank you." She accepted the cup.

"To what do we owe the honor of your company?" Dillon poured another cup of coffee.

"My father told me about Mr. Tone. I wanted to offer my condolences."

"How sweet of you." Caitlin smiled. "'Twas truly a striking blow to Ireland."

"Have you heard anything from your family?"

"Not yet." Caitlin's eyes misted over. "I'm so worried about them."

"I am sure they are fine. They will write when they have time." Dillon wanted to reassure her, but the possibilities of them being caught by England were great.

"I did not mean to bring up painful memories." Sarah walked around the table and hugged Caitlin.

"You did not." Caitlin wiped her eyes. "Reading about Mr. Tone's capture and death did."

"Do not worry." Sarah patted her hand. "God's protection is great."

"I guess." Caitlin sniffed.

"Here." Dillon handed her a handkerchief. He waited until she dried her eyes, and then kissed the tip of her nose. "I am going to work, so you two can have some time alone."

"Take care." Caitlin waved the handkerchief.

Sarah fidgeted impatiently, waiting for Dillon to leave. Once he was out of earshot, she bombarded Caitlin with questions.

"What is up with you two?" Her blue eyes widened with interest. "Are you in love? What happened to change your mind? Is he a good kisser?"

"Whatever do you mean?" Caitlin smiled playfully.

"Do not give me that." Sarah sat back, crossing her arms in a huff. "The last time I was here, you could hardly stand to look at him."

"It has been a while since you came for a visit," Caitlin commented.

"Yes. It seems a lot has changed."

"To answer your questions." Caitlin held up one finger. "One, we are married. I believe you were maid of honor." She held up another finger. "Two, yes, I'm in love. Three," she added another finger. "I guess God changed my mind." With the fourth finger came a huge smile, "And, four, I do not believe the word 'good' is adequate to describe Dillon's kisses."

Sarah's black curls danced over her shoulders as she shook her head, laughing. "And to think I quit believing in miracles."

Caitlin's expression sobered. "Do not ever stop believing. My family needs a miracle right now."

"I did not mean to imply I'd ever stop believing. I pray for Brogan and your parents every night. I pray God will bring them home safely."

"Your faith has always been stronger than mine," Caitlin sighed.

"No. You just don't let yourself believe in things you cannot see. I know once you find God's love, your faith will be ten times greater than mine." Sarah tilted her head to the side. "The fact that you went to church last Sunday and gave God credit for changing your heart about Dillon, already tells me that you are starting to believe."

"'Tis true, however I'm still struggling with the idea of war. I cannot understand how a loving God would allow all this tragedy."

"Did you understand why you had to marry Dillon?"

"You know I did not."

"Was that not a great tragedy in your life?"

Caitlin hesitated. Her feelings for Dillon had drastically changed over the last week. She now felt ashamed for all the hatred she had directed towards him. "At the time it was."

"Things are different now?" Sarah asked.

Caitlin nodded.

"My point is this." Sarah leaned against the table resting her folded arms in front of her. "You hated the thought of marriage, but, God had a plan all along, and look how it turned out. We do not always know why things happen, but we must never take our eyes off God. The Creator of this universe will always be in control."

"You sound like Dillon."

"He's a smart man." Sarah sat back in her chair. "Now, I am dying to hear all the juicy details of this change of heart. And, you have to fill me in on your trip to Mr. Jefferson's."

"I fear 'tis such a long story. I will have to give you the abbreviated version." Caitlin cocked her head toward the door. "Mr. Barclay and his men will be here soon."

"I guess talking you into a day trip into town is out of the question?"

Caitlin shook her head sending the fiery curls bouncing. "I cannot do anything until this house is finished."

"Can you not hire someone to do that?"

"I like having things done my way."

"Therein lies the problem. God wants us to give control to Him. He cannot direct our lives if we hold the reins."

"Are you going to sit there preaching to me all day? Or, are you going to take a tour of the house, so I can show off what's been done?"

Dillon trudged through the town streets, stopping briefly to help Mrs. Olsen into her buggy. Then he went into the general store. Mrs. Johnson greeted him warmly, as she always did. After all, Dillon was the richest man in town. And, he'd been splurging more since he'd gotten hitched.

"How nice to see you, Dillon." Her wrinkled face split into a smile.

"Hello, Mrs. Johnson. I wanted to check and see how that gift for Caitlin was coming along?"

"Oh, splendid, just splendid. Wait until you see it." She went around the counter, motioning him to follow.

When they came out from the back room, Mr. Mosely was waiting at the counter. If Dillon had been back there with anyone else, it might have looked improper and been topic of town gossip for months. However, Mrs. Johnson was old enough to be his grandmother. Besides, he'd just married that pretty, little Gallagher girl. There was no reason for him to be looking elsewhere.

"Dillon, how are you?" Mr. Mosely tipped his hat.

"I'm fine, sir. How about you?"

"As well as can be expected. You know this cold weather makes my bones ache."

"I'm sorry to hear that. I will remember to keep that in my prayers."

"No need, son. God already knows what's ailing me. But thanks for the gesture, just the same." Holding up the folded paper he asked. "Since when do you waste time writing about things like the social?"

"'Tis only an idea I'm trying out, a new column announcing social activities."

"Seems there's plenty to write about that's more important."

"Yes, sir." Dillon stifled a smile. "'Twas Caitlin's idea. I am letting her try a hand at writing."

"That doesn't seem quite proper." The lines in his face set in a deep frown.

"There are plenty of women writers. Did you find something wrong with how she writes?" Dillon crossed his arms.

"No. The writing was fine. 'Tis just that a wife's place is in the home taking care of the young' uns and all." He fidgeted under Dillon's watchful gaze.

"We have only been married a few months. We do not have any children yet." Dillon uncrossed his arms, smiling in his easy manner. "However, I will keep your advice under recommendation when we do have little ones running around."

Mr. Mosely smiled. "Yes. Yes. Of course, guess it won't hurt nothing to let the little wife to do some writing until the babies come."

Dillon bid his farewells and headed back to the shop. The jingling of the bell irritated him every time he opened the door, but he was tired of Henrietta sneaking up on him. And, after she read the paper, he was positive she would be by.

"Good night, boss."

"Good night, Johnny." Dillon watched him cross the street, and then went back to checking the invoices.

A few minutes later the bell warned him of company— a very unhappy, highly emotional guest.

"How could you?" Henrietta's advance was swift and agitated. "That was my article, and you published it under your wife's name."

Dillon stood, grateful the desk blocked any further advancement.

"You're a prig! A no-good thief. And believe me you'll have the devil to pay."

"Henrietta, will you calm down?" His loud voice out-matched her whiny pitch. "That is not the piece you wrote. I have not stolen anything."

"Just because your little wife rewrote my article, doesn't make it hers. That was my idea. My words. And you had no right stealing it from me."

"I admit the idea was yours. But, Caitlin did more than switch a few words. She completely rewrote the whole thing using her own words."

"It didn't need any rewriting."

"It needed a writer's touch." Dillon tried to be gentle, but had to be honest.

"And that was your wife?" The disgust in her voice spilled out.

"Caitlin is a very accomplished writer."

"What has she ever written?"

Dillon felt the trap, and wasn't about to fall into it. "She wrote the article on the social."

"My article. Has she ever written anything of her own? Or, does she merely steal other people's writings?"

"I will not argue this point any more. I am sorry if you're upset, but I have done nothing wrong." Dillon took his stand, arms behind his back.

Henrietta paused a moment. She loved that particular stance. The white, linen shirt fit snug across his chest, detailing his strong arms. His broad shoulders pulled back like a general in command. It was an all-powerful, take charge pose that sent her pulse racing.

Although his brown hair was pulled back in a ponytail, some strands hung loose, curling around his angled face, softening his deep set brown eyes, which were hard with anger. Her eyes lowered to his lips. His, dark, full lips may have been set in a harsh line, but she assumed they were tender when kissed.

If only I could get him to change his mind, she desperately thought. She would give anything to feel those strong arms circled around her. His soft lips pressed to hers. However, he had humiliated her more than once, having thrown herself at him, only to be refused. The sting sharpened when he turned to Caitlin.

"Dillon." She softened her tone, rounding the desk, and laying a gloved hand on his chest. Pressing her body close to him, she tried physical persuasion to get the answers she desired. "Why won't you confide in me?" She lowered her lashes over her hazel eyes, feigning hurt. "You know I forgive you for the article. I have not told a soul. Yet, you refuse to reveal the source of your anonymous writer."

"Why are you so intent on prying it from me?"

"Why are you so secretive?"

"Because it's none of your business." Grabbing her wrist, he jerked it off his chest, flinging her arm down. "An editor never reveals his sources."

"The whole town knows that Caitlin wrote it," she said, rubbing her bruised wrist.

"I do not care what the town thinks. It is all speculation."

"You'll pay for this, Dillon." Henrietta spit in his face, turned on her heel and marched out the door, the jingling bell angrily echoing each footstep.

Outside the cold night air tugged at her long, fur-lined pelisse. Henrietta paid no notice. Her thoughts were on Dillon, Caitlin, and revenge. Stepping off the wooden boardwalk, she rounded the whitewashed buildings lined up along Main Street. The brisk pace was out of sheer anger more than fear of the stranger following her. Finally catching up to her, he grabbed her upper arm bringing her to a halt.

"Where are you dashing off to in an all fired hurry?"

Yanking her arm away from his grasp, she replied, "I suppose you heard that."

His dark mustache twitched. "I didn't hear much. The window was closed, and you were too far away."

"I couldn't sneak you in because of that bell above the door. Besides, he didn't reveal his source."

"That leaves us back at square one."

"Correction. That leaves you back at square one." She lifted her blue skirts and started walking away.

"I'll get him, Henrietta. Then you'll have to pay."

She stopped short, her head snapping up. She turned, a seductive smile playing on her lips. "'Tis not Dillon you are after. It's his wife, Caitlin."

"I am after whoever is committing treason." His teeth gleamed from under the handlebar mustache. "I will be collecting my payment when the job is done."

Her smile faltered under his cold, dark gaze. However, she kept the bravado up. "You shall be collecting nothing if you do not get Caitlin Cade out of my way."

"I figured this was a personal matter. I hate to interfere with your plans, but it looks like your beloved will be going to jail."

"My plans and my reasons are none of your business. If you want me to follow through with my end of the bargain, then you'll do as I say."

The tall, stranger stepped closer, his boots crunching the dirt with each eerie step. His dark, menacing glance, pierced through her, "I am the one in charge, and I will call the shots." Brushing right past her as if she weren't standing there, he continued down the alley.

"The house is coming along splendidly." Dillon ran his hand along the wooden mantel. "I especially love this fireplace." The picture of Jesus and the Last Supper, imprinted in plaster on the front of the mantel, was gilded in gold.

"Do you truly like it?" This fireplace in the sitting room was her pride and joy.

"Aye. I believe even Thomas Jefferson will envy it."

"Truly?"

"You did a wonderful job designing it. I'm very proud of you." Dillon watched as the flickering firelight brought out the gold-leaf pattern imprinted on the cream wallpaper. "The cost is well worth it. That look in your eyes is all the reward I need."

"Oh, Dillon." Caitlin encircled his waist. "You are too good to me."

"I told you price was not a hindrance. Money will never be an object to stand in the way of your happiness."

Caitlin's unexpected withdrawal left him dumbfounded. "Is something the matter?"

She shook her head, but paced a few steps away.

"Caitlin?" Dillon cautiously approached, gently turning her to face him. He felt his heart stop when he saw the tears shimmering in her eyes. "What is the matter? Did I say something to upset you?"

"Nay, my lord." She smiled. "I am not sure why I feel so weepy all of a sudden. 'Tis really not like me."

"I know. Tell me what is the matter."

"I do not want you to think I'm after your money— that I am only here because of what you can give me." She looked him in the eyes. "I do not want you to feel that I am using you."

He breathed a sigh of relief. Why is it every time she cried, he thought she would leave? "I would never feel that way. I am amazed that you have come to love me at all. Our circumstances for marriage were not made out of love. I feared you would hate me for the rest of your life. The idea of having a true marriage with a happy home is beyond my expectations. You have never once taken advantage of the situation, always asking before you made any purchase. You even sought permission for this fireplace because it would cost a great deal."

"That was Mr. Barclay's idea," she confessed.

"My point being this." He took both of her hands in his. "I freely give you anything you want out of love. It is my gift to you. I expect nothing in return. I harbor no ill will or regrets when you purchase things that make you happy."

"'Tis my point." She withdrew her hands from his grasp, smoothing the front of her blue, linen gown. "You make it sound as though I need money and things to be happy." Her jaw set in a tight line. "I do not. I grew up with enough money to be comfortable and more than enough love to be rich."

"I fear we come from different circumstances. I grew up with a minimal amount of love, and as much money as royalty. I am sorry if I have offended you. It's just that money is all I knew as a child. 'Tis the only way I know to show love."

"I only want you to realize that you offer me much more than money. Your wealth is not the reason I love you."

"No amount of money in the world could compare with the joy I feel at those tender words." Dillon swallowed the lump in his throat.

"That is what I mean. Why would I care about money when you make me feel so cherished?" Caitlin went into his embrace, tenderly touching his cheek. "You treat me as if I were a queen, even when I'm angry at you." Fighting the tears in her eyes, she added, "What right do I have being married to someone so wonderful?"

"That, my dear, is the same question I ask myself." Dillon kissed her, a slow tender kiss that melted her on the spot.

Caitlin broke the kiss. "I cannot believe you would even think that after the way I treated you so unfairly."

"'Twas not your fault. You were put in an impossible situation." He kissed her again. "The past does not matter. We need only look to the future." His lips traveled down her neck.

"Aye." Closing her eyes, she surrendered to his kiss. She suddenly withdrew from the kiss again. "I almost forgot. I have a special present for you."

"I would rather be kissing you than opening a gift."

"It is in the downstairs parlor." She took his hand and led him through the halls.

Upon entering the room Dillon stopped short, staring at a picture of a young woman that was now placed above the fireplace.

"Do you like it?" Caitlin asked.

"Wherever did you find that?"

"In the attic. I knew instantly 'twas your mother. You look a lot like her."

"She was quite beautiful." He sounded choked up.

"I hope you don't mind that I hung it up."

"The gesture was most gracious." Dillon kissed her. "'Tis just that I have not seen her face in a long time."

"Why did you have her portrait stored away?"

"I am not sure." He sighed. "It just hurt too much remembering."

"Do you want to take it down?"

"Nay. I like being able to see my mother now. In an odd way, it almost feels like she is here with us."

"I am sure she is watching over you from heaven."

Whistling happily as he tethered his horse to the wooden hitching post, Dillon patted his steed on the neck. "That's a good boy." Jumping up the few wooden steps, he opened the door to his shop, still whistling.

Not even the gray, dreary weather could dampen his spirits. The Lord had been good to him, abundantly better than he deserved. The newspaper subscriptions were up to one hundred and ten. He had a beautiful wife, who seemed to be warming up to the idea of marriage more every day.

And, although he was not a materialistic man, he had money, land, and a nice house. Even that had been made better by the entrance of Caitlin. The house was transformed into a pleasant palace. Soon it really would be a Regal Hall. He preferred coming home to the lively, warm, and cozy atmosphere that Caitlin produced, rather than the empty, drafty, and dreary shell that he once called home.

No matter how many good things Dillon could name, there seemed to be a needling apprehension in the back of his mind that perhaps life was a little too perfect. The fear that something could go wrong seemed to intensify. Where did this trepidation come from? Perhaps it emanated from his childhood.

He remembered feeling that same kind of contentment when he was young. As a child he had everything he ever wanted. Life was happily humming along. Then his mother was killed and everything came to a screeching halt. His secure life had been shattered.

Dillon had not thought about his mother in years. He seemed to be thinking about her more and more since marrying Caitlin. He smiled at the remembrance of always feeling loved by his mother. He had been the center of her universe. That spot only being shared with his father.

Although they were upper-class people, his mother never looked down on the lower classes. She used to say that God loved everyone, no matter how much money they made. She even helped several families find jobs and get suitable housing. His mother's heart had been too big to be confined to one social class.

Caitlin reminded him of his mother, although not in looks or temper. His mother had been sweet, demure, and submissive. Even though Caitlin did not possess those qualities, she had a light that shined brighter than the sun. Her love was all-consuming, and her confidence all-powerful and she made him feel loved. He felt certain his mother would have approved of Caitlin.

Dillon sifted through a few letters on his desk, but couldn't seem to switch his mind to work this morning. The comparisons between his wife and mother kept running through his head. Eventually his thoughts settled on how beautiful Caitlin looked when she slept. Her hair splayed out like a fire in the night, and her bare shoulder gleaming in the moonlight.

The ringing bell drew his attention from his bride to the door. He watched as a tall, wide-shouldered man crossed the floor.

Dillon stood and rounded the desk, positioning himself in front of it. "How may I help you?"

"Sheriff Edward." He tapped the badge on his chest; not liking the fact that Dillon did not seem intimidated by him. "I'm looking for Dillon Cade."

"'Tis I." Dillon worked hard to conceal his emotions. However, his gut tightened, his worst fear coming true.

"I'm afraid I have to place you under arrest." The sheriff held up a newspaper. "This here article gives me cause to arrest you for treason." His black mustache twitched under his grin.

Chapter 15

Caitlin paced in front of the fireplace. Each agitated step thundering against the hardwood flooring. Every couple of steps she stopped to brush out the wrinkles in her gray gauze gown, or push a loose pin back to hold her curl.

She'd received the missive two days past, only one day after Dillon had been arrested. Her mind already abuzz with worry over Dillon, how was she expected to deal with the arrival of his parents?

A commotion in the hallway caused her to stop. She sucked in a breath through parched lips. A moment later the butler stood in the door frame, his long, angular body casting shadows over the walls and floor. "The stable boys have returned, ma'am. There wasn't a sign of Lord Cade."

"Thank you, Mr. White. I suspect it is a bit too early, considering we only received the written missive two days ago. The time of their arrival will depend on the haste of their packing and boarding." She sighed, one born more of relief than boredom. "'Tis nothing to do but send the boys out on the morrow."

"As you wish, milady." With a curt bow, he left.

Caitlin resumed her pacing. Her focus should be on the daily tasks at hand, but soon fretting about Dillon consumed her thoughts once again. She had already gone to her father's office and begged the help of his lawyer friend. Beyond that she hadn't a clue what to do next. She wanted to see Dillon, but now had to wait on his parents' arrival.

"Blast it all!" she fumed. "Why should I wait on them anyway? 'Tis not as if we invited them." On the contrary, his parent's arrival was more of an intrusion. After reading those nasty letters, she had no desire to meet his stepmother. Caitlin sent silent thanks up to God that Bernadine was only his stepmother and not related by blood.

Her pacing and thoughts were once again interrupted by a loud clearing of the throat.

She looked up startled. "Mr. Barclay, I am sorry I did not hear you."

"Clearly not." He cleared his throat, quieter this time. "A matter has arisen, and I must speak with you."

"Of course, come in and sit down." Caitlin waved her hand to the settee.

He took a seat. His dark eyes darted around the rims of his glasses as he took in the sight of the room. His chest swelled with pride. This room was much more pleasant and cozier than before.

"How can I be of assistance?" Caitlin took the wing chair opposite of him.

"Well. Umm… about the kitchen." He fidgeted with his hands, not knowing what to do with them. He tried resting them in his lap, but almost fell over as he sat nervously perched on the edge of the small couch. Using his hands for balance made him look awkward.

"Oh, the kitchen." Caitlin laughed, and waved her hand. "Do not worry about that room. Martha, the cook, has begged me not to touch a thing in there. You see that is her space, and she has it set up exactly the way she likes it. I fear it would be terribly impolite of me not to abide by her wishes."

"I, too, believe that would be wise."

"Good. I'm grateful you see my position on this. The only other room not to be touched is Dillon's study. He begged this of me before we started the plans for remodeling."

"Very well."

"The rest of the house, Mr. Barclay, is in your capable hands."

The compliment and her smile made his round cheeks turn red. "Shall I proceed with the game room?"

"That would be fine."

"And what are your plans for it, Mrs. Cade?"

Caitlin sighed and rubbed her temple where the beginning of an ache was coming on. "I'm sorry, Mr. Barclay, but I cannot think upon that right now. My thoughts are with Dillon at the moment." She didn't want to stop the work, but concentrating on the house was out of the question at this time.

"I am truly sorry for your troubles. I pray that Mr. Cade will come through this ordeal unharmed."

"Thank you for your concern and your prayers." Caitlin stood, walking over to the window. "So many people are praying. I only hope that God hears them."

"I am sure He does." Mr. Barclay stood. "Am I to assume that the rest of the remodeling is on hold until Mr. Cade is back home?"

"Aye. I have no other choice. I cannot possibly concentrate right now." Her smooth brow furrowed with worry and regret, for she truly wished to have the entire house completed soon.

"If it would not be too forward of me, I would like to make a suggestion."

"But of course."

"I have worked with you long enough that I believe I have your taste and style down. I believe I could do the game room in a style that you would find most acceptable." He walked closer, excitement dancing in his dark eyes. "And if you happen to not like the work, I would redo the room to your liking free of charge."

Caitlin's lips puckered and her brows drew together while she pondered his offer. "Mr. Barclay, I know that we had our differences in the beginning of this project. However, as we've worked together over the past weeks I have come to trust your judgment a great deal." She smiled. "But I fear I am the type of person who likes to control the situations around me."

"This I know." His smile seemed more like a leer. His thoughts went back to the first time they met and the awful things he had thought about her. Although, he had come to highly respect her in the last month. Her talent far exceeded most men in the area of remodeling. "However, I believe I can get the room done."

"I have no qualms about you redoing the game room. Every task I've given you has been completed with great craftsmanship and in a timely manner."

"Thank you, Mrs. Cade." His chest filled with pride once again. "If you entrust this task to me, I swear I will not let you down."

"It is a very generous offer."

He held his breath until she started to speak again.

"My plans for that room are slightly different than the previous rooms, however. I've done the rooms thus far on a more feminine basis. My husband, being a true gem, has allowed me extravagant leeway. But not every man is as sensitive to decorating style as Mr. Cade. Therefore I want the game room masculine enough for the men, and yet, stylish enough to hold the ladies' attention."

"Yes … yes. I get the picture. Perhaps shades of brown and tans." Mr. Barclay started to envision the room. "With leather upholstery."

"Aye, but not too many dark colors. That would make the room depressing. We still need slashes of bright colors to liven things up."

"Perhaps a red, or royal blue upholstery on the chairs."

"And the curtains on the window must match the color on the chairs."

"Yes, of course."

"Very well, then. You may get started, and I shall attend to my husband's needs."

"Thank you, Mrs. Cade." He shook her hand vigorously.

"And just what do ye think yer doing?" Martha huffed. "The lady of the house is not to be in the kitchen."

"But I need something to do or I will go mad." Caitlin wiped the flour off her hands using the edge of the apron.

"I understand the feeling, but you must be able to find something else more ladylike to take yer mind off yer troubles."

"I already tried my stitching and pricked my finger five times." She pushed a few red locks back under the blue cottage cap. "I've never very good at needlepoint even when I have full concentration. Now that my mind is full of worry over Dillon, I fear I cannot handle the hoop at all."

"If'n yer mind is full of worry, you best be sittin' down with the Good Book and read for a while. God doesn't like us worrying over things that are in His control."

"I know," Caitlin sighed and then went back to kneading the dough. "I did try to read, but I needed something to do with my hands so I made a batch of scones."

"I know you are having a hard time with this situation. However, you must give it over to the Lord. He will direct you in what to do."

"You just want me directed out of your kitchen." Caitlin smiled warmly. Martha's advice was good and should be heeded. She must learn how to rely on God.

"I ain't saying that," Martha laughed. "Although you are in the way."

Caitlin piled the dough in a circle on the baking dish. "There now I'll leave this to you to finish baking, and I'll go read my Bible for a space."

"I would suggest you clean up a bit first. It looks like a bag a flour exploded on you."

"I never said I was an efficient cook." Caitlin washed her hands in the basin.

"Mrs. Cade, there you are." A chambermaid entered the kitchen. "I have been looking all over the house for you." She rushed on breathlessly. "First I searched in the game room, but Mr. Barclay had not seen you all day. Then, I looked upstairs but to no avail."

"Calm down." Caitlin laughed at the urgency in her tone. "You have found me now. Whatever is the matter?"

"Ma'am, you have company."

"'Tis a little late for a morning caller." Caitlin took off the apron and handed it to Martha, a cloud of flour spilling into the air.

"'Tis Lord and Lady Cade, ma'am."

"But I sent the stable boys out this morning and they came back saying that no ships had docked from England."

"Apparently the ship was later."

Caitlin followed the servant to the sitting room. "Mary, you run along and get some tea and sweet treats for us, please."

"Yes, ma'am."

Caitlin fidgeted with her cottage cap and tried dusting off more flour from the front of her gown. Taking a deep breath, she stepped into the parlor. "Mr. and Mrs. Cade, I'm sorry to have kept you waiting, but…"

"You will address us as Lord and Lady Cade, young lady." Bernadine Cade drew up to her full height, making her tall, thin frame tower over the other occupants. "And I have no need to speak to another maidservant. I wish to address the master of the house." Her shrill voice went on. "I dare say, Roderick, it is so hard to find good help, especially in this Godforsaken country."

"I assure you, *Lady* Cade, that God has not forsaken this country or any other. As the Bible clearly states 'I will never leave thee, nor forsake thee'." Caitlin smiled tightly. "As for the hired help, I can attest to the fact that we have the most capable staff around."

"How dare you speak to me that way!" Her thin crow like nose elevated several notches. "If you were my servant I would have you horse whipped for being so disrespectful."

"'Tis a good thing I am not your servant." Caitlin tried to be respectful but she'd already developed a strong dislike for Bernadine Cade. She had hoped that a personal meeting would alleviate some of that tension. Obviously not! "As for how Dillon and I handle the servants, that is our concern. 'Twould be greatly appreciated if you kept your opinions to yourself."

The deep intake of Bernadine's breath was released with a louder gasp. "I don't believe it! Dillon has gone and married a scullery maid." She smoothed some loose, black tendrils into place.

Caitlin wiped at the front of her gown before nerving herself to take a few steps closer. The rustle of her gosslin gown preceeded her outstretched hand. "I'm Caitlin Cade. Pleased to meet you, sir." She pasted a smile on her face. "I am sorry about my appearance. I was not expecting company, and decided to help out in the kitchen."

Lord Roderick Cade's laughter was the last thing Caitlin expected. His hearty laugh reminded her of Dillon, as did his deep-set brown eyes. Other than that, the similarities stopped. He stood several inches taller than Dillon but had added extra pounds to his frame. His short cropped hair, thick eyebrows, and bushy sideburns were whiter than the snow. His face was much rounder with jagged angles, whereas Dillon had a softer, more oval face. Nonetheless, Roderick was very handsome for a man of fifty-plus years.

"'Tis a pleasure to meet you." His handshake was firm. "I apologize for the intrusion. We should have had the foresight to send a missive telling you we had arrived."

"'Tis no intrusion at all, my lord." Caitlin felt the need to curtsey. Roderick had a very masculine, commanding presence that demanded respect.

"Only unexpected." He winked. The lines and wrinkles fanning out from his eyes deepened.

"'Tis a most pleasant surprise." Caitlin smiled, and fidgeted with her blue dress.

"How very charming, no wonder my son hastened to marry you." The sincere compliment brought a blush to her cheeks.

"Hogwash." Bernadine Cade crossed her arms under her small chest. "There is only one reason to rush into marriage." Her small, blue eyes were hard and penetrating. "Especially when someone of the lower class is trying to snare a husband of such wealth."

"I can assure you, Mrs. Cade, that I was not out to snare any type of a husband. Dillon and my father arranged this marriage." Caitlin held her gaze.

Bernadine stiffened at the causal address. The insult of someone of lowly birth not giving her the rightful title she deserved hit like a slap. "I will get the truth out of Dillon. Where is he?"

"I regret to inform you that he is confined at the moment."

"What do you mean?" Bernadine advanced like a raging bull. "What have you done with my son?"

Caitlin held her ground, neither showing fear nor yielding to the contempt and disdain of her guest. "I have done nothing with him. Dillon has been arrested."

"For what?" Roderick's bushy white brows rose in surprise.

"Treason, sir." Caitlin demurely folded her hands in front of her blue gown.

"How did you manage that, you little twit!" Bernadine's eyes blazed hotter than a fire. "Where is my son?" Bernadine raised her hand to slap Caitlin. "I will beat the truth out of you."

"'Tis enough," Roderick snarled. "If you want people to treat you like a lady, then try acting like one." Stepping between the women, he maneuvered Caitlin to a chair. "Now, sit down and tell me the whole story."

Bernadine's anger rose even more. *How dare my own husband take her side!* she silently seethed.

"The audacity of the little nitwit," she grumbled to herself. "I will have her gone before we sail for England."

Dillon sat on the cot, his back up against the hard wood wall. He strained in the dim light trying to read the book of Psalms, but not even passages of comfort were helping him right now.

He knew God had a reason for everything. He had told Caitlin the very same thing in an effort to help her overcome doubts. Those words now seemed hollow in the dreariness of the jail cell. His faith was being tested, and he wondered if he had the strength to overcome his own fears.

'Be of good courage, and he shall strengthen your heart, all you that hope in the Lord.' The words from Psalm 31 leapt off the page, smacking his heart with the truth.

He flipped to Proverbs 3 and read, "Trust in the Lord with all your heart; and lean not unto your own understanding. In all the ways acknowledge him and he shall direct your path."

Suddenly the enormity of God overwhelmed him. Surely the Creator of the universe wasn't too small to help him with his problem. He only had to trust in God's promises. Dillon bowed his head and prayed out loud.

"Oh, Lord, please forgive me for my unfaithfulness. Help me to trust in You. Deliver me from my troubles. And may Your name be blessed as my enemies are trampled under your foot. Please be with Caitlin and give her strength as well. I miss her, Lord. Watch over her and keep her protected from harm. I pray that it is your will to release me soon. But if not, give me the strength I need. As Jesus once prayed, 'Not my will, but your will be done.' I now find myself in the same predicament. I pray the same prayer. In your name, Amen."

"Dillon." The soft, angelic voice floated down the corridor, penetrating through the iron bars.

He couldn't believe his ears. Surely that wasn't Caitlin's voice. His imagination must be playing tricks on him. He'd been cooped up for days with nothing but his thoughts and a Bible to keep him company. The only time he saw the sheriff was when he brought his meager meals. Being left alone with only visions of his beautiful wife running unending through his mind must have taken its toll. Now the visions were becoming audible.

"Dillon. Oh, my love." Caitlin rushed to the bars, and gasped when she saw him on the floor. "Are you hurt?"

He knelt on the floor, staring up at her. "Caitlin?"

Standing, he rushed to where she stood. Reaching through the bars, he touched her hands, feeling their warmth.

'Tis not a dream." He smiled. "You are here."

"Of course I'm here, you silly goose. I am working on getting you out."

"The Lord answered that prayer quickly. I didn't even have time to get up off the floor."

"Is that what you were doing? I felt faint when I saw you. I thought they had beaten you or something."

"Nay, my pet. I am fine. Just missing you like crazy."

"I have been out of my mind with worry. Dillon, what are we going to do?"

"Do not fret. The Lord will provide."

"They are holding you because of the article I wrote. I'm responsible for you being here." Tears shimmered in her eyes.

"Do not say that again. And, do not ever admit to writing that piece. You are not to blame. I have done nothing wrong."

"I'm so afraid. What if they find you guilty of treason?" Caitlin dabbed at the tears rolling down her cheek. "I shall go mad if I have to spend another night apart from you."

"I seem to recall a time when that would have suited you quite well." Dillon smiled, but the playful tone didn't fit the mood.

"Stop teasing me, you cad."

"I am sorry, my dear. I know you are distraught. But I have faith that God will work things out." He reached through the bars and wiped a tear away.

"Oh, Dillon," she cried. "How can your faith be so strong when you are being treated unfairly?"

"It was not that strong a while ago. But, then, I remembered how Jesus suffered unfairly, and how it was all part of God's plan. Should I not have complete trust in the Lord of the world? In the Lord who created everything including us?"

"It has been so hard to keep the faith."

"I know; we are being tested. The only thing left to do is decide if we are going to pass the test or fail it."

"You have never failed at anything in your life," Caitlin sniffed.

"Neither have you. I believe your faith is stronger than you give yourself credit for."

"I just want you home." She put her arms through the bars and embraced Dillon as best as she could.

"I want that also." Dillon kissed her. "I have missed you terribly."

"You need a shave." Reaching up she cupped his face with her hands. The five day stubble scratched her palms. "And a brush for that hair."

"I must look a fright while you look like an angel."

"I never picture angels wearing pink." Cocking her head to the side, she let the pink plume in her bonnet tickle his chin.

"Angels come in many shapes and colors." He plucked the feather out.

"Dillon Cade! You ruined my hat."

"You were teasing me, madam."

"That gives you no right to destroy my property."

"I will buy you another hat when I get out."

"You better."

"I better buy you a new hat? Or I better get out of here?"

"Both." She kissed him again and tried to snuggle into his embrace, but the iron bars stood in the way. "I only hope your father will be able to convince the judge of your innocence."

"What?" Dillon pulled back. "My father?"

"He arrived two days ago and has been working with a lawyer from my father's office."

"How did he know?"

"I believe they were already en route here."

"They?"

"Aye. Your stepmother accompanied him."

He threw his hands up in surrender. "I prefer to stay in jail than face the two of them."

"Why, Dillon Cade! That is the rudest comment I have ever heard, especially after we have come all this way to visit you." Bernadine's shrill pitch grated on his nerves. "Do you have any idea at all of what I went through on the trip here?"

"I do not care."

"Well, I can see that the time spent in this dense town has done nothing to improve your rude behavior." She pushed a few pins back into her black hair, and straightened her brown and white hat. "Just look at my new hat. It is all bent out of shape from the awful trip. The feathers are ruined and it won't sit correctly on top of my head."

"That is a hat? I thought a rooster was resting on top of your head."

"How dare you!" Her chest puffed out. "You were brought up with better manners than that."

"I have more important things on my mind right now than your hat."

"Of course you do." The brown silk of her gown rustled as she neared the cell. "Now, where is a kiss for your mother?" She pressed her cheek close to the bars.

"You are not my mother." Dillon fought the urge to slap the offered cheek.

"Perhaps not biologically, but I raised you." Hurt etched her thin, pointed features.

"I was almost grown when you married my father. 'Twas only four years I lived with you before I moved here."

"But I have been there for you, and I have come all this way to see you."

"You have only come to meddle in my life, and I will not stand for it."

"Any advice I give is only for your protection. Why are you treating me like I'm the enemy?"

"I have no need of advice from you. I stated that in my last letter." Dillon protectively slid his hand through the bars and around Caitlin's waist. "Caitlin and I are married and there is nothing you can do about it."

We'll see about that. Bernadine stiffened. She didn't like his new little wife, and was determined to split them up. "Why, Dillon, you make me sound so cold and calculating. Perhaps your father and I only came to help."

Dillon quirked his eyebrow. "Perhaps."

The entrance of Roderick with Sheriff Edward halted further comment. The sheriff unceremoniously put the metal key into the lock. Dillon's breath froze as the clang of metal resounded through the small space. Only when the lock clicked open did he breathe again.

"You are free to leave, for the moment," Sheriff Edward stressed the word moment. "But I will have you locked up for good."

"You have no grounds on which to arrest him," Roderick stated. "Even the judge agreed with us."

"For the moment." His black mustache twitched. "But I am watching."

"You can watch me leave." Dillon stepped through the open door.

Caitlin rushed into his embrace. It felt so good to hold him without the hard, cold bars in the way. "Dillon, you are free to come home."

He kissed her briefly, then turned to his father. "Sir, I do not know what to say." He held out his hand. Dillon felt unsure of what to say or do. Although this man had fathered him, he was still a stranger. He had no warm or fond memories of him. Roderick had always been a distant figure in his life, much the same as a trustworthy servant.

Roderick shook Dillon's hand. "Shall we go, son?" He clasped him on the shoulder and said, "I am eager to see your town and your printing shop."

Bernadine looked on, feeling quite miffed. It seemed everyone else was getting Dillon's attention. He spared not one second for her. *The ungrateful little snob!* However, Bernadine Cade was not one to be put off. Pushing her way through the small crowd, she rubbed up against Dillon, cooing softly, "'Tis so good to see you, son."

With the woman clinging to his neck, he had no alternative except to give her a brief hug, which led to her accidentally rubbing her chest against him.

"The horrible trip was worth it now that I have seen your handsome face." Her fake delightful expression turned sultry as she squeezed his biceps. "My, how much you have grown."

"And how you have not changed." Dillon yanked his arm away. He then looked at his father who was talking with Caitlin and missed the whole exchange. "I need some air."

Dillon squinted against the bright sunlight. The frosty air nipped at his nose and ears. Inhaling deeply he relished the cool, clean and fresh scent of the outdoors. "It feels wonderful to be free."

"'Tis wonderful to hold you again." Caitlin snuggled into the crook of his arm.

"Come now, shall we find somewhere to dine?" Bernadine slipped her arm through Dillon's other arm. She wasn't about to let Caitlin hold all of his attention.

Dillon felt like tugging his arm away, but could not do so without causing a scene.

"If you don't mind, I prefer to go straight home."

"'Tis such a long trip, and we need nourishment to continue. Besides, I can tell you have not eaten properly." Bernadine rubbed her hand over his stomach. "No meat on you at all."

"Surely Martha 'twill have a large feast prepared at home. Besides I am not exactly dressed for dinner." Dillon groaned inwardly. He hated having her hands on him. To the casual observer Bernadine was merely making motherly contact. Only Dillon knew what her true intentions were.

"I am a bit on the hungry side also." Caitlin smiled up at him with pleading eyes. "'Twas a long trip here. Besides, the only one you need to look handsome for is me. And I am pleased with your appearance just as you are."

"A short pause to sup will not hurt anything," Roderick commented.

"It seems I am outnumbered."

"Let us sup at the tavern over there." Roderick pointed to the wood building down the street. "I doubt anyone there will care about your appearance. We will be on our way in no time at all."

"That old building does not look fit for a lady," Bernadine whined. "Can we not find someplace more suitable?"

"Nay. We will eat there or not eat at all." Dillon's tone was brittle. "Sir, 'twill give you time to explain how you happened to be here and what role you played in my freedom."

"'Twas nothing really." Roderick laughed. "Your lawyer had things under control."

"Hogwash!" Bernadine sputtered. "You threatened that judge with your influence in the House of Lords. If not for the fact that your father is from nobility, you would still be imprisoned."

Caitlin gasped out loud, "I had no idea you were from the English Parliament. Why, you are the very body that makes the laws of England."

"'Tis true. However I am a normal man." Slapping Dillon on the back, he added, "Must be why my son never mentioned it to you."

"I believe, sir, he did not make mention of it because of my loathing the English. The fact that you and I are on opposite sides of how to handle Ireland can only lead to adversity."

Bernadine smiled triumphantly. She would not have to do a thing to break up this marriage. The Irish bogtrotter was going to do it all on her own. "I dare say, I have never heard such disrespect in all my life." Bernadine started to swoon and clutched Dillon's arm even tighter.

"Nonsense!" Roderick's sharp tone shot through the icy air. "It is not disrespectful to have a difference of opinions. We hardly ever agree on anything in the Parliament. 'Tis natural for people to see things differently. Problems only arise when people are too stubborn to discuss things rationally." Gently touching her arm, he steered her down the street. "Now, my dear, why not enlighten me on your opinion of this Irish uprising."

"That, sir, could be much more than you are capable of handling." Dillon laughed. "The quality I love most about my wife is her spirit." Dillon followed behind with Bernadine attached to his arm like a leech.

"I look forward to the challenge." He patted Caitlin's hand, which rested in the crook of his arm.

Cocking her head, Caitlin smiled sweetly. "If you two do not stop talking about me as if I were not here, I shall knock you both in the noodle."

"Disgraceful." Bernadine muttered under her breath.

Caitlin figured since she now had the undivided attention of a member of the House of Lords, that she may as well take full advantage of the situation. "Lord Cade, I cannot comprehend how any person could possibly see an advantage of holding another person against their will?"

"'Tis not England's stand to hold anyone hostage

"Then why do you fight against us? Why not let Ireland be free to make her own choices?"

"First of all, Ireland is part of our country. 'Tis like your arm being part of your body. If you cut off your arm, it would be no good. The same principle applies with land. If Ireland were to separate, they would struggle economically."

"'Tis not economics that we struggle against. 'Tis the Catholic Church."

"Dear God, she is a heathen also." Bernadine faltered forcing Dillon to support her. "What have you done, Dillon? Why have you married this …this, thing?" She waved her handkerchief at Caitlin.

Dillon disentangled his arm from her, hoping she would fall. But she managed to catch her balance, glaring at Dillon. "You treat my wife with the utmost respect or be gone from here." Taking his stance with arms behind his back he stated, "I am no longer Catholic, either. Most people are Protestants here. They are just as God-fearing as you, if not more so." He glared at his stepmother.

"'Tis not only the church we fight against. In principle, Ireland has as much right as any other land to be free. We deserve to make our own decisions. America fought for freedom and is doing just fine. These colonies have not suffered at all since getting out from under England's thumb." Caitlin's pace quickened as she talked.

"My dear, I fear I am an old man. I pray you take pity on me and slow your pace." Roderick had tried to keep up with her steps, but was now out of breath. "If you continue at this pace, I may never catch enough breath to refute your comments."

"I am truly sorry, sir." Caitlin stopped, allowing the rest of the group to catch up. "I had not realized that I was walking so fast." Her cheeks flushed red, partly from the wind, and partly from embarrassment. "I forget to pay attention when I ramble on so."

"'Tis no problem at all." Dillon kissed the tip of her nose as he drew up alongside her.

Caitlin smiled, silently thanking him for the support.

"No problem at all." Roderick agreed, a bit breathlessly. "I have not had such a spirit-filled debate in years. I fear all us old men are getting too tired to fight anymore."

"Sir, you are far from old." Sincerity brightened her green eyes.

Roderick laughed. "You and I are going to get along famously, even if we are on opposite sides of this war." He held out his arm for Caitlin. "Besides, we are now family."

"Aye." Caitlin smiled, placing her hand on his arm. She was now sandwiched between her husband and father-in-law. Nothing could have made her more content except her own family returning someday.

The three of them walked on leaving Bernadine to follow behind, her anger seething at being left out. Her hatred of Caitlin intensified, and the loathing of her husband continued. She wished the old goat would have a heart attack.

If not for needing his help in ridding the family of that Irish riffraff, she would have done away with Roderick on the boat. She contemplated the ship ride home. After Roderick helped talk Dillon into divorcing the white trash, she could still arrange a little accident. Then she would be free of his sniveling, miserly hand, leaving her and Dillon together, comforting each other.

"Oh, victory would taste so sweet," she muttered to herself.

Chapter 16

Dillon rubbed his hand over Caitlin's shoulder and down her arm. He loved the feel of her soft, smooth skin. "I could touch you all night long and never get enough." He planted a kiss on her bare shoulder.

"Perchance, do you think we could add a kiss or two?"

"Aye, my love, whatever pleases you." He captured her lips with his.

"I did miss you so," she murmured against his lips. "Promise, you will never leave me again."

"I cannot make a promise I don't know I can keep. But, 'tis a promise that I will never stop loving you. If I go, 'twill be by force." His eyes were serious, making him look older.

"Can you not lie to me just this once to make me feel better?" Caitlin pouted.

"What kind of trust would that build between us? I only want honesty in our marriage. That is how God designed marriage. Any untruth would not only undermine our relationship, but would be a sin against God."

"'Tis true, I know." Caitlin sat up, propping herself against the pillows. "I just wish sometimes that we could live a normal life. We have not had much normalcy in our marriage."

"We have only been united for two and half months."

"'Tis all?" Her pink lips puckered. "Seems much longer."

Dillon couldn't resist kissing those puckered lips, "Perhaps because we are always fighting."

"Not always," she corrected with a grin.

Dillon quirked an eyebrow. "You are my temptress. I believe the Lord has sent you to torture me."

"Torture?" She slid closer, running her fingers through the dark hairs on his chest.

"Aye." He kissed her. "Sweet torture." His lips moved down the column of her throat. "I remember when this frightened you."

"'Twas not really intimacy that frightened me. 'Twas giving my heart to another person. I was most frightened by the thought of giving up who I was."

Dillon stopped kissing her. Looking into her emerald eyes he asked, "Does that still frighten you?"

"Not with you as my husband," she confessed. "You have shown me that I can be someone's wife and still be me also."

"I would not want you any other way." He kissed her forehead. "I do believe that a comment like that shows maturity, or that the Lord has been working in your heart."

"Perhaps a bit of both." She started planting kisses on his chest.

"I also believe you would be bored to death in a normal marriage. You, my love, thrive on controversy."

"Perhaps the old Caitlin did." Her tone turned serious, and eyes misted. "However, we have dealt with one upheaval after another. The new Caitlin wants only to settle down in a boring routine and grow old together."

"I fear that will never be possible."

"Why?"

"Because when the children come along, our lives will grow even more hectic and be more disheveled than now."

"But they will grow up." She kissed him, reveling in the tenderness he possessed. "Then we will be alone."

"'Tis when the grandchildren come along."

She smacked his shoulder. "If you do not wish to be alone with me, then why did you marry me?"

He caught her wrist in his hand, bringing it to his mouth where he softly bestowed kisses across her knuckles. "Because we could not do this until we were married." He smiled, mischievously. "Or this." He kissed her. Slow at first then more passionately. "Or this." His soft breath slid across her delicate skin as he placed kisses over her shoulders and chest. "Besides, there is one advantage to quarreling."

"Pray tell?"

"Making up." His brows arched playfully over his dark eyes.

"You are a cad!" She teasingly pushed him away before surrendering to the passion he brought to life.

"I do declare, Martha, how are we ever going to eat all this?" Caitlin studied the sideboard overflowing with everything from hoe cakes, eggs, fried potatoes and oatmeal to sausage, bacon and a whole ham. The usual toast, biscuits and scones were present with butter, honey, molasses, and strawberry preserves.

"I figured ye would be needing your strength." She ladled the grits into a ceramic serving bowl.

"Oyster stuffing." Caitlin's brows arched. "Since when is that served for the morning meal?"

"'Tis master Dillon's favorite."

"You spoil me, Martha." Dillon slipped up behind the women. He almost felt like an intruder. He'd been watching them talking for several minutes. They certainly were getting along better. His life seemed to be falling into place. If only he could get rid of his parents quickly and stay out of jail, his life would be perfect.

A commotion of voices drew their attention to the entryway. Bernadine stopped short at the sight of Dillon with his arms around Caitlin. He looked so happy with her. How would she ever break them apart? "Such public displays of attention are inappropriate."

Dillon's good-natured humor evaporated like steam off boiling water. "We are not in public. We are in my home— where you are intruding."

"Well, I never would have thought you capable of so much disrespect." Her pointed nose elevated as she crossed the room in a graceful sweep of black velvet. The black hat, trimmed with jewels, sat perched atop her head like a crown. Her raven tresses were pulled back in the chignon so tight that her face looked like a snake. "Why do you think we traveled all this way, if not to spend time with you?"

Dillon bit his tongue, not wanting to start a debate over the real reasons she had come. "Is there something I can do for you?"

"How about offering some hospitality?"

"If you want to visit, that's fine, but mind your manners."

"I am not the one in need of manners." Her posture stiffened even more. Taking in Caitlin's white gauze morning dress and cottage cap, she added, "And you might try putting on some respectable clothing."

"'Tis nothing wrong with my clothing." Caitlin's temper flared to life. "I am wearing proper morning dress."

"I have seen fancier night gowns than that rag you are wearing."

"Just because I do not parade around in jewels, and fancy material, does not mean I am any less of a person than you. At least I follow the proper decorum of the dress code." Caitlin crossed her arms, elevating her nose in mockery of Bernadine. "I am not the one wearing an evening gown in the morning."

"'Tis almost noon," Bernadine righteously informed them. "And I have never been one to dress cheaply. There is nothing wrong with looking your best, no matter what time of day it is."

"I would rather look cheap than walking around looking like I'm in mourning."

"Hogwash!" She advanced toward Caitlin with her fist raised. "I will show you mourning."

Dillon stepped in front of Caitlin, taking the blow to his chest.

"Bernadine, stop it!" Roderick shouted.

Dillon grabbed her wrist. It took every ounce of self-control not to squeeze it hard enough to break it. "Do not *ever* touch my wife or speak to her in that manner again."

"Did you hear her, Roderick? Did you hear what that Irish trash said about me?" Tears flowed down her cheeks. Some from anger. Some from pain.

"You started it." Roderick's tone was indifferent. "If you would learn to keep your mouth closed, people wouldn't get so upset with you."

Finally freeing her hand, Bernadine glared at her husband with stone-cold eyes. She was tired of him never taking her side. Never defending her. His indifferent attitude had gone beyond annoying and now bordered on animosity. "'Tis a sad day when a husband is too feeble to defend his own wife."

"If his wife were ever in the right, he might try defending her. I do not defend the guilty."

"I need a chair. I feel as though I shall faint." Bernadine swooned, but no one came to her rescue.

"There is a chair over by the table." Dillon nodded his head, but never moved from his spot to offer assistance.

Giving up the act, Bernadine stopped swooning and stalked to the nearest chair, only to take up the act once more. Leaning back in the chair, she put her arm across her forehead and moaned, "I need some water. The room is spinning."

Roderick knew the storm brewing now would be unleashed on him later. Sighing he filled a goblet and took it to her hoping to at least lessen the vicious attack she would bestow upon him.

She took the water, glaring at him, but since they were in the presence of others, she managed a very tight-lipped, "Thank you."

The awkward tension drew tighter than a pair of new leather boots. Dillon decided that if he ever wanted to eat his meal while it was warm, he'd better do something.

"We were just about to partake of the morning meal. Would you care to join us?" he offered.

"'Tis a bit late for the morning meal." Bernadine noted. "In my household the morning meal is served promptly at seven."

"Then kept warm for you until you roll out of bed sometime past noon." Roderick knew angering her more was treacherous territory, but he was determined to defend his only son.

"That is hogwash and you know it," she yelled. "You no-good, lousy, self-righteous, pompous, old man."

"Careful, my dear, they may be family, but they are still witnesses." Roderick had become accustomed to the loathing in her eyes. She only managed to tolerate him while in the company of others. Then she'd put on the show of her life, acting the part of a loving, dutiful wife. However, it seemed lately that not even the attendance of guests could keep the contempt out of her attitude.

"If you do not mind, son, I am famished. We have not had our morning meal, and it smells absolutely delicious."

"As you can see there is more than enough." Dillon took a plate and started filling it. Caitlin and Roderick followed. When hunger finally won out, Bernadine got up and fixed a plate also.

They were all seated and enjoying the meal when Martha bustled in. "'Tis about time you all stopped arguing and started eating. The food is growing cold."

Bernadine waited for someone to reprimand this servant. When no one said anything, she felt it her rightful duty to put the help in their proper place. "No servant in my household would dare speak so freely. 'Tis disrespectful for someone of such lowly birth to project themselves at the same level as us."

"Seems to me God created us all equal. 'Tis what the constitution says." Martha folded her large arms under her chest, daring Miss High and Mighty to say another word.

"Bernadine can you hold your tongue for five minutes and allow us to eat in peace!" Roderick's temper reached the boiling point. His wife's attitude lately had grown unbearable. He couldn't take much more.

"If we are to stay here then things must be run properly. I will not dwell in a household where servants say and do as they please."

The clang of silverware hitting the china plate resounded through the room.

"Stay here?" Caitlin had been silent, allowing Dillon to deal with his stepmother, but she managed to find her voice before Dillon who looked stunned.

"'Tis customary to stay with the relatives you have traveled to visit. How else do you expect us to have time together?" Placing a gloved hand across the table, she squeezed Caitlin's hand in a friendly gesture and smiled. "Don't worry, dear, 'tis not your fault you do not know how to run a household. I will teach you while I'm here."

"Caitlin runs the household magnificently and needs no help from you." Dillon cleared his throat. "So you might as well stay at the inn. You would be more comfortable there."

"What?" Bernadine's mouth fell open. "You are not offering us a place to stay?" She shook her head in disbelief. The black plumes of her hat waving a mournful rhythm. "What has the world come to when your own kin won't offer hospitality? Especially after all you have done for him, Roderick."

Dillon rolled his eyes, groaning. "The fact of the matter is you were not invited. You took it upon yourself to come without any warning."

"It had been too many years since we have seen you," she explained, coolly. "And we did send word. It arrived several days ahead of us, but you were not here to receive it. You can ask Caitlin if you like."

"We are remodeling, and the house is a mess. No bedrooms are prepared." Dillon looked straight at Bernadine. "Perhaps if we had had *sufficient* notice, we would have had time to prepare."

Bernadine arched a finely tapered, raven brow. "We did not know it would be so burdensome for you." She sighed, deciding to play the poor downtrodden victim. "We were in such a hurry to see you and find out how you were getting along that I did not think ahead."

"'Tis no problem to stay at the inn," Roderick suggested. "We have quite imposed ourselves on you as it is."

"Nonsense. You may stay here for as long as you wish." Caitlin surprised everyone.

"But we have no rooms ready," Dillon persisted. Bewilderment creased his forehead.

"I am sure Mr. Barclay can stop working on the game room and prepare a bedroom rather quickly."

"That seems like a lot of trouble. 'Twould be much easier to stay where we are," Roderick insisted. "Besides you would have to prepare two bedrooms."

"Hogwash." Bernadine laughed. "I do believe that I can endure your snoring for a short period of time." She wanted to appear as a happy, devoted couple. Perhaps that would spike Dillon's jealousy.

"I do not believe it will be possible." Dillon stood firm.

"Why not?" Caitlin asked.

"Would you two mind if I have a private word with my wife?" Dillon stood.

"Not at all." Bernadine tasted victory. She knew the power of persuasion that woman had over men. Caitlin would have him eating out of her hand. Then she would be living under the same roof with Dillon. Soon she would have him eating out of the palm of her own hand. That image alone excited her more than any lover she'd ever had.

"Caitlin, are you crazy? I do not want that woman in this house."

"What about your father? Would you not like to spend some time with him?"

"My father never had time for me when I was growing up. Why should I care now?"

"Because you are a kind, caring person, and whether you want to admit it or not, you do love him."

"'Tis not like we would have much time alone anyway. You forget that Bernadine comes with the package. She will make life more miserable than you can imagine. What you have witnessed so far is only the start."

"Leave her to me. You forget, sir, that I can handle myself."

"Not when it comes to Bernadine." Dillon placed his hands on her shoulders, forcing her to look him in the eyes. "She has only one purpose for being here. That is to destroy us. She wants our marriage annulled."

"I know what her plan is. However, I have strength in our love. God has brought us together, and you said yourself that only death will tear us apart."

"It would not be beneath her if she tried that. She is a woman who goes after what she wants full force. There is no stopping her."

"Come, Dillon." Caitlin smiled. "She will be a headache, no doubt, but I can handle the insults and swiftly give some back. I guess the question is do you believe our love is strong enough to last?"

"'Tis not a question of our love." Dillon stared into her eyes. "I do not want you to be subjected to her. She is the devil."

"'Tis sweet that you worry about me." She reached up on tiptoes and pecked his cheek. "However, if she truly is possessed by the devil, then is it not our Christian duty to show her love? Perhaps that will chase the demons away." Crossing her arms, she added, "Is that not what Jesus did? The Bible commands us to love our enemies and pray for them. Besides, we are talking about your own flesh and blood."

"I left England to get away from her." Dillon sighed. "I hate when you use the Bible against me."

"'Tis because I am right, and you do not want to admit it." She smiled, knowing she'd won.

"You are sure you want this?" Dillon gave her one last chance to back out. "Bernadine is spiteful, deceiving, temperamental and obnoxious."

"You forgot controlling, self-absorbed, self-centered and hurtful." Reaching up, Caitlin cupped his cheek. "But I will endure it all for the chance to visit with the man who sired my husband."

"My father is English, and the two of you are on opposite sides of this war."

"You forget that you are English also." Caitlin arched her rust brows, playfully. "And he is still your father. Besides, what better chance will I ever have of helping Ireland? I will be able to debate and possibly persuade him onto our side."

Dillon laughed. "That, my dear, will never happen. He is very stubborn."

"Just think of all the fun it will be trying." Mischief glimmered in her eyes.

Dillon drew her fingers to his lips, placing a soft kiss on them. "If it means that much to you, I will abide by your wishes."

"Thank you." She threw her arms around his neck, drawing his head down to hers. With enthusiasm she kissed him.

"If that is how I am to be rewarded, I shall give in to your demands more often."

They entered the dining room and told the Lord and Lady Cade the good news. Everyone resumed eating; Dillon with relish. It had been a week since he'd had a good meal. "I did miss Martha's cooking while I was in jail." He got a second plateful.

"I believe she missed you just as much," Caitlin informed him. "I fear I was a dreadful dinner companion by myself. I could hardly eat a thing I was so worried about you."

"No more fretting, I am home now." Dillon leaned over giving her a kiss.

"Honestly, Can you two not show proper respect?" Bernadine's rivalry increased. She hated watching him kiss Caitlin all the time. "Such attentions should be displayed in the privacy of the bedroom, not at the table with company present."

"Perhaps that is how you like things. But in this house we kiss where and when we want." Dillon lifted a brow. "If you cannot handle it then feel free to leave."

"Let them be," Roderick commanded. "They are newlyweds after all."

"I still cannot believe our son grew up into this untamed, disrespectful animal." Bernadine sadly shook her head. "It must be this desolate country that did it to him."

Dillon clenched his teeth so hard that the muscles in his face almost went into spasms. He didn't know why she kept insisting she was his mother.

"Excuse me. I did not know you were still eating." Mr. Barclay entered the room. "Mr. Cade it is very good to see you, sir."

"'Tis good to see you also, Mr. Barclay." Dillon stood and shook hands.

"Mr. Barclay." Caitlin gave him her brightest smile. "How is the game room coming along?"

"Very well, ma'am." He cleared his throat. "I see that you are busy. I will talk to you later."

"Wait, please." Caitlin came around the table and stood in front him. "I have an urgent matter and must speak with you at once."

"Oh." His round, beaded eyes lit up. "How may I be of assistance?"

"We have had an unexpected, but wonderful surprise."

"Besides the fact that Mr. Cade is home safely?" he inquired.

"Yes. That is an answered prayer, is it not?" She waved her hand to indicate Dillon's father. "This is Lord Roderick Cade, Dillon's father. And this is his wife Lady Bernadine."

Mr. Barclay nervously nodded to both of them. He had never been in the presence of nobility. "Good to meet you both."

"And this is the mastermind behind the remodeling. This house is being artfully transformed by his brilliant mind and hands."

"You are too kind, Mrs. Cade." He sheepishly looked down to the ground.

"Nonsense. You have done a remarkable job." Caitlin went on. "Lord and Lady Cade have traveled all the way from England." She paused for effect, also to let the news slowly dawn on him. "However, I fear we have not a spare bedroom ready. We cannot just stuff them into an empty, unfinished room, especially after they are accustomed to much finery in England."

"Oh, no. That would not do." Mr. Barclay shook his balding head.

Caitlin sighed. "I fear, 'twould be inhospitable to make them stay at the inn after they have come so far to visit with us."

"I agree. That does not seem right."

"But what am I to do?" Caitlin wrung her hands in helplessness.

Mr. Barclay looked deep in thought then said, "Perhaps we could ready a room for them."

"That would be wonderful." Caitlin brightened. "How long do you suppose it shall take?"

"We will have to stop work on the game room and focus our full attention on the bedroom. I have some wallpaper with me now. If you like one of the patterns, we will be able to finish the walls today."

"You are the most prepared man I know, next to my husband, of course." She smiled cleverly at Dillon.

"Thank you." His cheeks brightened. "As for the furniture, we will have to scout out the other bedroom and see what we can find." He nodded to Dillon, "with your permission, sir."

"Of course, whatever you need." Dillon waved his arm. "The entire house is at your disposal."

"Thank you, sir." Looking back at Caitlin he continued, "I would say maybe a day. Two at the most, and we should be able to move them in."

"'Tis wonderful!" Caitlin exclaimed. "I knew you would come up with the perfect plan."

"I will get started right away." He left without further ado.

Caitlin sat back down, smiling.

"Very well done." Dillon winked.

"Thank you."

"'Twas amazing how you made Mr. Barclay think that redoing the bedroom was his idea." Roderick applauded her. "The innocent, distressed act was beyond words."

"'Twas not really an act," she defended. "I have come to understand Mr. Barclay's personality. He works much better when the matter is his idea. When it comes from a woman, he rejects it simply because he does not feel it appropriate as a woman's job."

"And you are fine with that line of thinking?" Roderick asked. It seemed to him that her headstrong attitude would fight against the injustice.

"Not at first. But I soon learned that I got more work done by appealing to his sense of pride."

"And stroking his ego," Dillon added. "You have him trained like a puppy."

"I can swallow my pride in order to get the job done," Caitlin said resolutely.

"'Tis a good business head you have," Roderick commented.

Bernadine seethed in silence. She could not figure, for the life of her, why everyone jumped and applauded Caitlin for being deceiving, yet condemned her for the same thing.

The day went chaotically along. First, there was a trip into town, where everyone stopped and talked and caught Dillon up on the happenings of town while he had been incarcerated. It was amazing how much had happened in only five days.

Roderick's respect for his son had grown even more while watching the townspeople respond to him. Dillon was a pillar of the community, and everyone wanted his advice or opinion. The respect for their newspaper printer was evident in the handshakes and hugs.

A few folks had fawned over Lord and Lady Cade as if they were a king and queen, to the delight of Bernadine, but most people were more concerned for Dillon's welfare than the fact that the aristocracy were in their presence.

Roderick had worried about his son going off to a foreign land. He now saw that Dillon had made quite a nice life here. Norfolk was very different from England. The pace slower, and the people friendlier and more respectful. They may not have the high-society museums or theaters, but they made do and were happy with what little they did have.

The Social was the talk of the town. People wanted to know if Dillon and Caitlin were going. It would be their first official engagement since their wedding.

"I had forgotten all about that," Dillon admitted. "I do not think we will have time to ready for it."

"I must confess that I am pretty tired also." Caitlin hid a yawn behind her gloved hand. "We were planning on a quiet night alone."

Bernadine who'd walked around with a scowl most of the morning, perked up at the news of a dance. This would be her chance to shine, to show these backwoods locals how proper women dressed. She was tired of being ignored. These common folk had treated them as if they were ordinary people.

"Dillon, I would love to see how your town puts on a Social." Bernadine fluttered her eyelashes. "Besides, I bet you could use the company after being locked up for so long."

"I am truly tired." Dillon took his stance with arms locked behind his back. Caitlin knew no argument would win against that posture.

"Please," Bernadine begged. "It has been such a long trip, and I long for some company."

"'Tis why you are staying with us," Dillon mocked. "Caitlin and I will keep you company."

I long for acceptable company, she thought. "You still cannot deny a woman the right to dress in her best finery."

"Come, Dillon." His friend, Stanly smacked him on the back. "The town was denied the privilege of seeing yer wedding. You cannot deny us the opportunity of seeing the two of you together at the Social."

Their marriage was still the big talk around town. Maybe after the Social, people would have something better to discuss. "It really has been a trying a day, however I will leave the choice up to Caitlin."

Caitlin's shock registered plain as day. "I have not even thought about what to wear. Nothing is ready."

"Gowns do not matter. Besides you would look beautiful no matter what you wore." Stanly blushed. "Anyway you have guests that want to come. It would not be the same without you two."

"How kind." She smiled. "I suppose it would be rude not to allow our guests see what a grand Social our town can throw." She looked at Dillon.

"I guess we could make an appearance." Dillon slid his arm around her waist. "But you realize that you cannot dance with Caitlin, now that she is my wife."

Dillon was aware that Stanly, like many others, had been an admirer of Caitlin. Some courting her, and even proposing marriage. Just about every single man under the age of sixty had been drawn to the fair redhead. How he had become so lucky as to marry her was beyond his comprehension. He just thanked God daily.

"Well, I will just go and take a rest for a while." Bernadine smiled with excitement. "What time shall we meet you for dinner?"

"Mr. Barclay, have you eaten yet?" Dillon asked.
"No, sir. I wanted to finish as much as possible today."

"Are you not hungry? Martha made more food than we could possibly eat in an entire week." Dillon waved to the sideboard. "Since you and your men are taking on so much responsibility, I would suggest full stomachs to keep up your strength."

"'Tis very kind of you, but we have never eaten with our employers before."

"But I insist."

"Dillon," Bernadine intruded. "Let the man be." She used her most parental tone. She did not want to sit at the table with a bunch of cheapened workers. At least Mr. Barclay had the correct disposition.

Martha bustled into the room and caught the last of the conversation. "Mr. Barclay, you sit your scrawny little bottom down and have some of this here food. I didn't cook all day just to have it go to waste."

"But ... "

"Don't even try arguing. You start your plate. I'm gonna go get the rest of your men." She left before another word was spoken.

Dillon and Caitlin exchanged surprised looks. Mr. Barclay did as he was told and went to the sideboard to fill a plate.

"I do not understand why he let her boss him that way." Caitlin's brow creased with perplexity. "He hated it when I did the same thing."

"'Tis a difference of servitude, my love," Dillon explained. "You were trying to challenge a position he holds as a man's job. Martha is the cook. 'Tis a woman's job."

"I see your point, although I strongly disagree with your theory."

"What theory do you have?"

"I can assure you that Mr. Barclay is not likely to be bossed around by anyone, especially a woman." Her eyes creased in thought. "Mark my words something is up with the two of them."

Chapter 17

Caitlin surveyed her appearance in the mirror, remembering how frightened and angry she had been the first time she wore this dress. But, tonight was a grand celebration, and she had plenty to celebrate.

"I think you look more beautiful each time you wear that gown." Dillon stood behind her, watching as she scrutinized her appearance.

"Do you think it too much for the Social?"

"Perhaps. However, I enjoy seeing you in it. Besides, I did not have the honor of helping you out of it on our wedding night." Dillon wiggled his brows. "I plan on rectifying that tonight."

"You, sir, are still a rake." She swatted his hand away. "'Tis not for your pleasure that I am wearing this gown."

"Then whose?"

"I believe half of the town is still upset at not being invited to our wedding. Apparently 'twas the big event of the year." She fiddled with the silver brooch. "I just thought that maybe feelings might be appeased if they saw me in my wedding gown."

He kissed the tip of her nose. His heart swelling with love as he realized the maturity she had gained. Caitlin was developing from a young girl into a grown woman. "As long as that is the only reason you are all dressed up."

"Well," she confided, "I am trying to make a good impression on your parents."

"Do not try so hard. Bernadine will more than likely be upset that you upstaged her."

"What about your father?"

"Why are you trying to impress my father?" His tone turned serious.

"Why, Dillon Cade, if I didn't know better, I would swear you are jealous." She crossed her arms. "And of your own kin. 'Tis as absurd as being jealous of Mr. Jefferson."

"We do not need a repeat of Thomas's party." Dillon laughed but the tone was not entirely playful. Especially remembering the hangover he suffered the day after.

Caitlin still had trouble grasping how her husband could use such a casual address with a man as influential as Mr. Jefferson.

"'Tis only that I know how many men have admired you."

"Most of them mere boys, hardly worth the time of day, especially compared to you." Caitlin encircled his waist with her arms. "'Tis no other man in this town, or any other town for that matter, that I want."

"As there is no other woman for me." He kissed her slowly, deeply.

"We could skip the outing tonight." She played with knot of his cravat.

"You will hear no argument from me. 'Tis not my idea to go, I would like nothing more than to stay home with you."

"As much as I adore the thought, your parents are downstairs waiting for us."

"Spending the evening with Bernadine is going to be pure torture," Dillon grumbled.

"I do not relish the idea either, but perhaps events of the night will keep her occupied."

"We can only pray for that."

Henrietta fumed most of the night as she watched Dillon and Caitlin together. It seemed nothing she did to break them up worked. All she needed was one last chance to prove to Dillon that she could make him happy. She'd never be able to show him as long as Caitlin stood in the way.

"You know, dear, a lady looks much prettier with a smile on her face." Bernadine smiled, small lines fanning out from her eyes. "That frown does not become you."

"What does it matter anyway?" Henrietta sighed. "The man I want will never notice me."

"Perhaps not, but I see a handsome fellow watching you." Bernadine nodded to a tall stranger, standing across the room.

Henrietta gasped when she saw him head her way. She glanced around for a place to hide, but found none. Not wanting to make it obvious that she knew him, she hid her fear and smiled.

"May I have this dance?" The stranger bowed.

"I would love to, however, 'tis not proper to dance with someone I haven't been introduced to." Her smile was forced.

"Allow me to introduce myself." He stepped closer, whispering into her ear. "'Twould be in your best interest to dance with me so we can speak inconspicuously. Otherwise, people will wonder what business you have with the sheriff."

"Why, yes, Mr. Oliver, I'd like to dance with you." Raising her yellow skirt enough to not trip over it, she walked to the dance floor.

The band began a waltz. She stood rigid in his arms as they circled the floor. The smile she pasted on her face never left as they continued their conversation.

"Really, sheriff, I have no idea why you are here, or what we have to discuss."

"We had a bargain, remember."

"Of which you did not fulfill your end." Henrietta felt the eyes of the onlookers ogling her. She smiled even broader.

"I did arrest the traitor. 'Tis not my fault his lawyer and father convinced the judge to let him go."

"Pish-posh." She twirled around. "'Tis a poor excuse to be sure. What power could they have over the judge? Treason is a serious crime."

"Lord Cade has plenty of power in England. Although we have our own justice system, the judge wasn't about to make an enemy of England, especially with weak evidence."

"Dillon's father is nobility?" She couldn't conceal her surprise. "To think of all that wealth and power going to that Irish imp. It should be mine."

The sheriff grimaced as Henrietta missed a step, the heal of her slipper landing on top of his foot. "I will try to consider that an accident."

"'Twas, truly." She glanced around the dance floor and found Dillon twirling Caitlin. "How did she manage to pull this off?"

"If I were you, I'd consider spending less energy on them and concentrate on our arrangement before I tell the whole town who put me up to arresting the town hero."

"Don't be absurd. Dillon is hardly a hero, and I never put you up to anything." The golden specks in her hazel eyes may have added color but no warmth. "Besides, our deal was for you to arrest Caitlin, not Dillon."

The music ended. She curtsied saying loud enough for onlookers to hear, "Thank you for the dance, Mr. Oliver." Then whispered for his ears only. "I have nothing further to say to you. Stay away from me."

As she turned to leave, he grabbed her arm. "Don't play games with me." His face grew hard. "You won't like me when I'm angry."

The commotion drew the attention of several couples. "Have a pleasant evening, Mr. Oliver." With head held high, she walked off the dance floor. Seeking solitude to formulate a plan, she headed to the punch bowl.

Bernadine joined her. "I have yet the pleasure of meeting you." She extended her gloved hand. "I am Lady Bernadine Cade."

"Dillon's mother." Henrietta almost choked on the berry drink.

"Stepmother," she corrected.

"Lady Cade, I'm honored to meet you." She curtsied. "I'm Henrietta."

"I do not mean to pry, but you seemed to be having a problem with that gentleman."

"He's no gentleman," she sniffed. "He's the sheriff."

"How do you know him?"

"I don't really know him. I just felt rude not giving him one dance. He is much too old for me."

"I also couldn't help noticing the melancholy look you have worn this evening." Bernadine followed Henrietta's gaze as she watched Caitlin and Dillon talking with a group of people.

"Look at her. How can she manage to have the entire town wrapped around her finger?" Henrietta looked at Bernadine. "I am sorry. I did not mean to be unkind about your daughter-in-law."

"Do not trouble yourself about it." Bernadine sighed. "I have no soft spot for the Irish. I have been surveying the crowd and noticed several more suitable companions for Dillon, including you." Bernadine had noted the spark of envy in those hazel eyes. She understood the longing and knew firsthand the determination it took to get what you wanted. "You remind me a lot of myself when I was younger."

"I do?"

"I know how it feels to be in love with someone who never notices you." She inclined her purple-feathered hat to indicate Roderick. "When he was married to Dillon's mother, he barely knew I existed."

"I find that hard to believe," Henrietta gushed. "You are most beautiful, and surely the belle of every ball in your youth."

"How very kind." She smiled, delighting in the compliment. "'Tis true I had lots of suitors, just not the one I wanted."

"But you ended up with him."

"'Twas only through tragic circumstance that I landed Roderick. After his wife died, he then looked to me."

"It does not matter how you get what you want, only that you get it."

"Truer words have never been spoken." Bernadine waved her fan. "So why are you sulking in the shadows and not going after Dillon?"

Surprise filled Henrietta's eyes. "How did you know?"

Bernadine laughed, the chilly sound rumbling over the sounds of the music, laughter and talking. "I have been watching you most of the night." Her cold, blue eyes bore into Henrietta. "I recognized the fire in your eyes. But as the night progressed and you made no move, I thought perhaps I was wrong about your feelings toward him."

"You figured right." Henrietta looked down at her folded hands. "'Tis only that I am tired of throwing myself at him only to be ignored."

"Well now, if you want attention, you must seek it out. 'Twill not find you while you're lurking in the corners. Not to mention that dress!" Bernadine stopped waving the fan, looking over Henrietta's gown. "Although the color is quite becoming with your light hair and fair skin tone, all that lace covers up your best assets. You need something with more flair and a lower neckline."

"I have already tried my best gowns, and all Dillon did was reprimand me for not looking like a lady." She sniffed. "Can you believe he prefers that pasty redhead over me?"

"'Tis no accounting for taste." Bernadine smiled slyly. "But you must not give up just because of a setback. You must fight harder."

"What else can I do?" Hopelessness carved a hole in her heart.

Patting Henrietta's forearm she advised, "Why not go ask Dillon to dance?"

"He'll turn me down, and I will look like a fool in front of the whole town."

"If there is one thing I know about Dillon, it is that he's a gentleman. 'Twould not be chivalrous to turn down a poor maiden who has sat alone all night."

"But I did have one dance, and with the sheriff no less." Henrietta could kick herself now. What if that one dance ruined Bernadine's plan?

Bernadine thought hard. "Perhaps we can convince him it was out of pity you danced with him. That is how desperate you are." Her eyes brightened as the plan formulated in her head.

"What about Caitlin? She will never allow him to dance with me. She has always hated me."

"That, my dear, can work to our advantage." Standing, she ordered, "Now you sit here looking as forlornly as possible. Leave the rest up to me." Walking toward the small crowd that had gathered around Dillon and Caitlin, she smiled to herself. *Let's see that little Irish trash out-smart me now.* She would certainly win now that she had an ally on her side.

"Dillon, may I speak with you for a moment?" Bernadine interrupted the conversation.

"I am in the middle of something."

"'Tis terribly important."

Dillon rolled his eyes then followed her to a quiet corner. "What is the matter?"

"I have been noticing a young maiden, sulking in the corner most of the night. I thought perhaps you could ask her to dance." Bernadine smiled.

"Have you forgotten that I am a married man?" He should have known she was up to no good.

"'Tis only one dance. 'Twill make her feel better to have at least one dance. It would be very chivalrous of you." She batted her long, black lashes.

"That coy look will be of no use." Dillon crossed his arms in front of his chest. "Besides, are you not getting too old for that eyelash thing?"

"Why, Dillon Cade, how rude you are!" she huffed. "However, I will not let personal insults stand in the way of someone's happiness."

"I do not care about any other woman's happiness besides Caitlin's."

"I am sure that if Caitlin saw this poor, dejected girl, she would insist on one dance, just to cheer her up."

"I do not think that possible," he sighed. "Where is this girl, perhaps I may have a chat with her without risking gossip."

"Right over there." She pointed. "In the yellow dress."

"Henrietta!" He crossed his arms. "Absolutely not. Besides she already had a dance." His eyes turned hard. "With the sheriff. Whatever game she is playing, I will not be a party to it."

"'Tis the problem." Bernadine fretted her raven brows together. "You see, she had no idea he was the sheriff until they were in the middle of the dance. She was positively horrified when she found out. Poor dear," she looked sorrowfully in her direction, "she now is worried that the whole town will be angry with her over a simple misunderstanding. She also fears that people will think she is associated with him, and that she had something to do with your arrest."

Dillon quietly sighed, not saying anything. He was not sure Henrietta hadn't had something to do with his arrest.

"Do you not see that one dance from you would alleviate the suspicion of the entire town?"

"'Tis not my problem or responsibility."

"Dillon, I am ashamed of you," Bernadine declared very loudly. "Where is your sense of Christian duty?"

"My Christian duty is to my wife only," he sighed.

"I cannot believe that Caitlin would be so heartless as to not help a poor soul in need."

"You do not know the circumstances. Besides, since when do you care about anything besides fashion and yourself?"

"I will have to speak with your father about your behavior. You are positively ill-mannered." The black and purple material of her gown stretched taut across her small chest. "I have had enough of your insensitive remarks. You have not seen me or your father in thirteen years, yet you stand there and judge me." Pulling out her fan, she frantically waved it. "I am a most generous person."

Dillon arched his brows in skepticism. "Only when it serves a purpose." He was not about to be taken in by her act or her use of guilt. He would never feel guilty about moving away, not when her advances had been the reason for leaving in the first place.

"I do declare," she acted faint. "I am not sure if this colony has given you a monstrous heart, or if it is your new wife?"

"You leave Caitlin out of this," he demanded.

"If your marriage is so unstable that one little dance with a poor maiden would cause so much turmoil, then maybe you shouldn't be married to that particular girl."

Dillon stepped closer, his tone icy. "Do not think that I underestimate you. I realize that your only purpose here is to destroy my marriage. I will not allow anything or anyone to come between us." His brown eyes turned almost black. "Is that clear?"

"Quite." Bernadine stiffened. "Let me make myself clear." Her blue gaze challenged him. "Caitlin is nothing but a mere mushroom who has transplanted herself from the lowly middle class into high society. I will not stand to have our good reputation soiled. You must start thinking with your head and quit these romantic notions."

"You have no right to speak to me of soiled reputations. You were merely middle class before you married my father. And your reputation has not improved one bit since then."

"How dare you!" Bernadine gasped. "I was much better off than that Irish chit. And I worked hard to improve our name and reputation after all the devastation your mother caused by having that affair and getting herself killed."

Dillon had to restrain every muscle in his body in order to keep from slapping her. "'Tis only that we are in front of the entire town that I will not hit you for that remark, but, be assured that if you ever speak another lie about my mother, I will not hold back my temper."

"I realize that as a young boy you would want to cling to the fantasies of your mother. However, you are a grown man now, and must face the truth." Bernadine did not back away from his advance.

"If you do not keep these corrupt lies to yourself, I will tell my father the real reason I left England."

"Is something the matter?" Caitlin hastily approached, placing herself between the two.

"We were just reminiscing about old times." Bernadine tried to make her voice sound lighthearted. "If you will excuse me, I need to go make apologies to a young maiden."

Caitlin waited until Bernadine was out of ear range before asking, "What was that all about?" She rubbed Dillon's shoulder. "You are more taut than the strings on a violin."

"That woman is the most irritating beast I have ever known."

"A beast?" Caitlin laughed. "Truly you are upset." She'd never seen him like this before. Not even when she was the one causing the quarrel.

Henrietta watched Dillon through the plate glass window of his shop, as he worked over the press. Pulling the silver timepiece from her reticule she checked the hour, hoping Bernadine would be on time. After all, this was her idea. The two of them hatched the plan early this morning and had already begun spreading rumors about Caitlin.

Bernadine had told everyone she met how Henrietta had sat all alone, except for the one dance, which turned out to be the sheriff. Then, explained how mean-spirited Caitlin would not allow Dillon to have one dance with the poor, miserable maiden. "Can you imagine being that heartless and selfish?" Bernadine drawled in her shrill tone.

Smiling at the memory, Henrietta took a deep breath and pushed open the door, bracing her ears for the shrill jingle of the bells. "Dillon, may I speak with you for a moment?"

"If you have something you want printed, forget it." His flat tone sent stronger chills through her body than the December winds.

"'Tis not about writing, but it is urgent." She glanced around the shop. "Is Johnny still here?"

"In the back." He stopped his work, finally meeting her gaze. "Why?"

"I wish to speak with you privately. Could you send him on break or something?"

"Nay. Whatever you have to say can be said in his presence."

"I have something important to tell you and cannot afford to have anyone else overhear." She pleaded with him.

"I cannot think of anything you have to say that is so secretive. Bernadine already informed me that you did not know the man you danced with was the sheriff. I am sure everyone in town will believe you." He wiped his ink stained hands on a dirty rag.

"I wish that was all I had to tell you." She nervously licked her dry lips. "But I have something else I must confess." Henrietta wasn't sure she wanted to inform him of her part in his arrest, but she had no other recourse to get him alone. "Please, Dillon. Send Johnny to lunch so we may speak alone."

Caitlin was tired of hearing Bernadine whine. She was bored. The workers' pounding was giving her a headache. The tea was too strong. The scones were cold. Caitlin didn't have the faintest idea how to run a proper house.

"Caitlin, go put on a proper promenade dress and let's go to town," Bernadine suggested.

"I have too much work. Mr. Barclay is working non-stop to finish your room."

"So let him work. That is why you are paying him. I do not understand why you insist that you must be here. Is he not competent to handle the job alone?"

"He is completely dependable. But since Dillon cannot be here to oversee the work, the responsibility has fallen to me."

"Pish-posh!" Bernadine waved her gloved hand. "Let the men do their work, and we will go shopping." Wrinkling her nose, she set the lemon square down. "Besides, 'tis almost one o'clock and I need some supper."

"If you wanted to be in town so bad why did we come out to the house?" Roderick white brows wrinkled in confusion.

"I wanted to spend time with Caitlin. We cannot do that if we are in town and she is here."

That statement drew surprised glances from everyone in the room, including Mrs. White, who was serving the tea.

"We do not have much time," Bernadine admonished. "Now hurry and change. I am not taking no for an answer."

"I truly am too busy," Caitlin protested.

"Nonsense." Bernadine crossed her arms, her stare penetrating. "Either you change your garments, or I shall drag you into town as you are."

Caitlin mentally counted as she vigorously brushed out the wrinkles in her gray cotton gown. She could not figure out why Bernadine was so against her appearance. The simple empire style was easy to move in. The pink flounce added style and she topped the outfit off with a pink cottage cap. It was most appropriate for morning. However, she did concede to the fact that it was almost noon.

She wished the woman would just leave her alone. Her chores would consume most of the day. She had no desire whatsoever to go into town. But, she did want to get into good standing with her mother-in-law. Biting back her temper, she merely smiled. "I will have Lucy help me change into more appropriate attire."

"Very well." Bernadine twisted her lips into a smug smile. "Make it quick."

"Why are you in such a rush?" Roderick asked.

"I want to get something decent to eat," she snapped.

"I will be down before you can miss me." Caitlin ran up the stairs.

Lucy helped her don a blue and yellow checkered, taffeta gown. After adding a blue hat with yellow plumes and blue gloves, Caitlin was most suitable in promenade attire.

Roderick whistled as she descended the staircase. "'Tis the fastest and most beautiful transformation I have ever seen." He was amazed how young she looked in the simple gown and ruffled cap, and how she now looked like an adult dressed in a fashionable gown. "'Tis the most beautiful young woman I have seen in years."

"I can now see where Dillon gets his flattering tongue." Caitlin curtsied.

Bernadine's impatient foot tapping and folded arms told everyone she was not elated by the metamorphosis. "Can we move it along before I faint of hunger?"

After loading into the carriage and wrapping tightly with the blankets to keep the chill away, they headed down the bumpy, dirt road.

"Has no one heard of stones," Bernadine mumbled. "I miss the cobblestoned roads in England," she sighed. "'Tis much easier to drive on."

"Speaking of home." Caitlin smiled sweetly. "When do you plan on returning?"

"Why, I never!" Bernadine pointed her beak into the air. "We have only just arrived and you are already throwing us out."

"I do not think that is what she meant," Roderick commented. "She was merely asking a question."

"And what do you understand of the female mind?" Bernadine quipped.

"Apparently not much," he grumbled. "At least not when it comes to you."

"Exactly what does that mean?" Bernadine crossed her arms. "I have done nothing but try to be the perfect wife all these years." She dabbed her eyes with a gloved hand. "And all I have ever gotten from you is disrespect."

Roderick rolled his eyes and looked out the window. He'd learned to not even defend his words and actions or it led to more squabbling. Instead, he tuned her out, and concentrated on the scenery. "'Tis beautiful countryside."

"'Tis nothing now." Caitlin waved a hand. "You should see it in the springtime. 'Tis most beautiful in the autumn."

Bernadine narrowed her eyes in anger. She hated being interrupted more than being completely dismissed. The two of them acted as if she were not even in the same carriage.

"We are near town. Where would you like to go?" Caitlin asked.

"I thought we could stop by the shop and ask Dillon to join us." Bernadine smiled which looked more a lopsided frown.

"'Tis a lovely idea," Caitlin brightened at the idea. She needed his moral strength to make it through another minute with her. Why had she deluded herself into thinking she could win over Bernadine? Any remote notions of them ending up like Ruth and Naomi fled.

The carriage pulled alongside of the boardwalk, and the driver helped the ladies out. They crossed the street a few buildings down from the printing shop. Caitlin was explaining who owned what shops and giving a brief history lesson of the town as they strolled along the boardwalk.

The cold wind blew through Caitlin chilling her to the bone. It stung her nose and cheeks turning them red. However, when she looked through the window of the printing shop and saw Henrietta in Dillon's arms, it was more than the winter weather making her shiver.

Roderick almost collided with Caitlin when she abruptly stopped. His eyes followed her gaze.

"Don't those two look cozy?" Bernadine's smug smile added more insult. She walked passed them, her steps so light it almost looked like she was skipping.

Roderick laid a consoling hand on her forearm. "Try to keep in mind that things are not always what they appear."

"I shall try." Her smile was weak, but she knew his words were true. She trusted Dillon. His loyalty and love were without measure. Henrietta was not going to destroy the bond that had begun between them. Whatever Henrietta was up to, she would find out.

"Dear Lord, give me wisdom and strength." She quietly prayed, before following Bernadine through the door.

At the jingling of the bell, Henrietta gasped and pulled away from Dillon. She nervously patted some loose tendrils of hair back into place and adjusted the flounce on her sleeves. Her actions the perfect picture of a woman caught red-handed. Her guilty look briefly turned deceptive when her eyes met Bernadine's.

"What on Earth is going on here?" Bernadine asked with as much disdain as she could muster.

"'Tis not what it looks like." Henrietta met Caitlin's eyes. "Dillon 'twas just being a gentleman. I started crying and well…" she wrung her hands fretfully. "He was only trying to comfort me."

"I assume, at the very least, you have your apprentice on hand." Bernadine's tone turned sharp. "So you two are not completely alone, and able to do who-knows-what?"

"Actually, Johnny went on break." Henrietta rushed on to explain. "I had a matter of utmost importance, and requested a private word with Dillon."

"Dillon, I am ashamed of you." Bernadine clucked. "One would think that since you are now a married man, you would respect your wife's reputation."

Dillon was about to remind her that it was she who wanted him to dance with Henrietta the night before. However, his defense was interrupted by Caitlin.

"My reputation is just fine, and Dillon need not defend his actions." She crossed the floor in a sure, swift manner, placing a long kiss on his lips. "I am married to the most generous, loving man. Of course he would want to help a poor, hopeless maiden in distress." She stressed the word maiden. Her green eyes narrowed at Henrietta, challenging her to keep up the charade.

"I am truly sorry for any inconvenience I have caused." Henrietta looked sheepishly at the ground.

Caitlin wanted to smack the look of guilt off her face, but instead she prayed for guidance and decided to ignore the whole situation. "Dillon, we have come to drag you off to supper. Bernadine is about faint from hunger."

"I am hungry as well." Dillon placed his arm around her waist, but noticed that she stood stiffer than normal. Her act of indifference may fool everyone else, but not him.

"I assume your business has concluded." Caitlin's pointed gaze dismissed Henrietta.

"Aye, 'tis done." Dillon acknowledged.

Henrietta's cheeks reddened with anger. She didn't like the display of affection, or the fact that she was dismissed so easily. However, there was nothing left to say. "I bid you good day." Nodding to Dillon, she crossed the wooden floor wearing a cryptic smile. She turned at the door. "Dillon, thank you for understanding." With a shrill jingle, she was gone.

She could only hope that the seeds of doubt would grow.

Chapter 18

"Caitlin, are we ever going to talk?" Dillon sat in his favorite wing chair beside the fireplace.

"Whatever do you mean?" She bustled around the room; straightening pillows, folding blankets, rearranging candles and vases.

"You have barely spoken a complete sentence to me since arriving home." He set his book aside. "Do not think you are fooling me. You played the part of a loving wife very well for the sake of my parents, but I know you better."

"I am your wife!" She faced him with fists clenched. "I do not need to play any part. That will be left up to Henrietta."

"Are you at least going to give me a chance to explain?"

"I do not need to hear any explanations." She set about shifting the candelabra on the table.

"I swear to you nothing happened." He took a deep breath. "She came to the shop insisting that she must speak with me alone. I had no intentions of sending Johnny away, but she persisted. I gave in. Then, she proceeded to tell me a long drawn out story before breaking into tears and launching herself into my arms. I had no choice but to catch her or we both would have toppled over. It was at that precise moment that you entered the shop. I am truly sorry for the way things looked, but I beg you to forgive me. I would never hurt you intentionally." He wanted to allow her to digest the information, and to catch his breath.

"Dillon, I said I needed no explanations because I trust you." She stopped fidgeting and looked at him. "I will admit to being hurt at first but I knew she was up to something. My only concern is finding out what her plan is."

"If you are not angry then why have you been avoiding me?"

"I am upset that you are overly nice sometimes."

"How can a person be too nice?" His lips twisted into a lopsided grin.

"Henrietta has done nothing but throw herself at you since we've been married, yet you allow the behavior to continue. You need to stand up to her and tell her to leave you alone."

"I do not want to hurt her feelings. Does that make me so bad?"

"Nay." Caitlin crossed the room, sitting in his lap. "'Tis the reason I love you. But your kindness is being taken advantage of, and only you can stop her."

"I shall try to remember that at our next encounter." He kissed her softly.

"You were absolutely brilliant." Bernadine cackled over the crackling fire in the hotel room.

Henrietta smiled. "And so were you."

"You should have seen Caitlin's face when she saw you hugging Dillon."

"I would give anything to have seen her expression. Your timing was perfect."

"I almost thought we would be too late to pull it off, Caitlin dawdled so." Bernadine sipped her tea. "Now tell me how you managed to get into Dillon's arms." She set her cup and saucer on the table, leaning forward in anticipation.

"It was not that easy, that is for sure." Henrietta leaned forward as if telling a secret that the rest of the world must not know. "I had to tell him about my role in getting him arrested."

"What?" Bernadine sat up straight. "Why would you do that? He will surely hate you now." She'd been impressed with this young girl's determination, but, perhaps her youth was working against her. She may have just ruined the whole plan.

"I had no other choice." Henrietta's hazel eyes darted around the room. "He would not send that stupid boy away. I had to make it worth his effort to be alone with me. 'Twas all I could think of."

Bernadine thought for a minute. "I suppose you are correct. How did he take the news?"

"He did not have much time to think about it. I explained that I ran into the sheriff and mistakenly slipped out information about the article. I had no intentions of malice and did not even think the sheriff would do anything. I was simply beside myself when I heard he'd been arrested." She batted her lashes, demonstrating the pathetic look she'd used on Dillon. "Then I began crying and inched closer. 'Tis when he put his arms around me." Her face transformed into sheer bliss. "How did Caitlin behave after I left? I bet she was madder than a hornet."

"I fear she seemed rather unaffected by the whole ordeal, but I suppose 'twas all an act. She is probably laying into him as we speak." Bernadine stood and walked over to the window. Pulling the flimsy material aside, she looked down the dirty, deserted street. "I cannot wait to get out of here," she sighed. In England there were balls, soirées and dinner parties every night. The theaters and restaurants stayed open until late, but this one-horse town was closed up by seven.

"I agree. The sooner you move into their house, the better we can plan our strategy."

"Let us just hope that not too much damage has been done by telling Dillon the truth." Bernadine took her seat once again. "And hope that we can break up this unholy union before any child is conceived."

"I will drink to that." Henrietta held up her teacup.

"To new alliances." Bernadine clanked her cup with Henrietta's.

"Mrs. Cade, the room is finished." Mr. Barclay stood erect, his round belly protruding over the waist of his pants.

"Already?" Caitlin set her fork down.

"'Tis only been three days," Roderick noted in dismay.

"I am sure the room will be plain. Nothing suitable can be accomplished in such a short period of time." Bernadine went back to eating.

"I am sorry to interrupt your supper. But I assumed that Lord and Lady Cade would want to move in by tonight."

"You have that correct. I cannot abide in that dreadful room one more night," Bernadine grumbled.

Mr. Barclay cleared his throat. "Perhaps you can take a look when you've finished eating."

"Nonsense, my boy. I am most anxious to see your work." Roderick wiped his mouth and stood.

Caitlin felt nervous. Bernadine would surely find something wrong even if it were perfect. However, she was correct— the room couldn't be very grand in such a short period.

Dillon put his arm around Caitlin's shoulders as they followed Mr. Barclay down the hall. Bernadine kept looking for signs of trouble between the two of them over the last two days but thus far hadn't seen any.

Roderick walked next to Mr. Barclay, asking questions. That left Bernadine to follow behind by herself, feeling like an outsider. This was *her* family, after all. She silently vowed to get rid of Caitlin by any means necessary.

The assembly entered the bed-chamber. Caitlin stood transfixed, her mouth open but words could not form. The transformation was beyond any expectation she held.

"'Tis a job well done," Roderick said.

"Amazing." Caitlin could not say anything else. Words failed to describe the beauty of the room.

"How did you accomplish such lavish curtains and rugs on such short notice?" Dillon asked.

"I called in a few a favors." Mr. Barlclay beamed. "I hope you don't mind that I painted the bed frame and dressers. The woods didn't match since nothing was in a set."

"Are you jesting? They are gorgeous." Caitlin loved how the bed and dressers' off-white color brought out the French style of the wallpaper.

"I white-washed the black iron frame then sponged a taupe color over it to give it the antique look." Mr. Barclay went on to explain every detail of the room. "I found most of these gilded frames in the attic. I exchanged some of the paintings for ones I had that looked more French."

"Please add the cost of the paintings onto your bill." Dillon shook his hand. "And add a bonus for a job well done."

"Thank you, Mr. Cade."

"I have never seen such fine craftsmanship." Roderick ran his hand over the top of the dresser. "'Tis amazing what some paint and imagination can do."

"'Tis much better than the hotel. Of course, that place is such a dump, anything is better." Bernadine strolled around the room. "However, I have certainly seen much grander rooms." She elevated her nose. "I suppose this will do."

After dinner, they retired to the parlor. Bernadine perched on the settee and started doing her needlepoint. Dillon started setting up the chessboard, and Roderick stood by the fireplace, looking up at the portrait.

"'Tis been a long time since I've had the privilege of gazing upon her face." He looked at Caitlin with sad, tired eyes. "Dillon reminds me of her gentle temperament."

Bernadine stiffened at that remark but held her tongue. Any fighting done now would only be proof that she had a disagreeable personality. "Roderick do not be drawn into the past." She walked over, putting a hand on his shoulder. "Nothing good ever becomes of memories."

"Depends on the memories," Roderick murmured. "My memories of Mary are always good."

Bernadine's face hardened. Even in death, *Saint Mary* still haunted her. She was Roderick's wife now and deserved more respect than he gave. Why did he pine away for a dead woman? *I could kill Caitlin for bringing that woman into my life again.* Fuming, she stomped over to the table and poured some amber liquid into a crystal glass. She would show them all she was a better wife.

"Here is your nightly glass of brandy." She handed it to Roderick while smiling to herself. Mary wasn't there to give him his drink. 'Twas her duty now.

"Where did you get the brandy?" Caitlin asked, surprised.

"I purchased it at the general store." Bernadine informed them. "I packed some for the trip; however, they broke."

"Yes, I had to go most of the ride here without it." Roderick took a drink. "I was hoping that the brandy here would taste better than back home."

"What is wrong with it?" Bernadine looked confused. "'Tis the same kind you always drink."

"Perhaps the stuff is losing its flavor to me." He took another sip. "It just tastes too strong." Sniffing he added, "and has a funny smell."

"Must be your old age." Bernadine laughed.

"Perhaps God is telling you to quit drinking," Dillon suggested. "That stuff is not good for you."

"Hogwash." Bernadine demanded. "'Tis nothing wrong with drinking, even the church says so."

"Caitlin! Caitlin!" Sarah rushed into the kitchen. "Sorry to interrupt," she wheezed, "but I must speak with you at once."

"What is the matter?" Caitlin noted the dirty hem of her green walking dress. "You look as though you ran all the way here." This anxious attitude was most unlike quiet, reserved Sarah.

Sarah held up an envelope. "I've just received a letter from Brogan."

"What?" Caitlin dried her hands on her apron.

Sarah was still trying to catch her breath. "I have one for you too."

"My family— are they all right?"

"Seems everyone is fine." Sarah took a deep breath. "May I have some water?"

"Of course." Caitlin untied her apron strings then started to pump the handle.

"I'll get it." Martha waved her hand. "You two go have a seat before Miss Sarah done falls over."

"Are you sure? I hate to leave in the middle of baking the bread."

"I'll get more work done with you out of the way anyhow. I'll bring some treats along with the drinks."

"Thank you, Martha." Caitlin and Sarah sat at the dining room table.

After Sarah caught her breath, she explained that she'd received the letter from Brogan. There was a second letter for Caitlin. Her parents thought it looked less suspicious sending it to her instead of Caitlin directly.

"I see their point." Caitlin ripped the envelope open. With blurry eyes, she read the contents of the two pages. Finally lowering the paper, she sighed. "'Tis not much to tell. Mother didn't want to give any specifics. But at least my family is alive." Caitlin hugged Sarah. "Thank God they are alive."

The morning dawned with a frosty breath of white so cold it could bite the nose off anyone daring to venture into its grip.

Despite the frigid temperature, Dillon trudged along the boardwalk with a brown wrapped package under his arm. Not many people were out and about today. The cold weather kept the sane people inside. Only the business owners and a few desperate shoppers dared to brave the winter.

"Dillon Cade, is that you under the thick scarf?" Henrietta tried to smile seductively, but only grimaced with pain as the wind blew into her face.

"Aye." Barely acknowledging her, he bent his head down, heading to his shop.

"Where are you off to in such a hurry?"

"To work, if it is any business of yours."

"You don't have to be rude." Her teeth chattered. "I was merely making small talk."

"'Tis freezing out." Dillon turned on his heel, walking away as quick as he could.

Henrietta huffed, and then stomped into the general store. Her only condolence was that no one saw the ill-mannered way he treated her. If he kept that attitude up in public, surely people would start asking questions. Not wanting the whole town to know she'd turned Dillon in to the sheriff, she would have to figure out how to win his favor again.

Perhaps Bernadine will know what to do, she thought as she went to the counter.

"Good day, Henrietta." Mrs. Johnson greeted with her usual wrinkled smile.

"'Tis nothing good about it." Henrietta pulled her gloves off. "I saw Dillon outside. He was in the foulest mood."

"Really?" Mrs. Johnson refilled the candy jars, sitting on the end of the counter. "He seemed most chipper while he was here."

"Perhaps 'twas the cold making him hurry off in such a frenzy." She waited for the storekeeper to agree, or, at least reveal what was in the package, but she said nothing. Mrs. Johnson had always been most forthcoming with information about Dillon. Why did she have to practically drag it out of the old bat now?

"Can I help you with something?" Mrs. Johnson closed the lid on the jar, coming to stand in front of Henrietta.

"I need a bag of flour, some sugar, and I'm hoping to find something fabulous for a new dress."

"I just got some new bolts in over here." Mrs. Johnson led her to the back of the store. She always got excited over new materials and making dresses, although it wouldn't show by her drab clothing. "Are you looking for something particular?"

"No."

"Any color in mind?"

"No." Henrietta browsed through the bolts.

"What kind of fabric do you have in mind?"

"I shall know it when I see it."

"'Tis a hard way to shop." Mrs. Johnson shook her graying head. "Most people have an idea of what they want before they come in."

"Perhaps practical people." Henrietta ran her hand over the fabrics. "But I am not practical."

"'Tis for sure," Mrs. Johnson laughed. "Not even when you were a little one."

Henrietta smiled at the old woman. This is what she wanted to do, remind the wrinkled old goat that she had known her longer than Caitlin. Usually, once you got Mrs. Johnson reminiscing, she would get a loose tongue.

"You know me so well," Henrietta laughed. "Why don't you help me pick something out?"

The plan worked perfectly. As Mrs. Johnson became absorbed in fabrics, patterns and colors, she started talking about everyone in town including Dillon and Caitlin. However, the positive remarks about her enemy didn't sit well with Henrietta.

Mrs. Johnson had been on her side when Dillon was forced to marry that mean-spirited redhead. Henrietta had managed to make people believe that Dillon was going to propose to her. When he suddenly married Caitlin, it made her look like a liar in front of the whole town. Of course, she played the victim, but the only thing that had really saved her reputation was when people found out it had been an arranged marriage. All sympathies had been with Henrietta then.

However, the mood of the town started to shift. People were starting to believe that Dillon and Caitlin were truly in love.

"You cannot believe the rumors about them being in love," Henrietta huffed. "I know for a fact the marriage is false."

"And how do you know that?" Mrs. Johnson's tone immediately turned stern.

"I have it on good authority."

"Really?" Mrs. Johnson's dark eyes pinned her.

"Yes." Henrietta tilted her head in regal demeanor. "I have been speaking with his stepmother."

"Hmph." Mrs. Johnson dismissed the name with a wave of her hand. "No one much cares for her around here."

"What!" Henrietta gasped. "She holds a title in England. She is the most elegant lady I have ever met."

"Her title means nothing here. She throws it around like a sack of flour. All she does is gossip, and I don't believe a word she says." Mrs. Johnson met her eyes. "The fact that she tried to make Caitlin look bad because she wouldn't allow Dillon to dance with some other girl at the Social only fostered resentment, maybe things like that are done in England but not here. No one in their right mind would expect a married man to dance with another woman."

Henrietta swallowed the fear rising in her throat. "Do you know who the girl was?"

"No. I doubt there was one. I think she only wanted to berate Caitlin."

Henrietta sighed in relief. At least Bernadine had the foresight not to mention her name. However, her plan was backfiring. Instead of making people turn against Caitlin they were now jumping on the *love Caitlin* wagon.

"I cannot believe she would be that vindictive to her own family." Henrietta had to save face for both herself and Bernadine.

"I wouldn't put it past her," Mrs. Johnson grumbled. "She is only trying to break them up."

"But it is not a real marriage in the first place. Why should Dillon not be free to marry for love?" Henrietta crossed her arms defensively.

"Have you seen the two of them together?" Mrs. Johnson's stare went right through her. "They are the most devoted couple I have seen in a long time. Why, Dillon just purchased a most expensive gift for her."

"Buying gifts does not equal love." Her stomach knotted at the thought of him spending money on Irish refuse.

"'Tis more than that. You can tell when people are truly in love."

"I know from personal experience that Dillon is not in love with Caitlin." She straightened her back. "Dillon was caught holding another woman in his arms."

"Rubbish." Mrs. Johnson bent her head over the fabrics, completely dismissing the thought. "I wouldn't be so accepting of the rumors if I were you."

"You don't believe me?" Henrietta asked, indignantly.

"'Tis time to move on." Mrs. Johnson tried to be gentle. "Dillon is not in love with you."

"I know that he is," Henrietta defended.

"That was evidenced by the way he ran away from you outside."

"'Tis with good reason he ignored me. Caitlin caught us together."

Mrs. Johnson wheezed as she clutched her heart. "I cannot believe you would make up something like that."

"'Tis the truth. You can ask Lady Cade. If you do not believe her, then ask his father, or Caitlin herself. They all saw us."

Dillon hid the package behind his back as he walked into the parlor.

"What is that?" Caitlin asked when she looked up from her stitching.

Dillon handed her the package. "A gift for you."

"It is not Christmas, yet." She took the package, deftly unwrapping it.

"It is an early gift." He sat beside her on the settee.

Bernadine and Roderick came closer to watch.

"Dillon, it's beautiful," Caitlin gushed. Standing she let the length of velvet material flow down to the floor.

"It will keep you warm while you're riding Spirit." Dillon held up an emerald coat. "I even had a matching spencer made."

"How thoughtful." Caitlin bent down and kissed him. "However, it is too expensive," she noted.

"Nonsense." Dillon stood and ran his hand over the fabric. "The color matches your eyes perfectly. And it is warmer that that old gray habit you wear now."

"I cannot believe you spent so much time and money on a riding habit." Bernadine sniffed. "Something that expensive should have been made into a formal dress."

"'Tis not your concern, Bernadine," Roderick reminded her.

"I will not stand by and watch while this woman robs him blind."

"Caitlin did not ask for anything. I had this made because I am worried about her riding the horse in the cold weather and catching an illness. Besides," he faced her with hard eyes, "'tis my money. I will spend it how I want, and on whom I want."

"'Tis your inheritance from your father that you are shelling out. As his wife, I may remark how it is spent. If you use it all up now, I will be left with nothing when he dies."

"My inheritance came from my mother. I have not touched so much as a sixpence of his money."

"What?" Bernadine was dumfounded. "You have all of this without any help from your father?"

"Exactly." Dillon stepped closer, towering over her. "I suggest you think twice before opening your mouth again."

"Roderick are you going to allow him to speak to me in that manner?"

"What shall I do?" Roderick looked innocent.

"Well do something!" she hissed. "Why do you always act like a spineless coward?"

"Why do you always ruin everything?" he countered. "You have destroyed the moment that Dillon worked so hard to achieve. He only wanted to surprise his wife with a gift and you turn it into a fight."

"I will bet anything that if someone had spoken to your precious Mary that way, you would have done something." With tears of anger, she fled the room.

Caitlin loved the feel of the velvet. Not only did it keep her warm against the winter cold, but it also made her feel elegant and graceful. The soft fabric swept across the floor as she made her way in from outside. She took a few steps, and then stopped and let the soft fabric float around her legs, allowing herself to enjoy the gift, no matter what Bernadine thought or said.

"There is my beautiful daughter-in-law." Roderick placed a fatherly kiss on her cheek. "You are freezing."

"I just came in from riding Spirit."

"No wonder Dillon bought you that habit. You will most certainly catch your death in this weather."

"Now you sound just like him," she pouted.

"It's a man's duty to protect the woman he loves."

"Since you put it that way, I shall not be angry at being treated like a possession."

"You, my dear, are too strong willed to ever be anyone's possession." Roderick offered his arm. "Shall I escort you to the dining room?"

"You may." She slipped her arm through his. "I am famished this morning."

"My stomach feels a bit queasy today."

"I do hope you are not coming down with something. I can send for the doctor."

"Nay. Do not fret so over a stomachache. I am sure 'tis nothing more than indigestion."

"You look tired and pale."

"I am an old man. That is how we all look. Is Dillon gone yet?"

"I do not believe so. We usually have the morning meal together. It can be so late sometimes before he comes home, that the morning is the only time we have together."

"Very well." He patted her hand. "I have something I must speak with him about." With that the subject of his health was closed.

"Mrs. Cade." The maid bustled into the sitting room.

"Yes." Both Bernadine and Caitlin answered at the same time.

"Oh. Umm." The maid was clearly flustered by the confusion. "Caitlin. Ma'am." The maid addressed Bernadine, then looked at Caitlin. "A package has arrived for you."

"From whom?" Caitlin's smooth brow furrowed.

"I do not know but this card came with the box." She handed the note to Caitlin.

"'Tis from Mr. Jefferson," Caitlin exclaimed.

"Who is that?" Bernadine asked.

"The vice president of America. Dillon is trying to help him get elected as the next president." Caitlin was on her feet and nearly flew down the hall. The whole staff stood excited as she opened the box. The excitement swelled when she pulled out the most exquisite set of silver goblets.

"Look ma'am, they are engraved with a "C"."

"He personally designed them." Caitlin rubbed the round cup with her palm, remembering a similar set he made for himself. "'Tis the most beautiful gift ever. I must write him at once." She ordered the glasses to be cleaned and set out with dinner that night then went to write the thank you note.

"I wonder why someone so influential would send such an expensive gift?" Bernadine was fast beginning to think Caitlin might be a witch. She had to be casting some kind of spell. She rubbed her chin in thought. "Perhaps I can use that to my advantage."

Bernadine watched how Dillon stiffened as Caitlin retold the entire tale of receiving the gift. "Are they not of the most beautiful craftsmanship?"

"They are quite handsome," Roderick offered.

"You should have seen how fast Caitlin flew off to write him a thank you note," Bernadine added. "She was the most perfect hostess in doing it so promptly."

Dillon picked up his glass and studied it. "Is the C for Caitlin?" He asked before sipping from it.

"'Tis for Cade." Caitlin shot him a look of displeasure.

"I find it hard to imagine that someone as busy and influential as this Mr. Jefferson would take the time to make such a gift for a woman he met only once." Bernadine smiled as she took a bite of her salad. "You must have made quite an impression on him, my dear."

Bernadine could feel the tension building between Dillon and Caitlin. *This may well be the factor to break them apart,* she thought. Jealousy is always the best weapon.

Dillon paced across the floor, reading a letter that had arrived earlier that morning.

Roderick watched each agitated step as he sipped his brandy. "Is the news that bad?" he asked.

Dillon stopped then looked up from his reading. "It is from Thomas Jefferson."

"I see." Roderick regarded his son for a moment. "The same Mr. Jefferson that has caught your wife's attention?"

Dillon's dark brows furrowed. "He has not caught her attention in the manner you think. He is very influential and Caitlin is not accustomed to such power."

"Are you jealous of him?"

Dillon waited a space before answering. "There was a time I envied him, but not now."

"'Tis good to hear." Roderick took a long gulp of his brandy. "You have a good wife who loves you very much."

"'Twas a time when Caitlin couldn't stand to look at me."

"Considering the circumstances, could you blame her?" Roderick swirled his glass.

"Nay."

"Things are different now, are they not?"

"Aye."

"Do you trust her?" Roderick asked.

"With my whole heart."

"Then do not let petty jealousies come between the two of you." A slow smile spread under his thick, white mustache. "Your mother and I were never jealous."

Dillon locked his hands behind his back and took a few paces before asking, "Do you ever wonder why Mother was in that part of town?"

Roderick set his glass down. "Every day." His gruff voice sounded thick. "But I have never believed that she was meeting a lover in that hotel."

"Then why did you not defend her honor when the papers attacked her?"

Roderick stood. "I did not feel the need. I knew the truth. That was enough. I also feared that saying anything would only fuel the gossip more. I just wanted the rumors to go away so I could let her memory rest in peace."

"'Tis good to know the truth." Dillon locked eyes with his father. "As a boy it looked as if you hadn't cared enough to defend her."

"If you are not jealous of this Jefferson fellow, then why the gloom?" Roderick needed to change the subject. He'd carefully schooled himself over the years to hide his emotions. The subject of his first wife and her gruesome murder were never brought up, although her memories lingered in the back of his heart.

The past few weeks spent with Dillon had encouraged the memories to surface. Dillon looked and acted so much like her. He was the living part of Mary, the element that continued even after death.

"He wants me to publish this in the paper." Dillon read on. "He says he has been working on a series of resolutions that were passed in the Kentucky legislature. James Madison is working on similar resolutions for our state."

"Do you disagree with the bills?"

"I agree with them. 'Tis only that the opposition against them will be great. If I am arrested again, I may not get out this time."

"I understand your fear, son. However there are times when a man must take a stand for the principles he believes in."

"Master Cade." Mrs. White's voice rang through the house. "Come quickly."

Dillon flew out of the study with Roderick fast on his heels. "What is the matter?" Dillon yelled as he jumped the last few steps.

Caitlin and Bernadine met the men in the hallway. Upon entering the downstairs parlor, they all saw the horror at the same time.

"Dillon, who would do such an awful deed?" Caitlin's eyes clouded with tears.

Dillon knelt on the floor next to the painting of his mother. The gilded frame had been ripped from the wall and smashed. His mother's serene smile greeted him through jagged slash marks.

The large slices crisscrossed, ripping the canvas and ruining the lovely image that had been preserved for over two decades.

Dillon reached out and caressed the painting. "I will find the culprit and have them whipped." Anger raged through him, visible to all in the room. His eyes met Bernadine. "Father was with me, where were you?"

"I was with Caitlin making a list of duties for the house workers." Her chest puffed at the insult. "I cannot believe you think me capable of this appalling deed."

"Who else would be capable?" He stood.

Bernadine waved a gloved hand. "You have a whole house full of people you do not know. Why not question them?"

"I will." His fists clenched. "If it is the last thing I ever do, I will find the person responsible."

Chapter 19

The rumors flew around faster than snowflakes caught in a gust of wind. Since Henrietta's announcement, everyone wondered what was the truth? Bernadine didn't help matters. Although the town folks didn't like her much, they also saw no reason for her to lie.

Dillon hated that Caitlin was the center of attention in this matter. He tried shielding her from most of the slanderous comments, but Bernadine seemed intent on bringing her to town and making her face the lies. It seemed useless for Caitlin to deny anything. The town didn't believe her. Why would the entire town believe the word of Henrietta over Caitlin? Something wasn't right.

"I have to get to the bottom of this." Dillon grabbed his great coat and topper, then walked to the general store.

"Good afternoon, Dillon." Mrs. Johnson gave her usual warm smile.

"It may be afternoon,but I am not sure how good it is."

"Every day the Lord gives us is good."

"Cannot argue with logic like that."

"Is there something I can do for you besides cheer you up about the weather?"

"Actually, there is a matter of some importance I wish to discuss with you." Dillon lowered his voice to a whisper, "'Tis personal."

"Of course." She led him to the back room.

"I am not quite sure how to begin." Dillon took his commanding stance with arms locked behind his back. "'Tis about the rumors going around about Henrietta and myself."

"I figured that was the matter on your mind."

"I am coming to you, not because I think you are a gossip, but because I need some advice. I have not a clue how to handle this situation."

"Thank you for trusting me with your confidence." Mrs. Johnson didn't waste time. She was a very direct person. That was what made her a good business manager. "Are the rumors true?"

"Of course not." Dillon paused. "Well, not exactly. Henrietta is twisting the truth."

"Why don't you tell me exactly what happened?"

"For some reason Henrietta has made it appear that I would have married her if I had not wed Caitlin."

"Is this not true?"

"Nay. I would never have married her. I do not understand how she got this schoolgirl fantasy that there was ever anything between us."

"'Tis easy when you are young." Mrs. Johnson started to see the problem. "I guess no one questioned the truth when she started saying things about the two of you."

"'Tis what I do not understand. Why is Henrietta's word worth more than Caitlin's?"

Mrs. Johnson's brows rose. "Perhaps because we have known Henrietta longer."

"'Tis not fair to Caitlin. She is just as much a part of this town."

"True, but, 'tis my experience that rumors cannot go around unless there is a ring of truth to them." Mrs. Johnson folded her arms across her chest, waiting for him to continue.

"Here is the truth." Dillon took a deep breath and told the whole story. Why Caitlin didn't want to be married. How they fell in love after the wedding. How Bernadine was trying to break them up, and, now Henrietta had started lying.

"I was not holding Henrietta," Dillon rebuked. "She fell into my arms and I had no choice but to catch her. I explained the situation to Caitlin and she understood. But now the whole town thinks I am betraying my wife."

"'Tis why the Bible commands us to avoid the appearance of evil," Mrs. Johnson reprimanded, softly. "The fact that Henrietta was in your arms, and that you sent Johnny away, would lead any righteous person to that conclusion."

"Aye, but Luke 6:37 tells us 'judge not, and ye shall not be judged: condemn not, and ye shall not be condemned: forgive and ye shall be forgiven.'" The battle of the Bible was on.

"Very true." Mrs. Johnson conceded. "However, Matthew 7:17 says 'every good tree bringeth forth good fruit; but a corrupt tree bringeth forth evil fruit.'" Her small eyes bore into him. "The rumors have been going around ever since you got hitched. A hasty wedding always breeds rumors. You gave Henrietta an open door, which she has been able use for her own agenda."

"So how do I stop her?"

"You just did." Mrs. Johnson smiled. "Telling people the truth will help. Truth is the only weapon we have against lies. Start showing people the good fruit and the evil fruit will be made known."

"Thank you, Mrs. Johnson." Dillon smiled. "I have some work to do."

"Mr. Barclay, you have done it again," Caitlin exclaimed. "This game room is exactly what I wanted."

"Good work, son." Roderick was once again impressed with the details of this room. "The colors almost invite you to sit down and play cards."

The red curtains and rugs offset the cream walls. Several square, cherry wood game tables were strategically placed around the room. Each table had four straight back chairs with bold blue, leather seats.

"I hate playing cards," Bernadine sniffed.

"'Tis because you always lose." Roderick laughed, which only earned him an icy stare.

"I cannot believe you completed the whole downstairs so quickly," Caitlin commented.

"You said it needed to be done by Christmas." Mr. Barclay seemed a little confused.

"I know I said it, but I truly did not think it possible," she confessed. "Now I will be able to have a Christmas celebration." She twirled around the room, her yellow dress swirling like a cloud.

Roderick smiled as he watched her enthusiasm. He could understand why his son loved her so much.

Bernadine brightened at the idea of a party. "How wonderful to have a soirée right here in our own home." She clasped her hands together. "Twill be the grandest celebration ever."

Bernadine noticed the scowl Caitlin gave her. "Do not fret, dear." She patted Caitlin on the arm like a pet. "I will show you how England throws a ball. You need not worry about anything. I will take care of every detail."

Caitlin counted to ten then pasted a smile on her face, and as sweetly as possible replied, "'Tis very generous of you. However, this is my first Christmas in my new home, and I will need the experience of planning a party." She patted Bernadine on the arm. "You are already an accomplished planner, therefore you do not need the skill as much as I."

"Precisely my point," Bernadine stated. "You can learn from me."

Caitlin silently groaned. She wanted no help from this woman, yet she wanted some peace. Perhaps Bernadine would be so involved in the planning of the party that she would forget about making everyone's life miserable.

Roderick's pride grew as he watched Caitlin handle the situation with grace and dignity. But, he did concede to himself that a party may be just the thing to bring his wife out of this foul mood she'd been in. Since the women were busy talking about the party, he took this opportunity to talk with the contractor.

"Mr. Barclay, my good man." Roderick slapped him on the back. "Would you be interested in coming to England and looking over my home? I like your work, and I want to hire you to fix up my place."

"England?" Mr. Barclay's dark eyes went bigger than the frames of his glasses. "It is a long way to travel."

"Aye, my boy." Roderick smiled. "All expenses paid, of course."

"A job of that magnitude would boost my credibility."

Bernadine overheard the conversation and flew to Roderick's side. "What do you mean come and do our place? It does not need redoing. 'Twill be a waste of time and money."

"It could use a little sprucing up. 'Tis been a long time since any work was done to the house."

"'Tis because I have it the way I want it. No work shall be done unless it goes through me." She folded her arms across her small chest.

"'Tis my house, and I will hire anyone I please to do any work I wish. I have lived with the awful color schemes you chose long enough. You redid the entire house without permission and I let it go. I have come to a point where I am tired of your gaudy, overdone look. I want the elegant, quiet serenity that used to be there."

"Are you suggesting that your beloved Mary had better taste than I?" She advanced toward him, her entire body shaking with rage. "I could kill you right now!"

Roderick ducked as the fist came at him. Bernadine stumbled, but regained her balance. "I have done nothing but care for you and your son for the past seventeen years, and this is how you repay me? Humiliate me in front of everyone? Criticize everything I do?" Her blue eyes blazed. "I swear, Roderick, if it is the last thing I ever do, I will repay you for this outrage." In a cloud of anger, she left.

"I am sorry about that," he apologized. "Caitlin, I do not wish to subject you to any more of her behavior. We will leave posthaste."

"Please stay," Caitlin begged. "I am sorry for your sake that she behaves so badly, but do not fret over me. I can handle her."

"I am beginning to notice that." Roderick laughed. "You are a very strong-willed woman, yet gentle and caring. 'Tis the perfect combination. "

"Thank you, sir." Caitlin curtsied. "Now I beg you to go make amends with Bernadine, and to stay for as long as you like."

"It is nice getting to know my son after all these years apart. I would value more time with him."

"Then stay and do not give Bernadine another thought."

Dillon held up the diamond necklace. "Do you think she will like it?"

"Why not? It is a beautiful piece."

"I am worried that she will be offended if I buy her too many gifts. She scolded me once already for thinking that she cared about money. She promptly informed me that she loved me, not things." He laid the necklace back in the box.

"You, my boy, are a very lucky man." Roderick placed a hand on Dillon's shoulder. "Caitlin loves you very much." His usually strong, powerful voice seemed subdued, almost melancholy.

"What about you, father? Does not Bernadine love you also?"

His laugh was harsh. "Your stepmother loves the title and wealth."

Dillon did not know how to respond. He was glad, however, that his father was not as blind as he thought him to be.

"Caitlin reminds me of your mother. Her strength and love was beyond measure."

The sudden nostalgic moment caught Dillon off guard. "Do you miss Mother?"

"Every day. Why would you ask?"

"I did not think you cared at all. You never mentioned her. You married Bernadine so quickly, it felt like you forgot about my mother." Dillon's throat constricted.

"I could not talk about Mary for a long time because it hurt too much. You were a mere lad, and I had no idea how to communicate with you. As for Bernadine, I married her for your sake."

"My sake?"

"Dillon, I had no idea how to be a father or how to take care of you. Your mother always took care of everything. I thought by marrying again, I would find someone to step into that role." Lord Roderick shook his white head.

"In truth, you married her so you could be discharged of the burden left to you." The hurt rang through Dillon's tone like a bell. He'd always felt like a burden. His father had been a mere stranger to him.

"I did not mean it that way." Roderick's brown eyes turned soft. "My biggest regret is that I was never involved in your childhood. The truth is, I felt scared to death when you were born. You were so tiny and squirmed all over the place. I didn't want to drop you, so I never picked you up.

"I remember watching while you slept in your cradle or standing across the room, looking on as your mother tended you." The memories were so overwhelming, that he almost felt faint. He walked over to a wing chair in the corner of the study and sat down, heavily. "But always watching from afar."

"I was not a baby all my life."

"No. The next thing I knew, you were toddling all around. Your mother and your toys seemed all you were interested in. That made it easy to believe that I was not needed. I allowed myself to get absorbed in my work, thinking that I would always have time for my family later. I would have time next week, or after the next important bill passed in parliament." His bushy brows drew together. "Then, suddenly you were a young boy, and your mother was taken away from me. In my grief and despair, I married Bernadine, hoping to get some kind of normal routine back in my life." Tears slipped out the corner of his eyes. "If only I would have known the truth."

"Truth about what?"

"Bernadine." His mellow tone turned hard. "She destroyed what little was left of my life."

Dillon finally saw his father in a new light, not as an uncaring husband and father, but as a confused, grief stricken man with nowhere to turn. "Has life with her really been that bad?"

"You have to ask?"

"And you had not any idea about her before you married?"

"I cannot complain overly much. I did not propose out of love. I knew I would never love another woman as I loved Mary. I only saw a need and thought Bernadine would be the solution."

Dillon walked over to Roderick, squeezing his shoulder in comfort. "I am truly sorry, Father."

"No, son, I am the one who is sorry. I made the choice to marry her. At the time I had no way of knowing how much of my life she could destroy." Roderick stood and walked over to the window. "'Tis not even the affairs that bother me, 'tis the fact that she drove you away."

"How did you know?" Dillon gasped.

"I did not figure it out for a long time. Eventually I recalled all the touching, the hugging and caressing. At first, I thought she was just being motherly. 'Twas not until after you left that I put two and two together."

"Why not leave her?"

"I am just trying to make the best of the situation. A divorce would only cause another scandal. Besides, 'tis against the laws of the church." Roderick gazed over the dead grass of the lawn. "It does not matter anyhow. You are better off here. You have done well, son." His eyes were full of tears when he looked at Dillon. "I am proud of you."

"I thought I would never hear those words from you." Emotion welled up so fast that Dillon had no time to think, he grabbed his father in a bear hug and cried. Years of pent up anger and sorrow spilling forth.

Roderick felt dizzy. He stumbled against the windowsill.

"Are you feeling ill?" Dillon noticed how peaked he looked.

"Just a little light headed." He looked into his son's worried face. "Nothing to fret over, my boy." However, he admitted, if only to himself, that he hadn't felt well the past few months. *Time may be running out.*

"Can you believe that old fool?" Bernadine sputtered. "He thinks he is going to redecorate my house." She paced across the floor. "I will show him who is in control." A wicked smile spread across her face. "Caitlin, too."

"But what can we do?" Henrietta asked. "We have already tried everything. Even the rumors have died down, now. No one believes anything I say since Dillon went and spread those nasty lies about me, as if I made the whole relationship up." She crossed her arms, miffed. "I am starting to hate him more than I ever loved him."

Bernadine was deep in thought. "There is only one thing left to do now." Her blue eyes turned darker than the sky before a storm. "Kill her."

"What?" Henrietta thought Bernadine had lost her mind completely.

"Think about it," she cautioned. "'Tis the only way to get Caitlin out of the picture completely. Even if we are successful in ending the marriage, there will always be another woman who had been his wife. She will forever be competition for you."

"I can handle rivalry," Henrietta stated. "But murder?" She shook her head.

"Listen to me." Bernadine's tone was sharp. "'Tis the only way. You once told me you would do anything it took. Now is your chance. Quit sitting around, whining. Go after the man you want."

"I cannot murder anyone." She wrinkled her nose in distaste. "It is so repulsive. Besides, I have not the faintest idea how to kill someone."

"You dimwit!" Bernadine admonished. "You do not have to actually kill her. You can arrange an accident if you do not want to get messy. You wouldn't even have to be around when it happens." Her voice grew more enthusiastic.

Henrietta thought a minute. "An accident would be nice and neat."

"There you go." Bernadine clapped. "An accident it will be. And Roderick shall join Caitlin on this ride of death." Her eyes gleamed. "We shall kill two birds with one accident."

"I will have no part in killing a Lord." Henrietta stood.

"You worry about Caitlin and I will deal with my husband."

"We will surely get arrested," Henrietta scolded. "Perhaps we can get away with killing Caitlin, but Lord Roderick will draw more attention than we want."

"Nonsense." Bernadine sat down on the chair. "All we need now is a plan."

Roderick entered the shop and blew on his hands to warm them up. "I think you need more wood on that fire. 'Tis freezing in here."

"Nay, father. You are merely cold from outside. You will warm up in a little while." Dillon pulled the handle down on the press. "Is there something I can help you with?"

"Aye." Roderick smiled. "I need you and Johnny to help me unload something from the docks."

"Bernadine does not have more clothing, I hope." Dillon grimaced at the idea of her staying longer, perhaps even moving here indefinitely. Although he would relish spending more time with his father, they were in essence a package deal, and he couldn't stomach much more of his stepmother.

"Nay. 'Tis something I ordered, but I cannot move it by myself."

"I will get Johnny."

The three men walked against the small flurries. The wind pulled at their scarves, hats and coats, sending a chill through their bodies. However, the cold seemed to bother Roderick the most. Although he said not a word of complaint, Dillon noticed the ashen color of his cheeks, and heard his labored breathing.

"Perhaps we could sit and rest a minute," Dillon suggested. "I am feeling a little winded."

"Of course," Roderick eagerly agreed. He sat in one of the wooden chairs placed alongside the main building of the docks.

"You know, sir, the ship isn't far. I could go ahead and get some crew members to help," Johnny offered.

"'Tis a good idea." Dillon knew Johnny had noticed how sickly his father looked.

"No. No. I am rested now." Roderick stubbornly stood, even though he still wheezed.

Dillon shook his head as he followed his father to the docks. When they arrived at the ship, Dillon was amazed at the size of the crate. "What is in here?" he grunted as he, Johnny and three sailors loaded it onto the flat bed of the wagon. "'Tis as heavy as a house."

"Just a little something for Christmas, my boy."

"'Tis the biggest present I have ever seen," Johnny commented.

"And the heaviest." Dillon added.

"Take it to the printing shop," Roderick ordered the driver.

"What?" Dillon's eyebrows rose in surprise. "I have no room for something that big."

"You will make room for this, son." Roderick's brown eyes gleamed. "'Tis a gift for you."

Dillon mentally tried fitting the huge box into his shop. There simply was not a space big enough to accommodate something of that size. "Father, I do not wish to hurt your feelings, but I simply cannot figure out what I would need that is so large."

"Wait until you see what it is." Roderick clapped his hands.

"A new printing press!" Johnny squealed.

Dillon stood stunned, not saying a word. The cast-iron frame gleamed as the fire from the hearth danced over the steel. "I cannot believe you bought this," he finally uttered.

"I noted how many times you complained about the old one breaking down. When I found out that the Earl of Stanhope made this press out of cast iron instead of wood, I had to get it for you."

"I had no idea that you even read my letters," Dillon admitted. Not only had his father been reading the letters, but actually listened to what he said in them. "You never responded, it was Bernadine who always wrote back."

"Writing letters is more of a woman's job."

Dillon ran his hand along the smooth, cool frame. "'Tis much sturdier."

"And 'twill not rot like the wood frame," Johnny added.

"Not to mention that you now have two presses. You can cut your printing time in half." Roderick pointed out.

"I do not have the words to thank you." Dillon looked at his father. "It is the most marvelous gift ever."

Roderick sniffed the glass of brandy. "Must be my old age but the smell of this is getting worse."

"It is God warning you not to drink," Caitlin said.

"Perhaps you are correct." He sat the goblet down with a sigh. "I have enjoyed a nightcap since I was nineteen years old. But lately the brandy has not been sitting well with me."

"Have you tried a different brand?" Dillon asked.

"I have no idea. Bernadine orders the stuff. She insists it is the same I have always drunk."

Caitlin picked up the glass and sniffed. "I am glad I have never had a desire for it." She wrinkled her nose. "I could never get past the smell, let alone the taste."

"You managed very well at our wedding," Dillon teased.

"I assure you I learned my lesson." Green eyes pinned him in place. "And what about you, my lord? I recall you having an inebriated spell as well."

"'Twas just jealousy." Dillon kissed the tip of her nose. "Now that you are mine completely, I shall never have need for strong drink again."

"If you can stop kissing your wife, perhaps we can play a game of chess." Roderick set up the board. "If I'm not having my night cap, I'll need something to take my mind off drinking."

Caitlin laughed. "I shall work on my stitching."

Bernadine waltzed into the room, silently joining Caitlin on the settee with her needlepoint. The quiet solitude broke only when Dillon or Roderick occasionally laughed.

Caitlin smiled at the two of them. It was nice to see them patch up their relationship. The old wounds and hurts of the past were left behind as they forged a new bond.

"What are you smiling about?" Bernadine asked.

"'Twas just thinking how well Roderick and Dillon are getting on."

Bernadine arched her raven brow and studied the two of them. "They are getting along famously." Her blue eyes narrowed. *A little too famously.*

"Master Dillon," The maid rushed in the room. "Word has come from Johnny that he needs you down at the shop right away."

"Did he say what the matter is?" Dillon took the note card she held and read it. "I fear I must leave for a while." Looking at Caitlin he said, "Make sure Father does not touch any of the game pieces. He likes to cheat."

Caitlin gave him a kiss. "I shall watch him."

"I hope 'tis nothing serious." Bernadine added, never looking up from her work.

"I am sure he just needs some help."

"I will come with you." Roderick offered. "Perhaps it is something with the new press."

"You need to rest, Father. If it is an urgent matter or I need you, I will send for you."

Roderick couldn't argue. He was not feeling well. He seemed to be getting sicker over the last few days. His breathing was hard and his heart felt like it would jump right out of his chest. "All right, but send for me if you need me," he offered.

"Very well." After a quick kiss to Caitlin, he was gone.

It was not but the space of half an hour later when they received another note. This one from Dr. Andrews stating that Dillon had been thrown from his horse on his way to town.

"Does it say if he is hurt?" Bernadine grabbed the letter out of Caitlin's hand.

"Nay. There is no information at all." Caitlin felt the panic welling up. Her hands trembled, and her legs went weak. She had never once in her life ever felt faint, but this descending blackness was about to overtake her.

Bernadine noticed the odd look and hurried to her side. "Quickly, get her sitting before she faints."

Roderick assisted, and after Caitlin was safely on the settee he asked Bernadine, "What shall we do now?"

"Get the carriage ready. Caitlin cannot possibly ride her horse."

"The stable hands are preparing the carriage as we speak," The maid informed them.

"Good. Now get the smelling salts." Bernadine took command.

"I do not believe we have any."

"No smelling salts!" Bernadine shrieked. "What kind of household has no smelling salts?"

"Well, ma'am," The young girl fretted. "Mistress Caitlin has never needed them."

"And I shall not need them now." Caitlin stood. "I will be fine. But I must get to Dillon." Although her legs wobbled, she knew she must be strong.

"Of course," Bernadine agreed. "But you cannot possibly go alone."

"I shall accompany her," Roderick offered.

"I believe I should be the one to go with her," Bernadine argued. "'Twill not look proper if you are with her alone at this late hour."

"Dillon is my son. I do not believe anyone would think it unsuitable."

"We do not have time to argue," Caitlin berated.

"Yes. Yes. Of course," Bernadine sighed. "Very well, but send me word as soon as you have news."

Lucy bustled around collecting Caitlin's belongs as fast as she could. "Are you positive you do not want me to accompany you also?"

"No use both of us being irritable from lack of sleep. You go back to bed, and I will be home as soon as I can."

"I will not be able to sleep one wink until I know how Master Dillon is fairing."

"Then be on your knees praying," Caitlin suggested. "He will need all our prayers."

Caitlin and Roderick whirled out the door and into the carriage, commanding the driver to go as fast as possible. Bernadine ordered the maid to bring some tea. "It will be a long night." She sat down to finish her stitching, patiently awaiting some news.

"Blast it all," Dillon muttered. "Who sent this note?"

"I do not know, sir." Johnny read the words. "'Tis not my handwriting."

"Why would someone want to tease me so?" Must have been someone pulling a joke, that was the only thing he could surmise.

"I have no idea, sir."

"I am sorry to have gotten you up so late." When Dillon found no one at the shop, he went directly to Johnny's house.

"It is not a problem. Good night, Mr. Cade."

Dillon, still running the whole situation through his head, happened upon a carriage, turned upside down. It looked as if it rolled over and tumbled down the steep incline of the cliff. Kicking his steed into a run, he headed down the hill.

As he neared the site, his heart plummeted to his feet. The black wreckage was his own carriage. "Caitlin!" he yelled. Only the deathly silence of the night replied.

Chapter 20

Dillon jumped off his horse and ran to the carriage. He tried to look inside, but the darkness prevented him from seeing anything. The half-moon floating overhead did little to aid his search.

Finally hearing a murmur, he followed the sound, stumbling over rocks and brush. He found Roderick about ten yards from the wreck. "Father, are you all right? Why are you out here? What happened?" Dillon rambled on in panic.

"The carriage rolled over." Roderick grunted in pain.

"Where is Caitlin?"

"Don't know." The raspy whisper was the last thing spoken before Roderick fell unconscious again.

"Father." Dillon shook him but got no response. He felt for a pulse and found one. "Oh, God, please let him live, and help me find Caitlin. Do not take her. I beg you. Do not take her away."

After stumbling around in the dark, frantically calling her name, he knew he had to get help. He would never find anything without some lanterns. He hated to leave the scene, but knew the chances of someone traveling this road at this time of night were remote.

Jumping on his horse, he headed to town.

"I found her," Mr. Johnson shouted. "She's over here."

Dillon and Dr. Andrews ran to where Caitlin lay unconscious. Dillon gazed down at her, fearing the worst. Her fair skin was now whiter than the paper he used at the printing shop.

Dark circles formed under both eyes, and blood trickled down her temple. "God, please let her be alive," he begged.

"I feel a pulse," Dr. Andrews informed him. "She has a nasty gash on her head, but I think she will be fine."

"Thank you, Lord." Dillon shouted. "Thank you. Thank you. Thank you." He felt like dancing.

"I don't feel any broken bones," Dr. Andrews continued his examination. "I believe she jumped clear before the carriage crashed."

Other men from town still milled around the accident. They found the young driver pinned under the wreckage. Using a large tree branch and a boulder as a lever to lift the carriage they pulled the young boy out.

"I'm sorry, Dillon, there is no pulse." Dr. Andrews hated to deliver the bad news. "He barely looks twenty."

"I want to know what happened." Dillon shouted in frustration.

"We can't do any more tonight." Dr. Andrews said. "We can investigate further in the morning. Let's get Caitlin and your father to the house so I can tend to their wounds."

"I tell you I am fine." Caitlin yelled in frustration. "I want to get out of this bed."

"You are not moving until the doctor examines you." Dillon stood firm.

"I have been bedridden for three days. I just want to stretch my muscles."

"Not until Dr. Andrews says you may walk."

"Then get him in here." Her green eyes glared.

"He will be by later." Dillon laughed softly. He was glad to see the spark of temper.

"Must I lie about all day? 'Tis three days until Christmas, and I have nothing ready." She crossed her arms. "'Tis bad enough that I have to postpone the celebration until after Christmas."

"I know you had your heart set on a Christmas celebration, but we will have one as soon as you are well enough. As for Christmas, Martha and Bernadine have taken control of the duties."

"Great!" she huffed. "My first Christmas and I cannot do anything for the celebration. I am not only missing the Lord's birthday, I am also missing my first Christmas as your wife." Tears rolled down her black and blue cheeks.

"You are not missing anything. You will be up and moving around by then." Dillon reached into his jacket and pulled out a long rectangular box. "Perhaps this will brighten your mood."

"You cannot buy me happiness." Caitlin smoothed out the wrinkles in the quilt, pretending not to care at all about the gift.

"I am not trying to buy anything; 'tis a gift."

"'Tis a bit early for Christmas."

"'Tis not for Christmas. We have been married for three months."

"You bought me a three month anniversary gift?" Her face brightened under the dark marks marring her face. She could no longer feign disinterest.

"Oh, Dillon, you shouldn't have." The round diamond pendent picked up the light from the bedside lantern making it sparkle with various colors. The diamonds placed evenly along the gold chain may have been too small to sparkle, but they added beauty and elegance to the necklace. "'Tis too expensive."

"Nothing is too expensive for you." Dillon leaned forward, gently placing a kiss on her lips, the only spot on her face that wasn't bruised. "What are these tears? Do you not like it?"

"'Tis most beautiful."

"Then what is the matter?"

"I did not get you anything. I hate to admit it, but I had not even recalled that we have been married for three months."

"All right, then." Dillon laughed. "Perhaps we can consider this a thankful that you're alive gift." His face grew serious along with his tone. "I will give anything and everything to keep you safe."

Caitlin reached up, cupping his face in her hands. "'Twill take more than a carriage accident to get rid of me."

Dillon kissed the back of her hands. "I do not ever want to live without you."

"Now where is your faith, my husband?" Caitlin gently reprimanded. "Are you not the one always preaching on faith in God?"

"I merely repeat what the pastor preaches on Sundays," he sighed.

"If God chose to take me home to heaven, he would surely provide you with the strength to endure without me."

"My head tells me you are correct, but my heart aches at the thought of life alone." He stared into her eyes. "'Twould be no fun or joy without you."

"You are speaking foolishness now." Her playful laugh ended the dreary conversation on a happy note.

Bernadine's entrance, however, breathed new life into the dark and gloomy mood. The rustle of skirts and tapping of heels forewarned them of her appearance. But, nothing could have prepared them for her cheerfulness.

Bernadine breezed into the room with a smile on her face and green boughs of pine and holly in her hands. "I have come to decorate your room," she announced. "I thought, perhaps 'twould brighten your attitude."

Caitlin and Dillon stared at each other in stunned silence.

"'Tis just awful how that carriage wheel just broke so suddenly." Bernadine started arranging the holly on the windowsill. "I cannot understand this situation at all." Turning to Dillon she sighed. "First you get called away on a bogus emergency, then Caitlin and Roderick receive a letter which sends them out into the night, where the wagon wheel practically falls off." She shook her head.

"The wheel did not fall off," Dillon stated. "'Twas tampered with."

Surprise filled her blue eyes. "You mean to say someone purposely tried to harm Caitlin or Roderick?" She looked about to faint.

"'Twould be my guess." Dillon made no move to help guide her to a chair.

"But why?" Caitlin questioned. "We have done nothing."

"Perhaps it was because of all these political matters with the paper," Bernadine suggested as she sat down in the nearest chair. Although miffed that Dillon hadn't offered to help, she was more interested in the information he had come upon.

"The government would not try to kill me, they would arrest me."

"Perhaps the person who had you arrested was angry at you being released?" Bernadine suggested.

Dillon's brown brows knitted together as he pondered the suggestion. "I doubt it," he finally said. He had not yet shared the information that Henrietta had blabbed to the sheriff. Moreover, he couldn't perceive her being so ruthless as to try and kill Caitlin. He doubted she was even smart enough to come up with such a complex plan. "Besides they went after Caitlin and my father."

"We have no idea who the intended victim was," Bernadine pointed out. "Caitlin and Roderick happened to be in there. 'Tis possible the carriage accident was meant for you."

"That is a valid point," Caitlin agreed. "You could have taken the carriage yourself."

"How do you explain the letter that led to you being in the carriage?" Dillon questioned.

"I do not have any explanations for any of the happenings lately." Caitlin shook her head. "Have you found out any more information about the painting?" She wanted to change the subject.

"I finished interviewing the workers but as yet have not found anything. Of course that investigation has been put on hold. My first priority is finding the person responsible for the carriage accident."

"How is Roderick feeling?" Caitlin asked.

"He is healing but still complains about pains." Bernadine informed her. "I am not at all sure that the pains are not in his head."

Caitlin started to say something, but Dillon's eyes warned her to keep silent. She looked questionably at him but obeyed.

"Are you positive the wheel was tampered with?" Bernadine noticed the exchange of looks and didn't like the silence. She wanted to know every move.

"Aye." Dillon stared at her. "Are you positive you do not know anything about my mother's painting?"

Bernadine's good mood quickly dwindled. She stood up in a huff. "I will not be treated as a common criminal. I did nothing, and I am sick to death of your accusations. All this fuss over a painting. 'Twasn't a very good work of art in the first place." She stomped to the door. "Mary this. Mary that. Mary, Mary, Mary. 'Tis all anyone talks about in this house." Lifting her red skirts she stormed into the hall still ranting.

"'Tis one way to get rid of her," Caitlin commented.

"I know she did it," Dillon stated. "I just can't prove it."

"Are you positive?"

"Who else would have a motive? Besides, you just witnessed her reaction to the mention of my mother's name."

"Seems to me 'twas more a reaction at being accused," Caitlin pointed out. "Is that why you did not want me to say anything?"

Dillon looked as far down the hall as he could from his position by the bed. "The painting is not the only crime I suspect her of." Dillon barely spoke above a whisper. "I think she had something to do with the carriage accident."

Caitlin gasped. "I will concede that she may well be responsible for destroying the painting, but trying to kill me? What would she gain from my death?"

"I do not know. 'Tis possible that my father was the intended victim. She would stand to gain his whole inheritance."

Caitlin shook her head. "Bernadine offered to ride with me. She thought it improper for Roderick and I to be alone. Are you sure you are not allowing your negative feelings about her cloud your judgment?"

"I do not have any answers." Dillon stood and paced to the window. "However, strange things have been happening ever since she arrived."

"I believe her capable of many things, but murder?" She couldn't grasp that anyone could be so evil, let alone a member of the family.

Caitlin popped her head into the bedroom. Roderick was on the bed with several large pillows propping him up. His eyes were open but he seemed lost in thought.

"May I come in?" she inquired.

"Caitlin." His usually somber tone was enthusiastic at the sight of her. "Please." He sat up straighter.

She carefully walked over and sat in the chair placed beside the bed.

"How did you manage to get permission to get up and walk around? I'm stuck in bed for another week."

"I didn't ask for permission." She leaned forward and whispered. "I snuck out when Dillon left."

"I am so glad to see you. I shall not say a word to give you away."

"How are you feeling?" She didn't like the sunken eyes and cheekbones. His skin was so translucent, she could see through it to his very bones.

"I feel like I have been thrown from a carriage." He placed a wrinkled hand on top of hers. "You, my dear, look as bad as I feel."

They both laughed. "I look positively frightful, but my injuries are relatively small. Just some cuts and bruises."

"I too have no serious injuries. Somehow my health problems are not due to the accident. I have been in poor health for some time now."

"What are you doing out of bed?" Bernadine's shrill voice startled both Roderick and Caitlin.

"I only wanted to visit Roderick."

"He needs his rest. And so do you." She advanced towards them with a crystal glass, which she handed to Roderick. "I brought you a glass of brandy. I thought it might help you relax."

"Thank you." He took the glass.

Bernadine turned her small eyes on Caitlin. "Get back to your room before I call Dillon."

"I am not a child to be ordered around." Caitlin crossed her arms defiantly.

"Do not treat her so unkindly," Roderick reprimanded. "She is not hurting anyone." He set his untouched drink on the night table.

"You are both recovering from a very serious accident which has claimed the life of a young boy already." Her slipper tapped impatiently against the wood floor. "'Tis my duty to care for you." Her blue eyes met his dark brown ones. "Now drink your brandy then close your eyes and rest. You are not permitted to have any visitors."

"'Tis my health and I will make the decisions. I will have whomever I wish to visit whenever I want. I will drink when I am thirsty and sleep when I am tired." His frail voice penetrated the room. "I am sick and tired of you interfering and ordering me around." Picking up the glass of liquid he threw it across the room. The smashing of glass was followed by the hissing of flames from the hearth. "I will not die a weak old man," he finally said, defeat in his tone. "I may have lived my life that way, but I refuse to die as such."

"If that is the way you feel, then I shall leave you to your rude behavior." Holding her head high she headed for the door. Stopping she looked back and said, "I have given everything to you. I have been a good wife, and all I have received is contempt and condemnation. I do not know what else I could have done to please you."

"Save the performance, Bernadine." Contempt poured forth. "You will need the strength to act as a grieving widow after I am dead. As for being a loving wife, the whole world knows that is a falsehood. The only interest you have ever shown is in my money." He watched her mouth gape open. "Close your mouth. You look like a bird waiting to be fed." He had no idea where the sarcasm had come from, but it felt liberating. "You look shocked, Bernadine." His brown eyes darkened under his white eyebrows. "I have spent too many years making excuses for your bad behavior, and turning a blind eye to your unfaithful activities, all in an effort to save face. I have tried to pretend that there was something, anything in our marriage worth salvaging. Alas, it has come to this." Sorrowful eyes clashed with angry ones. "I no longer have the time or effort to pretend any longer."

"You dare speak to me of unfaithfulness in love." She stormed toward the bed. "You never loved me." She pointed to her chest. "It was your precious Mary that always occupied your mind. I was nothing to you. You never allowed me to be anything. You ignored me and treated me with contempt. Then blamed when me when I sought comfort elsewhere one time." She pointed her index finger at his face. "You are the one to blame for this marriage souring. Take that to your deathbed." Her straight back and lofty attitude carried her out of the room.

"I am sorry for that improper display," Roderick looked at Caitlin. "You should have taken the opportunity to leave when it presented itself."

"Nonsense." Caitlin tried to make her tone sound light. "We are family and you cannot keep secrets from family. Besides everyone can see what an old sourpuss she is." She took her father-in-law's hand. "Do not blame yourself. She only wanted to cast blame off herself."

"I know." He kissed the back of her hand. "Thank you, Caitlin."

"For what?"

"For bringing sunshine back into my life again. I am glad you married my son. I shall die knowing he will be well loved."

"Enough talk of you dying," she scolded. "You shall get better. You and Dillon have a lot of time to make up, and we are just beginning to get aquatinted. You cannot die when you have so much to live for."

"I have no say in the matter. 'Tis up to God."

"I do have a say in the matter. God listens to every prayer. I shall start asking for your health forthwith." She immediately knelt by his bedside and started praying.

Christmas dawned with a vengeance. The sun did little but cast a gloomy despair of the whole state of Virginia. It was not only the winter weather outside that held dimness. The household inside had dark secrets which were working in the hearts of everyone.

Dillon had not yet confided that Henrietta had had him arrested. Even if it had been accidental— which he still wondered about— Caitlin would certainly not see it as such. Too many hostilities ran between the two women.

Roderick and Bernadine were barely speaking. Although Roderick seemed to be getting better physically, which Caitlin attributed to God answering her prayers, his mental contentment seemed a little shaky.

Roderick had been pondering the faith of his son and daughter-in-law. They were in an intimate relationship with their God, turning to him with every need and seeking diligently for answers with a wondrous hope that He would grant their petitions.

After Caitlin had started praying for his health, Dillon had joined them, kneeling and taking over the praying. Their love and commitment had astounded him. He wanted to know the same God they knew. He had stayed in the marriage because the church did not sanction divorce. Now he wondered if it was time to look past the church and seek God for himself. Only the Creator of the world could give him the answers he sought.

Caitlin had been in a sour mood since Dillon wouldn't allow her to attend church service on Christmas Eve. She'd missed the "sticking of the church". Helping put up the boughs of greens and decorations had always been her favorite part of the service. Of course, it was because as a little girl she had been allowed, on that one night, to stay up past her bedtime.

Now, as an adult, her favorite part was singing the Christmas carols. She was still too sore and bruised to play the pianoforte, and not in much of a mood to sing without music.

However, the gloom seemed to disperse for a while. Dillon read the Christmas story from the gospel of Luke. Then everyone enjoyed the huge dinner Martha had prepared. The Christmas menu, looking fit for a king, consisted of: Holiday eggnog, Virginia ham, beaten biscuits, corn pudding, pumpkin chips, chicken and oyster pie, and cucumber pickles. The dessert table was laden with mincemeat pie, filbert pudding, plum pudding, and honey flummery. To wash it down, coffee and tea were served after dinner.

Henrietta briskly walked through the street grumbling under her breath. Although Bernadine had promised her an invitation to the big New Year's celebration tomorrow, as of yet, she had not received it.

"Since the confounded carriage accident didn't work as planned, she has barely spoken to me." She continued on, ignoring some of the drunken partygoers who'd started celebrating early. "I don't know why she blames me. It was not my fault they didn't die."

She listened to some men banter good wishes back and forth. As if there were anything good about the forthcoming year. It was shaping up to be as dull and lonely as this year had been.

The cold wind seeped into her fur-lined pelisse. She snuggled deeper into it and headed for home. She shouldn't be out this time of night. Not only was it too cold, but the riffraff came out at night. However, needing a walk and fresh air to clear her muddled mind, she'd decided to take the risk. It wasn't like sneaking past her parents' had been difficult. Her father had been passed out as usual, and her mother had retired to bed early. But she needed to get back home before she was found out.

Turning the corner and hearing the sound of crunching ground behind her made her think twice about the wisdom of this walk. Her heart raced faster. Looking behind, she saw the outline of a man. Hiking up her skirts, she started running but hadn't gotten far when a large hand halted her progress.

"Going somewhere?" The dark voice matched the dark face.

"H.. h.. home," she stammered.

"How about I escort you." Sheriff Edward tipped his hat. "'Tis part of my job."

"No thank you. I can manage on my own." The fear started to ebb, but anger was quickly taking its place. She jerked her arm away and took a couple of steps.

"Not so fast," he drawled. Grabbing her arm and yanking her back. "We have some unfinished business."

"We have nothing left to say." Besides, he couldn't say anything about her without incriminating himself.

"We have something to do." His smile turned wicked.

"You cannot be serious," Henrietta gasped. "Right here on the street?" She needed a plan. If she could evade him one more time, maybe she could leave town, and he'd never find her.

Pasting a seductive smile on her lips and rubbing closer she cooed, "How about we meet tomorrow night? My parents are going to a celebration, and I'll be home all alone."

She watched his hard face soften.

Reaching up, she coyly played with a button on his vest. "'Twill be so much better in a warm, comfortable bed than on the hard, cold ground. Do you not agree?" Although her smile promised him all the pleasures a man could want, her mind was working on how best to escape before she had to follow through with his demands.

"Sounds very tempting." His black mustache twitched.

"I promise, 'twill be worth the wait." She batted her long lashes.

His mouth descended with such a crushing force that she tasted blood. Squeezing her body next to his he hungrily kissed her.

She pulled away in terror. "What are you doing?"

"I want a sampling to see if you will be worth the wait." He smiled shrewdly.

"You cannot handle me so roughly." However, she tasted victory. *One more night. That is all I need.*

"I will handle you however I want." His eyes hardened, "Has your Dillon Cade ever kissed you like that?"

"'Tis absurd. Dillon is a gentleman."

"Yet you throw yourself at him like a cheap whore." He grabbed her wrist as the slap came near his face. "You are going to learn that you can't use your body and make promises that you don't intend to keep."

His hand covered her mouth as she started to scream. Picking her up, he carried her into a nearby horse stable. His eyes gleamed as he threw her down on loose straw.

"You cannot get away with this!"

He unbuttoned his shirt. "You forget; I am the sheriff. Who is going to believe your word over mine?" He knelt beside her. "Besides, I am only taking what you owe me." His fingers undid the clasp of her pelisse.

She screamed and he slapped her. "One night of passion for arresting Dillon Cade, remember?" His harsh whisper whizzed by her ear.

"The deal was for Caitlin," she sobbed.

"The deal was for the traitor. I arrested him." He ran a finger over her shoulder and down her arm.

Her body shivered. Some from the cold. Some from fear. "Oh God, how have I gotten myself into this mess?" she cried.

"Greed," he whispered, forcing her back onto the pile of hay. "Pure greed."

"Are you sure you are feeling well enough to attend the party?" Bernadine asked. "You look a bit pale."

"I am fine." Roderick fiddled with his cravat. "Just frustrated with this thing."

"Let me help." She tied the black strings into a perfect knot. "You need something to calm your nerves." She left the room, returning a few minutes later with a drink.

"I am not drinking anymore," he grumbled.

"And you are as sour as a lemon." She handed him the glass, knowing he couldn't refuse the smell. "Besides, you don't want to be on edge for Caitlin's party. She has worked so hard planning it."

"I guess you are right." He took the drink, downing a third of it in one gulp. It tasted worse than he remembered. He took a few more sips before setting the glass down.

"Is that all you are having?"

"Aye. 'Tis enough."

"I agree." She smiled in the mirror as she brushed some powder on her face, watching him closely. "More than enough."

Within the space of ten minutes Roderick started feeling dizzy. He sat down on the bed, holding his head. "I feel like my head is going to explode."

"Oh." Bernadine continued fixing her black tresses in place.

"I feel nauseous, also." He put a finger into his cravat and tried loosening it. His heart beating so fast he thought it might jump up in his throat. "I think I need Dr. Andrews."

"He cannot help you now." Bernadine finished patting her hair in place then turned to face her husband. "You see, my love, you are dying."

"What?"

"My poor Roderick." She perched the blue hat on top of her head. "You have just ingested a lethal dose of Hemlock." She tied the ribbons under her chin. "But do not fret. Death will come quickly."

Roderick struggled to talk, but his tongue felt heavy, and the words wouldn't form.

"I see that paralysis of the tongue is already starting." She folded her arms across her chest and walked closer. "Central paralysis will set in soon. It will start with your feet, travel up your legs, then 'twill spread through your torso and arms. Next, it will render your swallowing useless. Finally the Hemlock will attack your respiratory system until your whole body shuts down."

She paced around the room, a triumphant smile on her face. "Everyone will think you died of a heart attack." She shrugged her bony shoulders. "'Tis the perfect plan, especially since you have been sick for a while now." Her eyes gleamed. "Of course that is because I have been slipping tiny doses of the poison in your brandy."

She laughed when his eyes darted to the half empty glass. "Did you know that Socrates died from an overdose of Hemlock? He drank the poisonous juice by his own hand after he was sentenced to death. I thought it poetic that you die the same way as a great philosopher. Only you did not know you were drinking poison. But all the same, you will die in the same manner."

Roderick could no longer sit up and fell back across the bed.

"Do you want to know how I came upon so much information about Hemlock? Or do you want to know why I did all this?"

She explained the whole sordid plan as she finished getting ready. "I had a liaison with an herbalist. Do you remember that toad-like fellow on the outskirts of London? He was nasty-looking, but he knew everything about herbs. Good and bad. I sweet-talked him into helping me. I got tired of waiting for you to die so I decided to help nature along."

She clipped a diamond pendent onto her dress, and then looked at Roderick. "Soon you will be with your precious Mary, and I will have all the money."

Walking closer to the bed and leaning over him, she observed how he stared straight ahead, his eyelids not moving. "I know you can hear me even if you are paralyzed.

"Why have I done all this, you ask?" Her mirthless laugh rumbled through the room. "I wanted you from the first day we met, but you never looked at anyone except Mary. The day you married her was a slap in my face. However, I am a patient woman. I bided time and formed my plan. I was brilliant. The way I befriended her. I knew her passion for helping others and used it to lure her to the hotel that day."

She licked her dry lips. "The feel of steel slicing through flesh. The blood. The confused look in her eyes before they went blank." She shook her head. "Nothing has ever compared to the emotions of that day. I knew with her out of the way you would finally turn to me. And, you did.

"How was I to know what an old bore you would turn out to be? How Mary ever put up with you, I have not the faintest idea. It must have been a blessing for her the day she died. I put her out of her misery. Now I shall do the same for myself. I have had enough of you and Caitlin too."

She walked to the door. "I will be rid of you both, and Dillon shall be all mine."

Her evil laugh lingered long after she was gone.

Chapter 21

"Is everything set for tonight?" Bernadine whispered.

"Aye."

"Good. I do not want anything going wrong this time." She gave a reprimanding look.

"'Twas not my fault the last time. I messed with the wheel so it would look like an accident, just like Henrietta asked."

"The job did not go according to plan. Dillon suspects someone tampered with the wheel."

"'Tis no proof."

"Perhaps. However, I want nothing left to chance." Bernadine folded her arms under her fur pelisse. "I am in charge now, and I will not tolerate any excuses."

She studied the stable boy. Early twenties. Wide shoulders and hard muscles. He was vital and strong and probably had the stamina of a bull. "Exactly how did Henrietta pay you?"

His brown brows drew together. "With money."

Her laugh caught him off guard. He'd never heard her laugh in the four weeks since she'd been here. She was always serious and sour looking. "No other benefits?"

"'Twas all business."

"Very good." Bernadine's smile spread, a night of anticipation already playing in her head. "Have you ever been with a woman?"

"Ma'am?" His pale face turned red. "What kind of question is that?"

"The kind I want an answer to." Her smile faded. "And I want the truth," she scolded.

He saw no rational reason for the question, but was scared not to answer. He certainly wouldn't lie either. She had a look that could cut the heart right out of your chest without the aid of a knife. "Aye, ma'am. I've been with a few women."

Disappointment briefly flashed in her eyes. "Why don't we work on that ma'am bit." Leaning in she devoured his lips with such a barbaric force that he tasted blood.

He broke away. "What are you doing?"

Her shrill laugh filled the barn. "If you do not know, then perhaps you lied to me about being with women."

"'Tis not what I meant," he defended. "Is this part of doing business?"

She arched a raven brow. "It can be."

"What about the plan?"

"We have plenty of time." She undid the first couple of buttons on his shirt. "I have informed everyone not to disturb Roderick because he is not feeling well and needs to rest."

"Will you not be missed at the party?"

"Nay." She smiled. "I made the excuse of needing some fresh air. I am supposedly taking a walk in the garden."

"In the middle of winter?"

"'Tis a poor excuse," she agreed. "However, I doubt anyone cares. No one has paid me any attention. They are too busy fawning over Caitlin." Her lips puckered. "Do not worry, everything is taken care of." She kissed him again.

"We are in the stables," he reminded her. "Guests are coming and going."

"No guests would arrive this late." She backed him up to the wall. "'Tis poor manners to leave so soon, besides the excitement is in the anxiety of getting caught."

"Lucy!" Caitlin yelled down the hall then rushed to the bed. She anxiously felt for a pulse, but her hands were shaking.

"What is the matter?" Lucy's head peeped around the door.

"Go get Dillon and Dr. Andrews."

Lucy stood frozen, tears filling her eyes as she saw Roderick's unmoving body and opened eyes. He looked dead.

"Quickly," Caitlin commanded.

Her mistress's sharp tone propelled her into action. She ran and found both men filling them in on what she'd seen.

"I need my bag from my carriage," Dr. Andrews said.

"Johnny," Dillon called. "Fetch the doctor's bag."

"Aye, sir."

Dillon and Dr. Andrews sprinted to the back of the house.

Caitlin jumped off the bed and ran to Dillon. "I decided to check on him, just to see if he needed anything."

Dr. Andrews went straight to the bed.

"Is he having a heart attack?" Caitlin asked.

Dr. Andrews checked for a pulse. "He's barely breathing, but I feel a heartbeat."

Lucy and Johnny entered giving the bag to the doctor. He pulled a long sharp object from it and poked around Roderick's hands and arms. "He's not responding. It looks like some kind of paralysis."

"Perhaps a stroke," Dillon suggested.

Dr. Andrews felt around his face and neck. "Both sides appear to be affected. With a stroke usually only one side is paralyzed."

"If it's not a heart attack or a stroke, what can it be?" Dillon restlessly paced across the floor.

"He is having trouble swallowing," Dr. Andrews noticed. "Has he had any abdominal pains in the last eighteen to thirty-six hours?"

"He hasn't said anything to me." Dillon looked at Caitlin. She shook her head.

"Have you eaten any shellfish within two days?"

"No." Caitlin answered. "'Tis been at least a week since Martha cooked shellfish."

"'Tis not shellfish poisoning." Dr. Andrews shook his head. "His face is not swollen." He sighed. "And food poisoning would have produced symptoms earlier."

"Not to mention we would all be sick," Dillon pointed out.

"Has he had anything to eat that you have not?"

"Not as far as I know." Dillon paced to the fireplace, mumbling. "What else would cause paralysis?"

"A good number of things." Dr. Andrews rolled Roderick's head to the side. "Has he fallen and hit his head at all? Some head injuries can cause such symptoms."

"'Tis possible. Where is Bernadine?" Dillon demanded. "She should know."

"I have not seen her for a while," Caitlin answered.

"She said he wasn't feeling well and wanted to rest." He turned grief stricken eyes to the doctor. "Why did she not ask you for help?"

Dr. Andrews shrugged. "I do not see any swelling on his head." He ran his hands along the sides of Roderick's neck. "Or his neck." The doctor scratched his own head. "Perhaps a bug bite," he finally suggested. "Help me look over his body."

Dillon helped the doctor undress Roderick and examine him for any puncture wounds. Caitlin went to get some comforters to help keep him warm.

Although it was not proper for a lady to see an undressed man other than her own husband, she could not bring herself to leave the room. Instead, she kept her gaze averted and paced the room picking up objects, folding clothes, and rearranging things, anything to keep her hands busy. "I wonder why he had this." She picked up the glass.

"What is it?" Dr. Andrews asked.

"Brandy."

"So?" He didn't see anything out of the ordinary about a glass of brandy.

"My father had stopped drinking. I showed him verses in the Bible that talked about not drinking strong drink and said maybe God wanted him to quit. He hasn't touched the stuff in over a week."

"Why start tonight?" Caitlin sniffed the glass and made a face. "No wonder he was sick from drinking this stuff. It smells positively dreadful."

"Brandy can be strong when you are not use to it," Dr. Andrews informed her, off-handedly. His attention focused on the patient and not on why he'd decided to take up drinking again.

"But it could be the one thing he had that no one else did." Dillon looked at the doctor.

"Let me see that glass." Dr. Andrews took the glass and sniffed. "Brandy does not smell this bad."

"Could the brandy be bad?" Dillon asked

Dr. Andrews sniffed again. "It smells bitter and mousey."

"Roderick had complained that his brandy had tasted bitter for months." Caitlin remembered. "He'd been feeling poorly for months also."

"'Tis something in here." Dr. Andrews couldn't decipher the smell. "I need to know what."

"Some kind of poison?" Dillon asked.

"More than likely." The doctor leveled his gaze to Dillon. "I need to know what kind of poison to give a proper antidote."

"What if there isn't one?" Caitlin fretted. "God please help us. Give Dr. Andrews the wisdom he needs to fight this evil deed."

She kept praying while Dr. Andrews and Dillon talked about different poisons.

"If I recall correctly there are several herbs that are poisonous." Dr. Andrews stated. "Hemlock grows wild in England. So does foxglove and aconite."

"Which one is in there?" Dillon demanded.

"I am not positive. 'Tis been a long time since I studied in England." Dr. Andrews thought a moment. "I believe that hemlock has a bitter smell and taste. So bitter in fact that animals leave it alone. There has never been an accidental poisoning like with the other poisonous plants. Animals stay away because of the smell."

"So this is no accident." Dillon realized.

"No." Dr. Andrews answered.

"How would hemlock get over here?" Caitlin asked.

"It could have been dried and ground up." Dr. Andrews informed them.

"Is there an antidote?" She wanted to know.

"Yes." Dr. Andrews listened to his heartbeat again. "We need more blankets. 'Tis imperative that we keep up his body temperature." He looked at Dillon. "I need someone to run to my office and get some supplies."

"I can send Johnny."

Dr. Andrews nodded his head.

A few minutes later the blond headed boy stood in the room, nervously playing with his hat.

"In the glass cabinet at my office you will find some glass vials. They are marked clearly. I need tannic acid, mustard oil and castor oil." He looked up at the boy. "Do you have that?"

"Yes, sir." Johnny dutifully repeated the list.

"Good. Now hurry. Ride as hard and fast as you can." Dr. Andrews looked at Caitlin. "I need one other ingredient for the antidote. Coffee, as strong as you can make it."

"Right away." She hurried to the kitchen.

"Coffee?" Dillon questioned.

"It is a strong stimulant which can counteract the poison."

"I think I should know your name," Bernadine mumbled. "I cannot keep calling you the stable boy."

"Wilson."

"You are not much of a conversationalist, are you?" She laughed and pulled the horse blanket higher as she sat up. "However, conversation is not what I require in my lovers."

She pulled some strands of straw from his brown hair. "Do I have any hay in my hair?"

He reached up wordlessly and withdrew a few strands. "You have more in the back." He sat up to reach better.

"Make sure you get it all. I do not think I can explain hay in my hair when I was walking in the garden."

"Your hair is a mess." He tossed a handful of hay on the ground.

"Thank you for your wonderful comment." Her tone turned icy.

He wasn't prepared for this emotional distress. He only wanted to do his job and get his money. However, keeping her happy was essential to getting paid. She was wealthy and after tonight would be even richer. It would serve him well to coddle her. A large reward would be worth the effort.

"I didn't mean to upset you." He kissed her bare shoulder. "I kind of like your hair loose and messy. It makes you look even younger." He lied so easily.

She pushed a few hair pins back in place. "How young?"

"At least twenty and five."

As they kissed, they fell back against the pile of hay, their arms and legs entangled. So caught up in their passion they didn't hear the footsteps.

"Good heavens!" A loud gasp startled them apart.

"Why, I never ever saw such a display." A woman cried.

"Miss High and Mighty with a stable boy." A man's laugh resounded.

Bernadine sat up, pulling the blanket over her naked torso. Her mouth hung open, but words failed. "'Tis not what it appears." She tried to reason with the small assemblage. "He... he forced me."

"Aye, you looked like you were struggling hard," someone mocked.

"Yeah, struggling to get underneath him." The group laughed.

Wilson sat up. "Liar." No amount of money would make him take the blame for a non-existent rape.

"Shut up," Bernadine hissed. "You will ruin everything." Why had she let her passion get the best of her? This was stupid!

How could she talk her way out of it? *What does it matter anyway? Roderick is surely dead by now.*

"Pardon me." A deep, gruff voice parted the joviality of the crowd. "Ma'am I have to ask you to get dressed now." The sheriff tipped his hat.

"I would love to, but I seem to be entertaining the crowd at the moment."

"Woo wee! That there is some entertaining." The man's comment drew laughter from everyone.

"All right, everyone settle down. I need you to leave so these two can get dressed," Sheriff Edward said.

"We want our carriage," one man insisted.

"I believe an arrest takes precedence over your leaving." Sheriff Edward looked at Bernadine.

"What?" Bernadine was bewildered. "Are you going to arrest me for adultery?"

"No, ma'am. Murder." He put his hat back on his head.

A collective gasp exuded from the crowd.

"Let's see you talk your way out of this one." Dillon came and stood next to the sheriff.

"I am quite sure I do not know what you are talking about."

"You poisoned my father. You also set up that carriage accident that almost killed my wife." Dillon stepped closer, rage flowing so hard that his body shook. "Why?"

"You have no proof." She stared him down.

"We will. Caitlin is going through your belongings as we speak. As soon as she finds the poison we will have you."

Bernadine smiled. *Good luck finding it.* She'd dispersed of the rest of the poison as soon as she'd given Roderick the overdose. The powder had been thrown into the winter wind behind the stable.

"You have no proof and you will find none." She arched a dark brow. "I am a very smart woman."

"Not smart enough," Dillon countered. "When my father recovers, he will be a living witness."

Surprise filled her blue eyes.

"That is correct. My father is still alive." Dillon glanced at Wilson. "And you shall be an accomplice."

"How is Lucy?" Dillon asked.

"She will be fine. Just upset from the turmoil." Caitlin sat down on the bed next to him. "I feel sorry for them. 'Tis not a very happy occasion to start off an engagement."

"It is not any occasion to start off a New Year." Dillon's lips quirked. "Why can nothing go according to plan for us?" His brown eyes misted. "Why must tragedy follow us?"

"Who says that this is not God's plan for us? Only God can turn tragedy into triumph." Caitlin smiled. "Is not our marriage proof of that?"

"Perhaps."

"How is Roderick?" Caitlin feared asking the question, not knowing if she wanted the answer.

"He is holding his own. Dr. Andrews said the next eighteen hours will be critical."

"He is a strong man," she encouraged.

"Stronger than poison?"

"You cannot give up hope." Caitlin got on her knees on the bed and massaged his shoulders. "God is in control."

"Aye." The half-hearted response surprised her.

"That does not sound like the faithful man I married."

"Perhaps I am too tired to care." He jerked away, stood and walked to the window. Looking out into the pitch black, he sighed. "Now I know how you felt when we married. Too overcome with worries, grief and anger to care."

"And the Lord worked everything out, did He not?" She slid off the bed, went to him, resting her cheek against his back. "I love you, Dillon Cade."

A small smile touched his lips. He turned to face her. "I love you, Caitlin Cade." He rubbed the pad of his thumb across her smooth, soft cheek. Just the feel of her skin was enough to uplift his spirit.

"God brought us together for a reason. Trust in His plan." Caitlin held him as a mother would a hurt child. "We found Roderick in time to save him."

"And spoiled Bernadine's attack against you." Dillon felt a chill wash over him, the immorality of that woman was too much to understand. "Wilson confessed to tampering with the carriage wheel and explained how they had planned a stable accident for you tonight."

"Why would Wilson betray us like this? He has worked for you for years."

"Money. Greed." Dillon's face hardened. "'Tis the only reason for any of this."

"'Tis hard to imagine that people could value money over someone's life." Caitlin shuddered.

"Only evil people," he replied.

"What I do not understand is why she tried to get rid of me?" Caitlin paced over to the fireplace. "I know she wanted your father's fortune, but what would she have gained from my death?"

"You were just an obstacle for her to hate. 'There is no reasoning in pure evil."

"Dillon. No!" Caitlin screamed as he tore off down the hall. She quickly looked to Dr. Andrews for assistance.

"Ready the carriage," Dr. Andrews advised.

Caitlin hurried down the hall calling for Mrs. White.

"Have the stable hands ready the carriage," she informed the maid. "Dr. Andrews and I shall be leaving." Caitlin silently prayed for courage. It had only been two weeks since the frightful accident. She wasn't quite over the shock yet. However, Dillon needed her, and love for him outweighed any fear.

When Dr. Andrews joined her, she hesitated only a moment before stepping into the carriage. As the four steeds transported the carriage over the frozen roads, Caitlin prayed they would catch up with Dillon before he did something crazy. She also prayed that all four wheels would stay intact. "God is bigger than my fear." She repeated several times.

After reaching the jailhouse, she ran into the building stopping short when she saw Dillon sitting in the hall. Their eyes met.

"I need to face her." Anger and hatred turned his soft features hard as granite.

Caitlin advanced a slow, soft stride. "What shall it accomplish?"

"I need to understand why," he said flatly.

"All right, Mr. Cade," the sheriff sneered. "You may visit with the prisoner now."

"'Tis about time." He stood, every muscle clenching.

Caitlin laid a gentle hand on his arm. "Do not do this. Please."

He considered her plea for a few seconds. "'Tis something I must do." With that, he walked back to the holding cell.

Bernadine sat perched like a queen on the small cot. 'Twas amazing how innocent she looked.

Dillon stopped in front of the open cell, fists clenched at each side. "How can you be such a monster?" The veins in his neck popped out. "How can you look so normal and yet be filled with wretchedness?"

"Dillon, how nice of you to come visit me."

Her nonchalant attitude made the wounds of grief even deeper. "'Tis not a social call."

"Pish-posh." She laughed. "Have you come to tell me that the old fool has finally died?" She stood, swaggering toward him. "Do not fret, love. I will use my inheritance to get out of here. Meanwhile you can get rid of Caitlin then we can be together." She traced a finger down the front of his vest.

He grabbed her hand squeezing so tight he felt the joints popping. "You have no inheritance. Father transferred everything over to me weeks ago." He smiled satisfied by the pain and shock in her eyes. "You see, all your evil deeds have been for naught."

"You are hurting my hand," she cried.

"Do you think I care?" He put more pressure on. "You have taken everything from me and my family." He twisted her arm behind her back. "I shall kill you before I ever allow you to touch my wife again."

"Don't you see, I did this all for us." She clenched her teeth. "He never loved you. Not like I do. I can make you happier than Caitlin ever will." Tears streamed down her face. "With both of them gone we can be together."

"You do not know the meaning of love." Dillon forced his hand open and allowed her out of his grasp. "I have never and will never love you. I cannot stand the sight of you."

"Why are you so upset over a weak old man?" She rubbed her bruised wrist.

"'Tis not my father's murder that you shall go to trial for. It is my mother's."

Caitlin turned furious green eyes on the sheriff. "How can you allow him back there? You know nothing good will come of this meeting."

"'Tis not my concern."

"You are the sheriff. You are supposed to protect the people of this town."

"I do my job with no complaints from other town folks. If'n your husband can't control his temper, then 'tis best he is in here. It will make it easier to lock him up." His mustache twitched as he grinned.

"You are only looking for an excuse to lock him up." She started towards the back.

Sheriff Edward blocked her path. "Only one visitor at a time. You'll have to wait your turn."

A piercing scream jolted through the air just as Dr. Andrews came through the door. "What in blazes is going on?"

"Dillon is back there with Bernadine."

"Let me pass." Dr. Andrews bellowed and pushed past.

Caitlin and Dr. Andrews found Dillon struggling with Bernadine.

"Dillon. Stop!" Caitlin cried. "Please, stop." Tears glistened in her eyes. "Don't do this. Think of our child."

Dillon heard the urgent voice of his wife, but her pleas fell on deaf ears. Hurt and anger had taken control. The strings of his heart pulled too tight. The pain of his mother's death had plagued him all his life. Only the love and forgiveness of Jesus Christ had kept his life in a respectable light. Now, when faced with the temptation, revenge felt stronger than his sense of right and wrong.

"Dillon, no!" Dr. Andrews tugged at his arm. "You mustn't do this."

Voices were raised floating around him, but he didn't understand what they said. Animosity blocked his hearing. Revenge blinded his vision. Hate obstructed his heart from love. "She killed my mother," Dillon sobbed. "In cold blood. She is evil and must pay."

Bernadine lay on the floor and Dillon started to wrap his hands around her neck.

"The justice system will take care of her." Dr. Andrews tried to soothe his wounds. "You cannot take care of the situation on your own. God will prevail."

"But God let her kill my mother."

"I'm sorry, Dillon." Dr. Andrews advanced, cautiously. "Would your mother want you to do this?"

Dillon started crying, then shook his head.

His hands froze on her neck. Bernadine made no move to get up. The slightest tick of a muscle could prompt him to start squeezing. Dillon had gone over the edge, and she did not want to push him any further. Perhaps the doctor and Caitlin could reach him before he killed her.

Dillon, think of our child. The words broke through his subconscious. He stopped, looking up at Caitlin. "You are going to have a baby?"

Caitlin advanced with a smile. "Aye."

"A baby." Dillon looked at his wife, then at Bernadine. He had a choice - his family or revenge. His hands were poised to destroy. His fingers itched, the muscles straining, wanting to apply pressure to that delicate neck until it snapped. But, he had a beautiful wife who was now carrying his child. God had indeed blessed him. Could he give it all up for revenge?

"A baby," he repeated. With a sigh and more mental strength than he possessed, he stood and embraced Caitlin. "A baby!"

Bernadine quickly stood. "I want that man arrested," she squeaked. "He tried to kill me."

"He did no such thing," the doctor informed the sheriff. "You cannot arrest someone for thinking about murder. He never touched you, so it cannot even be considered attempted murder."

"Technically he's correct," Sheriff Edward grudgingly admitted. "As much I would love to arrest him, I have no grounds. Yet."

"His hands were wrapped around my neck!" Bernadine screamed.

"I didn't see that," Dr. Andrews lied. "Do you have proof?"

"Look at my neck?" She walked to the doctor and pulled the lace around her collar down.

"I don't see any bruising or redness." Dr. Andrew sighed in relief. Thankfully Dillon hadn't squeezed enough to leave any marks. "It is your word against his."

"I wanted to kill her," Dillon admitted. "I could have done it."

"But you didn't." Caitlin brushed a long strand of hair away from his face. "It is human nature to want revenge. When there is injustice, we want to make it right. Every heart holds the capacity to kill." She looked at Bernadine. "A heart that gives can take away. If you can love, you may also hate. If you are capable of making a life," Caitlin laid a hand over her stomach, "you can also destroy one."

She allowed him to digest what she said. "There are two sides to every coin and two choices in every heart. Bernadine chose a path of destruction, but you have chosen a life of love."

"It is nothing to fear now." Caitlin smiled. "Your father is on the mend, and Bernadine will pay for her crimes. Even Henrietta has left town without a word to anyone." She kissed Dillon. "God has worked everything out. We can now start our life with no interference from anyone."

"Thank you, Lord." Dillon whispered the praise over the top of Caitlin's head. "Thank you."

Epilogue

Caitlin waited anxiously. The late August breeze blew the red tresses into a mass of tangles, but she didn't care. Clutching her hat onto her head tighter, she linked her other arm through Sarah's.

"I can hardly believe it," Sarah cried. "The Lord has brought your family and the love of my life home."

"Believe it." Caitlin smiled. "'Tis all those prayers we sent up."

They watched as the passengers disembarked. Finally Caitlin noticed her parents. "Mama, Papa!" She waved and jumped up and down as much as her large, round belly would permit. The baby kicked as if sensing the excitement of its mother.

"If you do not stop all that jumping, you will surely deliver the baby right now and not next month," Sarah admonished.

"Caitlin, my darling." Kathleen embraced her daughter. "What is this?" She stepped back, noticing the big bulge.

Caitlin protectively laid a hand across her stomach. "'Tis your grandchild."

"Papa." She threw herself into his open arms. The familiar smell of cigars and musk overwhelmed her. "You are home at last."

"Aye, my child. Thanks to you and your husband."

"'Twas not our doing. President Jefferson changed the law."

Alin laid a gentle hand on Caitlin's stomach. "Am I to assume your marriage is no longer in name only?"

"'Tis true." Caitlin laughed. Then looking more serious added, "You were right, Papa. I only had to give Dillon a chance."

"I knew he'd make a good husband."

"He is the best husband a woman could ever want. Thank you for choosing him for me."

"Did I hear my name?" Dillon approached with a little girl in his arms.

"'Twas just telling Papa what a cad you are," she teased.

Dillon slipped one arm around her thick waist. "Aye, and you are still as stubborn as always." He kissed her cheek. "I would not have you any other way."

She laughed, playfully nudging him in the ribs. "That sweet talk shall not work on me, sir." Turning her attention to the girl she added, "Mama. Papa. Meet your grand daughter, Mary Elizabeth."

"Two grandchildren," Kathleen exclaimed. "I think I shall faint."

Alin's rigid composure creaked some. His gray eyes misted. There was no mistaking the girl's curly red hair, and bright brown eyes. "I am a grandfather two times and you did not see fit to send us word."

"Oh, Papa, please do not be angry. I wanted only to surprise you."

Alin smiled. "I am not angry, just shocked."

"Where is Brogan?" Caitlin asked. "Did he not come back with you?"

"Aye, he is collecting the trunks and gathering the servants. He shall be along shortly." Alin looked at Dillon. "How is the newspaper business?"

"Fine, sir."

"I assume since Thomas Jefferson is now President that the election went well."

"'Twas a close call, sir. Jefferson and Aaron Burr received seventy-three electoral votes each. Congress had to reconvene and pick either Jefferson or Burr to be the next president."

"That too ended in a scandal," Caitlin added.

"How so?" Alin was intrigued.

"'Twas a deadlock in congress," Dillon continued. "That is until Delaware's congressman, Mr. Bayard, decided to abstain from voting for either person. That gave Mr. Jefferson the most votes."

"Why would anyone not cast a vote in such an important election?" Alin was baffled at the thought.

"Exactly," Caitlin quipped. "Although Mr. Bayard stated several reasons for his decision, Mr. Burr still believes that he made a deal with Jefferson. Of course Mr. Jefferson has denied all claims."

"Sounds like an exciting election," Alin said.

"Truly it was." Caitlin rattled on. "'Tis still being talked about six months later. 'Twas an exciting end to an exciting campaign."

"My dear, I am very impressed with your knowledge of politics," Kathleen intervened. "I never thought you paid any attention at all to your studies."

"I fear my studies bored me, Mama. However, since Dillon has me writing the columns in the paper about the very subject, I became proficient in the subject rather quickly."

"You are writing for the paper?" Kathleen's green eyes widened. "I never heard of such a thing."

"Caitlin and I are a team, in marriage and in the business of the paper. She is a most excellent writer. I believe people prefer to read her writings over my own."

"But who takes care of the children while you are gone?" Kathleen was of the notion that a woman's place was in the home.

"We have a whole staff who adores Mary, especially our cook, Martha and her husband, Mr. Barclay, treat her like their own granddaughter. Mr. Barclay even decorated the nursery free of charge."

"And my father has moved here as well," Dillon explained. "He adores watching her."

"Not to mention that Sarah is always wanting to sit with Mary. I fear sometimes there are so many people wanting time with our little Mary that we have to fight to have time for ourselves." Caitlin laughed.

"Perhaps with two of them there shall be enough children to go around." Dillon laid his hand on her belly.

"It still seems highly improper," Kathleen sniffed.

"But it works for us, Mama. Our marriage may be different, but we are happy." She kissed Dillon just to prove her point. "Besides now that you are home you shall be clamoring for the grandchildren's attention also."

"Perhaps." Kathleen's sour look brightened at that. And when Mary reached out for her grandmother, willingly jumping into her arms, Kathleen melted on the spot. "Oh, how precious." She hugged her tight, forgetting all about improprieties.

"Brogan," Sarah's scream bellowed over the crowd.

Tears filled Caitlin's eyes as she watched them embrace. Brogan picked Sarah up, twirling her around. A jumble of pink skirt and black hair flew into the air. Tears of relief and joy flowed down her cheeks.

Brogan set her on the ground, kissed her, and then, bending down on one knee asked her to marry him.

"Looks like we shall be having another wedding in the family," Caitlin smiled.

"We are to be married as soon as possible," Brogan announced as they approached. "I have wasted too many years of my life on this war. 'Tis time I start thinking about my own life and not the war in Ireland."

Caitlin hugged her brother. "Of course, the fact that the war is over and Ireland lost has nothing to do with this soul searching decision," she teased.

"Of course not." Brogan arched a dubious brown brow.

"Are you all right?" Dillon slipped a handkerchief out of his pocket.

"'Tis the happiest day of my life." Caitlin wiped the tears away. "God has truly blessed my family."

"The day is full of surprises." A familiar voice sounded in her ears slapping Caitlin a sharp blow. She turned slowly, not believing her eyes. Surely they were playing a trick on her.

"Dwayne?" The whispered name was barely heard over the wind.

"'Tis I, Catie pie." He stood tall. Erect. His light brown hair looked darker, aged with time and misery, but, his blue-gray eyes held all the life and mischief that she remembered.

"I thought you were dead." Caitlin wondered if she was looking at a ghost.

"I was captured and held until after the war." He held out his arms.

With tears streaming down her pale cheeks, Caitlin ran into his embrace. His body felt warm and hard. *Definitely not a ghost,* she mused.

"I don't believe it!" She hugged him tight. "I thought you were dead." She had a hard time grasping this. "'Tis nothing short of a miracle." God was more merciful than she could ever imagine.

"With God all things are possible," Dillon quoted scripture. After shaking Dwayne's hand, he slipped his arm around Caitlin's waist. "All you need is a little faith."

About the author:

You may find out more about Candy Ann Little and her next projects online at:

Blogsite:
http://candylittle.wordpress.com/http://candylittle.wordpress.com/
Facebook:
https://www.facebook.com/profile.php?id=1372216486
Twitter: https://twitter.com/#!/candyannlittle
Goodreads:
http://www.goodreads.com/author/show/4672789.Candy_Ann_Little
View Trailer:
http://www.youtube.com/watch?v=vFjmES8CB9g

If you enjoyed Unforgiving Ghosts, visit
Inknbeans Press for other books by this author
and many others.

Inknbeans.com

www.ingramcontent.com/pod-product-compliance
Lightning Source LLC
Chambersburg PA
CBHW061319170626
46817CB00001B/236